Once Upon A Time

In

Baghdad

I.M.Hussaini

I.M.Hussaini

DEDICATION

During the civil unrest that followed the war, more than 100 thousand Iraqi were killed, most of them by terrorist groups.

This book is for their memory…

Novels by I.M.Hussaini:

Once Upon A Time In Baghdad
The Detour – Edward Fleming's Series #1
Echoes Of Fatima – Edward Fleming's Series #2

To know more about I.M. Hussaini's books, news, or if you just felt bored with a lot of spare time, then you might want to check out his website: www.imhussaini.com

I.M.Hussaini

Although most of the events in this book are based on true stories that took place in Iraq, all the characters are fiction; any similarity between them and real characters is a mere coincidence.

Yeah, right

ACKNOWLEDGMENTS

Special thanks to Wahab Almurib for his unlimited support. The author also would like to thank Mr. Al-Muhalab Shiaa of Asahi newspaper for all the valuable contributions, details, and statistics (blame him for any mistakes), Ali Tabla for his efforts, Robert, Kais, Ali Al-Judi, Terry, Rebecca Snarski, Khalil, Sarmad, Omar, Firas, Adnan, Mohammed Kasim and Basim for being the early readers. And to Susan, without her this book wouldn't have taken this shape.
Thank you everyone...

Prologue
Place: Baghdad – the Iraqi capitol
June 10th 2005
Time: 4:00 PM

A cloud of black smoke rose high.

Alarming the heavens; more victims to come. In the silence shouting at humanity's conscience, a convoy of the dead started their journey in body bags.

The smell of death filled the air. Ashes of depression covered those who survived.

The sirens of ambulances mixed with the screams of pain and agony, the wailing of the mothers, and the invisible servants of death barking for more killing.

The lovers arrived to say their final farewells, saluting the burned bodies, kneeling in front of loved ones to apologize that destiny chose them to survive to moan and cry.

It was just another day in Iraq's battle against terrorism.

The battle of innocent bodies against bullets and fire. Another day when the desire for life struggled against ideologies of death and extremism.

Today, he knew death had prevailed. Desperation had triumphed. He arrived too late. Everything around him screamed with what he refused to accept.

Captain Abdul Hasan stared at the bombing site. He had failed. It was his fault, his alone, and no one else's. He could have stopped it.

Abdul Hasan pushed his way through frenzied firemen, their water hoses pointed at the fire and blood ponds. People passed by traumatized; eyes wide, looking everywhere and nowhere. Everyone on his own quest, searching the bodies, trying to identify relatives.

He could recognize some. A doctor from Karada Hospital looking around, ready to let out a cry. A member in the Iraqi Parliament shouting at his guards with madness. The American officer with his soldiers, lifting the body of a wounded American civilian, putting him in their armored vehicle.

A young man with a scarred face accompanied by a young lady. Both looked as if they had been resurrected from the grave to come running to the scene.

Of course he recognized them; he knew them from yesterday.

Yesterday, when everything had started...

-1-
Place: Baghdad – Karada Hospital
June 9th, the day before the bombing
Time: 5:00 PM

Those eyes again.

Concerned and tired and... familiar. He did not recognize the face amidst the blur that covered everything. Were her lips moving? Maybe. Why was there no sound? Just the deafening noise.

He looked at the eyes again. His mother's eyes. The worry, the suffering, the protection. The pain was back, again. Abdul Rahman opened his mouth. He wanted to scream. His mouth was dry, so damn dry his tongue felt like a strange object.

"I need that anesthetic...NOW!" The woman shouted. She wasn't his mother. But the worried eyes never moved away from him, as if afraid of losing him.

He could see her face better now. The wrinkles beneath her eyes, the delicate eyebrows, the rounded face, and the white Islamic head cover matching her white clothes.

Who was she? More importantly, where was he?

Abdul Rahman had a vague recollection of what happened to him. He remembered waking up to see people carrying him. He remembered being tossed around from one car to another. Then the hospital. He was in a hospital. Someone brought him to a hospital. How could that happen? He wasn't dead. Not yet, at least.

He wondered if he should feel happy for this, for being alive. His bafflement did not last long. A white, paralyzing pain shut down all his senses. Everything went into a blur again. Seconds later, the pain subsided. Abdul Rahman saw the woman again, talking to someone next to her. "For God sake, let someone run to the pharmacy and bring me something to drug this poor young man."

"Who will do the surgery?" a male voice asked.

"I will," she said.

"But Dr. Zainab, you don't really mean that you will take the responsibility, for this--"

"This what?"

The man's answer made the hair on the back of Abdul Rahman's neck stand.

"This man is a terrorist, doctor."

They knew.

"You don't know that, Kassem. Just because he was brought up with another man who wore a face mask doesn't mean that he is a terrorist."

Kassem sneered.

Pain. Unbearable pain. Abdul Rahman's entire body was on fire. He moaned. He felt ashamed but couldn't stop the moans. He needed some sound to block the pain. The bullet. He was shot.

"*Satakoon Bekhair,*" (you will be okay) Zainab said looking back at him. Not only her eyes were like his mother's, her voice was, too.

"Where am I?" Abdul Rahman asked.

"Sweeeeet... He is a Saudi," Kassem scoffed recognizing his accent.

"What's your name?" Dr. Zainab asked him.

"Abdul Rahman," he said without thinking.

"Abdul Rahman, you were shot. Do you understand? The bullet is below the lower ribs, you were lucky it didn't hit a vital organ." She spoke as if to a child; it felt stupid, yet comforting at the same time. "I have to take it out before you get an infection. But we are running out of anesthetic, so I might need to perform the surgery while you are awake. Do you understand?"

He looked at her wide brown eyes and nodded. Then felt a pang of fear, "Will it... hurt?"

"A lot," Kassem said.

Zainab glared at Kassem, her lips tightened. "Very brave, Kassem, very brave."

"What? It's not me who came to blow himself up among the women and children to marry virgins in heaven."

Zainab sighed. Kassem stepped in front of his bed. Abdul Rahman could see his young face and the unshaven beard and the wire-rimmed glasses. He didn't like the smug look and the way he stood putting both hands in his white blazer.

"What's the matter, hero?" Kassem said, "You missed dinner with the prophet when you didn't die?"

"Stop it, Kassem!" Dr. Zainab shouted. "Get out of here right now."

Kassem shrugged. "What about the other guy? Mr. Scar-face. Will you do the surgery for him as well? His wound is deeper and it looks serious."

Zainab closed her eyes, her lips quivered. For a moment Abdul Rahman thought she was going to cry. "I need you with me, Kassem," she took a long breath, "Please."

Kassem nodded, avoiding her eyes. "Let's wait for five minutes, the nurse said she might be able to get us some drugs across the street."

Across the street? What sort of hospital was this? Abdul Rahman almost complained but... hey, they were treating him for free.

"Is your family in Baghdad, Abdul Rahman?" Zainab asked, running a large chunk of cotton across his forehead. He was sweating. He felt cold. Cold and numb in the legs. Not a good sign.

"Abdul Rahman, stay with me," Zainab said. "Where is your family?"

"I ....have ....no family."

"Are they in Saudi?"

He did not answer. She nodded, caressing her lips.

"I found some!" An enthusiastic female voice came behind them. A large, dark skinned woman, a very large woman actually, with shoulder-length black hair, peered from the door. Her face was of someone who had just discovered Mammy's make-up drawer. She extended a hand that could be easily mistaken as a couch to Dr. Zainab, giving her something.

"Thank God," Zainab said.

"Anything for the Mujahedeen." The large nurse smiled at Abdul Rahman. Her heavy, red lipstick along with layers of white powder made Abdul Rahman wish she wouldn't smile again. "You have done well yesterday by attacking those American tanks."

Abdul Rahman had no idea what she was talking about, but managed a faint smile.

"Don't fall in love with him," Kassem told the nurse, his hands still in his pockets. "You will break the hearts of the virgins waiting for him in heaven."

She stuck out her tongue, then turned back to Abdul Rahman. Her white blazer was big enough to double as a sail and yet it was stretched over her waist. "You were luckier than your friend." Abdul Rahman had no idea who the other guy was. He tried to turn his head to see the adjacent bed, but a sharp pain in his neck made him change his mind.

"Leave now," Zainab told the nurse.

The nurse frowned. "I'll be in the cafeteria. Lunch." She made a gesture with her hand as if biting on something. It reminded Abdul Rahman of Jurassic Park, the T-Rex attack.

The room became immediately empty. Zainab turned to him, "I am not sure what sort of bullshit they stuffed in your head," she said, walking to him now with a needle in her hand. "But I know that anything that allows the killing of innocents is not a religion."

Everyone was a damn philosopher.

She stuck the needle in the plastic bag next to the bed. It was the first time he'd noticed it there.

Minutes later he was sleeping.

-2-

Karada district - Baghdad
June 9th
5:30 PM

The sun was about to go down. The orange disc shyly hid behind the curtains of dust that hovered slowly, engulfing the horizon and warning of another stormy day. The howling sound of the wind swelled from time to time, covering the loud roar of bumper-to-bumper cars in an endless queue in Karada's main street.

Luay glanced at his watch, late for his appointment and yet to find a parking lot. Not an easy task in Karada at this time of the day. Finally, he decided to double park the car behind a white Nissan Sunny.

At least he did not double park next to an ambulance.

Luay stepped out and walked toward the nearby, large, white-marble building that looked shiny even in the dusty weather. He glanced furiously at the grungy guy who came flying out, demanding parking fees. Unemployed individuals often imposed parking fees on free parking areas, claiming they were assigned by the city to guard parked cars.

Okay, put on the game face. Luay frowned and punched his left palm with his right fist. Grungy passed him, giving him a quick and shy smile. It always worked. How could it not? Over six feet of muscles and a face that, even when smiling, could be mildly described as intimidating. His large jaws, thick neck, and wide forehead made him look like a middle-eastern version of the Hulk. Luay was born this way, he never took steroids or anything like it. Yes, he worked out regularly, but not more than half an hour a day. He wasn't bad-looking. Large and gigantic, yes, but his features worked well with each other. It was probably his eyes that intimidated people around him. People seemed to always avoid him when they passed. As if an aura of destruction surrounded him wherever he went. Or maybe that was only the impression he got, given his past.

Luay headed to the five-story, white building across the crowded street, glaring at the silently approaching sand storm. The air felt heavy and had that intense smell of dust.

Shit…this day couldn't be better.

Once again, he remembered why he came here… his appointment. How his life was going to change if he got the job. He wouldn't have to work with Abu Ayob and his gloomy-faced cult. He never liked them, and they didn't like him either… not that he cared.

Funny, Luay had fought a lot of battles, his life was a series of continuous action. Yet, he never felt nervous the way he did now. One part was the interview, but mostly it was the change to his life. Too many possibilities, too many things to be done; life could be fun if he wanted to enjoy it.

Which just made the trepidation worse.

Instead of living like a hired gun, carrying orders of killing people and protecting others, risking his life in the process, he had to live now like any other person. Working in an ordinary job where the only thing to worry about was making his boss happy. Maybe even get married. Kids. Home. The money he had saved from the operations he'd done would provide a good start.

He could live with that.

Luay never understood why people cherished this boring way of living so much. The life he always saw in the eyes of those whom he was about to eliminate. He couldn't understand it, especially when they pled for mercy with words such as, "I have a family." What pleasure did they find to make them so attached to life, so afraid of death to the point of humiliation?

Never a complainer, he always used to think of himself as a warrior. One who treasured living in danger and trusted only his weapon. But everything had changed lately. His boss, Dafer Al-Dayni, a big-time politician and the leader of a coalition of parties in the crap they called the government, had changed a lot since his last trip to Dubai three days ago. The old man had become absent-minded. Nothing seemed to attract his attention anymore. Not even the undercover operations with Abu Ayob's group in which Luay acted as a liaison.

This morning, Luay had a chance to speak with Dafer in private. Luay told him about the job interview. Dafer didn't listen; he kept nodding slowly all the time. Then, when Luay finished, Dafer shocked him when he asked if he had seen Omar. Omar, Dafer's son, was with him in Dubai. Dafer then told him about how his son saw him with his mistress in a five-star hotel in Dubai.

"I am afraid that Omar will soon find out that I married her recently," Dafer told him, looking genuinely sad for the first time. Maybe there was a heart inside the old man's chest after all. "I gave him one of my best companies to run, I gave him everything he wanted, even before he asked. And now...now he doesn't pick up the phone when I call him."

Luay, who couldn't care less about the situation, asked Dafer if he wanted him to whack someone. Dafer gave him a long look then dismissed him.

To hell with him, who the hell did he think I was? Dr. Phil?

He stopped in front of the glass entrance to the elegant building covered by white marble and took the stairs to the first floor.

The golden plaque on the office door read:

Al-Sadiq Trade Company
Member of Al Ghadeer Group

Alsadiq and Al-Ghadeer! The ethnic background of the owners couldn't be more obvious.

Pressing on the small doorbell, Luay waited for a while. A sixty-ish wiry man opened the door. His eyes were sunk deep in his skull. The snow-white hair covering his head made him look even older.

"I have an appointment with Habib," Luay said.

"And your name is?" The old man looked upward to the gigantic Luay. His Adam's apple bounced up and down.

"My name is Luay, I have a job interview...my friend, Haj Ahmed, told me--"

The old man nodded slowly; his scrawny neck looked as if it were going to fall if he did it any faster.

"One minute, please." The old man disappeared behind the door. After one long minute he came back, gesturing Luay in. "This way, please."

Ah, the elegance of the place. The simple and yet luxurious interior design. In the reception room, two leather couches, plumped up to the point that Luay thought he could dive in them made his muscles relax just by seeing them. A table of dark-colored glass and leather of the same color next to the couch. A dark glass cupboard with too many shelves had a wooden statue of something that looked like a dancing man.

Modern stupid art.

Instinctively, Luay remembered his father's office in the regional branch bureau of the Baath party he used to manage. The big man had spent a lot for the office to look opulent and distinguished, but it was no more than a grocery shop in comparison with this.

"Hi, how can I help you?" A young lady behind a desk asked him in a sweet tone, tilting her head. Her long dark hair fell over her shoulder like a shampoo commercial. Hot was an understatement. Her attractiveness added more elegance to the office interior. But after spending all this time with Abu Ayob and his group, even a female prison warden would look hot.

"M...m...my name is Luay, I have an appointment with Habib at 6."

"Sure, one minute please." She smiled. Luay looked at the phone with envy as she picked it up with a hand so small, so soft and so white it could be on a hand cream commercial.

What was with him and commercials today?

"Mr. Habib, I have Luay here, saying that he has an appointment with you but I cannot see it in your agenda… oh… okay, one minute please."

Even his name was sweet on her lips.

With her hand covering the speaker, she addressed Luay again, "You came based on the recommendation from Haj Ahmed, right?" Luay nodded, she passed on his confirmation to Habib and hung up. "Please have a seat." She smiled at him with ardent dark eyes. He neither could look at them nor move his gaze away, "Habib will see you soon."

Luay sat on the nearest couch, smiling back at her. His smile widened as the couch started swallowing his body. For the first time during this tiresome day, Luay relaxed. He welcomed the puff of cold air from the air conditioner. When was the last time he sat in a room with the AC working? Two, maybe three days. Electrical power wasn't good after the war.

As he leaned his head back on the couch, flashes from his last twenty-four hours forced their way to his mind. A photograph with blood stains covering the edges lay near a beheaded body. The acrid smell of gunpowder filled the air. The fuming smell of death. A man cried in agony, another pled for mercy. Luay shook his head, opening his eyes.

Once he closed his eyes again, other images rushed back like an uninvited guest. He was at the truck bed of the group car. Engulfed by the darkness. The wool sky mask itchy against his two-days-unshaven beard. Fire shots disturbed the otherwise silent night. Two masked men accompanied him. Another two inside the car, the man next to him screamed in agony. Blood splattered. They kept firing toward the police patrol car. Triumphant cheering mixed with cursing and swearing. Blood everywhere. The flare of bullets occasionally illuminated the darkness of the night. One soldier down, then another, and another. The rest of the Iraqi policemen ran away. Luay walked toward a wounded soldier, pressed the gun against the man's forehead. He couldn't see the man's face because of the night goggles and the blood that covered the young man's face. Who cared? Pleading… begging… crying. The same worn-out clichés he got sick of, family, children. The soldier's hand reached to the front pocket of his jacket, Luay shot. The young man's blood splattered on the pavement. He took another look at the dead body, the man's hand was still in his pocket. Luay reached for it. A photograph. A young man with a newborn child. A loud thump sounded in Luay's chest. His heart beat loud in his head. With shaking hands, he removed the night goggles from the soldier's face and wiped off the blood. Swearing. He told him not to join the Iraqi army.

He cursed himself.

How couldn't he recognize him? At least the voice?

Another masked man approached him, the blade of his knife glittered in the dark night. He cut off the dead soldier's head. Carrying it high by the hair then threw it in a nearby garage with a victorious hurrah. More swearing followed.

Luay couldn't look at the photograph anymore, he tossed it near the now-headless body of his cousin.

"You can see him now," the cheerful sound of the receptionist came to him from a distance, bringing him back to reality.

Luay stood, embarrassed he had snoozed on the couch. He headed to the room where Miss Gorgeous pointed and opened the door to find himself in an even more luxurious room. It wasn't as big as the lobby, enough for six people, maybe eight. The only wall in the room was crowded with paintings Luay couldn't comprehend but they matched the room interior. The other wall was a big dark-glass cupboard filled with books, antiques, a flat plasma TV screen and another wooden statue of a dancing man.

Maybe it was a wholesale deal.

A large window overlooked the crowded Karada's main street. Close to the window stretched an oval-shaped, dark-wooden desk where a man with a five-o'clock shadow sat. He was in his early thirties, in-shape and wore a white shirt buttoned all the way up. No tie.

To Luay's right extended a coach of similar black leather where another young man with a reddish face sat watching the TV in front of him. The man behind the oval desk stood, extended his hand with a plastered smile, and introduced himself as Habib, the manager of Al-Sadiq Company.

Luay murmured something and sat on one of the two chairs next to the oval desk. "I came based on Haj Ahmed recommendation, regarding the job of the customs expediter."

Luay looked at the big red ring on Habib's finger, remembering his training a decade ago when he'd first joined the secret service. Learning to distinguish between different ethnic groups and sects was an essential part of his training... his life, actually.

And the signs were not good now.

For Luay, mottos such as the Iraqi brotherhood and we-are-all-brothers were… well...just mottos.

"Yes, Haj Ahmed told me about it." Habib leaned back in his chair crossing his legs. "You did a hell of a job there."

In fact it wasn't much. When Luay went to the customs office to help Haj Ahmed he found one of his old contacts from his days in Sadam's secret service. The man still had an influence there. Strange, despite being members in the old and now-prohibited Baath party, some people kept their jobs by simply switching sides to another party.

"Oh, it was nothing, really." Luay chuckled, he liked being modest. "All that you need is some connections and to know how to approach them."

Habib nodded.

"And you have to be smart as well, sometime even the people you know want to take advantage of you." Luay added, "You have to pay under-the-table money, in one way or another, but the tricky part is how much and how?"

Okay, maybe being modest wasn't his best skill.

"I don't remember someone called Haj Ahmed working for us?" Reddish-face asked Habib.

"He is the customs facilitator who works for Al-Ghadeer corporation," Habib said.

Luay didn't like the tone Habib referred to Haj Ahmed.

A knock came on the door. The same white-haired old man came in and stood in the middle of the room. Habib asked Luay if he would like tea. Tea, and not just any tea, the Iraqi black tea was perfect in winter when the temperature was below fifty degrees Fahrenheit. But now? In the summer, when it was almost one hundred? Just the thought made Luay sweat.

"Yes, tea will be nice," Luay said. He couldn't say no to Iraqis' favorite beverage or to his potential boss for that matter.

The old man nodded and left.

"So Luay, tell me about your experience. Where do you work now?"

"Huh?"

Luay had never had a job interview before. One didn't need to do interviews to work for the elite forces or the secret service of Sadam.

"I … I am not working now."

"Hadeeka?" Ruddy-face smirked, his gaze still fixed on the TV.

Luay was familiar with the term. The modern Iraqi lexicon was a fast-evolving subject. Hadeeka, which meant garden, was a man who lost his job and has nothing to do but to tend his home garden.

A simper filled with smugness tied down on Ruddy's thin lips. Would that stupid grin still be there if he punched him in the stomach?

"I worked as a taxi driver... I have my own car, you know."

Habib nodded. He wrote something on a paper. Luay hoped it wasn't the Hadeeka notion. Habib then grinned at him, maybe trying to be friendly. But Luay didn't like the patronizing look.

"And before the war? Where did you work?"

Shit!

Why did they keep asking about his old work? He would work as a custom's facilitator and he had already proven himself.

"Well... I worked for the government."

Habib's friendly grin evaporated. Many people in Iraq were cautious about anything relating to the old Baath government.

Shit... Shit...

Even Ruddy-face arched an eyebrow. But that was for a brief second, then he turned back to watch the TV.

"Where in government, exactly?"

"Habib, look at this!" Ruddy pointed at the TV. "Ministry of Planning is finally holding that conference to discuss the new investment legislation."

"This convention should be in the Ministry of Health, not planning." Habib chuckled.

Luay cracked a smile to complement but didn't know what Habib was talking about. Ruddy's mouth gaped in confusion.

"What? You didn't get it?" Habib laughed. "They will all need a brain-transformation surgery before making a new law."

"Or maybe they need a map," Luay added, laughing in the same way Habib did. "To help them find their brains."

Both Habib and his friend laughed.

To help them find their brains. Well, it wasn't very bad for ass-kissing. Making fun of the new government was one of Luay's favorite subjects.

"Okay, Luay, so what did you used to do for the government?"

"I...I worked a desk job."

"In?" Habib made a circular motion with his hand, beckoning him to continue.

"The government," Luay said with a smile. Habib's young face became serene. Luay had to come up with some place; he couldn't talk about the secret service or the elite forces, so he lied.

"The passports administration."

"The passports administration!" Both Habib and ruddy face exclaimed in unison.

Shit ... shit ... shit.

The passports administration was a Ministry of Interior division. Although it was a five-star spa compared to where he used to work; still, only people from certain ethnic background were allowed to work there and only those with ranks in the Iraqi army or other security agencies. Not a good thing in the resume, come to think about it. Not when being interviewed by someone with a big red ring on his right hand.

"So you worked for the Ministry of Interior?" Habib said, he subtly examined Luay as if searching for places where he hid his guns.

"Can we talk about how clumsy the new government is instead?" Luay smiled sheepishly.

No one laughed. The air felt tense and heavy.

"So... you don't have any experience working with logistics before?" Habib asked.

The room felt smaller. Isolated. Luay couldn't hear the noise coming from the street anymore or the muffled sounds of the chattering outside on the reception desk.

"No... not really."

Habib and Ruddy face exchanged glances. Luay used to exchange the same one with his superior in the old days when they were interrogating someone. His boss would give him the "look" and he would punch the man in the kidney or kneecap or even whack him dead, depending on the look. The Sadami version of good-cop/bad-cop, except with them it was a bad-cop and the-son-of-a-bitch-cop.

"What about experience with the private sector?" Ruddy asked.

Luay shook his head. The walls got even closer. How silly. Worrying about two civilians he could neutralize in one minute.

Neutralize?

He shook his head. The work with the secret service was over.

Ruddy face asked some follow-up questions.

14

Luay answered with another shake of his head.

A great interview technique, to keep shaking your head. Why hadn't the suspects they interrogated in the secret service used that instead of the worn-out phrase of "I swear by God I did nothing."

"Do you know how to use the computer?" Habib asked.

What the hell was he thinking coming here with a suit and a tie? He tried to loosen his tie a bit. "No… but I can learn." He wanted to add that he learned in no time how to use Playstation2 but he thought better of it.

Why had he even considered working for a private company? He did well working as a liaison between Dafer's party and Abu Ayob's group. To hell with the normal life. He couldn't spend one more minute being questioned by these haughty civilians. And then, unconsciously, his hand reached to his gun. But none was there. For the first time since he turned eighteen he walked unarmed.

Cold sweat covered his forehead, his breath became shallow, his knees buckled. Luay felt naked, surrounded by these probing eyes and twisted questions trying to embarrass him. He tried again to loosen his tie, it wasn't easy. Something boiled in his chest. Drums thudded inside his head. Why did he take his younger sister's advice to wear a tie?

From far away, Habib apologized with his phony manners. "I am sorry, Mr. Luay, but you see, I need someone with better experience with private companies."

To hell with them! He wanted nothing but to get out of this place. Luay murmured thanking Habib for his time and almost sprinted out, crashing into the old man who came bringing them tea. "Keep it to yourself," he muttered under his breath, slamming the door behind him.

Outside, Luay filled his lungs with the fresh air. Okay, dusty air, but anything was better than that cage. He walked with his head down. What happened there? Couldn't he come up with better lies? Inventing any company name? And why all this anxiety? He wasn't the sort of a man who feared walking through gunfire, so how could two naïve civilians trouble him the way they did? Was that black magic, a spell they cursed him with?

Who knew? Those people could do anything.

The traffic was better, fewer cars and more people walking. Karada Street was one of the best places to walk in Baghdad. It wasn't too luxurious, but wasn't low-class either.

Some of Baghdad best fashion shops were there. But there were also the affordable ones. Restaurants ranged from the fancy one-hundred-dollar-meal to the casual two-dollar-meal, food quality was the same. Luay particularly enjoyed the food stands. He used to buy his lunch from those stands every day when he worked in the secret-service's branch office in Karada.

The fashion shops' owners opened their stores, welcoming the evening customers. A group of young men stood in a corner gazing at passing-by young women, throwing meaningless comments as pick-up lines.

Good to see that some places were still the same after the war.

At the nearby pavement, a young man squatted, sorting a bunch of books on a white sheet to sell. Luay scrutinized the book titles. "Shia And The Rulers", "Emam Hussain's Revolution", "Stories Behind Prison Bars", "Sadam's Secrets" and what have you. Rage built in his chest again. What happened to the people? The way they turned their backs on the old regime, denouncing it, even condemning it. As if it were a plague of some sort.

All because of Iran. Iran was, and always had been, trying to push Shia against their own countries. But those idiots couldn't get it. He spat. Anger burned inside him, his hands tightened into fists.

Something vibrated in his pocket. His cell phone. Luay answered automatically still staring at the pavement filled with books.

"*Naam*," (Yes) he answered.

"Luay, *Oreed An ARaak*," (I want to see you) the voice at the other end said. "Immediately."

"But... I ... Okay, will be there." Luay sighed ending the call.

On the small screen of his cell phone, the words appeared:

CALL DURATION 0:43

CALLER ID: ABU AYOB

-3-

Baghdad International Airport

June 9th

5:45 PM

Captain Abdul Hasan stared at the distant ceiling made of green arches and chandeliers. Impressive. After twenty years, Baghdad airport still had its touch. The water fountains were not working as in their heyday but with what this airport went through, it was still admirable.

The Airport café had the closed sign next to the empty cashier. The two Kurdish men who ran the cafeteria yelled at the janitors, probably because they missed a spot here or there. In front of him were the duty-free shops. Promotion signs hung from the ceilings and behind the shiny glasses. For a moment, Abdul Hasan considered buying something for his son's birthday. Tomorrow he would be fourteen and he had always asked for a cell phone.

It sounded appropriate. But he soon dismissed the idea, almost scowling at himself.

He had an important mission to accomplish. Since he had been promoted to a captain in the Ministry of Interior Commandos Forces, aka MICF, Abdul Hasan never had to go on field missions. Convenient, considering his five decades, of which he spent more than a half in the army – both the old one and the new one.

But today's mission was exceptional. His unit had confirmed information that a Syrian young man, who miserably failed to detonate the bombed car he drove after getting cold feet, had arranged for a forged passport and was about to leave the country, back to Syria from the airport.

When Abdul Hasan first heard the story, the terrorist's stupidity astonished him. Leaving the country by the airport? With a fake passport? Those kids watched too many American movies. Probably he thought of himself as DiCaprio in *Catch Me If You Can*. It gave him and his lieutenants a good laugh. But now when Abdul Hasan thought about it, it was… sad. They were just kids. Kids who were taught to hate rather than to love. Kids who, for God-knew-what reason, decided to end their lives killing hundreds of innocents.

In normal circumstances Abdul Hasan wouldn't give a dime to chase a runaway terrorist such as their target today. As a matter of fact, he almost decided to ignore the tip before Hussain, a bright lieutenant on the team, pointed out that given the location of the attempted explosion, the young Syrian might have worked with Abu Ayob's group, a legendary, blood-thirsty terrorist, whose very existence was questionable. Abu Ayob was suspected to be an 'Ameer', the equivalent to a General in the Qaeda terminology. His group was suspected to be responsible for several killings, kidnappings, and terrorist attacks, including the two car bombs last week.

The myth —as it was the closest thing Abdul Hasan could think of— suggested that Abu Ayob had slaughtered over three hundred men, often with beheading. Because Al-Qaeda customs used killing records as the base for promotions, this number made him a rising star in the dark and gloomy sky of Al-Qaeda.

According to another myth the CIA was still working on, Abu Ayob was also suspected to be involved --if not the mastermind-- behind a couple of deadly attacks in Afghanistan and Yemen before coming to Iraq.

Needless to say, there were no verified sightings of Abu Ayob.

"No sign of him, Sir," Lieutenant Shaker reported with a hint of a smile. Shaker couldn't be serious. Well... except about money. He was tall and strong, his wide torso and dark skin, along with his fitness and cheerful mode, made his colleagues nickname him Kala, Tarzan's ape mother.

Abdul Hasan nodded, motioning for Shaker to sit on the chair next to him. The situation was a bit awkward. As the airport security was under the US army, Abdul Hasan had to go through tons of paperwork to allow his team to search the airport for the Syrian fellow. He had filed a request to the passport control office in the airport and another to the joint security committee with members of both Iraqis and Americans. But without a photo to the report, there was little chance that anything could be done, assuming the Syrian would be smart enough to change his real name.

Instead of leaving the case there, Abdul Hasan took two of his best lieutenants and came to the airport. The American officer in the airport was kind enough to let them in on the condition they gave up their weapons.

So there he was, sitting in a metal chair in the departure hall scrutinizing all passengers' faces for a young man with average height and built, asking for their passports and papers, hoping their uniforms and serious faces would provoke the Syrian terrorist to do something stupid.

It didn't happen. The only ones who looked stupid were him and his team running around from one group of passengers to another like headless chickens.

The second lieutenant, Hussain, came back, head down and shoulders slumped. Abdul Hasan scanned the departure hall. Over two hundred passengers. Women, children and old men were excluded. The possibility that their target disguised himself could be safely eliminated. Those things worked only in movies.

The Captain could count thirty, maybe forty men who fitted the general description. And he was sure they had covered them all. So where was that poor bastard? Did he get cold-feet again and finally realize it was too risky to escape Iraq from the airport? After all, most of the terrorists came through Syria by land. They should be familiar with the land road and naturally it should be their first option to leave.

Of course, leaving the borders by car required the same arrangements with the Syrian authorities and whatever gangs on the borders. The more Abdul Hasan thought about it, the more he leaned to the conclusion that their target felt trapped and hunted by his own group. Maybe because he dropped the cause. Or maybe because he knew too much. After all, the young man was supposed to die blasting himself up with the car. When he didn't, he suddenly became a man who knew too much. An immediate threat.

Maybe the bad guys got to him first? Why not?

Abdul Hasan's gaze settled on a scene outside the departure hall. Through the glass wall he could see a man with an Arabic white Dishdash and a red Shimag --the men's headcover people in the Arabian gulf areas wore.

The man in the Dishdash argued with two airport security guards. Something about him was odd. Abdul Hasan never had a spider-sense-like intuition before but this time he felt something. The uneasy sense of déjà-vu, a distant alert. Unsure why, he walked outside the departure hall to the entrance where white-Dishdash argued with the security guards. Hussain followed.

The matter resolved. The man in the Dishdash walked away waving threats with his hand. He turned toward the security guards, shouted something. They did likewise. They were laughing, he wasn't.

"What is going on?" Abdul Hasan asked one of the guards dressed in blue with full body armor and silver sun glasses. Give him a silver helmet and he would be RoboCop. An Iraqi version anyway.

RoboCop glanced at Abdul Hasan's uniform then said in a defensive tone, "He is the one who started it, Sir."

"Started what?"

"This clumsy idiot had lost his way and he wanted to enter the departure hall," the guard answered.

His colleague, who wore the same uniform and the same silver sunglasses but was a bit shorter, added, "Yeah, we tried to explain to him that arrivals should proceed to the other gate where they can find taxies and buses to town center."

"Arrivals?" Abdul Hasan asked.

"Yeah, his plane came from Saudi Arabia."

A Saudi. Abdul Hasan's mind went on overdrive trying to remember when or where he saw this man.

"He kept saying that he usually got dropped off at this spot, and he want to use the same route," RoboCop added.

"Dropped here? How?"

Civilians had to walk from the checkpoint one hundred yards away. But the answer came from the guard.

"He said he is a Saudi diplomat."

"A VIP." Short RoboCop sneered.

"Well yeah, he is a Very Idiotic Person," the taller added and they both laughed.

Abdul Hasan could hear the sound of 'click' in his mind. He remembered where he saw this man. His name was Saud and he was a diplomat, sort of.

"Isn't that..." Hussain said, looking at Saud now.

"Yes, Saud," Abdul Hasan added.

Saud engaged in another argument with another guard who kept pointing at a different direction to where Saud wanted to go.

"The man from the Saudi Red Crescent. We were assigned to protect his convoy three months ago," Hussain said in a monotone.

"Well, he is not working with the Red Crescent anymore," Abdul Hasan added, remembering seeing Saud on the TV shaking hands with Dafer Al-Dayni after a conference in Turkey where the later shamelessly asked for funds to support his sectarian war.

"But why he is alone?" Hussain asked, massaging the back of his neck. "Isn't he supposed to be with his security guards, like the previous time?"

A damn good question. Abdul Hasan had no doubt a man like Saud was some sort of liaison between highly influential people in the Arab Gulf region and other party leaders in Iraq. It was also quite possible he had links to armed groups. He remembered well finding a gun with a silencer in one of Saud's companion's bags, along with tremendous amounts of cash.

They stood there for another two minutes watching Saud in the street in front of the entrance to the departure hall, arguing and shouting with everyone around him. He looked funny trying to walk fast holding his table-cloth-like Dishdash with one hand while holding on the red Shimag with the other as if his head were on fire.

Finally, the airport security managed to put him in a taxi. Abdul Hasan asked the guard across the street about the destination.

"To Al-Adel district," the guard replied.

Al Adel district, where Dafer Al-Dayni and his small militia of personal security force controlled the area. No surprise.

What deal had Saud brought to Dafer this time? And why did he come alone with no staff and no security?

Good questions, but Abdul Hasan had no time for playing Sherlock Holmes, he had enough on his plate already.

They went back to their chairs next to Shaker, watching the people next to the check-in counters.

"We still have ten minutes for the plane to depart," Abdul Hasan told them, looking at the information board in the airport. Then he realized that half an hour ago, when they first arrived, the board showed only fifteen minutes before the plane to Syria departed.

He rubbed his chin, hmm... interesting how time works in the airport.

Shaker looked at the board and smiled. "I am willing to bet my next promotion that the monkey controlling the info board is busy chatting with his girlfriend."

"Putting in mind the success of this mission," Hussain grinned, "I doubt you will see any promotion for a long time."

Shaker's eyes popped up, his jaw dropped. Then he looked at Abdul Hasan. The Captain looked at the ceiling with a crooked smile. Normally, he didn't allow them to involve him in teasing each other, but he needed some distraction from the desperation they all felt. "But, Sir... I ...you ... I mean..." Shaker shook his head. "Come on, boss, you are not really going to let this affect my evaluation."

"Why not, what have you done lately anyhow?" Hussain sneered.

"Reports." Shaker said, his chin up. "I wrote lot of good reports."

Hussain waved him off. "Reports? I'd rather watch the paint dry. Nah, they won't grant you a promotion. No one likes them anyway."

Shaker waited for Abdul Hasan to say something. The Captain faked a sorrowful nod.

"There are lot of things no one likes doing but it has to be done," Shaker said, stepping forward to help an elderly woman by putting her luggage in the trolley while still talking to them, "like paying taxes or going to a public bathroom. Who can stand the smell there, but hey, if nature calls..."

Abdul Hasan's pulse quickened as he saw the smile evaporate from Hussain's face. The lieutenant looked like someone who just remembered he left the gas open at home.

"Shit!" Hussain slammed his forehead.

Abdul Hasan saw the answer in Hussain's eyes. The bathrooms. They did not check the bathrooms. Hussain sprinted toward the public bathrooms. Shaker called after him, laughing, "Man, I told you use the bathroom before we start the mission."

The veteran soldier followed Hussain, walking as fast as his body allowed. When he reached the end of the waiting hall, he could hear Shaker's voice: "Shit! we did not search the bathrooms."

Several passengers and janitors gathered in front of the men's room, not a good sign. Abdul Hasan pushed them aside, entering the room, Shaker followed. On the floor, Hussain sat on his knees holding a young man in a white shirt and blue jeans, both soaked with blood. Three black holes were visible in his chest. Knife wounds. He wore white sneakers, the same ones Abdul Hasan bought his son a week ago. The Captain could only imagine this kid going to a picnic with some friends, getting drunk and getting home late at night.

The young man looked at Hussain's eyes with urgency, sweat fell down his thick eyebrows. He grabbed the lieutenant's uniform as if holding life itself. His mouth opened in a silent cry.

"Please... don't let me die."

"Clear the room, and call the ambulance," Abdul Hasan told Shaker in a resolute voice. Shaker pushed everyone out.

The Syrian young man kicked at the air frantically as if he wanted to stand. "Help me."

"Don't move. You'll be okay," Hussain told him, biting on his lower lip, his eyes moist.

Two men from airport security came. They froze at the bathroom door, staring at the blood. Abdul Hasan kneeled next to Hussain, looking the young man in the eyes. "Son, tell me where I can find the one responsible and he will pay for what he did."

Hussain took out his vest and covered the kid.

The kid nodded, eyes closed shut, his face contorted in a cry. "Please."

And then he started talking.

It was Abdul Hasan's turn to gasp.

After all these years, the Captain never thought he would hear anything that could scare him like this.

-4-
The Green Zone - Baghdad
June 9th
6:15 PM

Enas stood in the portable cabin assigned to the procurement and contracting department of G-Plans, one of biggest American companies in the Green Zone area in Baghdad. She carried three heavy binders, trying to sort them in the big shelf on the wall in front of her. The binders were all quotations for the recent bid G-plans announced to enhance the drinkable water service in Baghdad's southern areas. Her task was simple: to sort out all the RFQs and RFIs—the Request For Quotations and the Request For Information—they had sent and received from various suppliers and contractors regarding this bid. A task Enas could finish in five minutes if she wanted.

But she didn't. Enas's full attention focused on the conversation between her boss, Robert Taylor, and a representative from Al-Ghadeer Company, a man named Ehab.

Robert examined the file on his desk. He thumbed down to the end and started reading. In front of him sat Ehab. Although she could only see the man's profile, Enas had no doubt how anxious Ehab was to discern any acceptance sign from Robert to the revised offer he'd just submitted.

Interesting. On one hand, Al-Ghadeer company, a local subcontractor, had a reputation of never losing any bid in water systems over the last ten years. The company owner, Ali Al-Kadumi, was a legend in the construction business. Ehab, whom Enas detested for many reasons, was an uncanny businessman himself and a shareholder in Al-Ghadeer Company. On the other hand, her boss, Robert, the head of the procurement department, was one of the best professionals Enas had ever seen or could imagine.

Robert was sharp, smart, and honest. Enas had seen him negotiating with several suppliers in the past three months that she had worked with G-plans. On every occasion, he managed to knock down the price given by the supplier, to sometimes half.

Enas liked her job. Working for a big construction company like G-Plans that was in charge of many big-time construction and infrastructure projects in Iraq made her proud. Due to the deteriorating security situation, American companies couldn't perform the work directly, and hence they started subcontracting local suppliers. Their department validated local Iraqi companies to be subcontracted.

"So your final price is seven hundred grand?" Robert closed the file.

"Well actually, yes... but—" Ehab spoke with a heavy English accent. Most of her fellow citizens did, and considering the anxiety Ehab was going through, it wouldn't be easy to tell for sure if he were speaking English or Swahili. "This the original price."

Ehab adjusted his seat and leaned forward, pointing at a certain paragraph in the last page in the file. "As you see here, we can save money if the cost was problem. The final price can be reduced to... umm... between five and four hundred grand only."

Enas winced. Hearing Ehab talking English was similar to when someone scratched his nails on the blackboard in school.

"Brilliant," Robert scoffed with a sarcastic tone, "so you took out the fire alarm system, emergency generators and reduced the pressure power of the pumps to sixty percent. I wonder why our guys didn't think about this."

"Come on, pumps can take the overload." Ehab chuckled, it sounded forced and nervous. "The specs is a recommendation only. And who cares about fire-alarm system while--"

"I do." Robert grunted.

This was the problem when you worked too long with the procurement department, you got used to the I-am-the-customer attitude. To his credit, Robert was modest and polite most of the time with the suppliers. Only crooks like Ehab got on his nerves.

"And do you know what I care about too? When I see one of our primary subcontractors trying to cut corners in such important projects."

Enas was done with the three binders in her hand. Too curious to leave, she went to the attached portacabin where the finance team worked. She asked her colleagues there if they had any invoices for her department. Less than a minute later Enas was back to the cabinet, careful not to look too conspicuous.

Robert gave her an inquisitive look. She pointed at the papers in her hand and then the shelves behind him. He nodded. Her boss had gotten used to her curiosity anyhow.

Robert had utilized the area allocated to his desk to its limits. In addition to the desktop filled with colorful paper organizers and a small laptop, cubical plastic shelves, similar to those one would find at Lego, were fixed to the wall behind his gray chair.

The shelves were labeled with small papers to indicate their content. A seven-inch picture of a group of African kids holding a football occupied the only small space left on his desk.

Enas started sorting the invoices in the corresponding folders, looking now at Ehab's face.

"Believe me, Mr. Taylor," Ehab said, his face flushed red. "This not the idea... no, no... never. We thinking... I mean, I thinking that I can show how flexible our company can meet your requirements."

We thinking? Enas frowned, she actually considered talking to Ehab later about his English. She just hoped he wouldn't argue that it was freedom of speech. People justified all kinds of bullshit lately with freedom of speech.

Robert shook his blond head, tapping on the desk with his large fist. Enas knew how much her boss hated this kind of salesmen, those with eyes in continuous movement, crooked smiles, and gray moral codes.

Robert once told her that during his ten years in the "third-world," he always came across a local subcontractor offering a bribe or another suggesting cost cutting by knocking down the specifications. Enas couldn't help but feel ashamed when an American was more sincere to help her country than the Iraqi who was trying to convince him to take shortcuts.

It was sad and pathetic, and she did not care if this showed on her face.

Her eyes met with Ehab's. He broke eye contact, looking at the desk instead.

"Okay it's my fault... I admit it." Ehab sighed. "But please, whatever your decision is, I wish this conversation don't reach to Mr. Al-Kadimi the chairman of Al-Ghadeer group."

Smart move. Ali Al-Kadimi had a shiny reputation amidst all the companies in Iraq. The man was known as an honorable and yet savvy businessman. The rumor was he had been approached by a major American company offering him a director position managing its operations in Iraq.

"You are saying that this is not your company's offer?" Robert asked, arching his eyebrow and looking Ehab in the eye.

"The proposal is from Ghadeer all right…" Ehab said with a sincere tone, leaning on the desk and looking Robert in the eye, no smile this time. "But to be honest with you, the second option, the one that you didn't like, was mine and Ali has no idea about."

Silence. Robert just sat there waiting for Ehab to keep talking. Something about salesmen, they always came with a suit and tie and a gene that made them keep talking.

"Mr. Taylor, I was afraid we will lose the bid because I know our competitors offer lower specs. And to be honest with you, you American companies sometimes always love to take the cheapest offer even if the specs are lower."

As if Ehab sensed some hesitation from Robert's side, he went on, "And you know Al-Ghadeer company, right? We finish the work in Al-Amel District water station even after the other company refused to lift the diapers and wreckage."

"I beg your pardon?" Robert said, sounding like someone trying hard to suppress laughter. "You mean debris?"

Enas slammed her head into the wall.

"Yeah, that…" Ehab said. "You can asked the project manager from your side, what was his name, Toroza, the project wouldn't saw the light if we didn't bear the extra cost. Now the station opening tomorrow and you can came and see for yourself our work and the quality of the project."

Robert nodded in silence then said, "You said the project launch is tomorrow?"

"Afternoon." Ehab nodded.

Enas had finish sorting the papers and had exasperated all the excuses to stay. No way she would leave before knowing what would happen. She sat in the corner.

Robert arched an eyebrow at her. Enas gave him her widest grin, waving. He smiled shaking his head. He had George Clooney's smile. Crooked and kind and charming as hell. The man looked like Clooney as well. Though his hair was blond, and his face slightly wider, maybe the eyes were smaller and his chin was somehow different. Okay... he did not *look* like Clooney but there was something common between them.

"I will come to the site tomorrow," Robert said. "I might even attend the opening ceremonies and I want you to arrange a meeting for me with Mr. Al-Kadimi."

Hold the phone. Enas opened her mouth, had she heard right?

Robert going out of the Green Zone? What about the security risks? And why? No one would question why he awarded the contract to the company that delivered the first phase. Not with the pressure the American government put on the companies to start delivering some results on the ground.

"You will be pleased of your visit, this much me can promise," Ehab said, eyes glittering as if he'd already got paid. "And by the way, we are arranging for a celebration during the project launch."

Ehab stood preparing to leave.

"That would be interesting, I haven't had the chance to try Iraqi dishes for months now."

"It's better not, at least to maintain your fitness." Ehab laughed, patting on his fat belly.

Ehab turned toward her. Enas felt his gaze x-raying her, taking longer when they reached bellow her neck. She felt naked. Ehab looked at her from the corner of his eyes, his thin lips curled slightly. Disgust, she always saw it in his eyes.

Enas had confidence in her looks. Her petite body, rosy high cheekbones and Angelina-Jolie-like lips made her a tad more than hot. Still, gazes from men like Ehab always made her nervous. They judged her. She could see it in their eyes even if they didn't say it. She could almost hear the accusation, that she claimed positions in her career as a result of another set of skills.

Enas tucked away a wisp of brown hair behind her ears, trying to hide her aggravation.

"What do you think, Enas?" Robert asked in a friendly tone.

"I don't know." Enas shrugged. "We will need to inform Heavy Waters to provide some security escort, won't we? I am not sure they will accept such short notice."

Ehab babbled something about everything being safe and sound. No one paid attention to him.

"We have to look into that... internally," Robert said, his face clouded at the mention of Heavy Waters. Their private security company was screwing them for more money.

After shaking hands with Robert, Ehab wished them a good day, opened the cabin door, and left. A gust of sandy wind came into the cabinet. Enas shut the door after he left a tad too violently.

"Interesting person," Robert said.

She hesitated. When she opened her mouth to comment, a massive explosion shook the cabin. She bent down involuntarily, watching the shaken windows with fear.

"Shit..." Robert said, walking away from the window.

They both fell silent, looking at each other as if expecting another explosion. Instead, gunfire burst from a distance.

"Where do you think it was?" he asked. Explosions outside the Green Zone hardly made the news now. As long as one didn't go out, he was safe.

Nevertheless, terrorists managed to compromise the Green Zone's security perimeter several times. Neither Robert nor his colleagues felt absolutely safe. Fortunately, Robert understood that whatever narrow-minded, bloody terrorists were behind these attacks, that had nothing to do with her or other Iraqis who just wanted to live in peace.

"Don't know, it sounded close." She looked at her watch with concern and added as if talking to herself, "I just hope it's not too close, otherwise I will be delayed even more."

Robert was about to say something when his desk phone rang. They both glanced at the big screen of the Cisco phone. The caller ID showed:

Incoming Call
Caller: Richard Barn 8626

Robert winced. "Speaking of the witch, Mr. Heavy Waters keeps calling me. The man wants to milk us for more money for the god-damned protection."

Richard Barn was the man in-charge of Heavy Waters in the Green Zone. Robert liked him about as much as cancer.

"Are you really going to go to the water project?"

The phone was still ringing. Robert did not move a muscle toward it.

"I don't think so." He sighed, putting his hands on his hips, looking at her from an angle with an off-centric smile. So George

Clooney. "I truly wish I could. I miss the action, the excitement of seeing regular people and seeing what we came here to help with, if you know what I mean."

She did.

The phone stopped ringing.

"Anyway. Mark my words, Enas, terrorism will not prevail. I have seen it before. The will of life will always find a way."

Enas forced a smile. Easy to talk about hope when you never experienced a power outage at summer when temperature exceeded ninety.

"I need to leave now." She remembered her personal curfew. "I am really late."

"Sure, take care, Enas."

"You too, Robert," she said, carrying her bag, covering her nose with a tissue. Enas embraced herself against the sand storm while opening the door. She took a long look at the gathering storm then turned to Robert with a smile. "It will be a hell of a night."

But it wasn't the stormy weather that worried her.

-5-

Al-Karada District - Baghdad

June 9th

6:30 PM

Captain Abdul Hasan was back at the MICF headquarters in Karada. A big house of three floors that used to be an interrogation facility operated by Sadam's secret service in the past. The past. Iraqis talked a lot about the past. Sometimes they used it to refer to the pre-Baath days in the 60s and early 70s when Iraq was in its golden era. Sometimes they used it to refer to the dark thirty years of Saddam's rule. Very recently, they had started using it to refer to better days, terrorist-free days.

As he walked the stairs to his office on the first floor, Abdul Hasan felt the same depression he always did when he entered the house. A heavy rock pressed on his chest. The Captain and his soldiers had tried everything. They had cleaned the house from all the torturing tools, washed the blood stains from the walls and the floors, then painted the house… twice. Nothing worked. The blood stains were not there but he, somehow, still smelled the metallic aroma. His olfactory sense triggered a deep and primal fear. He could see nothing and yet his ears screamed in his head, swearing they heard cries of the tormented souls echoed deep inside the walls.

"You have guests, sir," his secretary, a soldier with a thick mustache, told him as he turned the knob of his door. Abdul Hasan didn't ask who it was. Too obvious. Who could get to his office except:

"General Kenani!" Abdul Hasan spread his arms, the two men embraced.

"Been a long time, Hasan." Kenani was the only one who called him Hasan, not Abdul Hasan. General Kenani was the higher commander of the Ministry of Interior Commandos Force, the MICF. The force was the first law enforcement formation in post-war Iraq, formed by the blessing of the United States ambassador to help the United States forces in their mission to establish order in Baghdad streets again. Right after the new Iraqi government was elected, the minister of interior started head-hunting for people to manage this force. General Kenani, an old veteran, was the man of choice. Kenani's father and Abdul Hasan's served together in the Iraqi army in the 60s as generals. He and Kenani served together during Iraq-Iran war. They both had resigned, Kenani for medical reasons, Abdul Hasan... well, Sadam had put him in jail as a political prisoner. Which meant his real crime was anything between offending the regime to something as simple as farting.

Kenani sat on the big L-shaped couch next to the wall. Abdul Hasan sat in one of the two guest chairs in front of his desk. He kept the office furniture simple and practical. Besides his desk and the L-shaped couch, there was an eight-seat meeting table that filled half of the room, a big cupboard in one of the walls where he kept some important files, a metal safe next to his desk, and on the other wall a large map of Baghdad's roads with over a dozen colored pins in various locations.

"How is the family?" Kenani asked.

"Fine." Then, "Oh, by the way, my son's birthday is tomorrow, we are having a small party, why not bring the family?"

"Sure." Kenani tried to smile. "The kids are too bored. School is over and there is nothing they can do. We spent a week in Kurdistan in the north. It was okay, but once it's over we're back to the same boring life." He frowned. "One minute... you sure this is not one of your ways to ask for a promotion?"

"Will it work?"

"Unlikely," Kenani said, "but I don't deny you the pleasure of trying."

Abdul Hasan put his hand on his chest and semi bowed. "Your generosity… it's just overwhelming."

They both laughed, for a second Abdul Hasan's memory jogged to decades ago, when he and the General were teenagers. Kenani paused abruptly, eyes wide. He looked left and right still holding his breath. "Did you hear that? The…" Kenani searched for the word.

"The whispering you mean, yes."

Nothing new, the room allocated to his office was exceptionally worse than any other room in the house. Footsteps, whispering, and sometimes muffled cries of pain could be heard.

"For God sake, Hasan, when are you going to change your room?"

Abdul Hasan shrugged. "If we couldn't stand a few harmless sounds, how could we stand fighting those bloody terrorists?"

Kenani made a face. "Isn't that a tad too cliché? Even for you."

"Okay, let's just say I feel sorry to give this room to another poor officer. You know my regiment couldn't fit in this house so we have to send half of them to other locations."

"So now you want more space?" Kenani shook his head and sighed. "That's what happens when you offer your friend a job."

There was a serious space issue with Abdul Hasan's three-hundred-soldier regiment responsible for the eastern part of Baghdad of which Karada was the heart. But that wasn't why he didn't want to give up the room. The truth was far simpler. Abdul Hasan got numb to lots of things that other people, ordinary people, were sensitive to. Compared to what he saw and had been through, a couple of lost spirits wandering around was the least of his concerns.

Abdul Hasan checked the clock on the wall. Tradition in Iraq was that the host shouldn't ask his visitors something like, "How can I help you?" before they are well seated and served, and never before one hour of meaningless pleasantries.

So he tried something else. "Would you like some tea?"

"Nah, your guys served me one already." He pointed at the small glass in front of him.

"So how can I help you?"

So much for the traditions.

Kenani leaned back, took a long breath, his face serene and all-business now. "Do you remember the day when I called you to offer you the job?"

He did. Abdul Hasan spent the years after jail running a small bookstore upgraded to a computer store during the rage of computers in Iraq in the late 90s. When Kenani called him to tell him about the offer, Abdul Hasan's first response was to apologize. He was satisfied with his life. That evening he drove his car for several hours through Baghdad neighborhoods. Abdul Hasan didn't get back home until midnight. The next day, he called Kenani and told him he had accepted the offer.

"You had your conditions and I accepted them," Kenani said, toying with the tea spoon. "I had only one condition, not to go overboard because of our friendship."

Abdul Hasan knew where this was going.

"In the last two months your regiment raided four houses without a warrant, two squads dressed up in civilian clothes ambushed a terrorist checkpoint to the south of Baghdad, and several arrests --all with no court order... for God's sake, you are a cop, not a vigilante. And to make it even worse, other captains in the MICF started following your lead, inspired by your achievements."

"I can't just sit there and watch while Baathists and Qaeda take over my city because of some bureaucracy."

"And what about today?" Kenani frowned. "They called me from the airport saying that you were there with two of your men."

"So? We can't enjoy a vacation?"

"Hasan, this is serious, you know how the situation is. Areas were split between us and the ministry of the defense. It's not our due jurisdiction."

After the elections, the Shia-and-Kurd-majority government were forced to include Sunnies in the process. Sectarian-based settlements and power sharing were forced by the US government. So, despite the elections' results, several important ministries had to be given. Ministry of Defense with jurisdiction of western areas of Baghdad was one of them. Another version of democracy tested. And proven failed.

"The airport is under the coalition forces' jurisdiction." Abdul Hasan shrugged.

"Which makes it only worse. Listen to me, Hasan, you don't need to do that. You are a legend, for God's sake, what your regiment did... what *you* did, brought hope to many people that there is a chance that Iraq can fight terrorism. Don't ruin this. Play by the rules, man."

"Play by the rules?"

Kenani shrugged.

"So why don't you or our honorable three-estate system play by the rules and officially charge me?"

Kenani shifted in the couch, "Well... It might happen, the thing is, the people like what you—"

"Cut the crap, Kenani, will you, we both know what is going on here, they know they will be exposed to media scrutiny if they stopped us, they know that people will see through all this bullshit and will understand that it's all part of the ass-kissing game between politicians that made issuing a warrant harder than a private audience with the grand Ayatollah."

Kenani's face reddened. The veins in his big jaw and wide forehead were more prominent. "Nothing justifies disrespect for the rules. If you continue on this road, soon enough you will cause more harm than the terrorists themselves."

"Mashi," (Okay) "let me tell you what happened today and you can decide for yourself."

Abdul Hasan told Kenani about the reason they went to the airport and how they found the terrorist stabbed in the airport bathroom.

"Oh mighty God." Kenani rubbed his face with both his big hands. "Someone had taken the risk of following him to one of the most secure places in the city and whacked him there. That's serious."

Abdul Hasan raised his eyebrow, giving him an I-told-you-so look.

"This Syrian son of bitch must know something important then. He must know about Abu Ayob." Kenani slammed the table in front of him.

"Well, he does, but the thing is, from what this kid said, Abu Ayob is not the real danger here."

"What do you mean, not the danger?" Kenani chuckled. "The guy is a fucking Ameer, it meant he killed at least... what was the number again?"

"Qaeda gives Ameer to the one who beheads at least fifty people. In Abu Ayob's case, the number is around 300." Abdul Hasan noticed how neutral his own tone was. As if they were discussing the statistics of last-night's match.

"Aha," Kenani said, "here you go."

"Except that the kid is saying someone else did most of the killing and accredited the points to Abu Ayob."

"Like donating air miles to your spouse?" Kenani said, his face contorted in disbelief.

Abdul Hasan had no idea what air miles were but nodded. "It looks like he is a real nutcase who enjoyed killing and truly believed in Jihad, he is not after any credit for his um… work."

"It's a fucking sport to him," Kenani said then as if remembering something, "what is his name?"

"Mujahid," Abdul Hasan remembered the fear in the kid's eyes when he said the name.

"No shit? As in *Mujahideen*?"

"Maybe it's just an alias." Abdul Hasan shrugged.

"A damn good one," Kenani said. "Okay, let me get this. You are saying that all those killings we suspected Abu Ayob of being behind turned out to be done by someone who looks at it as a hobby?"

"It's worse," Abdul Hasan said.

Kenani waited.

"You remember the attacks in Haifa Street recently? The two bombed cars and the road mines, according to our kid, Mujahid was the mastermind of those attacks. He was also behind the kidnapping of the Iraqi Taekwondo national team who were captured on their way back from Jordan."

That got Kenani. Sixteen of Iraq's best athletes, coming back from a training camp in Jordan, were kidnapped in the road near Fallujah. The sixteen athletes, all below eighteen, all preparing to participate in the next Olympics… were never found, till now.

A scar on the face of the Ministry of Interior. Nothing to make the minister resign or even interrupt his holiday, but still, for the people who cared it was unforgivable.

"Hold the phone here. This cannot be."

"Oh, you mean because we know that the Taekwondo team were kidnapped by TAWHEED and JIHAD group and Abu Ayob's group is part of Qaeda?" Abdul Hasan said with a sad smile.

"Yes, this Islamic States of fucking Iraq."

"I can't believe that you put Islamic and Iraq and Fucking in one sentence."

"Fuck... what kind of world are we living in? it's just..."

"Fucked up?" Abdul Hasan ventured.

"I just don't understand," Kenani sighed, "how a man who's supposed to work for a group that operates in Hay Al Amel and works under Al-Qaeda's new formation is also related to attacks done by other groups like Tawheed & Jihad, or that one in Haifa Street, I think it was the Army Of Sunnie Supporters or whatever crap it was."

Abdul Hasan let Kenani speak and went to his desk and picked up a bunch of red pins and walked to the map on the wall.

Kenani kept talking. "I mean, we know that despite that all these groups are made of a mixture of Jihadist and ex-Sadam's secret service and Baath party members, their leadership are not on the same wave. They compete like any other business competes. They fight each other if someone steps in the area of someone else. How could this fucking Mujahid work in all those places without causing a..."

"Jurisdiction issue?" Abdul Hasan teased him. Kenani said nothing so Abdul Hasan went on putting pins on the map.

He put two in Haifa Street, three in the road between Baghdad and the city of Dyala. And half a dozen in different locations in Baghdad.

When finished, Abdul Hasan stepped back and examined his work then turned to Kenani and said, "Those are the areas where we believe Mujahid has done some... work."

The map was full with red pins.

"My theory, which is based on the bits and pieces I got from that kid, is that Mujahid is the type of man who truly believes in the bullshit Qaeda and other groups are trying to sell. He is not looking for a position so it kept him away from the struggle the leaders are having with each other. On the other hand, it kept him close to the Mujahideen themselves. He still had his good connections with many people and if you add to it his loyalty, craziness, and some planning capability, he would fit perfect to be chosen by different groups to help them pull attacks here and there."

Abdul Hasan came up with this as he spoke. It made sense. Recent attacks against either US or Iraqi forces had some sort of planning behind them.

"A fucking charismatic psychopath with a mind," Kenani said, rubbing his face. "As if we need more shit. So where the hell is the boy now?"

The boy... Abdul Hasan stopped for a while picturing the sixteen-years-old kid lying on the dirty bathroom floor, his young face filled with stark fear. He wanted the image to be registered in his memory so not to dissolve. He wanted to remember the pain he felt and his promise.

"We sent him to the hospital. I doubt he will make it."

Another neutral tone, another match statistic. Was it all just business? Was he really getting numb after all the killing he saw?

Kenani nodded. Then he checked his watch, "I must leave now, but there was a man here to visit you. He comes with a reference from the Minister of Construction about some information on a possible threat."

"Another tip about the conference?" Abdul Hasan pointed at the file with over a hundred pages on his desk. There had been a lot of reports and tips and all sorts of warnings of attacks against the conference the Ministry of Planning was holding.

Kenani shrugged, "Probably. But please be nice to him. Listen to him and then send him home with the impression that we care."

Abdul Hasan wanted to say "We do care," but let it slide.

Abdul Hasan used his desk phone to talk to the secretary, asking him to send whoever was waiting.

"Oh, by the way," Kenani asked walking to the door, "what are you going to do about this Mujahid guy?"

Abdul Hasan took out a blue pin, held it in the air for Kenani to see, then fixed it in the map in Al-Amel district area.

"This is the most valuable info we got from the Syrian kid," Abdul Hasan said. "We don't know why, but Mujahid will be at a specific address in Al-Amel area today in the afternoon."

A man of average height and unshaven beard opened the door. He had Kevin Costner's retreating hairline. He looked confused, even scared.

Kenani introduced them. His name was Ayad. Abdul Hasan asked him to take a seat and make himself comfortable while walking with Kenani to the end of the hall.

"So what are we going to do about Mujahid?" Kenani asked slowly, he must've realized the dilemma now. Al-Amel district was in the Ministry of Defense jurisdiction. Then he added, "You know what, I don't really want to know."

"Wise."

Kenani gave him a long look then he was off. Before Abdul Hasan got back to his office, his cell rang. It was Hussain.

"Sir, we are in our positions. I have eight men with me all in light arms and civilian cars. We will wait until he shows up and then nail that son-of-a-bitch."

-6-

The Green Zone - Baghdad

June 9th

6:40 PM

Enas walked toward the checkpoint in the Green Zone, trying to get back home before dusk.

She was late, too late.

Today is not my lucky day, she sighed, irritated by the sandstorm.

First the delay at work and then this weather. Since childhood, she suffered from dust allergies. Once her nostrils caught the smell, she fell into a frenzy of sneezing and watering eyes. She was miserable.

Enas opened her handbag and took out another pair of tissues. Getting closer to the checkpoint, she prepared for the boring daily search process.

Through her watery eyes, she could see what was left of the trees and the green areas of the compound. Since the establishment of the Green Zone after the war in 2003, it had evolved into a small, and stand-alone city. Enas had lots of memories about this area when it was occupied by Sadam's palaces. The best areas in Baghdad were chosen for his three enormous mansions. In the 90s, he ordered his close administration staff, ministers, and security service to live in compounds closer to him. Enas remembered well the day when her family moved to the luxurious district assigned for high-profile Baath party members. Gradually other districts were added for servants and other low-profile staff who worked in those palaces. The resemblance to medieval monarchy systems was clear. While millions of Iraqi suffered poverty, the former ruler of Iraq built palaces and artificial lagoons for him and his clan.

After the fall of the regime, the coalition forces turned the area that spans across more than thirty square kilometers into a secure compound. Ironically, the coalition forces enjoyed the advantages of the security barriers made by the former regime and the strategic location in the middle of Baghdad to start their campaign of renovating Iraq.

Soon after the war, the American embassy and the buildings for the new Iraqi government settled there. The Green Zone then became a showcase for future Iraq. A small city within the big city of Baghdad, self-contained and benefitting from the best services the mother city missed.

Other American and international companies from around the globe found a safe haven within the area. Not only the Americans, Enas thought, still walking toward the checkpoint, their old neighborhood was now occupied by people who used to work as servants in the palaces. They preferred to stay there enjoying the protection of the US troops.

We shouldn't have left our home, she muttered.

After the regime collapsed, Enas' father, being one of high-profile Baath members, was arrested by the coalition forces waiting for trial for many charges. Right after her father's arrest, her brother, who worked for Sadam's secret service, decided to leave the neighborhood, fearing he, too, would be arrested.

Enas could see the house she used to live in, the tall palm tree in the garden, the rectangular white window of her room. Who was living in her room now? Not a boy, please. She hated the things boys did with walls in their rooms, all the posters and sports equipments they hung on the walls ruined the painting. Not that her family was going to get that house again, she winced. It was only leased to her father by the former government.

Despite all she witnessed of the unspoken brutality of Sadam and his family, Enas had to admit that she and her family had seen better days during his rule. Memories from the previous era represented her shiny past, her happy childhood living in a rich family. The ominous war songs and hymns the Baath party insisted on broadcasting all the time jogged her memories of the days when she enjoyed her father's indulgence. The days when she felt safe.

However, most Iraqis would strongly argue about that.

Enas didn't care.

Ironically, before the war she always dreamed of life in Iraq with more freedom. Like everyone else, she wondered if they could have a satellite TV showing channels other than the national TV. If they could travel to other countries or have cellular phones, or of a way to express an opinion without losing one's neck.

How foolish and naïve. She regretted those dreams. Hatred consumed her thoughts while she watched the once-exiled and condemned by Sadam coming back to Iraq as victorious.

Enas didn't like the new government. She despised the new Iraq, the new freedom, and everything that came with it. But most of all, she hated the traditions and customs, and the way people twisted them to serve their purposes.

Her society took everything from her, giving her nothing. So it was only fair for her to walk her own path, not giving a damn about society. And so she had dropped college, confident that she could find better opportunities with foreign companies. And maybe she could show everyone how she could serve her country better than anyone else.

I am a survivor, I will find and take back what was taken from me. That was what she told herself three months ago. Now, well, she wasn't very sure that was the right decision.

Enas walked faster, hoping the queue at the exit checkpoint wouldn't be so long. Very unlikely. The number of people coming to work in the Green Zone increased phenomenally during the last months. Double the pay, more professional and organized environment, something most young Iraqis found attractive. If not for the fear of terrorists and kidnapping gangs, Enas had no doubt that thousands would pour into the Green Zone looking for jobs.

Her hopes of getting home before nightfall quickly evaporated when she took the turn in the street. At least fifty people were queued at the gate.

"What happened?" Enas asked another woman standing in the line, who'd just finished chatting with a soldier.

"They found a gun with one of the girls while searching her," the woman replied, scanning Enas from top to toe. She was in her thirties, wearing a tight shirt... too tight with large pink letters that read "I love Jordan," a short skirt, and high heels. She smoked a thin and long cigarette, sucking it as if it were a life-supporting tube. Enas was open-minded and liberal and everything, but... well, being judgmental is another word for being Iraqi. So she settled for the I-know-what-you-are look.

Tight-shirt smirked. "They suspect she stole it from an American soldier, and now the other ladies are refusing to go through the search, complaining that the American lady officer in charge is harassing them." Tight-shirt blew smoke in Enas's face. "Lame excuse to avoid the search."

Half a dozen young women argued with the Marine officer at the checkpoint. Enas watched then asked tight-shirt, "But why do they want to avoid being searched?"

"Oh, come on." Tight-shirt giggled, a piercing and high-pitched giggle that made several people, men, around them turn. "The search will get harder and you don't know what kind of stuff those sluts are hiding."

This wasn't the first time she'd encountered such a thing. Troubles were common, especially at the checkpoints. Once someone did something wrong, security measures suddenly became tighter and American forces grew nervous and extra cautious. Soon other Iraqis would start complaining about the tightened security measures, which caused more tension. It would go on until a high-ranking official from the Iraqi government or the US Army mediated.

But not before the salivating Arabic-media reporters got their circus and a chance for exaggeration. Enas checked her watch, tapping nervously on her purse. She was late, again. That meant she had to go through another fight with her elder brother.

Oh God, get me out of this mad house, Enas prayed, knowing that she had nowhere to go. Her father didn't maintain good relationships with their relatives.

After several long minutes, she was finally out of the Green Zone in the main Karada Street.

Enas pressed the hankie harder on her nose and mouth, desperately blocking dust. But she had stayed outdoors for a long time, sand particles covered her body, filling her nostrils and her hair. Where were the damn taxis when you needed one? She fell into a frenzy of sneezing.

Enas kept waving to the passing cars. With her watery eyes it was hard to recognize taxies from others. At least she didn't have to see to whom she waved, everyone worked as a taxi driver now. So many people lost their jobs after the war.

But her luck compass still pointed south.

"Something is seriously wrong with me today," Enas muttered, watching the fourth car she stopped driving away. Why did no one want to go to Al-Amel district? Her anxiety about her brother questioning her for getting back late was superseded by a more intimidating one. Soon night would fall. She glanced at the dusty scarlet horizon where the sun disappeared. People working at the Green Zone were primary targets for kidnapping gangs. Two men across the street stared at her. Come on, girl, you are tougher than this. Her heart accelerated. A lot of people gathered near the Green Zone exit. But everyone was moving or doing something. Only those two stood there and stared in her general direction.

A black Mercedes stopped next to her. Did Mercedes owners start working as taxi drivers too? This wasn't the first time Enas observed a classy car being used as a taxi, but a Mercedes, well... now she had seen everything.

The driver lowered the side window. Enas leaned toward the car to ask him if he would drive her to Al-Amel district as she did with the four previous drivers. Not like the others, this one was a good looking blond, in his late twenties. His muscular arms were visible from his short-sleeved shirt. The driver smiled with shiny white teeth and tried to talk, but she cut him off, fighting a strong urge to sneeze.

"*Min Fadlak*......aa-choo!" The sneezing started. "I... am... sorry," Enas said, her cheeks must be rosy flush now. "I just need... aa-choo!" the sneezing continued frantically. The embarrassment was overwhelming.

"Never mind." The young man flashed another shiny smile. He leaned toward the dashboard and pressed a small button. The faint click as the door lock disengaged. She searched for the door handle. Through her moistened vision she saw no rear door. A two-seated car! Not accustomed to taxi drivers driving sport Mercedes, she stood confused, fighting another surge of sneezing.

"The other side, please," he said, leaning toward the side door and opening it. Enas glanced at the other side of the road, the two still there. Grudgingly she sat in the only other seat available, next to him. Between standing there outside the Green Zone while darkness fell and the people thinned by the minute, and riding with a stranger in a one-hundred-thousand-dollar-car... not a very hard decision. Shut up girl, and close the door.

And she did.

-7-
Al-Karada District - Baghdad
June 9th
6:30 PM

The man named Ayad was still in his office when Abdul Hasan returned. The Captain gave him an apologetic smile. Ayad still looked... odd. He tapped nervously on the floor with his foot, his gaze fixed at something on the floor.

Abdul Hasan sat on his chair.

"How can I help you, Mr. Ayad."

No, pleasantries, no chit chat. He didn't have time for those now.

"It's the same room," Ayad said, looking around.

"*Afwan*," (I beg your pardon.)

"I was brought here before... five years ago. For interrogation," Ayad said in monotone as if reading from a paper. "There were two other men, I don't know them but they were brought here as well."

"I see," Abdul Hasan said, not sure what else to say.

"It was the annual memory of Imam Kadum," Ayad went on, "I still remember the day as if it was yesterday. I was going to visit the holy shrine in Kadumya, on foot, as it was customary at such occasions. Unfortunately for us, the Baath regime was vigilant about it so they start arresting anyone who tried to walk to Kadumya."

"Yes, I was living in Al-Adel district and I couldn't reach the main street that led to Kadumya that day." Abdul Hasan found himself talking. Memories from these days, despite the sadness, they made some kind of bond. It was as if they were members in some secret brotherhood fighting against the injustice. Which, in a way, was the case.

"They were abnormally tolerant with us," Ayad sneered, still looking at the floor, "they let us finish the visit rituals then arrested us afterwards."

"So at least you had the chance to do the Zyara."

"They gave me this... as souvenir, they said." Ayad pulled up his sleeves. Abdul Hasan saw a white spot that stood out from the normal skin color. No hair, as if someone used an eraser and wiped out everything on his arms. Burn marks.

Abdul Hasan bit on his lower lip. He didn't know why he asked but he guessed it was the punch line. "What happened to the other two men?"

Ayad lifted his stare from the floor to look at him, "They put them in the pool... over there." He pointed to the corner where the couch was.

"What pool?" But he knew the answer already.

"The acid pool," Ayad said, staring at the spot in the corner.

"God..."

Silence. Ayad finally turned to Abdul Hasan. He looked better now... normal, as if saying it dropped it from his chest.

"I really still cannot comprehend it," Ayad said, "why Sadam's regime kept insisting on oppressing all our religion practices; they were always peaceful. And the regime was so powerful in the years after the first gulf war that it shouldn't care even if whatever left of the opposition exploited these practices."

Abdul Hasan rubbed his chin. "Maybe it wasn't because Sadam was afraid of a direct threat. The idea was to oppress Shia, keeping them down and coercing them to the point where they couldn't even think of mutiny. In a way it was similar to what lions tamers do --they starve the lion, lock it in a small cage for a long time, and deny it even the simplest things, they even use electrifying sticks on it."

Ayad nodded slowly.

"At the beginning, the monsters resist and revolt, but sooner or later their wild spirit dies. The wild lions turned into tamed cats. The tamers could recognize the tamed animal from the wild one, preparing it to entertain people in the circus."

Abdul Hasan spoke in a calm, all-natural tone. As if it was just another fact about another people living on another planet. Despite what people accused him of --taking the battle against terrorism too personally-- he was very pragmatic. It was a matter of simple math. Ba'ath and Qaeda lived on hurting everyone around them, they had to be exterminated. He had seen enough of such ideologies and experienced it first hand to safely decide that it was a simple equation of us or them.

"That sucks," Ayad finally said.

"By the way, it wasn't only Shia," Abdul Hasan added, "they got the biggest share of the coercion, but other sects in the Iraqi society got their share as well, Kurds are one obvious example."

Ayad nodded absent-mindedly, staring at the floor again. Abdul Hasan made a mental note to ask someone to clean it.

"I believe you have some information," Abdul Hasan said. His team were ambushing a dangerous terrorist. Okay, he wasn't going to do anything from this place but still.

"Yes, I was actually trying to meet someone here, someone to be trusted." Ayad hesitated, he tapped on his knee with his fingers. "I think I have some vital information about a terrorist attack."

"Terrorist attack?" Abdul Hasan tried to sound surprised and concerned. It didn't work.

Ayad said after taking a long breath, "I have a Sunnie neighbor, a decent guy, I trust him. I have known him and his family for years. Anyway…"

Ayad looked at him, Abdul Hasan motioned for him to go on "My neighbor had divided his house into two parts. Living with his family in one half and renting the other as many families did to get another income. Three months ago, my neighbor hosted a refugee family from Faloja. At least that's what he told us. Weeks later, another family came in, then two men. Finally we lost track who was living in this house. People came and went, suspicious men, often armed."

"How do you know they are not families anymore?"

"Well, there were no kids, no women. Only men, no senior people, just men between twenty and forty years old. What happened is my neighbor's son got involved with this group, whatever they were, and that's why his father came to me asking for help."

"Your neighbor told you about the terrorist plan?"

"Yes, I think his son told him or he knew somehow. But the man was almost certain the group is up to something big and soon. He was worried that his son might join them."

"I see. Did your neighbor tell you what the target is?"

Ayad shook his head. "He heard them talking with his son about a big operation today or tomorrow, something the government will not forget, using his own words."

"Big, as the annual conference of Ministry of Planning?"

"Why not?" Ayad replied. "I mean look at it, the government is trying hard to attract foreign investors to spin the wheel of the big projects and investment in Iraq. Everyone knows that once this starts, unemployment would be over, people would find jobs and terrorist groups would find no one to hire."

Abdul Hasan winced, looking at his watch. Why didn't Hussain report yet?

"Did he tell you that this group, whatever it was, was targeting the ministry?"

"No, but it's--"

"And for that matter you don't even know if this group you are talking about is really dangerous."

Ayad frowned. "Of course they are dangerous, they carried weapons."

"And who doesn't?" Abdul Hasan smiled. "They could have contempt for the government for any reason. People are bluffing about mutiny against the new government and threatening a lot these days but that doesn't mean they are terrorists."

"But my neighbor was sure about it."

"This is not evidence." Abdul Hasan shook his head. "Maybe he wanted to get rid of the tenants and he couldn't find a better way."

"What kind of evidence do you want the man to give me? A bomb!"

Abdul Hasan let out a heavy breath. "Ayad, this conference is one of the most important events this year, and the security measures we took were phenomenal."

"Oh, that's a relief," Ayad snapped. "Phenomenal like the one you took during the last Zyara to Imam Al-Hussain when hundreds of people got killed? Or during Zyara to Imam Kadum where the people died at the bridge?"

It was a low blow, too low. Abdul Hasan felt the corners of his mouth turn up, his eyes looked down.

"I am sorry," Ayad said. "I didn't mean to--"

Abdul Hasan waved him off, no point of apologizing. "Terrorists had spread rumors between the pilgrims in Zyara to Kadumya about a man with a bomb. People got scared and we all knew what happened. Rampage, people fell over the bridge into water. The point is, those terrorist were supported by former Sadam secret service agents. And psychological war is not new to them. They have used it before and they can use it again. Especially for this conference. If they managed to scare the shit out of people, investors will not attend and the minister of planning will end up drinking tea with his fellow ministers, if they weren't scared as well."

Ayad nodded. "I understand your point."

Abdul Hasan stood and walked to where the map was hung on the wall. There were no windows in the rooms, so he stared at the map instead. He glanced at the blue pin representing the place where Mujahid might go. Was it possible they engaged with some armed group there? Or maybe with the ministry of defense forces?

"That's why we started hearing lots of rumors, tons of tips, about plans to attack the conference..." He paused then asked, "Where do you live by the way?"

Never too late to play Mr. Detective.

"Al-Amel district."

He thought about the mission and Mujahid again. He asked Ayad to show him his house on the map. Ayad did. Nope, too far from the place where they were ambushing Mujahid. Only God knew how many terrorists were in that part of Baghdad now.

"My neighbor tried to ask them to leave the house and to keep his son out of this," Ayad said. "You know what they told him? My neighbor swore to me that the terrorists told him that if he did the simplest thing such as opening his mouth again he would wish that the reaper himself came to take his family before he got to them." Ayad paused. "Do you think that the man would lie about that?"

"Did he use those words?"

Ayad nodded.

Abdul Hasan's cell phone rang, he picked it up.

"Sir," another young officer said. They were all young. Or maybe he just got too old. "I just got a call from the hospital we left the Syrian terrorist at. He didn't make it."

Abdul Hasan pictured the kid once more.

"Okay, thank you."

The Captain hung up and turned to Ayad. "It might be worth taking a look at this group. I am not sure how serious they are and it's not our jurisdiction area. But we will try our best." The words sounded hollow and empty even in his own ears.

He then stood and said, as if ending the meeting, "I will ask you to go downstairs, an officer will be waiting for you to open a formal record. We will do what we can."

We will do what we can. We will do our best. Iraqis heard a lot of this crap every day.

"One final request," Ayad said,

"Your identity will be totally protected," he assured him with his understanding smile.

Ayad thanked him and left. Abdul Hasan picked up the phone and dialed his secretary's extension. "Get me Hussain or any one of his squad, I need to know what in God's name happened to them."

-8-

Al-Amel District - Baghdad

June 9th

6:40 PM

Lieutenant Hussain tried to relax in the front seat of the white Nissan Patrol. He glanced through the windshield between the red sky and the narrow street. The palm trees swayed in a hypnotic rhythm with the growing storm. The street was deserted except for another unmarked police car some hundred yards away. The howling of the wind grew louder occasionally. Plastic bags tore past, reminding him of old western movies.

We just need the bad guy to show up now to have our movie, Hussain thought, realizing that surveillance wasn't his best way to spend time. One hour had passed since he and his partner started watching the house.

"And the most hilarious part is that he still thinks I am the best one to do police paperwork," Shaker said. "Can you believe it? I write only the first page and for the next twenty pages or so I just attach papers from my younger brother's psychology lectures. You remember my brother, don't you?"

Shaker's big dark eyes moistened with laughter.

As if the boring surveillance wasn't enough, he had to endure Shaker's sense of humor. Hussain tried hard not to roll his eyes.

"You put school lectures instead of the police report and the Captain didn't catch you?" Hussain asked in fake amazement.

"You don't really think anyone actually reads the reports, do you? Besides, I would rather work as a gangster than doing all this paperwork." Shaker laughed.

How could his partner be so energetic despite the boring and tiresome work all day? First the long search at the airport then the mind-numbing waiting here. Hussain closed his eyes. He saw the

Syrian kid. It was as if the boy's terrified eyes were engraved on his retinas.

"You know what," Shaker said in monotone, staring at the empty street while lighting a new cigarette, the third in a row. And no, Hussain wasn't a smoker. Thanks to the smoker-friendly Iraqi culture, it was totally acceptable to smoke, even in a gas station.

"If I was that good at writing reports, I wouldn't be here in first place."

"So," Hussain ventured, afraid this was one of Shaker's jokes.

Shaker sounded dreamy. "I would be a schoolteacher."

"Schoolteacher? Why the hell is that?" Hussain tried not to blast with laughter now. "I mean, normally all children... um... childhood dreams are always about being an engineer, doctor, you know, something important."

Shaker stared at him like a big child now, his wide eyes blinked twice, both his eyebrows raised. Shaker was always something of a child, a ruthless fighter, a man who feared nothing, yes, but beneath that, just below the surface, was the big heart of a child.

"I don't know." Shaker scratched his head then his left ear. Okay, now Hussain knew where the nickname Kala came from. "I wasn't so bright at school, maybe that's why I didn't have any ambitions of great jobs. On the other hand, I had that English teacher, I still think he is the greatest man in the world."

"He had a charming character?"

"Not really, it's just the idea that one man can teach hundreds of kids like me to speak English was something marvelous... even more." Shaker smiled with embarrassment. "I don't know."

"Indeed," Hussain murmured, trying to imagine Shaker ten or twenty years younger. "So how did you end up working with the commandos' force?"

"I didn't pass high school." Another shrug. "So I had to serve in the army for five years during the first Gulf War and the years after." Shaker blew the smoke upward, gazing at the white cloud. "When I was finally discharged, I couldn't find any job, so I worked with my uncle as a taxi driver between Baghdad and Amman, you know. That was a good business for some time. Until five months after the regime fell in 2003."

"What happened?"

"I was sick that day, and the business was so tough. Due to competition, we couldn't afford to say no to a customer. Anyway, my uncle got this family who wanted to travel to Jordan and he had to drive them to Jordan without me. At that time, Faluja unrest was in its very beginning."

Shaker blew another puff of smoke. His fingers trembled on the cigarette pack. "At that time we didn't have cell phones. So we used to call home from a gas station on the road. That day he didn't call. We waited till the next morning and still no call."

Another pause. Hussain stared at the approaching giant red cloud. Everything around him was red, blood red, like the way the conversation was going.

"Anyway," Shaker continued, "three days later, we found his body along with the family who hired him, all slaughtered at the throat. With a paper nailed to their foreheads, even the six-year-old kid, with one word... Kafer."

Infidel, the one-word death-sentence. Hussain focused on the giant sand cloud. The extremists Wahabbi gangs who controlled Faluja for a long time accused everyone who didn't get along with them, including by default all Shia, of being infidels. A death sentence that allowed the extremists to kill, rape, and confiscate all possessions of the condemned.

"Psychopath bastards," Shaker grumbled. Then he added with less tension, "Imagine one of those maniacs approaching a six-year-old kid to nail a paper to his forehead because his parents follow a different sect or prayed to God in a different way."

Shaker laughed despite the bitterness in his voice. He continued with his usual joyful voice, "Shortly afterwards, the Iraqi security forces started recruiting with good salaries and benefits, saying also that we would do joint patrols with American forces."

"And what's so special about joint patrols with the Americans? You want to learn English from the American soldiers?" Hussain teased him, happy to move to a more cheerful subject.

"Learn... hmm, maybe," Shaker said with a crooked grin, "but definitely not the language and not from male soldiers." He burst into joyful laughter and went on describing his fantasy.

"Hey Romeo, back to reality, will you. We are trying to arrest a terrorist here, remember?"

The two-way radio crackled to life. "Bravo team to Alpha team, possible target approaching. Ten o'clock. Over."

Shaker reached for the radio, with a wide grin. Hussain snapped it from his partner's hand and pressed the transmit button.

"Roger, Bravo team. Do not engage, I repeat, do not engage, over."

"Hahaha, target at ten o'clock." Shaker burst into more laughter, his eyes moist with tears, mocking the other soldier's voice. "What would happen if he just said slightly to the left. You guys are hilarious, you take the job so seriously. Ten o'clock and thirty minutes. Hahaha, we are late for dinner, what if I have a digital watch, ha?"

Hussain rolled his eyes, unable to believe how relaxed his partner was. They were in the middle of an area controlled by terrorist groups trying to arrest a dangerous terrorist and he kept joking. "Can you see the guy? It's so sandy outside," he asked, trying to get Shaker serious.

"No, but what difference would that make?" Shaker shrugged. "That son of bitch will come to this house, this is what that poor bastard told us, right?"

The images flashed again. Hussain knew the kid didn't make it. What did the Qaeda teachings consider such death? Would this kid still make it to heaven and enjoy the virgins? Or would he go to hell because he was killed by one of their men? Does friendly fire count as being martyred? What about the thousands of innocent people the terrorists -Jihadist- killed? The women? The children? Do they go to heaven or to hell? How could both the murderer and the victim go to heaven? And what in God's name was this heaven that accepted scumbags like those who came to fight in Iraq?

"Yeah, yeah." Hussain sighed, sounding more worried than he intended. "For all we know this guy is the mastermind of the new terrorist group of Islamic States of Iraq, which means he is smart, and we should not underestimate him."

"I swear by Imam Abbas," Shaker murmured through clenched teeth, shaking an angry fist, "he won't escape today."

Let's hope this for the sake of all of us, Hussain wished, squinting at the empty street. He finally saw the silhouette of an average height male. The man got closer. He was thin, white skin, high cheekbones prominent on his shaved scrawny face, his eyes sunk inside two dark holes. The man wore gray velvet pants and a white shirt.

He matched the description. The man crossed the intersection of streets five and twelve. The marked house was the first in street six. So he still had to cross one block. The suspect got close to the first car that was parked in the intersection of the 5th Street. Hussain's

Nissan Patrol was parked in the intersection of the 6th Street, closer to the marked house.

"Do you think he's our guy?" Shaker's fingers nervously trembled on his gun.

The suspect passed the first vehicle. His steps quickened. He turned to the sixth street with the marked house. His hand reached into his pocket.

Shaker removed the safety pin from his M16 machine-gun. Hussain's heart pounded. At any moment the man would enter the house, meaning he was their target. But to their surprise, the man continued walking, slightly adjusting his steps to normal speed again.

The radio crackled again breaking the heavy silence. "Shall we engage, over."

"Hussain, you have to decide, man," Shaker said. "We will lose him."

Thank you, that was just what I needed to concentrate.

"Let's arrest him," Shaker said, "and if he isn't our guy, we can let him go."

"Hold on," Hussain ordered. His brain was trying to analyze the situation. Shaker was right about not having time. On the other hand, if they chased the guy they'd blow their cover and lose any chance to catch the real guy. He scrutinized the man again, something said he was their target, not the description, not the clothes. Maybe the way he walked? Nah, it wasn't that either. Before the man disappeared in the dusty 6th Street, Hussain felt a rush of adrenalin. He was their target, Mujahid.

Instinctively he reached for the radio and yelled, "All units, target confirmed, engage, I repeat engage!"

"*Jameel!*" (beautiful,) Shaker cheered and launched like a panther in a hunt.

Hussain sprinted after his partner, gun in hand, gaze fixed on the suspect who broke into a run. From the other side of the street, another soldier appeared across the road.

"He has a gun!" Hussain yelled.

Without slowing, the terrorist fired two rounds toward the soldier who dashed to the ground.

"You bastard!" Shaker growled, throwing his machine gun away to sprint at full speed after the terrorist. Mujahid aimed his gun at the downed officer. "By Abas, you will not escape!"

"Shaker, no!" Hussain called after him. "Not without your weapon!" Shaker was already ten yards away, the words muffled by the wind.

Startled by Shaker's voice, the terrorist turned and trained his gun at the speeding large man. Shaker leaped at the terrorist with a battle cry. The terrorist fired another round. It whizzed past Hussain's head. Shaker tackled him sending both of them to the ground. The man tried to shoot again. Atop of him, the big lieutenant hammered Mujahid's head with both fists.

"You cowardly son of a bitch! You terrorist!" Shaker kept yelling, working his fists on the man's face.

The terrorist coiled in agony, dropping the pistol.

"Stop it, Shaker," Hussain commanded, helping the third soldier to stand while another approached, preparing to handcuff the terrorist.

Shaker let go of the man, leaving him with fat lips and a bleeding nose.

"We better leave this place," Hussain said, looking around at the nearby houses. He watched the closed windows in the neighborhood with concern. "The sound of gunfire will alert all the terrorists on this street and we don't have time or enough men to engage in a fight."

Plus, this particular area was not under the jurisdiction of the MICF.

"You, come with us," Hussain commanded one of the soldiers. "The rest of you go to the other car."

......

The two cars headed to the headquarters of the MICF in Karada district. From his front seat, Shaker turned toward their prisoner who was securely bound, teasing him, "Ahlan, Ahlan, Mujahid, that's your name isn't it?"

The man kept his gaze down, while Shaker went on, "Come on, don't be shy now, you will stay with us for quite a long time, being shy won't help. Come on, we know your name."

The terrorist lifted his head, looked at Shaker, and smiled. "And I know you had garlic soup for lunch."

"Shut up, we have very reliable intel about you, we know that you--" Shaker paused as if remembering something. He turned toward Hussain who was driving. "By the way, back there when we were watching him... How did you know that he was our guy? He passed the house and didn't go in."

Hussain smiled. Although this was the first operation he was in charge of, he did well. There were no casualties, the operation went smooth. And most importantly, the part of identifying Mujahid was a blessed moment for him. "Well, that was sheer luck."

"*Kafi Tawadou*," (stop being modest) Shaker chided him, "Come on man! We know you are not the modest guy here so tell us how you recognized him."

Hussain slowed down to take a turn, then he said, trying to hide his delight, "At first, I noticed him changing his walking speed when he got closer to the house. However, that could be a coincidence. What really turned him in was when his hands reached to his pockets."

Hussain paused. Taking advantage of the empty street, he looked at their prisoner. "The act was so instinctive and fast that I couldn't notice in the beginning. But when he continued on his way, I realized how awkward the entire thing looked and he actually put his hand in his pocket to get his keys out, the normal thing anyone would do when reaching his home."

The man fumbled in rage, glaring at Hussain.

Shaker whacked the terrorist on the back of his head. "Hey, Mujahid, we heard you are a clever guy. But you know what, we have Hussain here who is smarter than ten stupid terrorists like you."

He is clever, Hussain thought, remembering how Mujahid had passed his house. He had sensed their presence somehow. The cars were unmarked and they hid behind the tinted glass, yet he managed somehow to blow their cover. No, he wasn't stupid at all, he just slipped and they were lucky.

Ten minutes later, Hussain crossed the first gate of the MICF headquarters.

. . . .

"Captain, they got him, Sir," his secretary told him.

Abdul Hasan looked at the man, his bushy mustache made it difficult to tell if he was smiling.

"And where are they now?" Abdul Hasan asked, pushing his chair back.

"Lieutenant Hussain said that they will be here within five minutes," Bushy-mustache said.

So they had arrested him. Mujahid. The terrorist the Syrian young man had told them about.

Abdul Hasan checked his watch. Almost 7. He should be at home by now. Not on such a day. If half what the Syrian kid had told them was true, this would be the arrest of the month, hell, maybe the year.

He hurried to the ground floor flanked by his secretary and another officer who probably had no clue what was going on and followed them hoping for any sort of action.

By the time he reached the entrance door of the MCIF headquarters, Abdul Hasan was followed by seven of his staff. He stepped outside. The wind howled like something out of a bad horror movie. Sand filled his mouth. A sandstorm. A bad omen if he were to believe in such nonsense. The Captain stood there, hands on his hips examining his little fortress.

A large concrete wall surrounded the house used as the MICF headquarters. Part of the pavement and the street got swallowed up by the wall. The area created between the concrete barrier and the house was enough for a small parking lot for some of their patrol cars. Iraqi forces were allowed to use pickup trucks with large machine-guns fixed on top. It wasn't the US-army Humvies, but it wasn't bad either. A double-layer tin sheet was wrapped around the truck, maybe so that they could call it an armored vehicle. Two of the armored trucks guarded the only opening in the fence where two metal barriers acted as a gate.

They didn't wait long. Two Nissan Patrols approached the gate. The cars' drivers flashed their headlights twice. A routine check conducted, the cars were swept for explosives, the drivers' IDs verified, and they finally let them in.

"Ahsantum" (excellent), Abdul Hasan said addressing Hussain and his squad members who just stepped out of their cars. Shaker dragged a man in cuffs. He must be Mujahid. Abdul Hasan wasn't sure what he expected, maybe someone with a short dishdash and a thick beard, maybe a heavily built man with an axe in hand. But Mujahid, if that was him, wasn't any of these. Skinny, average height, his scrawny face was completely shaved, no thick, bushy, black beard. Another cliché blown to hell. He wore velvet gray cotton trousers and a white shirt, reminding Abdul Hasan of an old school uniform. He had short black hair, nothing special about it either. Despite his fat lips and traces of blood on his nose, the man was quite normal. Abdul Hasan looked at their prisoner's eyes. He searched for a suspicious look, craziness, or even superman's heat-vision. Nothing. His gaze locked with the terrorist's for a brief second. The man gave him a faint smile that looked awful with the way his lips had blown up.

"Take him to the interrogation room," Abdul Hasan commanded. Two soldiers took the suspect inside.

"Do we have a positive ID on him?" Abdul Hasan asked Shaker and Hussain.

"He was at the same address the young man gave us. The time also matched," Hussain said. "He also fired at us, no one was hurt, thank God but—"

"I see," Abdul Hasan said, rubbing his chin. The identity of the target had to be confirmed before they could really do anything about him. Arresting him without a warrant and outside their jurisdiction further complicated matters. Not that he cared. Formalities were the least of his concerns now. To know what this man knows and what sort of attacks he and his group were planning was the key. With such organization, once someone at this level was arrested, other leaves of the tree would follow.

"And I assume he didn't say anything during the ride here?"

They both shook their heads. Hussain said, "He kept flashing this stupid smile at us. I mean suspects normally yell and plea they are innocent, this man kept quiet."

"Damn Hollyood movies," Shaker said, "they keep showing that part of 'you have the right to remain silent,' what good does that do anyway?"

"You better start writing the operation report, Shaker," Abdul Hasan said returning to the house.

"Naam, Sayedi." (Yes, sir.)

Abdul Hasan heard muffled laughter. He turned back facing Shaker. "And if I find any psychology lectures in the report, I will make sure you spend the night in a prison cell."

Shaker's boyish smile evaporated. But that was for one second only. The big officer grinned. "What about history lectures, Sir?"

-9-
Outside The Green Zone - Baghdad
June 9th
6:55 PM

Enas felt as if she stepped into another world. All sounds from outside were muffled, the air-conditioned breeze was a relief for her sweating body. She was the only grimy object in that super-clean environment.

The Mercedes roared down the street, pushing her back in the leather seat. Instead of the comfortable feeling of going back home, Enas had another nagging feeling now. What had she done? How did she sit next to the driver? When a lady hired a cab, she ought to sit in the back seat. Sitting in the front seat was not acceptable unless she knew the driver. Was he flirting? She bit on her lower lip, cursing at the complicated customs. Relations between men and women in the conservative societies were always beyond her comprehension. Between the strict social rules that looked with great suspicion to any relations outside marriage, and the suppressed normal desires boosted by the esteemed western culture in the media. It was always confusing what she should do.

I am in Iraq, she reminded herself. Despite that many Arabic societies now had a great deal of tolerance for different degrees of relations between the two sexes, Iraq did not. Whether that was because Iraqi society was closed for the last thirty years of the Baath rule, or because of the strong Islamic culture that was at its peak in Iraq in the last decade; it was immaterial. She knew better than getting involved in any kind of relations in public. The slightest hint of such would raise a wave of nonstop gossiping and questions, pushing many of those relations toward secrecy and forcing them to live in guilt.

However, her worries now weren't of breaking the rules, but worrying that such behavior might send mixed signals to the guys, who interpreted it into a bad meaning.

Aware of her physical attractiveness, Enas refused the idea of giving herself to a man who enjoyed only temporary sexual relations only to dump her when the relation couldn't be hidden anymore. This wasn't what she wanted.

Enas pushed the hankie away as the inconvenient allergy ended. She wiped away the tears from her eyes.

"Are you heading to Al-Amel District?" she asked the handsome young man behind the wheel. *Assuming you are a cab driver*, she thought, doubting it.

He smirked. "I was wondering what the handkerchief was for." His gaze shifted to the rear mirror then at the road ahead. "Now I understand,"

Oh, God, was something wrong with her make up?

"With a pretty face like yours, you have the right to hide it," the young man teased her.

Enas felt her cheeks flush. She didn't expect a compliment. Not after half an hour in this sandstorm. He was flirting with her. Tucking a wisp of hair behind her ear, she reminded herself of the rules of her conservative society. Stupid rules. She fought the urge to smile.

Enas mocked his teasing voice. "Do you use that line with every girl who steps in your car?"

"Well, not every girl who steps in my car has a handkerchief covering her face."

"No?"

He shook his head.

"I thought you only drive people with emergencies."

"Well ... yeah, you could say that, when I drive next to a group of girls, they faint. So as a courtesy, I have to take them to the nearest hospital."

"They faint because of your car?"

"My car? No. My handsome face, it's irresistible."

"Please. Such a show off."

"You are embarrassing yourself," he said shaking his head. "You don't have to hide it."

"Oh."

"You cannot take your eyes off me, I don't blame you anyway. I learned to live with my exceptional beauty."

"Unbelievable!" She laughed. "Anyway, you know what they say about beauty."

"What?"

"It's only skin deep."

He stuck out his lips and frowned, then shrugged. "It's still good enough."

"So self-absorbed." She waved him off.

Enas was about to add more but stopped. Was that the best she could do? Now he was going to think she was flirting with him as well. It was always a trick for a girl to keep a guy around without sending him a signal that she was one of the easy girls with whom guys could have relations without marriage.

"Al-Amel district, you said? Where do you want to go, the 7th-of-April Street? Or the southern side?"

"7th-of-April Street, but..." She paused, not sure what to say to give him the right impression about her.

The car stopped at a crowded intersection. He tilted his head. Their eyes met. She broke contact and looked ahead. There was something in his look, she couldn't put her hands on it. Something beyond confidence and self-assurance.

"But what?" he asked, raising a blond eyebrow.

"It's nothing." She shook her head. Let him think whatever he was going to think. He was just a stranger.

"Do you work in the Green Zone?" he asked.

Her heart skipped a beat. Working for the Americans or the Iraqi government in the Green Zone was a common cause of death, more than bombing as a matter of fact. Ex-Baath gangs considered them traitors. Islamic extremists looked at them as infidels. As for kidnapping gangs, well, everyone knew how much people working in the Green Zone earned.

Another thing she didn't like about admitting her work location was that it would give him a very wrong image. Especially with the way she got in his car. According to this society's conservative standards, a lady working with the Americans and accepting car rides from strangers was dancing on a very fine line of the limited society tolerance. *A slut*, she told herself, *that's what he is going to think about me.*

"Do I have to?" she replied with her best poker face.

"Umm, I don't know." He shrugged. "You were there outside the camp. And at this time, it's just--"

"Being there doesn't specifically imply I am working there."

The blond young man did not comment. His handsome face showed no emotions. The air intensified. The uncomfortable silence would not break except with an apology. She shouldn't be so defensive. He was only after casual chatting.

"What about you? What do you do for living?" Enas asked, breaking the awkward silence.

"Civil contracts, I have one of the biggest firms in Baghdad." The way he said it, he must have said this line several times a day.

Certainly not a taxi driver. The fancy car interior, his clothes, and his big golden ring, were all too obvious.

"So," she smiled batting her eyelashes, "you work in the Green Zone then."

"Sometimes, depends on the contracts," the young man replied with a confident tone. Then he teased, "Why? Do I have to?"

Enas let out a laugh, happy that he didn't take her defensive response personally. Confident. Everything about him was hardly resistible but his self-confidence was atop her list.

"Al-Rasheed Company, right?" Enas guessed, peering at the business cards next to the gear box.

"Yes, but...how?" He crested his forehead looking suspiciously at her, slightly shifting in his seat.

She pointed to business cards in front of her.

"Oh," he exhaled with relief and handed her one of the cards, "sorry, I forgot to introduce myself." He offered his hand, flashing a smile. "My name is Omar."

"Enas," she replied, shaking his hand. Feeling the warmth of his hand, she quickly pulled hers away.

"We are based in Mansur district, I bought a big house and converted the ground floor to an office. I am still using the upper floor for my own accommodations."

He went on talking about the house, his work, and life.

Rich, has his own business, funny, and confident. Enas was doing her checklist of the right man.

She felt something. It wasn't a jolt in her chest or blood rushing to her cheeks or her heart pounding. Just an image flashed in her mind, so vivid and so colorful. But it didn't last long enough to grasp what it was.

"I work for a contracting company as well," Enas said, feeling suddenly happy and light-headed.

"Really? And what do you do?".

"Business development and management." She lied.

"Wow," Omar exclaimed. "I don't even know what that means but it sounded like ... um..."

"Like wow."

They both laughed.

Enas described her work, how challenging it was and how happy she felt doing something important.

Omar just nodded. Enas leaned back, watching the road, they were getting close to her house. Houses got smaller and lower, streets were dirtier, the poor neighborhood. They passed by a local electric generator, one of those operated by the residents to provide power when the main power goes down, which meant... always. A web of black electric cables spread from the generator to the nearby houses. The scene raised many questions. Such as how fire didn't start with all the mess of short circuits, or how people maintained such a network, more importantly for how long Iraqis had to worry about electricity while the rest of the world delivered fiber-optic connections to homes. Enas closed her eyes, wishing she could just fast forward this year, or maybe this decade. Who knew.

Enas decided to ask him to drop her a few blocks away to avoid the neighbors seeing her with a man. Enas wasn't in the mood to be the center of the neighborhood gossip.

Omar's cell phone rang. He pressed a button on the steering wheel. A beep sounded then a man said through the speakers, "*Marhaba*, Omar," The man's voice was raspy and tired.

"Bluetooth speakers," Omar whispered, wiggling his eyebrows.

"Show-off."

"*Hala*, my friend, tell me you have good news for me." Omar talked to the microphone that was apparently somewhere in the roof but she couldn't spot it.

"Ana... *Asef*," (I am sorry) the man said, "I think... we lost the project."

Omar's face turned red. "What! After all the arrangements we have done."

"I am sorry, Omar." The man's voice was fainter.

Omar reached to his bulky cell-phone and snapped it open. The car speakers immediately muted.

"Who got it?" Omar demanded, talking directly into the phone.

Who ever got the job, he wouldn't be invited to Omar's birthday party. Omar bit his lower lip, his face contorted in anger. He slammed the steering wheel twice, mumbled a swear then grunted, "I will burn them all."

Burn them? Nope, definitely not invited.

But something in Omar's voice, agony maybe, made Enas feel a strange compassion despite his scary rage.

"This guy is doing it on purpose," Omar added. "He is working on no profit margin just to make me lose the job."

Omar listened and nodded slowly, his full features showing a glimpse of hope that quickly turned into a grin of a boy promised a present. "Okay, I will discuss this with my father." He ended the conversation.

"Troubles at work?" she ventured.

He let out a long sigh, his face slackened. "Are you sure you want me to drive you to the 7th-of-April Street?" Omar asked after a bit.

Was he offering to take her somewhere else? How dare he? But his face showed nothing.

"So you have a better idea then?"

He grinned, "Well, if you like--"

"Listen, I don't know what you think of me but..." She paused, feeling undignified.

"If you'd like me to drop you somewhere that would be nearer to your home, I don't have a problem." He looked at her square in the eye, no hint of smile.

For the second time, Enas felt she had overreacted. She opened her mouth, but nothing came out. Finally she said in an apologetic tone, "*Almakan Munasib*, (the place is okay) drop me after the next intersection, please. And... thank you."

He said nothing.

Staring through the window glass, she watched the dirty street, the beaten-up cars and pedestrians, people in rough clothes and shadowed faces. One thing was common... poverty. Al-Amel district wasn't the luxury neighbor she grew up in.

There were moments in life where one had sudden clarity. When the illusions we make to block out the bitter reality disappear, leaving us naked, facing our fears. When one looks at the mirror and can't recognize his own reflection.

This was one such moment. During the last two years, throughout all the changes she had to endure in her personal life, starting from the arrest of her father, then leaving their big house and high-class neighborhood, replacing the drop-off to college by her father's chauffeur with taxis and then public transports, somehow her perception didn't register the ramifications of the transformation to her social life. She didn't see the new Enas --the poor girl from Al-Amil district.

At least I should try being modest, she thought, filled with resentment.

A child crossed the street in front of the car. Omar slammed on the brakes. They both jolted.

"*Ghabi!*" (idiot) he muttered with rage.

"I am sorry." Her voice was trembling, she didn't even recognize it.

"It's not your fault."

"Not this… I mean, I am sorry for the misunderstanding." She paused, feeling lost. "I just feel tired of the work pressure."

She had gone too far in a desperate mission to pursue her illusions, a dream of living her old life again, the rich life. She had dropped college, worked with the Americans, and she had no idea where she was heading.

To her surprise Omar started laughing. "You worry too much," he said, tilting his blond head and his muscular upper body toward her, slowing the car, and looking into her eyes with his… blue eyes. How had she not noticed them before? He wasn't laughing now, but wasn't angry either. "Enas… take it easy. A smart and good-looking girl like you shouldn't keep worrying about what she is saying."

She was too confused now to analyze whether he was flirting with her, insulting her, or simply trying to make her feel better.

"Maybe." She nodded absent-mindedly. Outside, a group of teens glared at the fancy car with suspicion.

No one fainted… yet.

Omar looked at the teens then stepped on the gas. "The protective boys-next-door?"

Enas gave a what-can-you-do shrug. "I think they came with the city blue-prints."

She always despised how men acted furiously when hearing that their girl-next-door started dating someone else while they totally accepted it if she dated one of them.

"Local girls should date local boys, this is their code of honor." She winced, trying to swallow the word date only to make it dissonant and clearer.

"I know." He heaved a long sigh, still grinning. "I've been there. I know the code."

They laughed. Enas felt a bit better now, amazed by his ability to smooth out the mood. "This is my stop." She pointed to the intersection, sorry she had to leave him.

He parked, keeping his wide grin.

She got out. "Thanks."

"*La Mushkila*" (no problem), he waved her a goodbye.

The car roared far down the street.

Show off. She beamed, watching the car until it disappeared in the dust.

Walking to her home, she felt something new, a vigorous enthusiasm. She didn't dare to call it hope but it was as close to hope as it could get.

She glanced at the small crammed houses, at the rusted doors, and peeling paint. To the ivory-covered fences, the grubby streets, to the stacked piles of week-old garbage bags waiting patiently to be picked up. Enas blocked the scene out of her mind. She would find a way back to the life she deserved. She promised herself, clutching hard on the business card.

-10-

Karada Hospital – Karada District

June 9th

7:00 PM

Voices came as if from another time. Another life.

Faraway, like cries in the middle of the night.

From everywhere, sounds surrounded him. What were they saying? One in particular was familiar. That soft voice. It was one of those moments where reality got mixed with dreams and memories. Was he remembering the sound, imagining it, or really hearing it?

How could she be here?

Her voice was faint, whispery... but he could feel it in his heart. The memory, the voice kept coming, repeating itself. Scrunching his heart every time it did, he felt suffocated.

Gasping for air, Abdul Rahman opened his eyes, panic consumed him. The lights where all turned on. White neon light. This wasn't his room. Why could he not feel his limbs? Was he dead? Was this heaven? And where in the name of God was this smell coming from?

The smell of hygiene and chemicals and something else, something he didn't want to know, filled his nostrils. He closed his eyes again, searching for that soft voice, escaping to the safety of her warm smile.

"Don't go, son." Her pleading voice came to him.

"It's just a holiday, Mom. One week I can take a nice break and get back." His heart crunched, as it did whenever he lied to those eyes.

"So why have you sold your car." She wasn't asking. Her voice was faint, but filled with reproach.

"Mom... I told you... I don't like it anymore, and I will buy the newer model once I get back."

The sad look in her glassy eyes, the quivering lips that failed to fake a smile.... she knew...

"Your father abandoned us years ago, dedicated only to his new house and second wife. Your elder brother is occupied by his work... you are the only reason I am fighting this ... this... disease. If I live, I am doing it because of you." Her voice was muffled, her eyes were watery, then the coughing started.

The resident Filipino nurse approached, she looked at his mother then frowned at him.

"Mom, you have God. And your life is within his grasp. You shouldn't say that."

"God will not take a son away from his mother," she fired back. "Those criminals filled your heart with hatred. Sometimes... sometimes I feel I don't know you anymore."

More tears, he resisted the urge to wipe them from her sunken cheeks as he used to when his father made her cry. But he could not do it this time. He was told that Satan would try to dissuade him from his intention in every way possible.

"They are my brothers in Islam, they are my family. They showed me the path to the real faith."

"Real faith!" she scolded. "Does the real faith says you have to abandon your own family? And why does this real faith look at everyone as an unbeliever?"

He had no intention of discussing this again. He'd had this argument with her hundreds of times. No use.

"I have a plane to catch," he finally said, taking his bag and heading to the door, still glancing at her through his peripheral vision.

"Promise me you will call me once you reached Syria."

He nodded.

"Abdul Rahman," she called him before he was out. Then she asked the nurse to help her stand.

With slow and tired feet, she dragged herself to where he was standing. Despite her hunched back and shrunken body, and the weakness and the trembling hands, she still made him feel safe. Overprotective, apprehensive, and suspicious as she was, she always gave him that feeling of safety. That she was there for him no matter what.

Her pale hands reached for his face. He bent over and let her kiss him on his forehead.

"Take care of yourself." She paused looking at his bag. With a troubled sigh she whispered while holding his head in her shaky palms, "I don't want you to live with the guilt of leaving me for the rest of your life. Maybe you are not feeling it now but you will … trust me. And I am telling you now that I forgive you for everything, I am not angry."

That was when his heart plummeted, when he started suffocating. He woke up again. This time he could feel his limbs, the numbness, the pain, and the smell of the hygiene.

"Make sure the morphine is replaced before you go," a female shouted at someone.

He was at a hospital.

A strong hand took his arm. Beefy fingers took the needle out. Ouch… a surge of pain… was this how you replace a needle?

"Are they awake?" a man asked. The voice came from the end of the room. "The police will come tomorrow morning, so it's better to keep them sleeping. I don't want trouble in my shift."

"They are out of consciousness, don't worry!" she yelled back, then added in a lower mumble, "go back and sleep, you lousy guard."

Thank God the nurse didn't notice he was awake. Minutes later, she was gone and he could hear her no more.

He opened his eyes, trying to adjust his position to have a better look at his surroundings.

The room wasn't big. White walls turned into gray from the accumulated dust and dirt. Next to his bed was another where a heavily built man lay unmoving. His good-looking face had a long scar beneath his right eye down to his chin. The man was wounded, and from the color of the bandages he could see that it was worse than his own wound.

Gradually, as if from the distant past, the doctor's words came to him: "The other person was found with a machine gun and wearing a face mask, he is one of them."

He was one of them... the Mujahedeen. At least there was one person he could trust, a person who shared the same situation.

Abdul Rahman couldn't stay here any longer. The police might arrive any time to investigate them. He wasn't sure about the procedures in Iraq regarding reporting gunshots, but the hospital administration had enough reasons to suspect them.

He would be sent to jail. Probably tortured by some sadistic CIA agent. Abdul Rahman felt a cement rock build up in his chest, his breathing got shallow. A voice in his head grew louder, yelling at him: you must run away, now!

The Saudi young man remembered the training he had in Syria. Don't let them catch you at any cost. Try to die and take as many people with you as you can. Abdul Rahman had no intention of letting them capture him, not when he could move, when he could still fight those infidels, those tomb worshipers. He had sacrificed all his life for this one purpose: to protect his religion.

What his teachers in Saudi Arabia told him about the enemy's threat had left him no choice.

"When we fight the Americans and infidels we are forgetting the real enemy... those who brought the Americans and are helping them, those who want to challenge the Islam teachings and replace them with myths."

However, yesterday's events were a setback. Abdul Rahman wanted to think about it. What really happened and why. He needed to.

But there was no time. He came here for a mission, and he wanted to finish it. He pulled himself out of bed, encouraged by the rush of determination. From the only window of the room, Abdul Rahman could see the main street. Few cars passed, stores were on both sides. Most of them were about to close. Across the street there was a pharmacy and a grocery shop. As far as he could tell, they were the only two shops with customers. Nothing gave him a clue where he was in Baghdad. The gloomy thoughts crept in his mind. He was a stranger, he didn't know anyone in this town. He had no money, no phone, and he was wounded.

Damn them.

Abdul Rahman shook his head, casting the memories away. No time for resentment or regret. He had to find an alternative. The answer was in the bed in front of him.

He walked toward the man, ignoring the slight pain in his shoulder.

"*Kum Ya Akhee*" (Wake up, brother), he whispered in the man's ear, gently nudging him.

The man with the scar was in his early thirties, his curled black hair was recently trimmed, his mustache was neatly trimmed as well. Although he was the same height as Abdul Rahman, the man had more weight on him.

He hadn't seen him before.

Scar-face moaned. Abdul Rahman tried again and again. And again until the man opened his eyes.

"*Mann... Ani?*" (Who are you?) Scar-face chided, his eyes the size of golf balls, he looked surprisingly hostile despite the weakness in his voice.

"I am your brother in faith, my name is Abdul Rahman."

"I don't know you." He looked around. "Where am I?"

It wasn't the brothers-in-arms greeting he had in mind. No hugs, no flowers, and no Allah-is-the-greatest.

Capitalism, it even got to the Jihadists.

"I am not sure where we are now," Abdul Rahman answered. "I am from Saudi Arabia, I came a week..." he paused, the man hadn't the slightest interest to know who he was or where he came from.

"Listen to me," Abdul Rahman said after Scar-face examined the needles and bandages on his body. "I heard the hospital staff talking about calling the police. I am not sure how much time we still have."

"The police!" Scar-face's gaze shifted toward the door. "I've got to go." He tried to stand up but was too weak.

"Akhee" (brother), "you can't walk. I can help you but I need your help as a brother in faith." Scar-face rolled his eyes. Abdul Rahman added, "See, I don't know the city, and I want to join the Mujahedeen."

The man looked at his chest then at Abdul Rahman. "Oh, I must've lost it."

"Lost what, Brother?"

Scar face smirked. "My name tag. The one that says I am the Mujahedeen recruiter."

Abdul Rahman didn't find that funny. He mumbled, "The group I was with... the Mujahedeen... there was a mistake, I am not sure."

"A mistake? Please don't tell me they shot you," Scar-face said in a sarcastic tone, yet Abdul Rahman thought he saw him wince.

"Well, not exactly," Abdul Rahman said. "It's a long story… by the way, I don't know your name."

Scar-face hesitated. Then he uttered, "My name is Malik."

Abdul Rahman smiled, extending his hand. Malik didn't shake it. Instead, he pulled Abdul Rahman's hand and used it to help him stand.

So much for brotherhood.

His injury must be serious, the way Malik stood, moving his legs out of bed one by one, the hunched back, the grimace with every step.

With some help, Malik reached the window. He peered at the street, his eyes glittered. "We are in Karada hospital, and I know how to get out of here unnoticed."

Alhamdu Lilah, Abdul Rahman thanked God. "Do you have a place we can go to?"

Malik chewed on his nails. Abdul Rahman wanted to point out that he should wash his hands first then decided better of it. Malik opened his mouth to say something but heard only the sound of Athan, raised from the nearby mosque calling for prayers.

The two men were silent for another minute. Malik finished one hand and moved on to chewing the nails on the other. He sat back on his bed.

When the prayers call finished, Malik said, raising his finger in the air, "I have an idea." Abdul Rahman truly hopped that this idea didn't involve chewing on his foot nails. "I know a friend who can help us. I will take you there and you can spend the night there. After that you are on your own."

Malik's tone left no room for negotiation. But one night was just what he needed, Abdul Rahman nodded. "*Ana Muwafik.*"

Malik extended his hand to him, and this time, again, he used it to help him stand.

-11-
Al-Ghadeer Cooperation – Karada District
June 9th
7:30 PM

Ali Al-Kadimi adjusted his seat, his neck sore from working on the computer for the past hour. Nothing like the old papers. A new pain, in his eyes this time. He inserted a blank CD in the CD-drive, moved the mouse slowly across the screen pressing on the Next button every time until the back-up process started. Nothing he could do now but sit and wait until the backup was over.

Ali pushed back his leather chair, tilting his head left and right. The computer techie in his firm had told him something about moving his arms and neck every half an hour when working on the computer.

Right.

In his late fifties, Ali had broad shoulders and was still trying to stay in shape. His bushy eyebrows matched his thick and wavy, black-turning-to-gray hair, something other men at his age envied.

Ali's tired gaze wandered around his office, which was designed by a famous Iraqi architect. Its three walls made of glass faced Al-Karada main street. There was some deep philosophy behind the design, the architect had explained to him during the construction. Something to do with sun and spirit… if he just hadn't fallen asleep during the discussion.

The view from Ali's office on the 6th floor was spectacular. The Tigris River made a turn around the land, giving the feeling that one was surrounded by water. Palm trees rose up on both sides of the river, the reflection of the long green fins danced in the water. There were no boats, and no people swimming in the river as before. But Ali could still see it in his childhood memories. He could still hear the cheerful songs, the sound of laughter. He wasn't sure how long he could hold on to his memories of Baghdad.

Today there was nothing more than the gathering sandstorm. He gazed at the yellowish scene below, a police checkpoint of Iraqi national guards with two police cars right under his window. The two cars parked horizontally in the street effectively blocked the three lanes and let only one lane pass. Three soldiers stood there just looking at the cars passing without any real inspection.

Maybe there was another deep philosophy behind this inspection. Who knew? One had to keep his mind open these days.

Over a hundred cars stuck in an endless traffic jam because of this road block. Ali looked at them, the hot weather, the old non-air-conditioned cars, and the sand.

A deep wisdom.

From this vantage point, the entire scene looked like a sepia photo. Especially with the red sand filling the air. The suffering, even misery was hard to ignore. He stood silent, looking at the drivers struggling to pass.

At times he wished he had his Nikon camera. Ali had a touch with photos. Not anymore. He quit photography the moment he got back to Iraq, some six or seven years ago. It just didn't feel right taking photos of what he saw. As corny as it might sound, the suffering was too much to be photographed.

Ali heaved a long sigh, turning back to face the only wall in the room. Photos of the company's delivered projects, along with certificates of different kinds filled the space. Ali had taken all the photos himself. Okay... he didn't *completely* quit photography. But taking photos of the projects they delivered wasn't about photography. It was also about the finished work. The promise fulfilled.

The memories spanned back to the last ten years, back to the first project his company had delivered. The water supply system in Al-Askari district in Najaf, his home town. It was during Saddam's era.

The photo he took that day of the people celebrating clean and drinkable water had a special place on his wall. And his heart.

Since then, Ali felt something beyond happiness. He was as happy as everyone else in his company to deliver the project and lessen the suffering of the people. But there was more to it. It felt as if he were creating his legacy. A tribute of his life. Something that when looked at, when remembered, made him feel that his life had a tangible value. One could not take money with him to the grave, but the happiness he gave to people's lives... it must count. He tried not to dwell more there. Ali didn't like the dreamy version of him much.

He was a businessman. Better to think this way.

On his computer monitor, the Windows-logo screen-saver was dancing. Teasing him that he would have to key in his password if he wanted to work on the machine again.

"Security measures," the computer technician would say pretentiously. Computers made people's lives easier, computer technicians, on the other hand, made sure it would be a hell.

Ali looked back at the photo on the wall, at the broad smile on an old woman's face holding a big jug of water in Najaf.

"I will pray for God every time I visit the holy shrine of Najaf to bless you and keep you safe and wealthy," the old woman told him, tears in her eyes, pointing to the big golden dome of Emam Ali's Shrine.

"Thank you, ma'am, but I am just doing my job," he replied, watching in embarrassment the woman's sons filling the big trunk with water, still afraid this clean water might not last long.

"Son, we were suffering for the last five years because of the lack of drinkable water. All the contractors who came here just took the money and did nothing."

He knew of the history of the project, which was almost the same in all the Iraqi cities. Despite that Iraq had "two great rivers," Saddam's government had succeeded in doing one thing none of the previous governments in Iraq could do... parching the land and people.

People gathered around him and his colleagues that day, told them how the city government made revenue of selling water to the people. The water that the government's job was to provide.

The people celebrated the clean water, washing their faces, pouring it over their heads, getting totally soaked with it.

Since that day, his company only did water-related projects. They gradually specialized in supply lines for refinery stations. He never lost a tender in this field. His profit margin was minimum and everyone in the industry knew them. Even if another company won the contract, soon they would either subcontract them or, when the project challenges started to pop up (which was the case with such projects in Iraq), they dropped the project and Al-Ghadeer Company stepped in.

When he was young, Ali's father kept telling him that as long as his goal was to help people, God would bless the money he made and more business would come in.

He wasn't sure if it was because of his good will or God's mercy or him not being greedy or some other mysterious reason, but Ali saw it firsthand --the amount of business he got was more than one company could handle. Other companies and branches were founded, and the once-small Ghadeer Company turned into a corporation with six different companies under its umbrella.

Quiet knocking came at his door. The door opened and Mahmoud, his driver, stepped in.

"I might need another twenty minutes," Ali said, checking the progress of the backup on the screen. "Have a seat while I am finished."

Mahmoud murmured something and sat in the chair in front of him. Ali started with the Iraqi's best ice-breaking line: "*Shaku Mako?*" (What's up.)

Mahmoud smiled and murmured, "Everything is fine."

The smile looked so forced Ali almost felt the effort it took Mahmoud to pull it. The old man looked tired and exhausted. His unshaven beard started to have more hair than that on his head. Black wrinkles formed below his eyes. He wore a white shirt that had turned yellowish, stains of odor were visible in his chest and under his arms.

"How is Yousif?" Ali asked. Yousif was Mahmoud's teenage son. The kid was a pain in the neck for his father. Staying out late, angry and introverted most of the time and hanging out with strangers. Probably typical teenage rebellion, except in his case he was hanging out with armed men who wore short Dishdash and grew thick beards.

"He's still lecturing me about Jihad every day," Mahmoud sighed, his mouth still smiling but not his eyes.

Shit, even teenagers problems were special in Iraq.

"It's all my fault," Mahmoud added, rubbing his face with his hand. "I was so furious about what happened in Abu Guraib that I start complimenting Jihadists in front of him."

"Don't worry, Mahmoud, once the summer is over and he is back to school he will forget about all of this."

Mahmoud nodded. "I am not worried about him. He is a man, he will handle it, I am worried about his sister."

Not worried about him because he is a man…hmm… Ali wanted to point out that this was sexism. But then he remembered he was not in the United States anymore. Mahmoud was just a member of the big group of sexists called Iraqis.

"Your daughter is in college now, right?"

"Senior in medical," Mahmoud said, puffing his chest up. "She is my pride, the way she studied despite the hot weather and no electricity."

Ali remembered her, he also remembered that she was about to get married. "So?"

"Her fiancé," Mahmoud shoulders slumped, "he disappeared. Two days with no sign of him."

Disappeared. A word that could mean anything from got in a car accident to kidnapped, arrested, or killed. Ali did not know how to respond to that so he settled for, "Oh."

"The man had no enemies, a very peaceful man, I don't want to say he is a prince but… I mean he is very good guy."

A prince… half of the men arrested by Iraqis or Americans were described by their relatives as princes. Even after bombs and heavy weapons were found in their places, they were still princes. Maybe it's a Robin-Hood-like prince. Ali shook his head. He had no right to judge people.

"I am sorry for that."

Mahmoud nodded. Another knock came on the door. Ali Al-Kadumi turned and saw the cheerful face of one of the female staff peering in.

"May I?" the young lady asked with a child-like smile.

During the past two years, Ali made it clear to all his fifty-something employees that they could come to him for anything. The open-door policy was not just a corporate slogan. It was a mistake.

"Sure, I thought you were already on your way home."

She was in her early thirties. Her long olive-green dress with a loose white shirt matched the scarf covering her head, leaving only her rosy pink face visible. "I needed some time to sort out my emails. I was so occupied with the modifications to the tender proposal for Mr. Ehab that he wanted to submit to G-Plan for the water project."

He gave her a congenial smile. Ali always appreciated the enthusiasm of his staff. When projects with the government and big American companies started to be subcontracted to Iraqi companies, people reacted in two different ways. Some considered it as a help to the "occupiers" to stay in Iraq and hence they fully opposed the work. Others, like his staff, considered this as the real chance to help build their country.

Albeit things got messed up later on, and that fine line between the two groups eventually evaporated, some people still looked to their jobs as a sacred task of building their country, something most young Iraqis were longing for during Sadam's regime. Another cliché, but like all clichés, it was dead on.

"It's past seven and the road is not safe," Ali said, watching the message on his computer. The backup was done. "Okay, tell you what. Mahmoud will drop me at home and then drive you to the nearest point."

"Fanan," she said.

Ali had no idea what that meant. His young staff kept coming up with new words, it made him feel old.

"You are welcome." Ali turned to Mahmoud. "Can you do that?"

Mahmoud made a half shrug. "I live in Al-Amel district. I will drop her at any point on the road."

-12-
MICF Head Quarter – Karada District
June 9th
7:40 PM

From the diaries of the abandoned city.

In the early '80s, a wealthy businessman decided to build his house on the piece of land he'd recently bought in Karada, one of Baghdad's most luxurious and oldest areas. The businessman, motivated by his life dream to build a house big enough for him and his sons and their future families, managed to build one of the biggest and most elegant houses in the district.

The fancy house, however, didn't bring the happiness his owner sought. Not only that, but according to the Saddami-intelligence-super-agent in charge of Karada in 1982, the only thing this house brought its owner was envy.

At that gloomy period of Iraq history, envy could materialize to something dark and dangerous like the report on the agent's desk that claimed this businessman had "religious interests". The report also claimed that the man had donated some amount of money to finish building a Hussainya –a small mosque of Shia - in that area.

The super-agent didn't buy the claims in the reports, not only for the lack of evidence but also because he knew that the report was written by the businessman's neighbor, who happened to be a new member in Al-Baath Party.

Reporting your neighbor was a common thing in the old days to get a promotion in the party.

However sure that the allegations weren't true, the agent, seeking a promotion himself, had forwarded the report to a newly formed community of members in the secret services and other 'secret' agencies.

A week later, the businessman was being sadistically tortured in one of the famous one-meter-by-one-meter cells of the Baghdad security administration. His wife was repeatedly raped in a cell in front of him. One of his five children died in the detention. And his house was confiscated.

Another common thing in the old days.

A week later, the businessman was exceptionally lucky that his brother personally knew one of the high-ranking officials in the security administration and managed to bribe him to get his brother out. Because the charges were minor, the bribed official agreed to set the man and what was left of his family free if he turned in someone else.

That, however, wasn't common. Normally you die either way. Just how you die would be different. Which still made it worthwhile for a lot of people to sell anyone they knew, for a less-painful death.

Another week later, the businessman and his family were deported to Iran. All their equities, money, and their Iraqi passports were confiscated.

The next month, two of his friends were arrested with their families and were sent for interrogation –read, torturing– to the new secret intelligence office that was now in the same big house the unfortunate businessman built.

The two families, convicted of participating in the Al-Dawa Islamic party, were the first to be thrown in an acid pool in that house.

After two months, the remains of the two families –those who were... luckier to get normal execution... were sent to Al-Radwanya to be dumped in one of the big holes already occupied by hundreds of rotted bodies.

The big house was officially turned into an office of Sadam's secret-services, mainly used for interrogations, and its original owner was working as a waiter for daily wages in a small Iranian city, trying to forget his old life.

Twenty years later, the new Iraqi government took over the house and it was turned into headquarters for the Ministry of Interior Commandos Forces –aka MICF– one of the first security forces formed by the blessing of the American ambassador.

The halls and corridors of the house had forgotten that it once held a family that lived with love. The rooms unwillingly replaced the cheerful occupants with those who were brought only to be tortured. Blood traces covered the walls and the floors. The repelling smell of death became part of the foundations. Cries of pain echoed endlessly in the-now-dark corners of the house.

Captain Abdul Hasan heard muffled cries of pain rising from one of the rooms on the ground floor. He let out a sigh. Did he make the right decision by letting Hussain and Shaker handle the interrogation with Mujahid? What if they had arrested an innocent who just happened to be at the wrong time and place? He heard another muffled cry, this time with Shaker's angry shouting.

Abdul Hasan went downstairs to the interrogation room. In the original design of the house, this room used to be a bathroom. It was modified to be used as a 'special' interrogation room during the last two decades. Bricks now covered the only window. Other utilities were removed to fit the new 'function' of the room.

Abdul Hasan stood at the beginning of the corridor leading to the interrogation room. Shaker and Hussain stood facing the chair where the suspect was seated.

Lieutenant Shaker roared, "Come on, you filth, speak up!"

Abdul Hasan checked his wrist watch. Time ran against them. Whatever information they could get from the suspect, it was only valuable for a brief time window. After which, his group would know about his arrest and what was compromised and act upon it.

"There is no point of denying Mujahid." It was Hussain, his voice was calmer than his colleague's. "We know who you are and what you and your group are up to, Kattan told us everything."

Kattan was the name of the Syrian kid. If the suspect was not intimidated enough to talk, the best way was to confront him with the evidence. A little bit of exaggeration wouldn't hurt.

"I have no idea what you are talking about," the man replied.

Shaker grabbed the suspect by his shirt and fixed him against the wall. Abdul Hasan couldn't hear what they were saying until Shaker yelled, "You Salafism bastard!"

Shaker then threw the suspect on the ground. A crashing sound. Cursing. Hussain tried to calm his colleague. Shaker's voice came panting: "For thirty years you treated us like scum, you called us Southerners. Yet we didn't avenge ourselves when the regime fell. We listened to our clergy; they said we are brothers and we kept quiet. We said why not, let's put it all behind us. And how did you pay us back? You bombed the pilgrims of Emam Hussain, you sent your fucking suicide bombers to the crowded Shia areas."

"*Kafa Ya Shaker*," (Enough) Abdul Hasan said, stepping inside the room.

Shaker spun around. His eyes had the look of a ten-year-old being caught by the principal fighting in the school yard. "He... He said, he was..." Shaker pointed at the suspect on the ground, "he wasn't talking, he refused to..."

"What was this speech about?" Abdul Hasan asked, still able to keep his calm tone. "Salafism, pilgrims of Hussain, and Southerners... have you forgotten what you are?"

Shaker stood silent gazing at the floor, again like a school kid.

Hussain helped the suspect to sit on the chair again.

"Tell me, what are you?"

"I am a soldier," Shaker said in a low voice, still gazing down.

"Where? In Sadam's secret service or a soldier in the commandos' force?" The secret was to keep the voice as low and calm as possible. Abdul Hasan didn't like shouting and yelling.

"In the commandos' forces," Shaker winced like a child being forced to apologize.

"And do you know what the difference is between the commandos' forces and Sadam's secret service?"

Shaker's lips tightened, his eyes looked everywhere but at Abdul Hasan.

"Tell me, Lieutenant, do you know the difference or were you so gripped by the old vengeance, forgetting what we are trying to do here."

His voice was getting louder now.

"We protect Iraqis, Sir. And they used to protect only Sadam."

"Iraqis? Are you sure?" The Captain's gaze shifted from Shaker to Hussain then back to Shaker again. They both stared at the ground. "Which Iraqis? The one from our sect only or all of them?"

"All Iraqis," Shaker murmured.

Abdul Hasan leaned forward, putting his face an inch from Shaker's. His breath grew heavy and slow. He said, grunting and pointing at the suspect who buried his head in his arms. "Are you sure?"

Shaker didn't answer.

Abdul Hasan shook his head and walked away. He felt disappointment, not only because of Shaker, for it was the same everywhere he went. Sectarian violence threatened to be an unstoppable force. He wanted to fight terrorists, he wanted his soldiers to believe how important it was. But above all, he wanted them to disassociate from the personal feelings and old vengeances.

"Do you know what is the scary thing about sectarianism or any goddamn intolerance?" he said after a long exhale. "That once you start, once you say I am with this group against that group, then you can't stop. Soon you will look at your own group and start seeing some differences. So you divide them into subgroups and so on, putting every one with a slight difference in faith or opinion in another group. And before you know it you will end up alone, unable to trust your closest friends as they might end up with some differences later on."

The Captain paused, looking at Hussain and the other soldiers who came to watch the scene from the corridor. "And then, there will be no victory. Even if we won the battle against terrorism. Because at that stage we would have lost the most important thing we were fighting for in the first place... the life, not any life, the good life that deserves living, the society that we want to build."

Some of the soldiers started nodding, some just stared at the floor.

Some people might object to his way of talking to his soldiers and officers in front of the suspects. But Abdul Hasan believed that the culture of human-rights had to be taught not only to the law-enforcement personnel but also to the suspects. Everyone must have the confidence that he would not be suppressed or mistreated.

"Don't you get it? It's not about winning a war, it's about not losing our values, our souls, our love. Call it whatever you like but for Mohammed's sake, don't forget who you are."

"Permission to speak, sir," Hussain said.

"Granted."

"Don't you think this situation is different, I mean with all due respect. We are almost sure who he is and what he did. And we need to get as much information from him as possible."

Abdul Hasan nodded. "I know that well. But do you think this way of interrogation is helping us getting anywhere closer?"

Hussain shook his head slowly.

"Besides," Abdul Hasan added, "this is hardly the point. Look at Sadir city for example, how many bombings happened there in the last month? Five, ten, even more. And after every bombing the streets are back with life the next day as if nothing happened, in the same spot the damn suicidal had blown himself up, you would find one or two new food stands. Doesn't that tell you anything?"

"Umm… people are… not afraid of terrorists," Hussain replied reluctantly.

Abdul Hasan shook his head. "That no matter how hard they hurt us, how often they committed those bombings, they will not take away of our will to live."

The Captain turned to Shaker, "But if they manage to drag our feet into their bloody fanaticism. If we become like what they have evolved to, afraid of the slight difference in opinion, antagonizing anyone who doesn't agree with us. Then I know for sure that we will end up killing ourselves. This is the real danger, not the bombing. Mark those words, we protect Iraqis, all Iraqis. We are not defending Shia against Sunnie or the followers of Najaf clergy against Al-Sader army."

The suspect sneered. Everyone turned toward him. "Nice speech," he said, wiping his bleeding nose. "I wish it was half an hour ago before your gorilla here beat the hell out of me." He spat blood from his mouth on the floor and looked at them defiantly. "Where is my right of getting a lawyer? Where is my right of knowing what are my charges? I did nothing."

"Hey, you!" Shaker yelled. "This is an anti-terrorist facility not fucking Hollywood. You can bitch about your lawyer when we are done with you."

Abdul Hasan shook his head. Pointless. Lecturing Shaker about human rights was similar to explaining Beethoven to a chair.

"Have you done the gunpowder test?" He asked Hussain.

"We will do it now, sir." Hussain motioned to one of the soldiers who left and came back carrying a small table with another soldier. On the table was the test toolkit, a transparent sleeve connected from one end to a vial with a chemical mix. Hussain removed the clip from the sleeve, took the suspect's hand, and put it in the sleeve. Then he asked him to crush the vial with his hand. The man did. Hussain took out the test strip and gazed at the vial. The color start changing to yellow, then orange, and finally settled on something brownish.

"Shit!" Hussain looked at the man, stepping back as if he were going to explode. "What the hell have you been doing? Using TNT instead of salt!"

There was no question about it. This man had dealt with explosive material and gunpowder, and in large quantities.

The Captain scoffed at the suspect. "So much for playing innocent, what do you say about this test... Mujahid."

The suspect sighed as if to declare that he lost a match. "Okay, Okay, I will speak everything but I will talk to the Captain only."

Shaker tried to protest, Abdul Hasan cut him off.

"I will grant you that, but in case this is one of your games, I promise you that you will wish you stayed with Shaker."

The Captain signaled for everyone to leave the cramped room.

Hussain watched, with worry, the Captain closing the interrogation room door on him and the suspect. Something about the way Mujahid was looking at the Captain made the hair on the back of his neck stand up.

"What the fuck was that?" Shaker said when they were alone.

Hussain shrugged. Everyone knew how the Captain liked to lecture.

"You know what," Shaker said in a low voice, "I heard he was once a lecturer in the military college. Before Sadam put him in jail."

"A teacher? Really?"

Shaker nodded with a conspiratorial smile. "I think we were lucky he didn't punish us with an extra ten pages of homework."

Hussain laughed. For a moment he forget his nagging feeling. It didn't last long. Before Hussain could leave the floor, the sergeant at the reception desk came dashing toward the interrogation room.

"Lieutenant Hussain," the sergeant addressed him breathing heavily while gazing at the closed door of the interrogation room and then at Hussain as if asking for help. "I have an urgent call for the Captain."

"We can't interrupt now," Hussain said, "the suspect is confessing." At least that was what they hoped he'd do.

"Sir, you don't understand, it's his wife. I think someone from the Captain's family was just kidnapped."

-13-
Al-Tawheed Mosque, Al-Amel District
June 9th
7:45 PM

The masses started leaving Al-Tawheed mosque after the sunset prayers. Several youths stayed, listening to the religious lecture that took place in the one-hour window between the sunset's prayers and the night's prayers.

Luay sat in the corner, waiting for the lecture to be over. The Egyptian sheikh was taking it seriously, his face reddened, his voice getting louder and angrier. He used his hands a lot, waving and pointing and threatening. Something about the entire scene reminded Luay of the pre-battle speeches in the Braveheart movie. If only Sheikh Abu Ayob was a hundred pounds thinner and wore a kilt.

Most of the attendees were adolescents. There were several unemployed men as well. Luay knew most of them from the neighborhood. Everyone was sitting on the floor, this was the tradition in mosques and Luay got used to it.

From his tone now, Abu Ayob had reached the end of his war-speech. He took a sip of water from a plastic glass next to him and spoke in a calmer voice:

"We had wished the practices of this deviant group were confined to practicing polytheism, and blessing the graves and the establishment of the so-called Al-Husseini mourning ceremony. But they took another dimension. Now, they feel safe and free to show their real faces. Yes, my brothers. They subsidized the infidels, began the occupation of our land, and allied themselves with the Persians and the Crusaders to destroy Islam from within."

Despite his resentment to the Sheikh, Luay appreciated the way the man talked to the young people. The way he prepared them for the real world, the way he warned them. It was essential. Back in the secret service, they used to have a full branch responsible for moral support and political education. Luay hated the long hours that he was forced to listen to and repeat Baath values over and over. But now he could see how important this was. How could he survive otherwise against the giant American marketing campaign?

Abu Ayob looked left and right, then leaned forward talking in a lower voice, his face was solemn:

"So we have no other answer for the continuous threat of the Bader organization and Al Mahdi army but to retaliate with force. We cannot let a bunch of Safavid destroy our religion. We cannot stand by and watch those misguided people help the Americans to infiltrate our lives."

Most of the attendees nodded. One asked the sheikh something Luay couldn't hear due to the distance. Abu Ayob smiled and looked at the rest of the audience. Some laughed. Then he answered with a chuckle, "Of course we are allowed to do that. It is Jihad."

The discussion went on in a low voice, everyone leaned forwarded and listened to Abu Ayob telling them a story of some sort. Abu Ayob liked telling stories. Luay heard fractions of it. He wished he could give Abu Ayob a torchlight to put under his chin.

When the lecture was over and people were dismissed, Abu Ayob called out for one of them. "Brother Amjad, I need to talk to you."

A tall young man with thick glasses nodded. Not like the rest of the attendees, Amjad did not wear the white, ankle-short Dishdash. His beard, however, was as thick as most. He had clean-cut hair and delicate facial features. His clothes were, at best, casual. Sky-blue trousers that looked so old even a charity organization might throw them away, and a dark green short-sleeved shirt. The miss-match of the colors was painful.

One conclusion, there were no mirrors where he lived. That, or he was colorblind.

Amjad sat next to the Sheikh and they talked for a while. The young man kept nodding. Finally they shook hands and Amjad left.

Luay waited for some time until everyone around the sheikh left. He stood up so that Abu Ayob could see him. The fat sheikh motioned to Luay to follow him. Luay did. Abu Ayob opened a white metal door in the corner of the praying hall. Luay followed him to a narrow corridor. Lit only by a small florescent light that buzzed loudly and kept blinking, the hallway was dingy and dark. It had the distinctive wet and mildew smell of the Bukhoor, although he couldn't see the incense burner, nor the white smoke of the Bukhoor but the smell of the burning wood-chips filled the hallway, making him feel dizzy for a second. Two closed doors on the right. A bathroom and a small kitchen to the left. Luay had been in this corridor many times, never once had he seen the rooms to the right opened. Yet, he had a good idea of what was there.

At the end of the corridor stood another white metal door. This one was a bit rustic. Abu Ayob opened it and ushered Luay to a wide room. The walls were covered with sheets of white fiber and carried different blood-red slogans inciting fighting Americans and unbelievers.

"I see you haven't changed the décor," Luay said.

Abu Ayob mumbled something. Luay examined the floor. No blood. "At least you managed to do some cleaning."

The sheikh winced and gave him an I-am-not-in-the-mood look. "Please sit, brother Luay." He gestured to the floor. There was nothing but a crimson carpet. Practical choice of color, knowing what the room was used for. Luay sat on the floor. Abu Ayob took a big pillow and used it as a hand-rest.

"I called you for something," Abu Ayob said, his voice sounded as if he was talking from the bottom of a well, which might as well be the case giving his 250 pounds. "However... something else... happened... and it's urgent. Very urgent and serious... very serious."

Luay punched his left palm with his right fist. There were few things in life Luay enjoyed more than listening to Abu Ayob, having his fingernails removed was one of them. And he knew that the Sheikh shared the same feelings with him. Nice to be in love.

"Okay, I got it, it's serious and I am here."

Abu Ayob took his rosary and started fiddling with the beads "It's... tomorrow's operation."

"Oh, shit!" Luay slammed his thigh. "I knew it... you want out don't you? Shit!" This was the second time in a week Abu Ayob's group let him down. First, the bombed car operation two days ago when the kid they brought chickened and ran away. And now this one. Six hours earlier he wouldn't have given a damn about it. But now, knowing that his plans of quitting this business were blown up, he had to make it work. His commission for each operation was enough to get him going for a month.

"La, La (no, no) it's not that!" Abu Ayob held up his hands, his eyes wide. He took a deep breath. "Mujahid had planned everything since last week. We prepared the car you gave us and set it up for the mission. And we were ready to do the operation tomorrow, especially with the valuable information you gave us."

"So?"

Abu Ayob's fingers moved faster on his praying beads. There was something fishy about this operation from the beginning. Mujahid had refused to share any information with Luay about how they were going to execute. He also made some strange request for classified information from the Ministry of Interior database.

"I got very bad news just now."

"From this guy you met? What was his name? Amjad."

"No, no." Abu Ayob waved his hand. "Amjad is a new recruit. You can use him if you want. He is very motivated and strangely willing to participate in fighting the enemy--"

"Abu Ayob. What was the bad news?"

The Sheikh made a lemon-sucking-face then said, "Mujahid was arrested."

"Fuck!"

"Luay! This is a house of God."

"The fucking son of bitch got fucking arrested... shit."

"Luay!" Abu Ayob yelled, looking at him in the eye.

Luay's palm clenched into a fist, he relaxed himself. "I told you, this man is not up to the trust you gave him, Sheikh."

Abu Ayob frowned. "You are underestimating him."

"Just because he killed so many people does not mean that he is good or anything." Luay pointed to his chest with his thumb. "You know how many men I killed? You have no idea what I did in the good old days, but you know what? I wasn't enjoying it. It was just a job. This fuc- this maniac is doing it for fun. He just enjoys killing people. He is not a pro."

"You know nothing of brother Mujahid," Abu Ayob said, his cheeks puffed making his rounded face look like an over-grown tomato. "He doesn't enjoy killing people."

"No? Oh, maybe he just wanted to keep his knife sharp."

"You don't understand." Abu Ayob shook his head. "Mujahid, likes to take away lives."

Luay rolled his eyes. Smart-ass Jihadist.

"Mujahid, likes to know the people he is killing. He wants to know everything about their lives, their dreams, their interests. What they liked and what not. He asks his …umm …prisoners, for their children's names, looks for photos in their wallets. They gave him everything he asks for, they are desperate and they think he sympathizes with them. Not that they have a choice anyway. So you see when he does the killing… he…"

"Takes away lives," Luay said. Abu Ayob nodded.

An image flashed from the last beheading they filmed in this room. He remembered the look on Mujahid's face. A shiver ran through his body. Something he hadn't experienced for a long time.

"How did he get arrested?"

"I am not sure." Abu Ayob sighed. "It was utterly surprising. He was going to the safe house where the Syrian kid was staying to clean up any evidence when the sinners from the commandos forces arrested him. Someone must have turned him in. Anyhow, we will cleanse the area soon."

Luay remembered the pending task he'd kept postponing for more than a week now. They should have started cleansing the area from all the opponents.

This lazy two-brain-celled Sheikh. Abu Ayob had wasted time playing around and asking girls for marriage. He should have taken care of his area if he wanted to be a real Ameer.

"Assign someone else to finish the job. Why do you need Mujahid?"

Abu Ayob made the lemon-sucking-face again. "He is the only one who knew about the location of the bombed car."

"Oh, shit." Luay pounded the floor with his fist. "And I assume that you want me to help get his ass out of the jail?"

Abu Ayob just nodded.

"And if I manage to get him out, you will carry on with the mission?"

"Tomorrow, we are all set. Except for the car and that's why we need Mujahid."

Luay looked Abu Ayob square in the eye. He believed him.

A muffled shriek came out from the adjacent room in the mosque. Luay gave Abu Ayob a quizzical look.

"Some naughty boys need discipline," the sheikh murmured.

"Uh huh." Luay never liked what Abu Ayob did in this room. It was unnecessary and felt wrong for some reason. Coward.

"*Sawf Uhawil An Osaed*," (I will try to help,) Luay said. "But I need to know more about the plan."

"*Ana La Aareff*," (I don't know,) Abu Ayob said. His eyes shifted. "Mujahid handled all the details – I really don't know."

"Listen, Abu Ayob." Luay fought an urge to smash Abu Ayob's head against the wall. "You need me, and I have instructions to help you. But if you and Mujahid kept showing me that you do not trust me, then I have to say that we cannot work together."

"This is absurd… we are not--"

"And you know what," Luay pointed in the Sheikh's face. "You know well that we are the only people who can support you here. We know the ground, we know the people, and if you want any further help you have to get us to approve your plans. If you want to play alone, then just tell me and I will go home and have some rest."

Abu Ayob's face was blood red. He opened his mouth then closed it. He pushed the big pillow away and sat with his back straight, scratching his cheek.

In a normal situation, Abu Ayob used to bluff about some other forces supporting him. But now with Mujahid gone and the ever-increasing competition with other Islamic groups, everyone claiming control over their territories, he simply could not risk it.

Luay made a move as if he were about to stand up and leave.

"*La, La*, (no, no) sit down, brother, please."

Luay waited.

"God knows how much I appreciate the help you are doing for the faith, brother Luay, but as they say, precaution rules."

Luay made a face. "Precaution rules?"

"It's an old wisdom."

"Uh huh. What was Mujahid's plan?" He sneered. Luay didn't like to brag, but he had a good reputation in planning. Assassination was his forte, but planning for a bombing wasn't that different. By all means it was easier, he didn't have to focus on one target and the more he killed the better.

"It is simple, we will drive the car inside the target and bomb it."

"Drive it? Why not use the valet service?"

Abu Ayob smiled. "Actually, it's very close to that."

"Stop the cryptic talking, tell me how you can pass the security defenses."

"They will drive it for us." The smile was still on Abu Ayob's face.

Luay didn't like it. He was the one who surprised everyone.

"You will bribe one of the Iraqi officers to let the car in?" It wasn't a bad idea and they had done it before, the problem was the government changed their procedures so that no one could know which officer would be in charge of the location.

"Bribe?" Abu Ayob shook his head. "We don't pay the infidels."

"So what is it?... if not money, then what could it be? Unless." Luay smiled.

Abu Ayob smiled back, maybe even winked.

"You will threaten the one in charge?"

Abu Ayob made a yes-no gesture with his hand. Luay still didn't get it. The same problem existed as with the bribe-- they had to know who would be in charge of the target.

"You remember the information Mujahid asked for and you managed to get from your friend, the politician?"

Luay nodded. Dafer had acquired the information from the Ministry of Interior database.

"We found a high-ranking commandos officer with access to all places, one who can get the car in, no matter who is in charge of the security."

Luay's jaw dropped. "But... But those people hate us. It is personal between them and us now. Threatening will not work. Unless... you've got his family don't you?"

Abu Ayob's smile reached his ears now. It wasn't a very pleasant sight. Two words, bad dentist.

"Come with me, I will show you something."

It took the fat Sheikh the good part of a minute to stand up. He ushered Luay through the door back to the dark corridor. The buzzing florescent light was off now, leaving the place totally dark. The muffled cries became clearer as they stood next to the first room's door. There was a big lock on it. Abu Ayob took a key from his dishdash pocket and opened the door.

The room was big, dark, and had no windows. It reminded Luay of the interrogation rooms they used to have. They would keep the suspect in the dark, and only during the interrogation would they switch on a red light. Very romantic. Ah, the good old days of Sadam.

Abu Ayob switched on a faint yellow light. It sent dancing shadows on the thick curtain that divided the room into two halves. In the front half, close to where they were standing, a kid was blindfolded, gagged, and bound to a chair.

"This is what will guarantee his cooperation," Abu Ayob said, pointing at the kid.

Despite the gag and the blindfold, Luay saw the purple bruises on the kid's face and neck. "His son, not a bad idea."

The kid started crying, probably because he heard their voices. He begged them for mercy, but the mouth gag muffled the sound away. Luay shook his head with disgust. He didn't like weak kids. This boy's father was in the army, he should be tougher.

Abu Ayob raised his fat hand and slapped the boy on his cheek. The hit was so strong that the Captain's son fell into a low weep immediately.

A different sound came from behind the curtains. This one was more of a moan. Abu Ayob answered Luay's suspicious look with a frown.

"Spoils of war," Abu Ayob said.

Luay decided to let it slide for now. "So the father should receive the news any minute now?"

"I think so. We kidnapped him less than an hour ago, in front of his mother actually. All we need is Mujahid to give us the car."

-14-
MICF Head Quarter – Karada District
June 9th
8:00 PM

Abdul Hasan hung up the phone with his wife. She was still sobbing hysterically. Her words sliced through his chest: his son was kidnapped. He tried to take a breath, to sit on a chair, to do any of the tips he normally advised people to do when he delivered bad news.

None of it worked.

During the last year, Abdul Hasan had delivered a lot of bad news to different people. Missing persons found dead, kidnapping, killing, and even decapitation. He watched with great sympathy how people collapsed when they first found out their loved ones were in grave danger or dead. He had experienced this himself, a long time ago. The loss of a loved one. With time he managed to disentangle from the sufferings he witnessed. Call it apathy or dispassion or emotional numbness, an inevitable result after so many years in the field. Abdul

Hasan wasn't sure if it was a gift, a by-product of all the suffering he saw, or a curse.

It didn't matter. Whatever it was, he didn't have it.

He was still as vulnerable and as ... human as anyone else.

He knew that from the nausea, the sense of being scooped out, the sickening feeling of the room spinning around him, the floor shaking beneath his feet, or was that his legs shaking?

I should be stronger, for God's sake. Young soldiers had died in his arms. Friends and colleagues lost in action. He learned how to deal with such crises. Or so he thought.

And then, exactly as he knew it would, his brain started searching for ways out. Escaping the awful truth. Denial.

Could it be all a big mistake?

His wife saw them forcing their boy into a car.

But she might be mistaken. Maybe that was his friends doing some sort of tasteless prank.

As he was still trying to reason, forcing himself to accept the truth –again– and to pull himself together, it hit him. The images of his son smiling. He couldn't block out the memories. He had to focus on the matter at hand. But another part of him wanted so desperately to hold on to those memories. To submerge into that world. Never to wake up.

"My dad is the bravest man in the force," he heard his son once bragging with his cousins. Now fourteen, he had passed the age where boys look at their fathers with blind admiration, the teenage rebellion did something, as it always did. But not to his admiration for his father; Abdul Hasan was still his son's idol.

"A black car abruptly stopped next to where he and his friends were playing," the quivering voice of his wife echoed in his mind. "It all happened so quickly... two men emerged... grabbed him... he tried to fight but... oh my God!"

His son was tough, strong, and athletic. But that didn't help him.

Abdul Hasan collapsed on the only chair in the interrogation room. Focus. He had to get his son back.

For a brief second his gaze locked with the terrorist's blood-shot eyes. The man was still cuffed, sweating. His once-white shirt was torn off, wet with sweat and blood. His look was not the sardonic, annoying one it used to be; rather, it was something else.

Anticipation... anxiety.

It reminded Abdul Hasan of the look he used to see at the explosions squad team when they were about to dismantle a bomb.

But why? Abdul Hasan didn't have the time to even speak with him.

Mujahid, or whoever this man was, was about to confess, at least that was what he said. Abdul Hasan couldn't totally exclude that he might just want some time out from Shaker's brutality.

"You wanted to make a confession." Abdul Hasan couldn't hide the weariness in his voice. Wishing nothing but to sprint out of the room and start a search for his son, a desperate one, he knew well. "Let's start with your name."

"Yes… yes... I will tell you everything about myself." His voice was now sincere, or at least trying to be.

Abdul Hasan nodded nervously, looking at the door. He shouldn't be here.

"Well, Captain, I know you might not believe me but I really know nothing about this Mujahid. But I am willing to share everything I know with you."

"Listen, I don't have time for games." He added in a semi-apologizing tone as if trying to avoid a boring meeting, "You will speak better with Lieutenant Shaker. And you can explain to him the amount of gunpowder on your hands."

Abdul Hasan started packing his papers, ashamed for feeling happy that the suspect wasn't really up to a confession and he could give him back to Shaker for more interrogation.

"Captain," the man called when he was about to leave the room. "May I ask what happened?"

"What do you mean?"

"That phone call you just received." Mujahid spoke the words very carefully. "It seemed to me that something wrong happened to your family."

Abdul Hasan tilted his head and stared at Mujahid in utter astonishment. The suspect's tone was sincere. Abdul Hasan looked at him square in the eye. The man held his gaze. No hint of smile on his beaten-up face, as if he really cared to help. Right.

No way a man who had decapitated more than a hundred men felt sorry for him. But, again, he wasn't one hundred percent sure about his identity.

"You really better keep your own business." The Captain headed to the door again. He yanked it open just before Mujahid's words hit him.

"I can help."

Abdul Hasan froze. Shaker and two soldiers stood outside, waiting for his signal to resume the interrogation. He could just tell them that the suspect was not willing to come clean and they had to keep pushing him. Even if he wasn't Mujahid, he would be someone who worked with him. After all, what Hussain said about the urgency of the matter was true.

On the other hand, this man probably had connections with many terrorist groups. If anyone in Baghdad could know something regarding his son's kidnapping, he would be someone inside those groups.

"Help with what?" Abdul Hasan asked in a cynical tone. "You have no idea what's going on."

"I am not stupid."

"So?" He stepped back, closing the door, avoiding Shaker's looks.

"The soldier said it was a call from your wife, and it was urgent. Then you were asking about your son as if something bad happened."

"Could be anything."

"True, but you were so eager to go, which means that you believe something can be done now."

"Maybe." Abdul Hasan tried to shrug but couldn't pull it. He fought to keep his emotion checked.

"My conclusion, your son was kidnapped," the man said, his narrow eyes glittering with pride. He wiped out some blood from his nose with the back of his hand, stared at it, then said, "And you have no clue where to look."

Abdul Hasan tried to reply. But his voiced choked. The man had put it plainly. His son was kidnapped and he had no damn clue.

"What can you do to help?" The words sounded as if someone else had spoken them.

"There are people who know about everything happening in this country. Maybe not directly but they have connections to other people who have other connections and so forth."

Abdul Hasan nodded for him to skip that part. He still couldn't believe he was actually listening to this man. Not only for the crimes he might have committed but also if he was really connected to such people it only meant that he might also know something about the next operation Mujahid was planning. If he wasn't Mujahid that is.

"No matter which group kidnapped your son, if this was the case, there must be someone who knows about it and not all of them know how to keep their mouth shut."

"And why exactly do you want to help?"

"Because you can help me get out of here… I didn't do anything. And I don't know this Mujahid."

They stood looking at each other as if one would acquiesce to the other. Maybe that was the case indeed.

"So I just give you my cell phone… you will contact your friends… and then we will sit and wait."

"Pretty much, yes."

"And you trust me? I mean you trust that I will keep my word after you help me and release you?"

The man looked down, then let out a sigh. "What other choice do I have? Your people will keep torturing me for something I don't know about. And maybe if I help you out you will convince them that I am not a bad man and let me go."

"So you just happened to play with some Play-Doh that turned out to be mixed with gunpowder."

"What can you do, tough childhood. I mean come on, this is Iraq, there is more gunpowder than bakery flour."

For the second time, Abdul Hasan felt his legs shaking. Tired and overwhelmed, he couldn't stop the images from jumping into his head. His son. The sound of his laugh. From a distance he thought he actually heard it. No, not a laugh, his boy was screaming, crying for help.

The man kept talking about being innocent. Abdul Hasan didn't have time for those games. He wanted to go and do something. Anything. He knew his search would be pointless without help from this terrorist. Merely thinking of it made him ashamed. Again what other option had he? None.

Abdul Hasan dragged himself out of the room. Shaker jumped toward him. The young lieutenant wasn't good at hiding his feelings. His sympathy was genuine. Which made it even worse.

"Sir, Hussain has assembled a squad to start searching for your son."

The Captain nodded. "Good luck."

"Did he say anything?" Shaker asked after a moment of silence, pointing with his chin to the room where the suspect was kept.

Abdul Hasan shook his head. He considered the man's offer for the second time. Every minute Mujahid gained without giving any information would render the information more useless. If they had any hope of defusing the terrorist's plan, whatever it was, they had to act as soon as possible, like... now.

"Do you want me pick up with Mujahid where I left off?" Shaker made a gesture with his fist.

"No, leave the suspect for now."

The large lieutenant opened his mouth, his eyebrow almost jumped off his forehead. "But Sir... time is running out--"

"I said... leave him... now."

The Captain closed the door of the small interrogation room, taking a final glance at the terrorist who sat with his cuffed hands in his lap, calm and silent. In the split second before the door closed shut, the terrorist nodded with appreciation.

A terrorist is feeling grateful to him. How great. Maybe he should do it more often, his good deed of the day, help a terrorist.

The veteran officer locked the door and headed towards the main door where three armored vehicles awaited him.

-15-
Al-Amel District, Baghdad
June 9th
8:15 PM

Enas had finished walking the two blocks to her home. It was safer for her to be dropped at some distance from her place to eliminate the chance of being spotted with a stranger by the neighbors, the honor and reputation and the Arabian chivalry sort of thing. But to walk in this weather again was unpleasant, especially when she kept checking her watch. Way late.

She was doomed this time.

So far she was able to sell her brother the idea that she was attending extra classes to recap on what she missed when her father was arrested by the Americans.

No college went this late.

She told her brother she normally finished her classes after 4, and then it took her one hour and a half of transportation to get home, which gave her until 6 to reach home.

But now it was past 8.

Doomed.

Her brother wasn't the kind of man who was easy to deceive. A human lie-detector, that's what he used to think of himself. And he wasn't exaggerating, not much.

But her elder brother underestimated her. She was way smarter than him. His blind ego kept him from seeing that. Men were always men.

Alas, today she wasn't herself. Her unexpected meeting with Omar opened some interesting possibilities. She couldn't explain what or why. Enas didn't believe in love at first sight. And she wasn't the immature high-school girl with the missing father figure who threw herself on the first man she saw... Okay the first rich, funny, and handsome man. And she didn't want her judgment to be clouded for any reason.

At the corner, piles of black plastic bags were all over the pavement, higher than ever. Even with this sand storm, the sour smell of the garbage guarded the street as a protective spell, casting everyone out. The buzz of the flies and the sound of the cats fighting over some leftovers greeted her. Home sweet home. The poor neighborhood they moved into was even poorer today. Paint peeled off the houses, showing a historical record of each different color the walls once had. The cumulative brown dust made the entire scene as if watching one of those old war movies. Add the audio effect of the windstorm, and you had a second-class horror movie.

A young lady, her age, was on the balcony of a nearby house collecting red and orange pieces of clothes from the clothesline. The young lady smiled at her, Enas smiled back. She could sense the boredom, the dullness in her neighbor's eyes. Would she be like that when she finished college? Would her brother allow her to work? Or would her only excitement be when she would go to the balcony to collect the clothes before the sandstorm?

There must be a way out of this life. A ticket to happiness. Somehow.

Enas thought about her life and her options while she tucked her hands inside her trousers to make sure Omar's business card was nowhere to be seen. This card was too dangerous to be left in her purse. She needed to stop thinking about him. Concentrate. Otherwise she would be beaten to death.

Enas opened the front door. The uncomfortable silence of electricity off. No hum from the refrigerator or the air cooler. The ceiling fan still. Enas racked her brain to come up with some bullet-proof excuse her brother could not verify. Too late, his large silhouette was in front of her, blocking the faded light coming through the window.

"Where have you been?" he growled, his tone like a boiling pot about to explode.

"At the college," she answered trying to swallow. "Luay, there was some--"

"Liar!" Luay exploded with an earsplitting shout. He slammed the nearby table with his fist, knocking over its contents.

Her heart skipped a beat.

Any other girl would break down and confess she hadn't been at college. In the conservative Iraqi society, a girl living on such a lie of working with an American company in the Green Zone, while her family thought that she was in school, could face only one fate if the family found out.

Severe punishment.

Different Iraqi families had different understandings of how to interpret the word severe.

Some would ground the daughter for a month. Another might ground her for life. Others would consider that their daughter had some serious issues and start working on understanding why she dropped out of college. And some -a minority really but for her bad luck... Luay was of this minority- would take the girl and beat the hell out of her. Then they would either lock her up, if she survived the beating, or force her to marry someone.

Enas knew what awaited her if caught. She managed to pull herself together. Luay's method of accusation and threatening might have worked with the unfortunate political prisoners Luay interrogated in his days with Sadam intelligent agency.

But not with her.

She had grown up in a house dominated by the Baath ideologies. A suspect was guilty until proven otherwise. And, everyone was a suspect until proven otherwise.

In his other hand, Luay carried his cell phone. It could be anything, Enas knew, but it also could mean that he called someone at her college to ask if she came to school today. She took her chances. "I... am... not... lying," Enas growled back, looking him in the eyes.

"Do you think I am a fool?" he shouted, moving in her direction. "What college stays open till this time, and don't try to tell me you went to some friend's house or any of this crap."

He kept shouting and breathing heavily. She prayed that it wouldn't develop into a beating. Not that she was afraid of the physical pain. She got used to it. Her father had beaten her -so did Luay recently- so ferociously she had to miss a couple of school days.

Three years ago, Luay suspected that she had a boyfriend. He couldn't prove it, she was smarter than that. But suspicion was enough. And Luay made sure that even if she had a boyfriend, she wouldn't be able to step out of the house for days.

Beating was a way of humiliation. Mortification. And she had enough of both.

"I am not lying and I refuse to be accused as a liar." She stared back at him. Her mind swirled with flashes of the memories from the last time he beat her. He was angry, just like now. She closed her eyes, imagining him slapping her. This was how it had started. "You could have at least called me to make sure I was all right."

That took him off guard. He stopped moving toward her. Didn't back up, but stopped. "What?"

"If you were really worried about your sister, you could have called to make sure I was safe. At least from the storm." Her tone was low and not challenging. Still, it spoke of pain. Enas didn't have to fake emotions, she truly believed what she was saying and everything came natural.

"Enas, I called you on your cell many times, it was out of coverage." His face was still red, the veins on his forehead about to pop out. But his eyes were searching for an answer. He frowned, "Please don't tell me it was the bad network."

Cell phone service, or lack of service to put it right, was an endless story of speculations, finger pointing, and recriminations. Some blamed the Egyptian service provider, some blamed the jamming devices suspected to be used by US Army vehicles roaming the streets to prevent terrorists from detonating explosions by using cell phones when they passed.

With Enas, it was much simpler; she switched her phone off to avoid receiving calls from Luay.

"Luay, I know you didn't call me."

"Really? How so?" He scoffed, hands on his hips, his eyes closed to narrow slits, his lower lip stuck out.

"Because I find it hard to believe that Luay suspected his sister of doing something wrong, unable to reach her on her cell, and when she arrived home you didn't beat her to death."

Luay frowned. He did that when he needed time to process.

"Luay, I know very well that you would rather die than to be challenged in the honor of your family."

Honor. Pride. Reputation.

What a crap. Especially when you live in such a dumpster.

Then she handed him her cell phone. "Here you go, call Wafa. I was with her all afternoon trying to get a taxi with no luck."

Wafa was her colleague at work. They made this arrangement to cover each other's back. While Enas wanted to cover going to work in the Green Zone, Wafa needed a cover when she spent the day with her boyfriend.

Luay hesitated, then took the phone from her. He gave it an examining look, more as if trying to figure out how to use this new model.

The landline phone rang. They both turned to the kitchen counter where the green phone was. She recognized the caller ID despite the accumulated oil stains on the screen. It was Luay's boss, whoever he was.

Luay yelled at her, pretending to be angry. "Now get of my sight and go prepare some dinner! I will see to it that you won't repeat this again."

She faked a protest sigh and went upstairs, concealing her triumphant smile. Even if he still remembered her after talking to his boss, all he could do now was to search her cell phone for suspicious calls or text messages. Nothing to worry about, all her work contact numbers and calls went through another cell phone, which he didn't know about.

She was safe, at least for now.

"Oh, by the way." She stopped in the middle of the stairs and turned to Luay who was on the phone already.

"What?" He covered the mouth piece.

"Aunt Selma called me this morning, her son was found dead... beheaded." Enas spoke the words with bitterness, careful not to hurt

Luay. He and Aunt Selma's son were good friends when they were kids.

Luay just nodded.

Enas continued up the stairs.

Before she got to her room, Luay called after her, "I am not done, Enas, I will call your college and get your schedule. I will find what time you really finish your lectures."

Shit...

She bit her lower lip, slamming the blackened wall next to her bedroom with her fist.

Once Luay called the college, he would know that she had dropped school months ago.

"You sick paranoid." Why didn't he leave her alone? Enas cursed under her breath, feeling the pain in her hand from hitting the wall.

She closed the door behind her. It would have felt much better if she could slam it shut. But that might provoke Luay. Enas leaned on the door and breathed.

Her room in this house was nothing like her old one. This one was small, tacky, and no matter what she did to organize it, things always looked untidy.

The exhausted girl sat on the edge of the bed to take off her shoes. Her father's portrait on her mirror table, with its metallic picture frame, had always been there. Sometimes when you get used to seeing something you stop noticing it. Today, for some reason, Enas noticed the photo. She had saved it from the old place. Her father looked so confident. He had that look of someone so positive that everything would be as he wanted it.

Her only protector. Despite his temper, she knew that he loved her and cared for her.

She broke into tears.

This situation! Not only the poverty that she had to endure now but her suspicious brother. Enas needed a way out of here. Anything to get her out of this shit hole.

She found the business card from Omar. Enas held the card, remembering the awkward way she met him, laughing through the tears at herself.

She read the card over and over. Something was familiar. And then she saw it, right in front of her. Blood rushed to her head, her heart skipped a beat.

"I'll be damned!" She put her hand over her mouth. Reading the Name on the card: Omar Dafer Al-Dayni.

"He is Dafer Al-Dayni's son!"

Luay stood in the kitchen talking on the phone to Dafer Al-Dayni.

"You will never guess who visited me today," Dafer said in his cigarette-raspy voice.

"Sharon Stone?"

"No, you pervert, Saud."

That was a surprise. Luay didn't recall any notification to prepare a security escort.

"But... how? I mean, why didn't you tell me, Dafer?"

"How the hell would I know, I just saw him on my doorstep. He said it was a personal visit. I don't think anyone from the big man's office knew about it."

"I don't understand." Luay scratched his head, Saud wasn't the type of man who came without a small army of bodyguards. "What do you mean, personal?"

"He didn't say it in the beginning," Dafer said then started coughing. "He sat there and didn't even drink his coffee." Another cough, then he added, "He finally told me what it was about and, oh, you know what was the other surprise?"

"Not Sharon Stone."

"My son Omar."

"Ah, so... you have sorted out your... um... problems."

"We talked, he was upset at me because I let this Ali Al-Kadumi from Al-Ghadeer company win the deal for the water project. Anyhow, I promised him that I would take care of the man so that he could win the second phase of the project."

"Do you want me to... take care of him?"

"No... no, not now. I told Omar that first he should talk to the man and advise him to fuck off."

"Nice advice." Luay chuckled.

"It's a courtesy thing." Dafer laughed, which turned to another coughing frenzy. "Anyhow, that wasn't the surprise."

"Oh, really?" Luay tried to fake interest.

"Guess."

"Don't know, Dafer, you sound like the stock market, full of surprises."

"Haha, funny, but shut up…" This time the coughing was louder. Luay switched the phone to the other ear. As if that would help. "It turned out that Omar and Saud were best buddies. They were talking about the time they spent in Egypt and Saud even asked Omar for a secretary."

"Secretary? How interesting." Luay yawned.

Fathers always assumed --for some mysterious reason Luay couldn't grasp-- that everyone was dying to hear their children's news. Most fathers somehow recovered from this stupid situation when their kids grew up. Not with Dafer though.

"Yeah. He wanted her to work for his office here in Baghdad, you know, the cover-up office. Saud told Omar that he wanted a good looking, single woman and he wanted her young, then Omar teased by asking him was he sure it was only a secretary. Why do you think Omar said that?"

"I don't know. Probably nothing." Luay rolled his eyes. Dafer looked at his son as an innocent teenager. Omar was almost thirty, and from what Luay heard he had more girlfriends than his father's party seats in the parliaments.

"So, is that why Saud came to Baghdad? To ask Omar for a secretary?"

"No, you imbecile," Dafer said, "It's something else… *personal*."

Dafer uttered the word personal in the same way one would say bomb or Arab in an airplane.

Silence. Then Dafer said, "Listen Luay, come to my office tomorrow, at the National Consul."

"The Perelman, shit… You know I hate that shit hole."

"I know it's too low for your normal standards but bear with me, Luay, its important."

"Will there be any belly dancing?"

"Shut up." Dafer chided. "This Saud guy is looking for someone."

"Looking for someone?"

"Yeah, a Saudi young man who came to Iraq from Syria."

"From Syria?"

"Yeah… for God's sake, Luay, shut up and listen and stop repeating everything I say."

Luay pulled a chair and sat. "Go on."

"Saud wanted this young man so desperately. And he wants him alive. He said he killed his brother or something so he wants to take him to Saudi with him."

Luay whistled. "It must be serious then."

"I told you, he killed his brother. Anyway I want you to come tomorrow to my office in the parliament and take the man's photo and name."

"You want me to find him."

"No, I want you to invite him for dinner. Of course find him, Saud wanted him within two days."

"Tell him to fuck himself," Luay said. "You know how many fucking Mujahedeen came through Syria every week?"

"Yeah I know, but this one came through your friend, the officer in the Syrian army. The one who brings Mujahedeen to your group."

Hmm. Maybe it wouldn't be so hard to track the man down after all. Besides, they would need one favor from Saud.

"I will search for the man Saud wanted, but we need Saud to help us with one thing in return."

"You mean besides paying your salary."

"There was a guy in Abu Ayob's group who got arrested and we need him to be released in order to go on with tomorrow's operation. I am sure Saud can help with this."

Silence again, then Dafer said, "Yeah, tomorrow's mission is important. I think I can speak with him about it, but you have to find Abdul Rahman for him."

"His name is Abdul Rahman?"

"Yeah, come to my office tomorrow and we will arrange everything. There is a lot we need to discuss."

-16-
Al-Karada District, Bahghdad
June 9th
8:20 PM

Ali held the TV remote, surfing through the channels in his house. Finally he settled for the Iraqia-TV channel, the official government channel.

It felt stupid.

With hundreds of news channels around the world to pick from, he was watching the national TV.

He couldn't bear to watch the Arabian news channels, with all the twisting and poisonous words. Focusing on the negative, and doing whatever possible to undermine the change in Iraq.

Why did thousands or maybe millions of Arab viewers enjoy channels like Al-Jazeera? Did people really like to watch this amount of intensified bad news, all focused around conspiracies, killing and poverty?

Or maybe the savvy Arab viewers found something he didn't?

You have to be open-minded, Ali told himself, flipping to Al-Sharqya, a-supposedly-independent Iraqi channel. A woman was being interviewed. Calling her a lady would be a broad use of the word. Her shirt was too tight on her busty body, her bra looked as if it was on top of the shirt. Her thick makeup looked as if she had dipped her face in a bowl of white powder. Even the way her body undulated and wiggled while speaking, everything suggested that the best job this woman ever had was working the late shift in a nightclub.

Now in tears, she was talking about how Iraqi soldiers had raided her house, looking for terrorists in the middle of the night. How they terrorized her and her old mother. And how they found nothing after all, just some rusty machine guns and some rustier grenades.

He flipped to the Arabia channel.

The same interview was there. But it was before the woman burst into tears, she was talking about herself. She described herself as an artist.

Close enough.

Ali Al-Kadumi shook his head. He didn't like to stereotype people. And it wasn't Islam ethics to judge others. This woman could have been really harassed by the soldiers. It happened. And despite the legitimate reason of chasing terrorists, innocent people shouldn't be harassed.

Innocent people with machine guns and grenades.

Ali dared to flip the channel to Al-Jazeera. And the same interview was there.

Okay, enough about being open-minded for one day.

He flipped back to the Iraqia, the national TV.

The good news about the Arabian news channels was they didn't have a hidden agenda. Their message was crystal clear. Against the change in Iraq, they didn't call it democracy, it was a change. A scary and reckless change.

No one liked democracy in this part of the planet. Check that, no one could afford democracy in this part of the planet.

Ali watched a special report in the Iraqia-TV about the Annual Conference of the Ministry of Planning to be held tomorrow.

The doorbell rang. He opened the door to see his brother-in-law, Ayad. They sat in the living room.

"How was your visit to the MICF today?" Ali asked.

Ayad shook his head. "They didn't take it seriously."

Ali had told him so, but as he didn't like someone to tell him the I-told-you-so line, Ali just nodded.

"I told them about Mahmoud and how this gang threatened him."

"And?" Ali asked. Mahmoud was his driver and Ayad's neighbor. It was Ayad who recommended Mahmoud to Ali.

Ayad shook his head again. "They said it could be anything. Maybe even Mahmoud was using this to get his house from the tenants."

"I told you so." He couldn't keep it any longer.

Ayad then told him he hadn't prayed yet, so he went to the other room and started praying.

Ali continued watching the report about the conference. Sometimes it's better for your health to watch the national TV where everything is just fine.

According to the report, the ministry succeeded in attracting many international and regional investors. The objective, with which Ali couldn't agree more as he was still in the national-TV-viewer mode, was to encourage foreign investors by the legislation of a new investment law that replaced Sadam's old one. The old law was bad for any investor seeking any guarantees.

He kept watching with increased interest, unable to block what Ayad had told him earlier about the terrorist group.

Were they targeting the conference? Or was this just a new terrorist scheme to use rumors to terrorize people when they could not execute?

Ali shut down the TV, resting his head on the couch. He wished to think about anything else. His gaze wandered around the living room. He liked this room. Despite his wealth, the room, the house actually, was characterized by simplicity in everything.

The living room had two comfortable beige-colored couches. The dimmed light from the two table lamps gave the room a cozy touch. Another floor lamp stood next to the bookshelf, Ali only used it when reading. His favorite part was the bookshelf that covered the five-meter wall. It contained books in Arabic, English, and French. Titles varied from classic literature to references and world encyclopedias.

He might have nice taste in room furniture, but what made the place comfy was the stuff his wife added, pictures in elegant black frames and small souvenirs scattered neatly on the bookshelf and small tables in the room. A miniature tour of the couple's life. Souvenirs from Eiffel, Saint-Clare and the coliseum surrounded the shrine of photos that showed their only daughter from infancy to graduation to marriage.

Ali always found solace staring at this wall. He felt content. Despite all the difficulties, their life was as close to happy as one could expect.

Somewhere on the wall hung a certificate of a master's degree in engineering with his name on it. And next to it another certificate for general surgery. With wife's name, Zainab Al-Mousawi.

Ayad came back and threw himself on the other sofa. "When is Zainab coming?"

"She had an urgent surgery at the hospital," Ali said. "She should be here any minute--"

The power went off. The room went silent, in darkness, except for the faint white light coming from the emergency rechargeable light. One of the gadgets every Iraqi house was equipped with.

"It's eight-thirty!" Ali protested, lighting two candles and putting them on the dining table. "Power shouldn't go off before 9. They are not following the schedule."

"How many hours do you get the main electric power here?" Ayad asked.

Ali wished he had a penny for every time someone asked him this. "Six a day... and then we get the power from our neighbor's electric generator. He is giving us twenty amps for ten dollar per amp, which is enough for most of the small appliances."

"Ten dollars per amp! Buy your own generator, Ali. At least you won't have to rely on someone else's."

"And bury myself with continuous maintenance? Do I look like I can change the oil and gas for these monsters? And worry about where to get the fuel from every day. Thank you very much, I am too old for this."

Ayad made a half smile. "Okay then, enjoy the darkness."

"Come on, we Iraqis are the most romantic people in the world." Ali chuckled, it was louder than he intended. "Look! Candlelight at every dinner."

"Honey. I'm home." Zainab's voice came from the entrance.

Ali noticed how Ayad's eyes glittered in happiness. The two were so close.

"We are here in the living room!" Ali shouted in the general direction of the entrance.

Later, they sat around the candle-lit dinner table. A variety of Iraqi dishes crowded on the table leaving no empty space. Aside from the salad and the must-have rice, Zainab had prepared breaded beef escalope steaks and fried chicken wings. The main dish however, was *dolma*. A special Iraqi dish that consisted of rice and minced meat wrapped in grape leaves and tomatoes, and dressed with special sauce.

A traditional everyday-Iraqi-feast. Ali smiled, starting to cut a big piece of escalope on his plate.

"So, how was the work?" Ayad asked his sister. He had started with the *dolma* dish. Ali considered the rate the dolma was transferring from the main plate to Ayad's plate and he wasn't optimistic about having some. The problem with this dish was that it took ten hours to prepare it. Something Zainab only did when her brother came to dinner.

"A nightmare." Zainab said, "We receive around twenty cases of gunfire injuries a day."

"It could be worse," Ayad said.

"Ask him about his visit to the police station," Ali told his wife. The best tactic to get someone to slow down eating was to make him talk.

"Oh, yes, how did your visit go?"

Ayad, still holding the knife and fork, briefed them on his visit and how the authorities didn't take his tip seriously. Ali commented that he told Ayad so while tasting the first piece of the grape leaves. Ah. It was juicy and sour and sweet and salty at the same time.

"Yes, you did," Ayad said. "But I still had to try. We can't just watch while they take us back to Sadam's days again."

Zainab poured a cup of orange juice for each of them. Ali and Zainab had a strict rule of no soda drinks in the house. Pepsi and Coca were strictly prohibited. Which didn't make them popular at dinner parties. Not that they threw any lately, given the current economic situation.

The lights came back again. Ali reached out to the remote control and turned on the air conditioner. A gust of dust greeted them. He forgot about the storm outside. Now, dust hovered on top of it, Ali felt sorry for the dolma, not that he was going to leave it to Ayad anyway.

"I am just still unable to comprehend the logic those who call themselves 'resistance' use to justify their attempts to undermine the economy," Zainab said, blowing out the candles. "I mean, come on, this has nothing to do with fighting the Americans and the government. They are fighting us, the people, and our future."

"Sister, they already passed that stage. The terrorists were using those excuses in the past to attract sympathy from the Arab world. But now, after their roots were deepened in this country, they declared their goal very bluntly."

Ali and Zainab both stared at him.

"What? Isn't it clear? Do you want to tell me that all bombing attacks were taking place in areas with Shia majority by coincidence? Sader city alone had more than fifty bombed cars this year. And how many bombed cars in the Sunnie areas? Zip. Nothing. Whether they are Al-Qaeda or the remaining Baath forces, their goal is only to eliminate Shia, just like Al-Qaeda did in Afghanistan by killing all the Shia."

The political process was a key event in the new life. The life after Sadam. Iraqis were deeply involved in the process. Criticizing, in most cases. But also evaluating, objectively and subjectively. Their gossip was about politicians, their celebrities were the political leaders, and their idols —at least for a good percentage of the population— were somehow involved in politics.

Ayad, like most of his fellow citizens, loved to talk about politics. Ali didn't mind it. After all, there wasn't much to talk about in Iraq

"I am not sure," Ali said, passing the pepper to Zainab. "Most importantly, I don't consent to blaming our Sunnie brothers for what their politicians are doing."

"What about you, sister. What do you think?"

Zainab shook her head, looking at Ayad and then back to Ali. "Honestly, I find it difficult to ignore the fact that most of the Arab-Sunnie parties from the moment the war was over till now –the last half of 2005– those parties are still trying hard to undermine the political process. Look how they are promoting Shia-Sunnie divergence and pushing for a civil war."

"I don't blame our Sunnie brothers if they supported a party like that of Dafer Al-Dayni," Ali said taking a sip of the juice, glancing at the TV. The Iraqia-TV news anchorwoman was on the screen. She wore a blue headscarf and a pink suite. She had a blue eye-shadow to match the headscarf. For some reason all anchorwomen the Iraqia-TV hired looked like Sumo wrestlers. It was either that, or their LCD TV stretched people horizontally. Ali looked at the male anchorman next to her, he had some weight on him, but next to his colleague he looked dried and scrawny.

Zainab looked at the TV and winced, probably at the color match. Ali couldn't blame her, blue and pink? Things like these made him long for the old black-and-white TVs.

"What excuse can you have to support a party led by a man who spent his life working for Sadam and signing execution orders against innocent people without a chance to stand in a court," Zainab said.

"Not to mention his bad taste of clothing," Ayad added.

"Especially the hat," Zainab agreed.

"Maybe we forced them to take that route," Ali replied. "Try to look at it from their perspective, okay? Most of them didn't like Saddam. But after the fall of the Baath regime, they were surprised by millions of Shia –sixty five percent of the population– revealing a side they didn't see before. I am not saying we threatened them. But what they interpreted was a threat to them. Overnight, the Sunnie start hearing us –their friends and their neighbors– talking about all the injustice, marginalization and oppression we suffered from at the time of Sadam. Of course, we had all the right to express what we had been through. But I think it had a bad influence on them. Look at our ceremonies and rituals related to Emam Hussain's martyrdom. They were intimidated by it."

"But it was peaceful, it had nothing to do with them," Ayad said.

Ali leaned on the table to serve himself some of the dessert. There were three layers of different colors with strawberry fruit on top. One of Zainab's new dishes.

What a waste of talent! Ali almost salivated over the dish.

"The entire political climate was not clear for them," Ali said while tasting the dessert. Yummy. Cold and light. Just what he needed. "They were torn between seeing their country invaded by foreign troops…"

"Liberated," Ayad corrected.

"Whatever you want to call it," Ali said. "And between seeing millions of Shia, united, organized, and asking for equity and compensation. And not to forget how Shia always looked organized and well lined-up behind their religious authorities, clerics like Ayatollah Sistani. Where do you think this will leave the Sunnies? Do you think they feel safe? Would you feel safe if you were a Sunnie?"

Ayad shook his head slowly, biting his lower lip.

"But Ali." Zainab paused for a second as if to choose her words. Doctors do that a lot, maybe years of relaying bad news to patients taught them how every word counts. She put her finger on her rosy cheek, after all these years, she was as elegant and as sexy as ever, "We all remember when some Shia individuals demanded some new mosques that the Baath regime built for the Sunnie in the Shia districts, Ayatollah Sistani sent a statement ordering those mosques to be handed over to the Sunnie."

"I think what Zainab is trying to say," Ayad picked up where his sister was. They used to do that when one of them spoke. They had that thing. A bond. Or some kind of brain-wave synchronization. "is that our leadership made sure that the message was clear to our Sunnie brothers: that we were not their enemy."

"Maybe," Ali shrugged, "but if you put the bad influence of some TV news channels and opportunists like Al-Dayni or Al-Dari who hit on this same nerve, stressing their fears, reminding them how unorganized they are compared to the Shia..."

"But Ali," Zainab said, "we didn't do anything to them. They are the ones who started the checkpoints and the road blocks, stopping the cars, and checking drivers' ID to kill any Shia they may find. We still have hundreds of Shia pilgrims going to Emam Hussain, killed in Mahmodya or in that bloody Death Triangle."

"What about the Sadder Army?" Ali raised his finger. "Didn't they attack Sunnie? Didn't they do what the Sunnie militia did? Both sects had their share of violence."

Ali didn't like Muqtada-Al-Sader Army. When it started in 2004, he thought that this was the worst thing that could happen to the Shia who were trying to rationalize the violence. The really sad thing was when the Salafism and Qaeda-like militia got into their killing spree, he -and many others- had to admit that having a Shia armed forces, like the Sader Army, was somehow a safety valve against full-fledge cleansing against Shia.

"But they started it," Zainab said. "The Wahabies, the Salafism, I know it's hard to prove. Especially with all the focused media campaign to provoke both sects for a civil war. But it was very obvious to anyone living in Iraq."

Ali wanted to say something but was distracted and turned to the entrance where he left his bag.

"Is that my cell ringing?" he asked then headed to his suitcase.

A familiar tone of the new Iraqi national anthem came from his bag where he'd left the cell phone. He took it out and answered it. Ayad kept humming the lyrics. Zainab joined him.

My home... My country.
Shall I see you
Safe and triumphant and dignified.
Shall I see you, where you belong?
High up in the sky.
My home... My country.

It was Ehab, his business partner. Ehab briefed him about his visit to the American company G-plans.

"We almost got the second phase of the project, Ali. I just need you to meet this Robert guy."

Ali had heard of Robert Taylor. He respected the man and truly wanted to meet him. "But Ehab, I don't know what we are going to show the man, the opening ceremony is simple."

Ehab laughed. "Oh, don't worry, I have invited some people from the government and the press as well. It's all being taken care of."

"The press! You know me, Ehab, I don't like changing the project into some political agenda."

"Ali, we are not doing it for politics, consider it as PR to win the second phase of the project. Don't you want to get that deal?"

"Sure I do."

"Okay then, stop worrying and just send me a photo to put in the news. I have pulled some favors here and there to get onto the first page."

First page? Ali didn't want to ask what kind of favors Ehab had pulled. They finally agreed that Ali would attend for less than one hour just to meet Robert Taylor and then he could leave.

Ali finished his phone call and joined them again at the table.

"That was Ehab. He wanted to make sure I would attend the opening ceremony of the water project in Al-Amel District. It looks like there is someone from the American company, a manager, who had promised him the second phase of the project on one condition."

"What condition?" Zainab squinted at him, her lips tight.

"He wants to meet me personally at the opening ceremony."

"The American manager?"

"Yes." Ali tried to hide the smirk.

"But that would--" Zainab stopped mid-sentence. "Do you want to go?" She reached to hold his hand. Her hand was warm and soft and... electrifying, as always.

"It will be safe," Ali said with a comforting smile. "Trust me, it's not a big event."

She nodded, her lips pulled in a smile, but not her eyes.

"Can you turn up the TV, please," Ayad said watching the TV where a man wearing a gray suit was talking to a reporter. At the bottom of the screen the subtitle flashed the words, "Breaking News."

"That is the interior minister, isn't he?" Zainab said, pointing the TV remote.

Ayad nodded, the volume was higher now and they could hear what the minister was saying.

"It's a serious matter and our ministry, with all its forces, is ready to secure the event. Our reputation as law enforcers is on the line here and we will not allow anything to threaten this conference."

Zainab shook her head. "What is he doing?"

"It looks like," Ali said slowly, "he just gave the terrorists another motive to attack the conference."

-17-
Near Al-Adel District, Baghdad
June 9th
9:00 PM

The taxi dropped Abdul Rahman and Malik in the intersection between Al-Jamea'a and Al-Adel district.

"Where to, brother?" Abdul Rahman asked, putting Malik's hand around his neck, helping him to walk.

"There. Just after the railway bridge. The first street to the left." He pointed with his chin to a large concrete bridge that crossed over the Jamea'a main street.

"Where are we going, brother Malik?"

"An old friend."

"Do you trust him?" Abdul Rahman asked. He could feel his breath getting shallow, and not from the dusty weather. This was the second time he trusted a stranger. The first time didn't go well.

"Yes."

Malik's weight was pressing on his neck and shoulders. Abdul Rahman needed some distraction. "Is he one of the Mujahedeen?" Abdul Rahman ventured.

"No."

"Oh, but he is one of the brothers, right? I mean... the good guys, you know, part of ... um... group."

Malik slowed down and turned to him. His eyes were black and expressionless. "No."

"But how can you trust him then? I mean, if he isn't a brother--"

Lights illuminated the dark street. Three cars... no, trucks with machine guns on top, passed next to them without slowing down. Iraqi Army patrol.

"One hour to the curfew, my friends, hurry up, it won't be safe," an Iraqi soldier called out.

"Burn in hell, infidel," Abdul Rahman murmured.

They crossed the street and walked into the alley. Faint lights came from the houses' windows. The noise from the generators covered the storm. Most of the houses were large with big garages and even bigger gardens. Except for the mess of electrical cables of the generator, and a big hole in the middle of the road, the neighborhood looked in shape and tidy.

"But you are close friends, right? I mean, you and this guy we are going to visit, you must know him very well."

"I trust him, okay?" Malik winced putting a hand on his waist. "Look, I was the one who convinced him to get into Salafism. His family is very liberated and he doesn't like them for that. He is not part of a group and he doesn't like violence but I still trust him. Do you understand?"

The question sounded rhetorical, yet, Abdul Rahman said, "Yes."

After five minutes of walking, Malik pointed at a nearby house with a white door. "There, this is the house."

"Brother, do you mind me asking why we didn't ask the taxi to drop us here instead of the main street?"

Malik laughed, then he grimaced, putting his hand on his wound again. "Do you think any taxi driver will be crazy enough to drive two men inside an alley at this hour? How do you think people get killed?"

Abdul Rahman nodded. They reached the house with the white door. Long tree branches dangled from the once-pink fence. Malik stood gazing at the house. He took a deep breath and knocked on the door. Nothing happened. Malik kept knocking.

Finally, a bearded young man wearing a green shirt and sky-blue trousers answered the door. Malik and the young man embraced.

"What a nice surprise, brother Malik."

"Glad to see you too, Amjad."

Amjad ushered them in. They followed him through a deserted garden with overgrown grass and a rusty swing. The house was dark except for one oil lantern in the corridor close to the stairs and another in the kitchen. Oil lanterns. Abdul Rahman had been told that he would see everything in Iraq, but oil lanterns?

Amjad used a flashlight to guide them to the stairs, he opened the door to one of the rooms and gestured for them to enter.

"No one is in the house at this time of the year," Amjad said, quickly clearing piles of books from the only sofa in the room for them to sit. "Most of the students are on summer vacation."

So this was a student's house. The room looked cramped and dingy. Another oil lantern sat on a table where books and flyers piled. A silver Dell laptop lay on the table. Laptops and oil lanterns. Iraq. Shadows danced on the empty walls and the curtains, and the old cupboard that too was filled with books and flyers. A loud howling sound came from the closed window.

"I will take the bed," Malik said, collapsing on the single bed in the other corner of the room.

"You are wounded!" Amjad said. He stepped closer and examined the bandages then hurried to the cupboard searching for something. He came back with a pack of blue pills. Abdul Rahman watched Amjad's bearded shadow on the wall, bending at the bed, and handing Malik the pills and glass of water.

"Take this, it will prevent infection."

Everything looked too… surreal.

Amjad then turned and examined Abdul Rahman. "*Salam Alycum*, my name is Amjad," he said extending his hand.

Abdul Rahman shook hands with him. "My name is Abdul Rahman."

Amjad's face lit up hearing his Saudi accent. "Please brother, make yourself at home."

Abdul Rahman thanked him and sat on the sofa.

"How did you get this bullet, brother Malik?" Amjad asked.

Malik looked at the ceiling for a while then at the sofa. "You haven't changed the furniture, my friend. How is your college?"

Amjad frowned, then his face was neutral again. "Thanks to God. I dropped college."

"What! But you were in senior year."

Amjad shrugged and sat on a white plastic chair next to the table. "You sure that the wound is clean and the bullet is out?" Amjad gestured with his chin to the bandages on Abdul Rahman's shoulder.

"Yeah," Abdul Rahman said. "A doctor in Karada hospital got the bullet out and closed the wound, she helped brother Malik too."

Malik squinted at the flyers on the table. The lines in his forehead deepened.

"Are these publications of Al-Kateb?" Abdul Rahman asked, he recognized the booklet that his teachers in Saudi gave to young people.

"Yes," Amjad said, taking one new booklet from a stack on the table and handing it over to Abdul Rahman. "This is his newest article about Jihad against those who helped the infidels."

"Cool." Abdul Rahman remembered he distributed the same books in his college back in Saudi. "Do you actually distribute them?"

"No, he uses them for the bonfire," Malik mumbled.

"Yes, these and others," Amjad answered. "After the regime defeat we have to work harder to warn all Muslim brothers from the crawling danger of Iranians."

"What is going on, Amjad?" Malik asked, using his elbow to lift himself so that he could face them. "I thought you didn't want to join any group, my friend."

"You were the one who kept taking me to join the Tawheed group... *Brother.*"

Malik nodded and went back to resting his head on the pillow.

"Everyone, everyone including those who called themselves the free world are carrying weapons." Amjad smirked. "Why shouldn't we? They said they want to protect the democracy; well, we want to protect our way as well. It's a jungle out there and only those with enough power survive. America taught us this."

Malik nodded slowly, his lips tight.

"The proof to what I am saying is the increasing number of Mujahedeen joining our cause," Amjad added, then turned to Abdul Rahman. "Am I right, brother?"

"Yes. Sure." Abdul Rahman rubbed his face. "But don't you think when too many people come in there is a chance that we... um... lose track."

"Lose what?" Amjad made a face. "What are you talking about? Malik, who is this man?"

"I met him at the hospital. We were both shot and brought to the hospital. He helped me escape."

Amjad nodded then turned to Abdul Rahman, examining him again, mumbling something about trust and security.

Abdul Rahman took a deep breath, he owed them an explanation, they knew nothing about him and had the right to be suspicious. "I am from Saudi Arabia, I joined Al-Tawheed and Jihad group in Syria where I got some basic training on weapons. After two weeks of training, they put us in a bus that took us through the borders to Iraq. From there another bus took us to Baghdad. We arrived at a place called Gazal district in Baghdad."

"Gazal means deer," Amjad said without smiling, "it's Gazalya district west of Baghdad."

"Yeah, so I was in that Gazalya district and I had to report to the Ameer of the group. We were twenty people. Five came from Syria with me, Saudis and some Pakistanis as well. There were also two guys from the old Iraqi army, some elite forces."

"Like always." Malik sneered.

"Most of the operations we did were about carrying out execution commands issued against people who were working with the new infidel government or the Americans. I wasn't doing much. I actually never had to shoot a bullet. Two or three guys jumped the target, put a bullet in his head, and left. Very simple." Abdul Rahman swallowed. "Then came my turn and… "

"Things went south?" Amjad asked with a flat tone.

Abdul Rahman nodded. "It wasn't my fault. The guy who used to work for the ministry of communications, a professor or something, he escaped his house before we knew about him. And even worse we found the Americans there."

"And you fought them?" Amjad said, his eyes glittering.

"We exchanged fire." Abdul Rahman nodded. "The two guys from the elite forces were with us, they always came to drive the car and drop us. Anyway, this time they couldn't run away. One of them was shot in the head and I got a bullet in the shoulder. Everyone left me. The Americans left as well. Then the second guy from the elite force came after one or two hours, I wasn't sure because I lost consciousness. He was checking out his dead friend and when he saw me alive…"

"He took you to the hospital," Malik said.

"No." Abdul Rahman shook his head. "That's the thing. He just searched my pockets and took the last hundred dollars I had. The Syrian officer who brought me to Iraq took my passport and most of my money. Anyway, I was in real pain, so I begged him to take me in the car. You know what he said?"

Abdul Rahman paused, the memory still hurt. Malik gave him a sympathetic look and nodded to him to continue.

"He told me: you shouldn't be alive, you are a suicidal. we brought you here to die not to live while we die. Then he drove away."

For several minutes there was silence. No one said anything. The only sound was the roaring of the sandstorm outside.

"We can't just judge people without listening to their part of the story," Amjad said.

"Really?" Malik said. "All that guy will tell you is that he took the one hundred dollars to buy some liquor. Or to do Jihad in some nightclubs on Abu Nawas street."

Amjad glared at his friend, his face not showing any emotion. "The resistance is still our right. Nothing will change that." Amjad then turned to Abdul Rahman. "But you have to choose your group carefully. What you mentioned is typical of Tawheed and Jihad, that's why they are not so powerful anymore."

Abdul Rahman asked, "But I thought they were the strongest organization in Iraq."

"Not anymore." Amjad poured some water and gave it to Abdul Rahman. "Since the last three months, the Islamic State of Iraq are not only doing more operations, but they have also an Ameer in every district except for Sader city and some areas on the east, like Karada."

Abdul Rahman still didn't tell them everything. There was something terribly wrong with everything in Iraq. Yet he still didn't know how to put it. "I don't know... it wasn't just that. I mean everything was different than I expected," he finally said.

"Don't worry, brother," Amjad said, "I will introduce you to the right people to join. Tomorrow, *inshalla* (by God's will) we will go to pray in the Tawheed mosque and I will introduce you to the Ameer of the Islamic State of Iraq in that area. Sheikh Abu Ayob."

Malik murmured something, his face darkened.

"Is he trustworthy?" Abdul Rahman's question was more to Malik. Malik just stared at the dancing shadows on wall.

Abdul Rahman didn't like the way the two supposedly-old-friends talked to each other. His impression of the relationship between Mujahedeen in Iraq was different from the one-big-happy-family he kept hearing about when he was at Saudi.

"Sure he is, I've known the man for some time now," Amjad answered. Then he turned to Malik. "And you, brother Malik? You have to come with us. When I introduce you to the sheikh, I am sure you will be so... proud."

"Sure. Why not." Malik smiled but it looked more of like a grimace, his gaze still on the shadows on the wall. "Now excuse me, I need some rest."

-18-
Al Amel District, Baghdad
June 9th
10:00 PM

She had no idea how long she had been lying on her bed, submerged in this quasi-dream. Picturing herself in a different time and different place, better, and fair to her.

Enas dreamed about a house in a luxury area… Karada or Mansor. Having her own car. Traveling abroad, once a year during summer. Living in the rich class, again. She even dreamed about the possibility of working in the private sector, some managerial position. Maybe in her future-husband's company.

Her thoughts hit a brick wall.

Whenever she tried to lose herself in that fantasy world, she found that it was conditioned by getting the right husband.

Had she found him today?

Enas had asked herself this very question a zillion times today. She still wasn't sure about the answer. Her mind kept telling her that one hour of a casual meeting could never be a proper way to know someone.

But there was something about him. Something she could feel but not explain.

Girl, stop it. Do you have any idea how stupid you sound?

But she couldn't help it. Maybe she admired the name. The son of a known politician. Having his own company was a plus. But it wasn't only about that.

There was something to do with his personality, something… deeper. Maybe his confidence. His cool attitude. Unlike other guys, Omar looked at her with total indifference. She was used to having everyone's gazes on her for a second longer. Sometimes even more. And she didn't mind it. Omar checked her out, but his eyes made her experience new feelings, ones she couldn't describe. Or was that only her imagination?

Enas wasn't herself today, but it wasn't a total disaster. She ran the sequence of events in her mind again. Was her being there at that time and in front of the Green Zone a source of confusion?

There was a certain reputation, a bad one, for everyone working in the Green Zone, especially females. Enas found this beyond racism and sexism. It was idiotic and close-minded, and other hyphenated words she couldn't think about now. One more thing to add to her long list of why-I-don't-like-my-culture.

She needed a plan. The generator-powered lamp flickered. That, and the small table fan were the only appliances working in her room. She felt sticky. The temperature must have exceeded a hundred Fahrenheit.

She was good with plans, she always had been. She was capable of doing anything as well. Some people might accuse her of having no moral deterrent. But wasn't that what people said about all smart fellows who could walk on the gray areas without being caught?

With relationships, it was a tad more complicated. She had to attract the man while keeping her dignity and honor and reputation and, well... virginity. With Omar, she wanted a chance to know him better. To understand her feelings better. To have a peek at him... at the real him. How to do that without hurting his feeling? What if she didn't like him after she knew him? Oh, well, she would cross that bridge when she came to it.

Anyway, who said relationships should be fair. In the culture she was raised in, men did not marry women with whom they had affairs. In most cases anyway. Some of her friends went down that road, the guys dumped them at the end. The society did not tolerate a woman who did not respect its rules.

Enas had always complained about this. Why was the woman who gave everything to the man she loved not considered trustworthy? While the one who didn't risk anything for him, who didn't give anything without marriage bonds, was more trustworthy?

Of course such discussion was only with her friends at college. The girls kept telling her some lame excuses about honor and how once lost, it couldn't be retrieved.

Enas never bought that. But she accepted that those were traditions and she was smarter than challenging them. At least in public.

An abrupt whiff of air from the table fan was followed by the refrigerator engine outside her room rumbling to life.

Electrical power.

Enas jumped to switch on the window-unit AC. She listened to the musical sound of the compressor, and despite the blow of sand that came with the first surge of cold air, it was far better than the stickiness of the table fan.

She stood in front of the air conditioner, enjoying the cold air on her face.

She needed to change her clothes. Her room was too hot for jeans so she started emptying the contents of her pockets. The business card she hid in her jeans came out.

Enas opened the small inner zipper in her purse where she hid her work cell. She flipped open the phone and entered a text message:

Thanks for the ride. Enas.

She entered Omar's number and hit send.

Before a minute passed, her phone beeped.

A text message!

Like a kid opening her Christmas gift, she pressed to open the message. It was from Omar!

No problem. Nice to meet you.

Blood rushed to her face. Her chest ached. What was this?

Don't be silly, you barely know him, she thought while writing another text to him.

Sorry, I wasn't myself today.

My work is making me nervous.

Maybe I should find myself another job.

She tried to reason with herself before hitting the send button again. So far nothing had happened between them. But maybe after this message he might send her something more personal. Maybe a compliment. Who knew, maybe he'd offer her a job!

It was silly and idiotic and naïve. But she didn't care. Her finger hit the send button.

Enas threw herself on the bed again, phone still in her hand, willing it to beep again.

Her mind drifted away. To the big house and the new car. To the new life. She finally fell asleep, still holding the silent phone.

-19-

From the diaries of the abandoned city

Darkness engulfed the city.

The night of Baghdad. The word used to have certain rhythm. Frequently associated with the famous One Thousand and One Arabian Nights erotic ambiance.

But Baghdad at night now could not be related to the old image. Not even the one of forty years ago.

That was so because of a curse… a disease. Iraqi intellectuals were perplexed about how to describe it.

They realized the results, noticed the symptoms, but when it came to the cause it confused them.

You can still hear the debate. On the radio, on the talk shows, in every single gathering where people flashed back to the old days, trying to understand what happened to their lives, to their city.

Some called it the Baath. Others were more specific and pin-pointed Sadam. Lately people added Al-Qaeda, the war, the huge oil reserve.

Whatever the reason.

Whatever the name.

The city knew that the famous, exotic and surreal nights were replaced with fear.

Baghdad knew that its calmness was replaced with anxiety, and the peace it was often described with was replaced with a thousand and one trepidations.

Baghdad knew this long ago, when it heard the cry of the prisoners in the endless tunnels of Sadam's secret-service underground prisons. When it heard the weeping of the mothers who lost their sons in the pointless wars.

The city knew that it would not be the same after it first heard the cry of the oppressed. Pleading to the god of heavens, having no one else to complain to about all the injustice. About a future that was confiscated. About all the money scattered at the feet of the ambassadors of the Arab League and the whores of Sadam and his sons. About that night when the so-called Arab poets came chanting of Sadam's glory, drinking toasts of blood from the skulls of thousands of Iraqis in a long night that lasted thirty years.

Darkness wasn't new after all.

Long ago it engulfed the city of Baghdad.

People had lost hope of seeing the dawn of the new day.

Tonight was another night of those continuous ones.

The nights of trepidation and fear.

The fears of the officer who realized that he was a father before anything else. That he couldn't go back home, couldn't face the inevitable and trivial question in his wife's eyes, asking him about their son.

The fears of the everyday citizen who was afraid that terrorists' plans would be carried out. Afraid that the old past and evil would triumph… once again.

Of the man who spent the night afraid of the people living next door. The people he brought in and provided shelter to.

The fears of a politician anxious that his plans might fail.

Or the young police officer who spent the night alone in his bed, wondering about what his life might have been if he was born in a better place. Looking at the alternatives and thinking about all the unpaved roads and the life that would have been.

Endless fears, in the endless darkness, Baghdad had yet to endure another night of fear.

And it was fear that forced Malik to sneak out under the cover of night.

He tip-toed, careful not to awaken Abdul Rahman and Amjad. What he heard today made him worried. Scared. He couldn't risk staying with Amjad any longer.

Malik stepped carefully to the door, opened it, and walked into the dark streets with his hand on his wound, careful not to tear out the stitches.

A safe distance away, Malik gave one final glance at the house he used to consider a safe haven.

He didn't ponder long on how and why it ended like this. There was no time. And Malik had more important things to do. To start with, he needed a plan. A plan to go back to his life. To the woman who was waiting for him.

But most importantly, he was seeking revenge.

Revenge against those whom he'd trusted with everything but rewarded him with death.

A death that came with the betrayal built from the back.

By the leader of his group.

Mujahid.

-20-
Place: One of Baghdad's streets close to Al-Adel district
June 10th, the day of the bombing
Time: 5:30 AM

The cold breeze felt good on Abdul Rahman's face as he followed Amjad to the Al-Tawheed mosque where they would meet the sheikh. Although still dark, sounds came from everywhere. American choppers, some distant gunfire, dogs barking and cocks crowing. The two last sounds fit in a surreal way with the scene.

"Isn't it interesting how the stormy weather turned into this cool breeze?" Abdul Rahman said, trying to break the awkward silence.

"Yeah, *Alhamdulilah Ala Kul Hal.*" (Thank God for everything.) The comment was flat. Abdul Rahman didn't have to see Amjad's face to know that he was frowning. Apparently, Amjad didn't take the news of Malik disappearing with much pleasure. The stern-face young man picked up the pace. Abdul Rahman tried harder to keep up but his wound was still hurting him.

"What's the problem now?" Amjad said when he turned around and saw him lagging behind.

"My wound, brother. I can't walk fast."

"We will miss the dawn prayers." More frowning.

"Is it far?"

"Yes, and at this rate we will not reach before the noon prayers."

Amjad explained again that they were in some area called Al-Jamea'a and they wanted to go to Al-Amel district. Abdul Rahman still couldn't memorize district names so he kept nodding.

He wanted to ask Amjad why he didn't pick up a closer mosque to pray in. It didn't make sense to walk all this distance to pray. But Amjad wasn't in the mood to talk now. Abdul Rahman didn't have to be smart to know that something was wrong between the two supposedly best-buddies.

A taxi came near, Amjad waved for the car. It stopped. They got in the taxi, heading for the Tawheed mosque.

The car went through the same main street, passing one military checkpoint where the soldiers just waved them through. After one cross over, they reached a poorer neighborhood. The houses were smaller, front yards were close to none. It was as if entering a different world. More people were in the street, more cars, but also the signs. White signs with red writing, all talked about Jihad.

Amjad gave the directions to the driver to enter an alley. They reached the front of a long fence six foot high. Houses surrounded them, the same small and crammed ones. Two men in dirty sweat suits were working on an electric generator the size of a van. Iraqis enjoyed working on machines. One of the men had half of his body buried under the big engine, he was yelling something at the other guy. Iraqis enjoyed yelling too.

Nothing was special about the mosque's façade. Only the upper part of the mosque building and the minaret were visible behind the fence. The white-sheet signs with the red writings were everywhere on the fence and the nearby houses as if some kind of big laundry party.

Abdul Rahman examined the writings on the signs. Most of it was against Americans, the government, and the Shia. It all made sense. Americans were supported by the traitorous Iraqi government and Shia.

Amjad hurried through the main gate. Abdul Rahman followed. Two men in white dishdash strolled the yard. Both glared at them, then when they saw Amjad, they turned and continued their walk. A patrol.

Once he was in the inner vicinity, he could see the entire façade of the mosque building more clearly. It reminded him of old mosques in Madeena back home. The main mosque structure had a smaller house attached to it. Despite the recent white paint, the walls' edges still had the old yellow painting. The wooden doors peeled off and turned to yellow. Another room jutted off to the right of the main gate. It smelled of urine and was dark with only one rusted door; he couldn't tell what color it used to be. The bathrooms. There was no warning sign enter-on-your-own-responsibility, but there should be one.

All the windows of the mosque and the small house were painted black.

Must be very cheerful inside.

The electrical generator roared. Black smoke rose behind the fence from where the generator must be kept.

The prayer hall was lit with two dozen florescent lamps on the ceiling. Four air coolers, the type that used water for cooling, roared, one in each corner. A few people sat on the floor waiting for the prayers to start. There were four or five old men wearing dishdash, several young men, most of them had long beards, and one kid who kept staring at Abdul Rahman as if he were from another planet.

Abdul Rahman did the prayers in the second row behind the fat sheikh. After it was over, Amjad went to talk to the sheikh. They both glanced at him from time to time. A large man, bordering on hulk, entered and walked directly to the sheikh without breaking a stride. They talked for a second, then went into a side door.

He had nothing to do but use his time to praise God. Tasbeeh. It was always a good way to spend time. Albeit, Abdul Rahman didn't find the peace he was seeking. Something occupied his mind. Fear.

A stranger in a hostile environment, he had the right to be scared. But it wasn't that. It wasn't even the fact that he was shot and left to die. How Malik's face clouded whenever he mentioned Jihad. Something was terribly wrong. Malik was from the Mujahedeen, no question about it. What he heard in the hospital backed it up. But everything Malik did suggested otherwise. He wasn't very enthusiastic when Abdul Rahman introduced himself to him at the hospital. They were brothers in arms for crying out loud and yet he treated him as an extra back bag. Malik had taken him to Amjad's house as a place he trusted. Yet, he ran out at night without even saying a word. What made him change his mind?

Abdul Rahman had stopped watching TV two years ago –his mentor's advice. However, he could still see the analogy of his situation and the stupid kid in the movies. The one who stepped into a vampire's nest and got eaten, or the one who trusted a serial killer. Something like that. He always found it hard to believe that someone could be that stupid and miss all the danger signs. Now he understood.

The Saudi young man looked at the door where Amjad went. No one came out. Maybe now was a good chance to get out. But what about Jihad? He would lose his chance of being a holy-martyr. He tried to remember how enthusiastic he was to die for God back at home in Saudi. He couldn't. Somewhere on his road from Saudi to Syria to Baghdad he lost his zeal. How his family tried to talk him out of what he was about to do. How persistent his mother was. She looked at every new thing he did with her skeptical eye. She didn't like him going to the mosque to attend the daily lecture. She didn't like the tapes he was listening to. She kept commenting about his long beard. About his short dishdash. The sad thing, the scary thing, was he missed all of that now.

He stood. Walked to the door, still praising God. His wound hurt. He considered what his mother would say if she saw it. Never matter. She would understand. Like she did three years ago when his girlfriend got pregnant. Another time in another life, that was the start of his transformation... redemption. Her mother covered it up. They never spoke about it but he knew she had to sell a good deal of gold to buy the poor family's silence.

"You are safe, that's all that matters to me," were her only words whenever he tried to talk about it.

Would she still tell him this now? Abdul Rahman never doubted it.

He could imagine her pain. For the first time, he thought of her. What his travel would do to her. Wasn't Islam's most important teaching to be good to your parents, especially your mother?

Two brothers put another white sign on the mosque. Something about how a Muslim should be perfect in everything he did, even slaughtering. Slaughtering. From all the things a man can do and should perfect they chose slaughtering. Maybe the amount of blood he lost recently made him light headed, but the word choice sounded like a bad joke, or something you would expect a butcher to hang out on a wall in his shop, maybe, but in a house of God?

The brothers should find a better marketing manager.

Somehow, he wasn't interested in all of this. None of the conspiracies between Shia and Iran and Americans and Israelis were of interest now. He needed some time out. Time to think this through. And most importantly he craved the safe haven of his mother's warm arms.

Iraq was a country of twenty million. So far, he'd never met anyone who was really keen to be a martyr. Everyone wanted him to sacrifice himself. Him. Not themselves. Even the clerks in Saudi did the same. They kept lecturing about Jihad and martyrdom. None of them bothered to go to Iraq.

Oh dear God, forgive me.

His thoughts were leading him to the very path his teachers warned that the devil might try with him. Just as they warned him that his family, his mother would try to stop him.

His mother.

He couldn't take her image out of his mind. Close to the door of the mosque, his feet picked up the pace. Soon he would be out. This wasn't a run-away. No. He just wanted some time to think. It was rational. He might even go back home. Jihad would be there next month. For heaven sake, given the way things were developing in Iraq, Jihad would be there for the next three years. And he would be back once he made sure he was on the right track. He opened the door.

"Akhee Abdul Rahman!"

No.

Maybe he could still make it. He could sprint out now.

He stopped and spun around.

"Where were you going, brother?" Amjad asked.

"Just outside... I needed a walk." Even to his ears it didn't sound very convincing.

Amjad frowned then forced a smile that looked anything but assuring. "God bless your soul, what walk? Come on, Sheikh Abu Ayob wants to see you."

Run now! He couldn't. Once again he saw himself as the dim-witted kid in the horror movie.

He had a feeling that he would regret missing this chance.

-21-
Al-Amel District – Baghdad
June 10th
6:00 AM

He never liked mosques. Maybe because they were always working places for him. Like the hotel manager who couldn't enjoy staying at his hotel. During his time in Sadam's secret agency, most of Luay's assignments were related to mosques. Shia and Sunnie mosques, depending on the political climate. And he did his job well. His instructions were simple --mingle with the prayers, get their trust, then watch and listen. What were the people talking about in the mosques? Who started the discussions? Who came regularly? What was the sheikh of the mosque talking about? Fridays were slightly harder, as he had to concentrate on the speech of the sheikh, The Khutba. Luay had to make sure the sheikh did not cross the red line. That is: criticizing Sadam's government in any way.

All Sunnie's preachers and sheikhs had to be appointed by the Ministry of Religious Affairs, and since Sadam made sure that all the ministry staff were directly employed by one of his secret-service agencies, only on very rare occasions did a sheikh go off on a tangent.

Shia mosques were more complicated. Even in Sadam's time, Shia's secret financial network was very active. Shia called it Khums. The name was very descriptive. It means one-fifth. Khums referred to Shia's teaching that every person should volunteer twenty percent of his annual profit to the poor. The problem as Luay saw it was that the Shia were always giving the money to the head of the Shia clergy, the Ayatollah, and he in turn distributed the money through the same network to God-knew-where.

Luay was told that the Shia preachers were all paid from this network. Which was why it became difficult for the government to control them. Luay and many of his colleagues were asked to gather as much information as they could about Khums. To understand where the money was stored, who controlled it, who distributed it. But that was almost impossible. Their records, if existed, were well hidden. They didn't talk about it, they just did it.

That was, by itself, enough proof of how dangerous the Shia were. Luay could understand why Sadam had executed two million of them during the '80s. The number seemed exaggerated but he wished it were true. Those people were a menace, out of control. Most of his Sunnie brothers did not realize this. They were fooled by the crap of the brotherhood. But he knew better. Part of his training was to understand all the dangerous groups that threatened the regime.

He sat in the mosque. Abu Ayob had just finished the dawn prayers. Luay headed straight to him but a young man, one of those long-beards, was talking to him.

He had no time to waste; he didn't come here to pray or to have a chitchat. "Al Salam Alycum," Luay interrupted.

"Alycum Al Salam, brother Luay," Abu Ayob replied, gesturing to the young man to wait.

"We need to talk, Sheikh."

Abu Ayob scratched his thick black beard and squinted at Luay. He finally said to both of them, "*Mashi* (Okay), let's go inside the house. Come with us, brother Amjad."

The three went to an empty room. The same room he was in last night with Abu Ayob. Luay checked the walls again. The same banners hung as when they filmed the beheading of the Australian businessman. Images flashed into his mind.

Might he have completely lost any empathy to human suffering? Luay credited that to his work for the elite forces. But certain moments —like the beheading of that Australian fellow— made him doubt it. The former secret-service agent felt that guttural pain of a long time ago. Not that he would help the infidel Australian, but for a brief moment he wondered why they didn't just shoot him and spare him the slow and painful slaughter.

"Brother Luay," Abu Ayob said, pointing to Amjad. "I want to introduce you to a new committed brother, Amjad. Who will join us from now on."

They shook hands. The young man was thin and wiry. His cheekbones, hell, all his bones were as if they were about to emerge from the thin skin that covered them. His long beard made his face even thinner. His eyes continuously moved, something Luay didn't like. The man was nervous, too nervous. But again, this was the case with all the guys Abu Ayob recruited. Was it the long beard that made them look somehow… off? Or was it the shaved mustache?

Hmmm… Luay rubbed his chin, then he dismissed the idea. Hey, even a Baathist can be open-minded.

"Brother Amjad brought us another brother from Saudi Arabia," Abu Ayob added.

"Oh really?" Luay punched his palm with his right fist.

Oh boy, those coming from the Arabian Gulf and Pakistan were the best suicide attackers. What did they tell or give or feed them there? They always came determined to kill themselves. A weapon no concrete wall could stop.

"He is still waiting outside," Amjad said. Luay perceived the edgy tone. This young man had issues.

"Good, go and fetch him," Luay said, then called after Amjad, "do you know how to use weapons?"

Amjad bit on his lower lip and blinked. "I have… took several shots during the …military training in … um…" more blinking. "The school, six years ago."

Another amateur.

"I don't have time for this, Abu Ayob, I don't have time to train people and you know that."

Abu Ayob muttered while flipping his rosary beads. He kept doing this for some time. Then he finally said, "Help him, we must."

That was the problem with watching too much Star Wars. Luay rolled his eyes. Every asshole wanted to be master Yoda.

All the Qaeda Ameers tried to be Jedi-wise. Come to thinking about it, Bin-Laden could do Obi-Wan pretty well.

"Please, brother Luay, I will do anything for Jihad. Anything," Amjad said, his narrow eyes popped out in horror. "I can watch, I can drive cars. I can do explosive charges."

Luay faked a frown. "We will see about that. Now go and bring that Saudi Jedi, Brother... I mean Saudi Brother."

Shit. Stop watching movies.

Amjad ran back to the mosque. Luay then turned to Abu Ayob, taking the chance to speak with him privately. "I am not very comfortable with Mujahid's plan."

Abu Ayob's face clouded. Not that he was cheerful before but Luay knew the man better now, he didn't like complications.

"So what do you want to do?"

Luay sat on the ragged floor, the only place to sit. "Nothing, we will keep to your plan but I will be ready with another alternative plan." He sighed, pointing with his thumb at his chest. "And when I feel that the circumstances change I will decide which plan to follow."

Man, I like my job.

"So what do you want to do with the kid we kidnapped?" Abu Ayob's question sounded more like shall we kill him?

Since Luay was instructed to work with this group, he noticed some differences between him and them. Luay wasn't very touchy about working with people whom he didn't comprehend. He was raised to follow orders. But he couldn't help but notice certain things. Like how blood-thirsty the entire group was. He definitely killed more people in his life than the entire group could ever do, but at the end of the day, he did it only following orders or to survive. Those guys killed as if to satisfy some need, to prove something.

God, I hate this job.

"The kid will stay here, maybe we will use him."

Luay had thought about this before. No matter how desperate the kid's father, he would not be that stupid to follow their orders and drive a bombed car into a heavily guarded area, and hope that terrorists would keep their word and release his son. He had seen desperate people do strange things when it came to protecting their families but in this case it was a long shot, especially from an army man. He'd better base his plan on the assumption that the father would refuse to comply at a certain stage.

"If the shit hits the fan," Luay said, "we might use him as a guarantee or a human shield. I am not sure. But for now let's stick with the plan and call his father and try to shake him a little."

"A little?"

Luay gave him a you-know-what-I-mean look.

"But what is this… second plan?"

"I am still putting on the final touches." Luay rubbed his chin. He searched the banners at the wall for some inspiration. A flow-chart of 'how to make a successful bombing' would be good. All he found were mottos about death, killing and slaughtering. "I need the car and I need to prepare the detonator."

"But... But only Mujahid knows where the car is."

"We are working on getting his ass out of the trouble he put himself into."

How Mujahid controlled everything was getting very annoying. Luay was so relieved that he got rid of him. Having to work to get him out was too much.

"I just need the car, I am not counting much on using this officer. But I have a plan to weaken the security. We can't do much damage to the building but many people will die."

"Infidels." Abu Ayob nodded. Another short-word-of-wisdom.

"I need those two new guys to work with me starting today."

"They are yours."

"Yeah, but I need you to speak with them both about suicide."

"Martyrdom, you mean."

"Yes that, I need you to…" Luay wanted to pick the right word. Damn, how he hated their language.

"You want them... prepared." Abu Ayob grinned, revealing yellow teeth and bad dental work.

Luay nodded.

"Consider it done." Abu Ayob chuckled, his belly flapping.

Rare was the time when he recalled seeing Abu Ayob this cheerful. He wished he never had to see it again.

Footsteps clattered in the corridor. The door opened and Amjad entered with another young man, same age, same beard but this one was a bit beefier. Other than the exhaustion on his face, he had a perfect athlete's body.

"Al Salam Alycum," Amjad greeted them again. They liked to repeat the greeting every time, Luay knew that. "This is brother Abdul Rahman."

They sat on the floor. Abu Ayob rested on the oversized pillow.

"Sheikh, we have a very important thing to finish today," Luay said, putting his hands on his hips. "How many do you have of your group?"

"Two, they are outside guarding the mosque," Abu Ayob said.

Luay wanted to ask about the others. But not in front of the rookies. Mujahid's absence surely had to do with the sudden decrease of the men.

He thought about postponing this thing but then, he didn't really need many men with him. "We have to start cleaning the area."

Abdul Rahman tilted his head like a dog who was unable to understand what his master was asking him to do. "What do you mean by cleaning?"

Abu Ayob glared at the young man, took a long breath, and then shook his head.

Luay simply explained, "That means the area has to be closed, security-wise closed. Everyone living in the neighborhood has to be loyal to us and under our control. Then we can enforce the law we want."

"Applying Sharia'a law," Abu Ayob added.

The Sharia'a law or Islamic laws had some exaggerated importance for Abu Ayob for some reasons Luay never understood. "Not only the Sharia," Luay had to correct this, "we need to move freely in our areas. We need to move weapons, people, hostages, leaders, and what have you. If the area is clean, or secure, we can do whatever we want."

There were other important reasons he didn't have to share with them. Like having one complete election area under their control, or controlling the projects, if any, in this area. They could decide who would do what and how much he would pay for them to do the simplest thing like fixing a broken window.

For months, Dafer repeated this theory over and over. Now when Luay thought about it, it was similar to what Sadam did when he surrounded Baghdad with small towns all filled with people extremely loyal to him. People who were still loyal to him now, in areas such as Mahmudya and Yousifiya. The Triangle of Death as they called it.

Abdul Rahman asked again, with a lower voice, "So, is this district secured?"

"*Al Hamdulilah*, it's much better now," Abu Ayob answered.

"No, it's not," he uttered, looking Abu Ayob square in the eyes. The man didn't hold his gaze. Then Luay added to Abdul Rahman, "Not like the other districts in this part of the city. There are still some infidel Shia and some disloyal Sunnie. If you ask me, that's who turned Mujahid in."

Abu Ayob raised his palms in surrender. "Mashi, Mashi. Start with the Shia infidels and then we will discuss the Sunnie."

"We will do that," Luay said. He stood up and addressed Abdul Rahman and Amjad. "You both come with me, we will start this now. Another brother will join us, he lives nearby and can help us identify all the houses."

Abdul Rahman looked at Amjad. His gaze seemed fixed at his friend's mouth as if hoping the other would say something. Amjad just stood and helped Abdul Rahman to stand.

"Don't forget about Mujahid," Abu Ayob whispered, getting so close he could smell his rancid breath.

"I am not." Only because of this damn bombed car.

-22-
Al-Bayaa District - Baghdad
June 10th
6:30 AM

"At least take this orange with you so you can eat it if you feel hungry during the day," his mother called after him for the third time on his way to work. Each time, she suggested him taking something different.

Lieutenant Hussain smiled at his mother. The way she stood at the doorstep wearing her black Islamic Abaya that covered her entire body and head, leaving only her face visible. Her face. The sixty years had left quite remarkable traces on his mother's cheeks and mouth. The way she stood, with her back slightly hunched, her shoulder slumped. The way she smiled. It wasn't the shiniest smile, half of her teeth were missing. The wrinkles in her face and neck all moved in an awkward way. Her eyes were watery, not tears, it was that thing with her eyes. And yet, it had a strange sense of déjà vu. It reminded him of his primary school. She always stood there watching him going to school. Embarrassing and over protective, and comfortable and warm, and no matter how big he was now, what kind of weapon he carried, nothing gave him that feeling of protection like her look.

"Thanks, Mom, I will take it." Where could he hide it? The two big pockets in his uniform were already filled with cookies and some homemade bread with meat that his mother handed him on the first two calls.

"Be careful, son."

He nodded. She used to kiss his forehead or cheek when he was younger. Another embarrassment. He wished he could hold her in his arms.

"I should be careful so the guys don't see me with all of this food."

She smiled. "If you hear the place you are working in is threatened, come back home." She bit her lower lip, looking at a car passing by, "Tell them, my mother is sick."

"Sure, Mom, don't worry." He gave her his best assuring smile.

Needless to say, Hussain didn't mention that he was working with the MICF. As far as she knew, he worked in some administration job in the ministry, where it was completely safe.

He lived this lie every single day. It wasn't easy. Looking in her eyes and then lying. But again, those deep lines under her eyes, her white hair under her head cover, those didn't come from her sixty years. His mother had lost three sons. His elder brothers. One by one, during Sadam's reign. In a photo taken twenty years ago with all four boys around her, her smile was of a happy woman who had everything she needed... or wanted. That smile, and the woman, were gone.

No matter his reasons, she would not be able to live with the fact that he was in the line of fire. Since childhood he had learned how to live with this extra dose of mother care. What she used to give for four boys was concentrated on one now, well, two counting his younger sister.

He kissed her on the forehead and stepped out of the house, still hearing her prayers for him.

The usual qualms started hunting him. That nagging feeling of responsibility. About what could happen to her if something went wrong.

Another car passed. His neighbor's old white Toyota, filled with kids as usual. School time. The everyday routine. The man honked, waving from the side window. The kids, smiling at him, made signs of guns pointed at him. Hussain could almost hear their giggles.

Everyone in his poor neighborhood knew about his job. Except his mother. And for the zillionth time since he started working with the MICF he pondered his options. He couldn't quit his job. He needed it. That was the only job he could find. During Sadam's days –the black days as his mother called them– being a brother of three executed men made it almost impossible to get any job. Whenever he tried to complain to any government official about being rejected, the only answer was a question as to how he escaped his brothers' fate.

He tried to explain what happened to his brothers. And that they were not against the regime for any reason. But that wouldn't help either.

For what it was worth, his elder brother was not executed, he was killed during the war with Iran. Forced into the draft, as was the case with thousands of Iraqis. The second brother tried to escape, he was caught and executed. And no one knew for sure why the third one was executed. Some said because of his brother who tried to escape the draft. Others said that it was a mistake.

It didn't matter.

The family was doomed. And he had to live with the continuous rejection.

For most of his life, Hussain worked in a TV repair shop. After the regime ended, he tried to find a more stable and rewarding job.

It wasn't easy. He had no qualifications. He had to drop out of school to support his mother. The repair shop wasn't very profitable, especially after his sister and her family had moved in with them. His brother-in-law was in a wheelchair after losing both his legs in a terrorist attack a year beforehand.

Practically, Hussain was the only provider for the big family. He didn't mind. At least now his mother could focus on her grandchildren. At least that was the theory. He looked at the orange, not sure if he should feel happy or guilty.

Two college girls passed across the street. He sneaked a glance toward them. They were looking at him, whispering something to each other. He was used to that –the grinning and smiling. Hussain was a good-looking young man, charming. Most of the girls in the neighborhood knew him and they knew that he wasn't married.

An attractive package.

"Hussain," his mother called again.

Now this was something new. He turned around; she stood at their front door. As all houses in their neighborhood –a glorified ghetto if there was such thing– it had no garden or outside fence, just the house and one door.

She beckoned for him to come back.

Hussain raised his hand, showing her the orange she just gave him. Was it to be an apple this time?

She kept waving for him to come.

Sigh…

"Okay, I'm coming," he called and walk back to the house. The girls giggled. Thanks, Mom.

At the doorstep, his four-year-old nephew peeked from behind his grandmother. Hussain smiled to the kid, who gave him a balloon to blow full for him.

"Don't bother your uncle, you little brat." She smiled at the boy, pulling him inside.

Hussain start blowing the balloon anyway, he was like a father now for those children. He waited for his mother to speak. Hoping that she didn't call him for the balloon.

"What time will you come back?"

He cocked his head still looking at her. "Should be around 4."

She made a crooked smile. "Can you come earlier? Can you make it before 2?" Another smile. Hmm... That wasn't very comforting.

"Mother, what's going on?"

"We have an appointment." She beamed, somehow reminding him of her photo. Her cheeks were rosy now. Her eyes glittered with joy and... hope?

"What appointment?"

"We are going to visit your aunt's neighbors in Kadumyah." The grin widened.

His aunt's neighbors. What was that supposed to mean? Unless… "Oh, Mom, you didn't, not again." He let the balloon go, all the air went out, making a funny sound. His nephew giggled.

Arranged marriage. His mother wouldn't stop trying.

"You didn't ask me who she is." She gave him another crooked smile.

"It's irrelevant," he said.

She nodded, keeping the crooked smile.

"Mom, I don't like arranged marriages."

"Okay." She shrugged, still smiling.

Was he missing something? She was chuckling now.

He didn't like this, for her to outsmart him. "And I am supposed to guess who she is, right."

A nod, and a chuckle. Then she nudged him on the shoulder. "Come on."

"But you've told me nothing, I don't know anyone in Kadumyah except…" He paused mid-sentence. "Sarah?"

She nodded, giving him a hug. He backed away in embarrassment, pretending to blow the balloon again.

Sarah was the first girl he had a crush on. They were neighbors. He loved her and she loved him back. He dropped out of school and had to work to support his family and she went to college. Four years later, he proposed to her. Her father refused. Not directly, they were neighbors after all, but the father gave difficult conditions. A house of their own and those kinds of things out of his reach. A typical romantic B-movie.

The real reason was the father didn't want his daughter to marry a technician.

Normally that was uncommon, but for a beautiful young lady like Sarah, no one could blame her father that he was asking for a better husband. Hussain had to accept the fact that she was beyond his reach and move on.

Recently, Sarah and her family moved to Kadumya area. That was why he didn't catch on at first.

"But how? Did her father changed his mind?"

Hussain finished blowing the balloon and sealed it. He handed it to the boy, who grabbed it and sprinted inside the house.

His mother explained how the father changed his mind. Apparently Sarah refused the men who proposed to her. And as Hussain had a decent job now, there was no reason to keep refusing him, especially since the number of men suitable for marriage was in continuous decrease. War, killing, migration, and all other reasons.

"I totally forgot about her," he said, trying to hide the flush. He never stopped thinking about Sarah.

"Well, I didn't. My only wish in life is to see you happy."

He promised her to come back at two in the afternoon.

He kissed her forehead again. And walked away. Her prayer still reaching him.

Hussain walked to the bus station with a smile. Maybe different from the one of his mother but equally happy. His life was taking another course now. A better one. His salary was very good. Abdul Hasan, his direct boss, had promised him a promotion. And marrying Sarah was... well... more than a pleasant surprise. Exactly what he was missing. Next month he would be thirty; perfect timing.

He reached the bus station. A group of college girls waited. Four or five. All the same height, same clothes. The college uniform of gray and white. Like those families who dressed their twins in identical clothes.

He smiled in their direction. None of them smiled back.

They must know he was about to get engaged today. Yeah; that must be it.

He smiled again. This time for himself.

For a long time he had believed that his family was doomed with misery. His father's death. Then the tragic loss of his three brothers. Even his brother-in-law's accident. Maybe the time of suffering was over. Captain Abdul Hasan was like a father figure to him. The kidnapping of his son seemed a bad omen. But now, it didn't look so. After all, this was life. Continuous ups and downs for everyone. Happiness, sadness, luck, tribulation were all temporary situations and never lasted for anyone.

A reminder from God that nothing lasted.

That true happiness, everlasting happiness, was God's gift for people who served him.

He believed that. But he didn't think about it much.

Now was his turn to be happy.

-23-
Al-Amel District - Baghdad
June 10th
7:00 AM

Flanked by Abdul Rahman and Amjad, Luay walked to the house Mujahid and his group occupied. It was ten minutes from the mosque and another ten minutes to his own house, which made the location very convenient.

The place was relatively big, the trees in the small garden blocked most of the house except for the upper white windows and the big water tank in the roof. There were two metal front doors. The big white one was the main one that accessed the garden and the main house. At the end of the gray fence, a smaller black door provided access to the other part of the house that was given to the group.

A white Mercedes was parked on the pavement in front of the house. The hood was open and Mahmoud, the house owner, leaned on the windshield wiping it with a piece of cloth, a small plastic bucket in the other hand.

Yousif, Mahmoud's son, waited for them next to a small olive tree across the street. He wore jeans and a blue shirt with red strips. Clean shaven and, despite being over twenty, his cheeks were full of pink spots and holes left by unhealed acne.

"*Jahiz?*" (ready) Luay asked Yousif.

The young man looked at Luay's companions and then in the direction of his father who had his back to them now. "Yeah, I got your text message." Yousif looked at his father again. "Let's go before he sees us and starts asking questions."

"Your father is a good man, he will understand the importance of what we are doing."

Yousif shook his head. "He is scared."

"Of what?"

"I don't know. Maybe of the government or maybe of the Americans, maybe even of the Mujahideen."

Mahmoud took another rag and started cleaning the tires. He still did not turn to face them.

"Look at him," Yousif pointed at his father with his chin. "He is over fifty now, and he still works as a servant for some fucking rich guy."

"Everything will change, Yousif. I told you that."

Yousif nodded.

"Okay then, let's get this done," Luay said, motioning to Abdul Rahman and Amjad to follow. "Yousif, I don't know the houses here and Abu Ayob wants us to start with the Shia."

"I know everyone," Yousif said.

"We don't have anyone working in the Army here, do we?"

Yousif looked at the houses to the left and right. Then he shook his head.

"Good," Luay said, "now take us to the nearest Shia house, Christian is better if you found one."

Yousif pointed at a house with a yellow door across the road, only two houses away from his own house. "This is the nearest one, his name is Ayad Al-Mousawi and he is a Shia. Then there are two other families on this street."

"So let's go, what are we waiting for?" Luay said, walking across the street to the house Yousif pointed at.

"Listen, Luay," Yousif called behind him, "I have shown you the house. My role is over. I don't want to stay. They will figure out, they know me."

"Oh, come on, put the shmag on your face. We all will cover our faces." Luay then turned to Amjad. "Hey, Amjad, give me the bag."

Abu Ayob had given them a bag with red shmags. It was the best way to cover the face. Luay took one and wrapped it around his face, leaving only his eyes visible. Amjad and Abdul Rahman did the same.

Yousif held the shmag and just looked at it. "Man, I don't know."

"Amjad, Abdul Rahman," Luay yelled, "hold your machine guns in front of you, like me, don't put it behind your back as if we are going on a trip." Luay took his AK47 and held it in both hands in front of him. "It's more intimidating this way."

They did as he said.

Rookies, at least they knew how to dress by themselves.

Before Luay could reach the yellow door and knock on it, the door yanked open and a man wearing sleeping pajamas and a white sleeveless flannel shirt appeared. Face reddened, as if about to yell, the man stopped short when he saw their guns.

"Are you Ayad Al-Mousawi?" Luay said.

The man raised his head to look at Luay. He opened his mouth, then closed it and swallowed. "I...what...you..."

Luay refrained from rolling his eyes. It was always the same response. Confusion.

Then Ayad saw Yousif, he hadn't had time to cover his face yet. Ayad's eyes popped out, his eyebrows rose up high. "You!" He pointed a finger at Yousif. "Yousif, why? We are neighbors and friends."

Yousif threw the Shmag on the floor and turned to Luay. "Shit, I told you I shouldn't be with you. See!"

"Does your father know what are you doing?" Ayad said.

Okay, this was going nowhere.

Luay stepped forward to Ayad leaning so that their faces were only inches apart. "Listen to me, you filth, you talk to me, okay?"

Ayad's adam's apple bounced up and down. "What do you want?"

"You have two hours starting from now," Luay said, poking Ayad's chest. "After that, I don't want to see your filthy faces in this area anymore."

Ayad squinted at Luay, his jaw tightening. Luay yawned. They both knew Ayad could not do anything. He was alone. Unarmed. Standing in the middle of four armed men.

"One more thing," Luay said, "you get away with your clothes only. No bags, no furniture, no nothing. You understand? Leave your shit here, understood."

"My son is sick, I just …"

Luay grimaced, why did people always want to argue and plea and postpone the inevitable? "Two hours, and consider yourself lucky that you got a warning," he said trying to fake an angry tone. He felt sleepy and bored. "You're worth nothing, you piece of shit. Nothing more than the price of the two bullets I am going to fix in your bald head."

Ayad shut his eyes and nodded.

Luay motioned to his group and walked away. They still had other houses to cover. He didn't have to worry what Ayad would do. He didn't have to worry about him calling the police or whatever forces. Ayad would do the same thing all his misfortunate neighbors would do today.

He would go wake up his wife and tell her to pack. He would look at his house, his furniture, his gym equipment, his tools, his clothes, his books and wonder what could fit in his trunk. He knew how it felt. Luay tested it firsthand two years ago. But he didn't feel sorry for Ayad or anyone.

This was just business and by noon, this area would be a step closer to serving their target.

-24-
Somewhere in Baghdad streets
June 10th
7:30 AM

He drove his car without purpose. He must keep searching. Anything but sit at home. Somewhere he might find something. A clue to where his kid was. Abdul Hasan had broadcasted the description of the kidnappers' car. Nothing serious came up. He couldn't quit.

The soldier next to him remained silent. Abdul Hasan understood and appreciated it. Nothing could be said to make him feel better.

His cellphone rang. His wife again? He glanced at the screen but didn't recognize the number.

Abdul Hasan hit the receive button. His heart raced. He pressed the phone to his ear. His heartbeat getting louder. The kidnappers?

"It's me, Shaker, Sir." Shaker's voice came, so vibrant, so alive, so painful. Abdul Hasan shook his head, it was just the way the young lieutenant spoke. He was the one on edge.

Shaker asked if he could resume the interrogation with the suspected terrorist.

"Have you changed your phone number?" Abdul Hasan asked, not sure what to say about Mujahid.

"No, sir. It's my other phone."

Many people had second cell phones through a different carrier. If one network was not working, the other could be used.

"Sir, is there anything I should do with Mujahid? I might be able to extract what we need."

Abdul Hasan felt something in the pit of his stomach. He remembered the Syrian kid's words. How he lay covered with his own blood. He remembered how determined he was to not let that happen to anyone else. And he remembered his son.

The terrorist they captured might really be able to help. There was still time for the kidnappers to contact him and then he would need the man's help. Unleashing Shaker on him would mean that he would lose any chance of his cooperation.

What bothered Abdul Hasan was that he didn't have any trouble choosing his son's life over the possibility of saving the lives of all the potential victims. The gift of numb feelings.

He hung up the phone with Shaker after ordering him to leave Mujahid for the time being.

The phone rang again. Automatically he hit the receive button. "What do you want, Shaker?"

"I am not Shaker," a tight voice with an Egyptian accent said. "If you want your son to live, you have to listen carefully."

Abdul Hasan felt as if a hand reached through his chest and squeezed his heart. He put his free hand over his other ear trying to isolate all outside sounds. The Captain parked in the middle of the street.

"We will send you a car today. I want you to drive it to a certain place. If you don't, your son is dead."

"What car! Where is my son?"

"I will call you later to tell you where the car is. If you don't--"

"Listen! Where is my son?"

Silence... Abdul Hasan thought that the man hung up. And then a familiar voice came in crying for help. The words slashed his heart.

"Dad! Dad, help me!"

"Son, where are you--"

Click. The call was ended.

Anger consumed him. This guy had his son. His dear son. The sound of his cry echoed in his mind, driving him mad. And he, the Captain in the most powerful Iraqi force, was unable to do anything. Abdul Hasan wasn't the type of man who expressed his feelings. But now he felt an urge to smash something, to yell, curse, anything.

"The kidnappers... sir?" The soldier next to him asked.

He nodded, biting hard on his lower lips.

Despite that he tried to convince himself that it might be a casual kidnapping for money, Abdul Hasan knew that his son's kidnapping was related to his work.

An image came to his mind that made the blood freeze in his veins. An image of a bombed car, one of many he saw almost daily in his work.

But this one was different. He was the one driving this car. This was what they wanted him to do.

-25-
MCIF headquarters - Karada
June 10th
8:30 AM

Abdul Hasan opened the door of the room where the suspect was detained. The man cupped his eyes as if the light coming through the door hurt them. The room wasn't dark, but he looked as if just awakened. Understandable for someone who was interrogated by Shaker.

Mujahid –or whatever his name was– scrutinized him. Abdul Hasan wondered if he looked any better than his prisoner. He didn't need a mirror to know that his face had that zombie-like-gray color. Sleepless night and fear, a recipe for aging.

"We need to talk," Abdul Hasan said.

The man looked up, arching an eyebrow as if considering it. "Why not, I am free today."

Abdul Hasan bit on his lower lip and took a long breath. He then closed his eyes and sighed, letting it go.

"You said you can help me find my son. Help me and I will set you free."

The man tilted his head, his narrow black eyes staring at Abdul Hasan. Abdul Hasan stared back but saw nothing. Emptiness. He would add, snake-eyes or shark-eyes emptiness but maybe it would be an exaggeration. Abdul Hasan blinked to focus. His son's scream echoed somewhere in his ears.

"I can help, yes," the man said, his voice sounded as if coming from a tunnel. "I need to make some calls."

"Some calls?"

Mujahid shrugged.

"Who do you want to call?"

The man put his hand on his chin and tapped his lower lip with his finger. "800KIDNAP… or maybe Mujahedeen local call center."

Abdul Hasan stepped forward, his hands tightened into fists.

The man stepped back, hands in the air. "Come on, I mean whom do you think I will call? I need to call my contacts."

Abdul Hasan stopped.

"I told you I have some friends who know everything happening in this city," the man said. "If your son was kidnapped by any local gang they will know about it. Nothing could be hidden."

"What do you mean by 'local gang', who else could've done it?"

Mujahid smiled. "Maybe the Americans."

"Bullshit," Abdul Hasan spat. "They weren't Americans. The man…" He stopped mid-sentence, something flickered in the man's eye. "You aren't going to make any calls. Give me the number you want to call and I will talk to the guys myself."

The suspect sneered. "Right, will you invite him to dinner as well?"

"Listen, you," Abdul Hasan pointed a finger at his face, "you are pushing my patience and believe me, I don't have any today."

"I can't give you the number," the man said as if he was apologizing for a mistake with a hotel booking.

"And why is that?"

"Well, first of all, I don't trust you guys. Second, do you think that they will talk to you at all? What are you going to say? Hello, I am a captain in the MICF. We have been kicking your asses for the last year but hey, let's forget about it for a while and help me find my son."

Abdul Hasan considered it for a while. Then he shook his head. "You don't understand."

"Oh?"

"They called me this morning." his voice, too, sounded as if coming from a tunnel. "A man, Egyptian judging by his accent, told me that I should drive a car to a certain destination. I think the car will be bombed and they want me to drive it to the place where they want to blast it off."

"Most likely." The man nodded.

"So… I think that I need some guarantee," Abdul Hasan said, looking at him square in the eye. "You."

"I am sorry," Mujahid spread his hands, "I don't do car dates. Why don't you try this Shaker of yours. I am sure he will be fun."

Blood boiled in his veins. A noise in his head as if a bee was in his ear. A dark curtain pulled in front of his eyes. "Shut up and listen!"

When he was able see again, he was holding the man's jaw against the wall, his other fist ready to punch. The Captain let go of him. He shouldn't let this man get on his nerves. He shouldn't do anything that would complicate things further. Maybe this was what the terrorist wanted. The terrorist. No matter what justification he tried to come up with, he was making a deal with a terrorist.

"I want a guarantee that after I drive the car they will give me my son," Abdul Hasan said. Every word felt like swallowing a razor. "So here is what you will do. You will work with Lieutenant Shaker to find my son and get him out before I deliver the car. I don't trust those guys. And I admit that we don't have enough intel about them or who they are. So you will be my leverage. You know their methods and you can help Shaker to get my son back. If I get him back, you are free. You have my word. If not…" he took a deep breath, "I give Shaker the orders to put a bullet in your head."

The man tried to force a smile, but the smug look was not there anymore. "I'm sure Shaker will be disappointed that he will not have the chance to beat the hell out of me."

"He might as well do it. Hell, I might do it now if you don't stop being a smart-ass."

The man made a tsk-tsk sound. "So much for the we-are-all-brothers speech."

"Cut the crap. Will you help me get my son back?"

Mujahid shrugged. "As long as you keep that dog of yours away from me."

Abdul Hasan nodded. "I will call Shaker in here and you will start working with him. I will ask him not to lay a hand on you. But if you keep that wise-ass tone with him, not even a direct order from the Prime Minister will stop him."

Mujahid nodded. Then he looked at Abdul Hasan and a smile, a real, happy, day-dreaming-like smile lit his beaten-up face.

Abdul Hasan felt his stomach roll.

"I will do whatever I can to help," the terrorist said, his tone surprisingly sincere. "By the way, perhaps when all this is over we can sit for a small chat... to get to know each other."

-26-
Al-Karada District – Baghdad
June 10th
9:15 AM

Ali Al-Kadumi arrived at his office late. For some reason his driver Mahmoud didn't come to pick him up, instead sending a short text apologizing and asking for emergency leave.

Today of all days he needed Mahmoud most. He had the project launch among a dozen other things on his to-do list.

Mahmoud was more than a driver to him. Ali had only known Mahmoud for less than a year when his brother-in-law, Ayad, recommended him for the job. But he was a man Ali could trust, which meant a lot these days.

Lately, mobilization in Baghdad had become a burden. Traffic jams and road blocks were one thing. Random explosions and military-convoy passage was another. But the most serious things were armed robbery and the increasing danger of kidnapping wealthy businessmen.

So for Ali and his group of wealthy businessmen, a driver became a must. And a trustworthy driver who could do a little bit more than driving could easily turn into the businessman's best... friend.

Ali tried to reach him on his cell but it was switched off. It could be anything. Most probably the network was temporarily down where he was.

"*Sabah Alkhair*," (Good morning) he greeted the group of young employees at the office reception area. Most of them were in jeans, much better than the suits and ties they used to wear when they started working for him. Suits and ties in this heat?

His company had bought a complete floor in one of Karada's newest buildings. Ali changed the interior architecture of all the office apartments to make one open space; a design style that wasn't common in Iraq. He liked it here, the greenish carpet that covered the floor, the off-white walls and the glass-partitioned desks made the place look bigger.

At least this was what people kept telling him. He doubted anyone would tell him the truth if they didn't like it. One of the things you lose when you are rich –people's honest opinion. He could live with that.

Large plants perched all over the place. Ones with those big green leaves. The keyword for the office was "green" but that was the farthest he could go with any environmentally friendly initiative. Hard to talk about environment to someone who saw blood every day, who had trouble getting enough electric power to turn on a fan with this heat, or who couldn't put enough food on the table to feed his family.

Ali tried to institute some ground rules in his office. Such as no unnecessary paper printing. He tried to talk to his employees about how important living green was, to reduce the carbon footprint, etc. Nothing worked. 'Green' didn't go well when your life was painted in the red color of war.

"Good Morning, Mr. Ali," his secretary greeted him. No one used last names in Iraq. She wore a pink shirt with a yellow scarf that covered part of her hair. She had done something with her hair or makeup but he couldn't tell what it was.

She flashed a smile. He wanted to pay her a compliment but she was already speaking. "I finally found the roses. My brother will pick them up tomorrow morning."

"Superb."

Roses were always his gift to his wife on their anniversary. Year after year, finding the red roses became more of a challenge. The last flower shop closed three months ago. And you don't have to be Albert Einstein to conclude that flowers, and more to the point, flower shops, don't flourish with TNT.

"Oh, and you have a guest, Mr. Ali." She pointed to his office.

A guest? "But I don't recall an appointment."

"Well, yeah," she said in an apologizing tone, "he showed up today and insisted on waiting for you at your office. Mr. Ehab was here and he said it was okay."

"So why didn't Ehab meet him?" He walked to his office. Her voice came behind him. "He is Omar, the son of Dafer Al-Dayni."

But he could see him now, sitting in one of the chairs in front of his desk. Omar didn't stand, just smiled smugly. He wore jeans and a bright-yellow shirt unbuttoned to his belly revealing chest hair. A golden locket dangled from his neck in the shape of the map of Iraq, which was all the rage in the young generation, mostly girls, or so Ali thought. Omar still had his sunglasses on. Ray Ban's new model, the one with all black plastic frames. Another all-the-rage piece.

The young man was dressed for a nightclub rather than a business meeting.

Ali frowned; he and Omar had a bad history. Their business competition wasn't very peaceful. At their last meeting, during a conference at the Ministry of Trade, Omar had threatened him in public.

"What do you want?" Ali tried to make his tone neutral. He wasn't very successful.

"To do you a favor," Omar said with a broad smile while chewing gum.

The office smelled of cologne. Omar must've showered with it. Old Spice, if he wasn't mistaken. "A favor? let me guess, you're gonna show yourself the way out?"

Omar made a tsk-tsk sound. "You should be happy to see me."

Ali sat, leaning back and tried to keep his emotions in check. He had dealt with Omar before. The guy was so over confident about his father's political influence that he was acting like a mobster. Rumors were that the father and son had their own small army of goons besides their alliances with some Qaeda-related militia.

"Omar, do yourself a favor and stop acting like a wiseass because you are not."

Omar made a bubble with his gum and blew it until it burst. Ali took a long breath, looking at his reflection in Omar's glasses.

"I have a message that is better for you to receive from me rather than one of my father's friends."

"Oh, so now you are a delivery boy, I thought you were here to do me a favor."

His secretary peeked in the door, gesturing if she should send the office boy to bring them coffee or tea. Ali waved her a no.

"Well, let's say the favor is I am giving you the message myself."

"Not one of your daddy's goons, you mean."

"Exactly."

"And what is the message?"

Omar took a tissue and spat the gum in it. "Your corporation has taken a lot of projects recently. We were bit concerned that this will affect the quality of the work, and it's also not a healthy thing for the economy when one group of companies takes half of the subcontracts of Green Zone companies."

Worried about the quality of the project. Right.

"You forget the background music," Ali said.

"What?"

"The background music, your speech will sound better with the national anthem as a background."

Omar took off his glasses and glared at him. First the gum, now the glasses. Ali hoped the next thing wouldn't be the shirt.

"You know how many men my father has working for him? Do you have any idea what those people are capable of?"

"Shiver."

Omar's forehead creased. He pointed at Ali with the index and middle finger. "You know what, forget about our people, look at yourself. Your name is Ali Al-Kadumi, your company name is Al-Ghadeer for crying out loud. Everything about you and your company screams that you are Shia and to top it off you are working for the Americans. Do you know if I want to give your name to the armed resistance how long they will need to pronounce you an infidel who deserves death?"

It was a cheap game, threatening a Shia with the armed resistance and threatening a Sunnie with the Sader Army.

"As you said I am a Shia, so technically, for them, I am a step below an infidel anyway." Ali snorted.

"Listen, Ali, withdraw from the water-supply tender and we will let you live. You have been warned."

"You listen to me, kid." The rage building inside him made his words sound like a low grunt. "Go tell Daddy that Ali Al-Kadumi is not afraid of him or his cheap mobster games."

They both leaned on the desk, their faces inches apart. Ali could smell Omar's breath. Mint. At least the man knew how to take care of himself. They stared at each other. Calm down. It wasn't wise to push Omar anymore. For one his face was turning to crimson red, he was agitated enough that he could fight now.

But Ali couldn't help it, the thought of someone the age of his daughter coming into his office to threaten him. Someone immature and as arrogant and as corrupt as the son of Dafer Al-Dayni. He just couldn't help it. Omar's blue eyes looked left and right, he was here just to scare him, it would be safer for everyone if Ali nodded and told him the message was taken. Not taking it seriously would only provoke Mr. Sunglasses here.

And hell if Ali didn't like to embarrass him.

Omar gave him another dagger-like glare. He wasn't about to let it pass. He would try to make it physical.

Ali snorted. Big mistake. That flimsy strain of sanity in Omar's eyes snapped. His arms moved.

The door opened. "Is there a problem, Mr. Ali?"

Three of his employees stepped into the room, all Omar's age. They wore piercing looks, as if someone was threatening one of their family members.

It was probably his ego— he was used to people trying different ways of ass-kissing. But the way the three guys looked at Omar, as if they were about to kick his ass no matter who his father was, Ali felt moisture in his eyes.

A drama queen.

"No," he managed to say, clearing his throat. "Omar was just leaving."

Omar shook his head in a sad smile. If acting, it was a good one. "You know, Ali, I tried to save you from this. You are an honest person. I respect you but you are leaving me no choice. For the last time, pull out and save your life."

A cold chill ran through him. Omar sounded very repentant. As if apologizing for signing the orders to kill him.

"Shut up, Dayni boy," one of the project managers, a tall guy from Arbil, a Kurd, said.

The accountant, a wiry guy from Basrah, stepped forward and closed the door behind him, whispering as if making sure the ladies in the office would not hear. "Go and take your threats and stuff it up your father's dirty ass."

The guys chuckled.

Another added, "Yeah, try to get it shinier the next time the big asshole appears on TV."

More chuckles.

Insults... If there was some international competition for best insults, some InsuLympic, Iraqis would harvest all the gold medals.

Omar glared at the three guys. They glared back. He stepped back, looking at Ali.

"Okay guys, stop this. No need for insults. Omar was about to leave now." He gestured to clear the way.

The Kurdish young man opened the door, gesturing to Omar to leave with something like a game-host move.

Omar stomped outside. Once he passed the receptionist, he spun around and shouted, pointing at him, "One bullet costs fifty cents nowadays, Ali, this is what you're worth now. Fifty fucking cents." Then he sprinted, slamming the door shut.

"That son of a bitch watches a lot of movies," the Kurdish project manager said.

His secretary approached him again. Ali frowned then thought that she had nothing to do with the unpleasant visit. He sighed then said, forcing a smile, "Yes Luma, any more guests for me?"

"No, not really, it's your wife... I mean she is on the phone."

"Did you tell her that I was with Omar Al-Dayni?" he asked slowly, trying not to intimidate her.

She winced and then nodded. "Sorry sir, but she said it's urgent. I mean she asked to pass her through and I suspected that you wouldn't like to be interrupted so I had to tell her--"

"Don't worry, you did right."

Great, just what he needed. Zainab was already uncomfortable about him attending the project-launch ceremony; if she got a whiff of why Omar was here she would make a scene if he decided to go.

"I will take it in my office." He tried to comfort the young lady with a smile. He wasn't sure he was successful. The tension in the office was thick. Twenty men and women all stood. All looking at him. Reading his face. He could sense their worries, their fears. His company was not the first to get a threat of this kind. And it wasn't the first to temporarily close or have to move inside the Green-Zone after such threats.

They were reading his face for answers. Trying to know what he was going to do with Dafer Al-Dayni and his son. Trying to figure out if they had to start looking for another job. If they had to be more careful when driving every morning to work. Ali would also like to think that part of it was worry about him. Him being the one who directly hired them and picked them personally, not only the man who signed their checks. He smiled, made a face as if to say "empty threats," trying to comfort them. He wasn't a good actor but he felt he succeeded in soothing the mood. Most of his employees had families and children to support and bills to pay, they wanted to believe that everything was okay.

"Yes, honey," he answered the phone after closing the office door.

"Ali, I need you to send me Mahmoud."

Zainab didn't sound normal. She was upset, weary, and even angry, he suspected that had to do with putting her on hold for all that long.

"He didn't come to work today... I had to take a taxi. Why do you need him?"

"Nothing that cannot wait." Her voice was not very convincing. "What did Dafer's son want from you?"

"Nothing."

"So he what... just came to say good morning?"

Ali wanted to tell her but thought better of it. "It's... complicated." He tried to sound vague, it felt stupid.

"They came after you too, that was it, right? They threatened you too."

Too?

But before he could speak, before he could answer her question or demand an answer, she said, "Sorry, love, I need to go. Ayad and his family are here. Bye."

"Love you too," he said, not sure if she heard him.

Weird. The entire phone conversation was weird. Why would his wife ask for his driver the very same day he didn't come to work? And why was Ayad and his family at their house? They rarely went out together because of their sick child. And what was that she said, "threatened you too"?

He wanted to call her back, but a knock came on his door. Mahmoud walked in. "I am sorry, Mr. Ali," The man stood at the door. "*Wallah*, I didn't mean to be late but... Something happened at home and..."

Mahmoud was babbling. He looked as if he aged ten years. His face muscles, his shoulders, his back were all... slackened somehow, as if something was pulling every piece of his body to the ground. His eyes had that glassy look that revealed a huge emptiness behind them.

"Are you okay, Mahmoud?"

The man nodded. Ali knew him better, he wasn't the kind of person who liked to complain but something was wrong. Very wrong.

Mahmoud apologized again for his delay. Ali waved him off, telling him that his house wasn't that far anyway and it was good to listen to taxi drivers' chatter from time to time.

Ali wanted to ask Mahmoud if he knew why his wife wanted him. But Ehab rushed in carrying a large file. He spread it across the big table in the middle of the room.

"*Sabah Alakhir, Shareeki,*" (Good morning, partner) Ehab said with a wide grin, pointing at the file. "We need to knock out some ten percent off our offer for the second phase of the project."

Ali frowned; he wanted to talk with Mahmoud. But again, he was here to take care of the business. Such deals secured his family and his employees' families for maybe another year.

"My contact at the American company told me that they are ready to give us the deal if we could show some flexibility. What do you think? Can we do ten percent? No? At least five?"

Ali nodded absent-mindedly. He turned to Mahmoud. "Would you please wait for me outside, we will go to my house now."

Mahmoud trudged outside. Every move he made was a cry for help. Ali remembered the phrase 'dead man walking'. He'd never seen someone fit that more than Mahmoud.

"Do you think there is something wrong with him?" he asked Ehab after Mahmoud left.

"Who, Mahmoud?"

"No, George Bush, of course Mahmoud."

Ehab gave him a get-real look. "Ali, the man has a family of six or seven children and his salary is one hundred dollars, and this is just because you are generous."

"Five." Ali said, looking out from the window facing the street, watching Mahmoud standing next to the white Mercedes.

"What?"

"Mahmoud has five, and they are not children. Two of them are in college."

"More expenses. My point is, of course he will look tired and depressed and bad, people at his age should retire and enjoy their sixties peacefully. But here in Iraq we have to work our asses off until we get lucky and die in some bombing."

Enjoy their sixties! Ali shook his head with a sigh. There were things he couldn't discuss with Ehab. The man had no sense of people's suffering or feelings. Or maybe he was just right and they should focus now.

"Let's talk about business."

-27-

The Iraqi Perelman – The Green Zone
June 10th
9:45 AM

From the diaries of the abandoned city.

Deep in the depths of the past...

Since over four thousand years... the farthest that mankind's memory can reach.

In a land in the south of Iraq...

The first civilization was founded.

Sumer.

On that land, the first city was built, announcing that man had left caves, hunting, the wild, his animal part, and become a distinctive species.

From the clay tablets of that civilization... Historical writing began.

But, and despite what wonders history kept of that civilization, it was forgotten. Modern-world culture, Hollywood culture, was not interested in it.

Not the Zakorat, that wondrous and mysterious type of pyramid.

Not the epics of its fifth king, Gilgamish.

Not the first temples of the moon and the sun goddesses... The first civil laws, the first civilized society.

Nothing incurred interest. Not even slightly close to historically-less-important civilizations.

Of course, Iraqis blamed everyone else in the world for that. Part of the "global conspiracy" against them.

The same conspiracy that left Sadam controlling the fate of twenty million Iraqis for more than three decades. The same conspiracy that made killing hundreds of Iraqis in a bomb attack worth the same time on the news ticker as the last statistics about extinction dangers for the rhinos.

Of course questions such as, how much did we spend on the last media campaign about Iraq history, or, when was the last time you promoted a campaign about your glorious history. Those kinds of question were never asked. Easier to blame the world.

Still, many real archeologists knew the potential of not only the civilization but also the unique philosophy of the Sumerians.

Everything was about life.

Starting from the inventions of electrical battery cells way before the Mayans, or the still-mysterious King Ornumo journals, describing his trip into space where the gods took him high in the skies and he described the Earth as a big hazelnut... The Sumerian civilization cherished life.

But most of the researchers agreed that the most remarkable thing about Sumerians was the story at the end of Gilgamish epic.

Even before the great king started his long search for the secret of eternity –yes, life again– when he was running the first kingdom of Sumer, Uruk, the city was under continuous attacks from a nearby kingdom. So Gilgamish (a man who was described as half-god) asked for an urgent meeting of the warriors consul to support him for his war. After they did, the king went to the senate's counsel, where they refused to conduct the war and forced the king (so much for a half-god-king) to pay the attackers.

The story goes into detail about voting, Perelman, politics, war and peace rules, and laws, the three authorities.

It all started there.

Civilized human life.

But the wheels of history rolled, and Sumer as a city was long forgotten. Only shadows remain.

A page of the British encyclopedia.

An image that stayed hidden in the memory of humanity.

A gene in the gene pool of the Mesopotamians.

A gene that evolution brought back again.

Call it a survival need. Call it history repeating itself, Darwin's survival of the fittest.

Doesn't matter.

What matters for the Iraqis —at least most of them— that the dome of their new Perelman (a real Perelman that could say no even to a half-god-king) was built again.

And this time they built it and elected its members with the ink that blended with their own blood and sacrifices.

What matters for them now is that they have managed to say their words.

To choose.

And they have chosen life. Again.

Apart from the frenzied media campaign of the very objective Arabic media organization, Iraqis (again, most of them) didn't care much which party won the election. Politicians turn out to be good only at promising.

What matters is they have, once again, scored a point against terrorists in the long match of history.

They have proven that the great first civilization is still alive, somewhere inside them.

Today, the Iraqi National Counsel, the Perelman, was conducting a regular session. The corridors and hallways were full of movement, men and women walking with papers, talking on phones, media people with their cameras and microphones running after big-shot senators surrounded by their bodyguards and staff.

Faxes, printers, and cell phones buzzed and beeped everywhere, all mixed up with the continuous defining hum of the crowd. Employees ran after their bosses, carrying papers for signatures or words of wisdom. Some were shouting to everyone around them, communicating top-secret instructions such as closing up a door or cleaning certain areas.

For some, Iraq was fairly new to democracy. You could hear that a lot if you just listen to any of the staff circles in the hallways. Iraqis like to talk in circles, the way they gather. Even Sadam's regime had to deal with it by issuing the No-Gathering law. Part of the thirty-year-martial-law situation Iraq lived in.

Young staff working in the Perelman often complained, during their gathering-break, that Iraq couldn't move to democracy within such a short time. Those complaints got really serious when fights, sometimes even literal ones, took place between Perelman members or when a security team of a big member physically assaulted another. Rule of the jungle. Even in the heart of the democracy.

And then there were those who believed that Iraqis were created with democracy and love of argument hardwired into their brains. Those are more or less the optimists, the young generation in awe of their great history. After all, Iraq was twice the center of the world, once in early history and then in the third Islamic state. Getting there again was an achievable hope –assuming this planet would survive another century and global warming would not consume the Earth.

Despite what they believed, whether optimists or not, all people in that building were busy. Making alliances, personal or on party levels. Negotiating deals. And, of course, playing games. Political games.

Luay walked through the eastern section of the parliament building, flashing his access badge every now and then until he reached the area allocated to the heads of big alliances. Dafer's office was the first one. There was no banner outside the office, not even a name plate, just one small metal desk where three of Dafer's body guard sat. The arrangement was temporary, Dafer and other parliament members of his party were supposed to get another office on the upper floors soon.

"*Hawytak*," (Your ID) one of the guards with a buzz-cut hair and something in his mouth that was bigger that a toothpick and smaller than a pen demanded.

Luay raised his middle finger, the three guards burst into laughter.

"Nice to see you too, boss."

Boss. They still called him that. Something in the corner of Luay's mouth cringed. He wasn't sure if it was a smile or a wince. He didn't remember their names, not even sure what their ranks were in the old army. It didn't matter. They knew and respected him.

Dafer's office was a lot of space. The entire scene looked like a new house where people had just moved in. Boxes stacked everywhere. There were two lines of brown couches next to the wall where a big banner with the party logo hung. A dozen of Dafer's bodyguards and staff sat there. All males, all between thirty and forty, and all stood up when Luay walked in. Some greeted him, some shook hands, some hi-fived him, some just nodded and mumbled.

"Just in time, Luay," Dafer said. He sat behind the only desk in the room. It was a wooden one, Luay wasn't sure what type of wood but it was filled with what looked like Arabic art, a mixture of calligraphy and drawings. "I was trying to explain to those imbeciles why that shit they call investment law is more dangerous than the Iraqi army campaign."

Despite looking much older, Dafer was in his mid-sixties. Clean shaven, his face had that old-man slack, to the point that it was almost impossible to imagine him smiling. He wore his strange triangular hat, an Ottoman Kuffya. Today's hat color was dark green, which, Luay guessed, had to do with the new brownish suit Dafer wore.

Luay sat on one of the two chairs in front of Dafer's desk. A young man in a gray suit and wire-rimmed glasses, Dafer's secretary, sat on the other.

Dafer pointed to a big plasma TV on the wall. "See... see... even those Sharqya guys were fooled by that shit." The TV showed a report from Al-Sharqya, one of the few good channels that were giving the new government a hard time, criticizing almost everything. "This new investment law has a life of its own now. I can't believe it. Months ago it was just demands, some shit from some shitty liberals. Now look at it, the government is pushing for it, the media is talking about it, the conference is tomorrow and everyone is talking about it."

"I was just saying that the Al-Sader army was getting very aggressive recently, wouldn't that be more... I don't know..." one of the bodyguards said, he was older than the others. He used to be a major in the old army.

Dafer rubbed his face. "Security shit will not last forever, you dimwits. Once all the parties agree on some power-sharing shit, investors will pour in like parasites on a dead body. Can you tell me who will work for the militia when easier jobs are there?"

The major shrugged.

"No one," Dafer said. "People will abandon Jihad and work for the new projects. And how can my company compete with some Chinese shit... no way."

Dafer's word of the day... shit.

On the TV the Sharqya reporter was interviewing the minister of planning. The reporter asked if opening the door for foreign companies would increase the fears of Iraqis losing their jobs. Good one. Luay couldn't agree more with this question. Why they should share his country's fortunes with some American or Chinese investor who didn't care —or to use Dafer's term, give a shit— about Iraq.

The minister told him that they expected more projects to come; new projects meant more jobs.

"Hey boss," one of the guards addressed Luay, a fat guy, so fat that his XXXL white shirt was tied up on his belly. His thin mustache looked even thinner on his big face. "They said that Iraq will be even better than Dubai or Amman, will that be possible?"

Luay sneered.

Another guard answered him, "Sure, you idiot, we have enough oil that we can afford to drink it instead of Cola."

"And we can get blond Russian hookers in the nightclubs?" Fat guy asked with a chuckle.

"Yeah," Luay said, "we had enough of watching your mother shaking her fat ass."

Everyone laughed, even fat guy himself.

"Enough." Dafer grunted.

They all fell silent, first-graders chided by the principal.

"Hey, cheer up, Dafer, it's not the end of the world," Luay said. He wasn't the least intimidated by him. Their relationship went ten years back. During his work with the secret service, his squad was assigned to carry out a series of execution orders for the regime enemies. Dafer was the Baath office representative. In other words he was the judge, the prosecutor, and the jury.

"Do you think the Kurd or Shia would give a shit about me if things were peaceful and quiet? They have the biggest share of the seats but they know well what will happen if they don't listen to my... err... our demands."

"We need to talk," Luay said.

Dafer nodded and gestured for his staff and guards to leave.

"You look like shit," Dafer said examining Luay's face, it was his idea of casual talk.

Luay shrugged. "Tough work, and my boss is an asshole."

Dafer rolled his eyes and sighed.

"What? We are alone, don't expect me to play your little game all the time, calling you Mr. Dafer and all."

Dafer needed him. Luay was not only the best of Sadam's elite forces Dafer could put his hands on, but he had good connections with all the Islamic militia in Baghdad. Something that gave Dafer his edge.

"I just want to make sure you don't have more fuck-ups like the one a couple days ago when your guy didn't blow up the car."

Luay made a tsk-tsk sound. "For an Islamic party member, your language needs to be improved."

"Shut up, Luay." Then, "By the way, what happened to that moron?"

"The Syrian? We arranged for someone to whack him in the airport."

Dafer raised both his bushy eyebrows then nodded with admiration.

"I hope you didn't bring me here to show me the new democracy system," Luay said, toying with the ink pen on the desk. It was a Montblanc Star Walker.

"Fuck you and the democracy," Dafer muttered. "Are you ready for today's operation?"

"This is one of the things that I need to discuss with you," Luay said. "Those idiots from Abu Ayob's group thought they wouldn't need us any more so they planned it alone."

"Which group was this?" Dafer always forgot the group names, it might be just his way of saying that he didn't pay attention to details, the focus-on-the-big-picture sort of thing.

"It's a new one, called the Islamic State of Iraq."

Dafer scoffed. "Yeah, right."

"I would take them seriously if I were you," Luay said, flipping the Montblanc between his fingers.

"Are they part of Al-Qaeda?" Dafer asked.

"Yes, I guess. They are organized and there is serious oil behind them, if you know what I mean."

Dafer nodded. He had a funny way of nodding, tilting his head left and right. "I don't like them," Dafer whispered, "I don't trust them."

"Well, they need us for now, they know nothing about the ground and that's why we are so important for them."

"For now."

Luay sneered. "You know, Dafer, they are not crazy about you either. Not with you on the TV shaking hands with the infidels."

"But ... But... I only do it for the sake of the higher cause."

"Whatever," Luay said, he held the pen in front of him. "Good pen, black resin and platinum."

"Huh?"

"You know you could kill a guy with this thing."

Dafer swallowed.

"Regarding tomorrow's job, I need your help," Luay said.

"Huh?"

Good, the change of subject got him off guard. "Your help, Dafer. The man who knew the bombed-car location was arrested yesterday and we need to get him out."

"Oh shit." Dafer rubbed his face, then said, "Forget about it, I cannot help you with that. I took lot of trouble last time getting your people out."

"What about Saud? The man is an octopus."

Dafer frowned, then his features relaxed into something that could be taken as a smile. "Can you get the man he is looking for?"

"Maybe."

"Then, yeah, I can ask him for a favor in return. But tell me, Luay, what is the plan?"

"Do you remember the information they asked us to get them about the MICF forces some weeks ago?"

"Sure, it cost me an arm and leg."

"It turns out that they used the info to determine which officer in the MCIF forces has a high enough clearance to get the car into high-security areas."

"So?"

"They kidnapped the officer's son and they want to force him to drive the car inside our target today."

"Not bad." Dafer almost whistled.

"Well, they fucked up big time when the mastermind was arrested yesterday. He is the only one who knows where the bombed car is."

"What is his name?"

"A blood-thirsty psychopath called Mujahid," Luay muttered hearing the bitterness in his own voice.

"A blood thirsty– god, I am sorry," Dafer put his hand on his heart. "I almost forget you were cutting tongues and ears off the prisoners in the old good days."

Luay looked Dafer in the eye, Dafer didn't hold his gaze. "It was business. Okay. This guy does it for... I don't know. He enjoys it."

"Or..." Dafer smiled. "you, my friend... are getting soft."

Dafer's secretary came, Mr. wire-rimmed glasses, asking him if he was ready for an interview with Al-Arabya TV channel. Dafer asked for ten minutes and then to usher them in.

The old fox couldn't turn on a big supporter like Al-Arabya, not after all the help with his media campaign in the elections.

"Anyway," Luay said, leaning backward and lacing his fingers together behind his head, "I don't think it's a great plan. Do you think this officer will be so dumb as to drive a bombed car in the hope that the kidnapper will keep his word and release his son?"

"He is dumb all right, why would he join the MICF if he wasn't dumb?"

Luay reached into his shirt pocket and took out a folded paper. "I have a copy of the file we shared with Abu Ayob. It contains three names, they have chosen one of them, I read it myself, the man is not that type."

Dafer chuckled. "What type?"

"It says here that he was a political prisoner for ten years, then he was released when the UN made that noise about Sadam's prisons."

Dafer waved it off. "Probably some liberal with the Iraqi communist party or a Shia from the old Daa'wa party. Most political prisoners were from either of those anyway."

"Well, here's the thing," Luay said, unfolding the paper on the table in front of Dafer. "This man was in our Army. A captain."

Dafer took the piece of paper. His face slackened, his lower lip quivered. "It can't be."

"What?"

"Shit," Dafer whispered.

"What is it?"

"Is this the guy whom they kidnapped his son?" Dafer asked, his breathing suddenly heavier.

"No, he is the belly dancer we are getting for your next election party."

"The photo is recent, but the face. His eyes... I know him."

"Dafer, You told me that your man in the Ministry of Interior sold you this information for a lot of money, I thought you already knew what names he gave you."

Dafer's shook his head.

Typical lazy-ass Dafer.

"His name is Abdul Hasan," Dafer said, rubbing his face, "fifteen years ago, at the beginning of the Iraqi invasion of Kuwait, one of the young officers stalled the execution of ten Kuwaiti soldiers, keeping them in prison, asking for a confirmation from Baghdad for the default take-no-prisoners-show-no-mercy orders. The word got to Ali AL-Majeed, aka Chemical Ali. He sent the order to take the young officer to a military trial. Which always meant execution, fast and painful and memorable.

"The young officer had an elder brother, a just-retired general who served in the Iran war and then was retired after getting injured. Some people who know the elder brother advised him to sign up for the new war with Kuwait as a sign of loyalty to the regime. The elder brother refused to join another pointless war."

Dafer stopped, he rubbed his face again, looked around, and then walked to the nearby water dispenser and poured himself a glass of water.

"Anyhow, the story ended by the younger brother being sentenced to execution by some recently invented gas. After one month, the word got to Sadam that his brother refused to sign up in a chance to save his brother, so Saddam sentenced him to life in jail. For the lack of fighting spirit, as stated in the court order. Except there was no court or trial of course."

Luay smiled. "Idealists, always a headache, but this is exactly my point, this man will not help us in the plan."

Dafer nodded still looking at the mug-shot in the paper. Luay understood this, ghosts from the past, part of the job description. He had learned how to deal with them. Or so he hoped.

"And I assume that Abdul Hasan is the elder brother?" Luay asked.

Dafer nodded. "I remember him well. I was the one who advised him to sign up for the army to save his brother."

Luay smiled. Right. He knew Dafer better now.

"And as you might guess," Dafer added unable to hide the nervous tone in his voice. "I was the one who reported him for not signing up."

-28-
Karada District
June 10th
10:00 AM

Ali sat silent during the way home. He wanted to ask Mahmoud why he was late coming to work, he wanted to ask him why Zainab, his wife, wanted to see him so urgently. But he decided to wait until they reached there. Silly as it might sound, but asking another man - even your driver- "Say, why does my wife want to talk to you?" was not going to raise one's stocks in the eyes of other men.

Zainab opened the door. Ali didn't know what to make of her. When he left her this morning she was... well, normal. Now, her eyes were blood red, her face had a solemn expression as if someone died, she even barely looked at him. Her gaze shifted immediately to Mahmoud who was a few steps behind him.

Ali tried to ask her what was the problem. She said, "Let's talk inside."

Zainab was what one might describe as an angry woman. She was caring and kind and funny, no question about it, but also easily irritated. Her face would turn red and her hands would shake for as simple a thing as her phone not working. Ali learned to live with it, and sometimes he even liked the angry lioness she came to be. However, today she wasn't angry. Defeated might be a better word.

They sat in the dining room, most Iraqi houses had one. A room used only for formal occasions. Zainab whispered to Ali that Ayad's family was in the living room and it was better to sit in the dining room.

Ayad walked in almost immediately after they sat. He wore a polo shirt and loose khaki shorts. Too casual, as if he just got out of bed. His face, too, was solemn. No one exchanged pleasantries.

Zainab took a deep breath. "A group of men came in today to Ayad. They have…" she paused as if trying to figure out a less undignified word. No need for that. Ali could tell what was it all about. "They told him that he had to leave his house immediately. Your son, Yousif, was with them." Zainab uttered the words as if making an embarrassing confession.

Mahmoud closed his eyes. He then nodded slowly.

"Mahmoud, you are not only Ali's driver, you are a friend of the family. Ayad had been your neighbor for a long time … And Ali has a very high opinion of you."

She was babbling.

"I didn't know…" Mahmoud said, then he turned to Ayad. "I am sorry, Ayad, I knew he was involved with the wrong guys, I …" he paused, shook his head, and let out a long sigh. "I am sorry, you know I wouldn't allow anyone to hurt you. I even told you about how I suspected my son to be part of a gang."

Ayad opened his mouth. Ali thought he was about to say something but his brother-in-law remained silent. His foot tapped nervously on the floor, making his entire body shake. There was no anger in his eyes, no frustration, not even pain. The only thing Ali could see was calmness. And in a way, it made the pain and anger more pronounced.

"But they are at your home, Mahmoud," Zainab said, "you are the one who brought them to the neighborhood."

Mahmoud said nothing.

Zainab went on, "Being Shia doesn't mean that we deserve being kicked out of our houses."

"Zainab!" Ali gave his wife a reproachful look. It was under the belt.

"Mahmoud, I know you have nothing to do with those people," Ayad said, his voice was low and weary. "I know you better…I just need one favor…" Ayad swallowed, bit on his lower lip, and then looked at Mahmoud. "If you could talk to Yousif to convince those people to allow me to take the medical equipment we had installed in my son's room… let them keep all the furniture, the house, but you see… that equipment is really important to monitor his situation."

Mahmoud shook his head slowly. "They have threatened me today to give my daughter to the Ameer."

"What?" Ali asked, then remembered how Mahmoud was late today, how he looked.

Zainab's eyes popped out, then she frowned with disgust. "I thought your daughter was married."

"No, just engaged. Her fiancé... disappeared two days ago," Mahmoud said, his gaze fixed at the empty dining table. Ali wanted to end the discussion but he had the feeling that Mahmoud wanted... needed, to talk about it. "The Ameer of the group said that her fiancé was arrested by the Americans. I know he used to work with them for some time. He said he quit for her sake. I am not sure."

Used to work for them for some time. A real prince. Ali wondered if the fiancé had, too, some rusty machine guns and grenades in his house.

"But you have to do something," Zainab said, "go to the police, to the Commandos forces, let them know about it. For God sake, we have to do something."

Mahmoud might have shrugged.

Recently the national TV showed daily interviews with the MICF forces after arresting several terrorists' groups. It gave some hope that someone was out there who could and was willing to chase down the bad guys.

Would Mahmoud dare to go?

Then Ali remembered Ayad's own attempt at contacting the authorities. Who knew? The threat he got today might have something to do with his visit to the MICF.

"And what did you tell the Ameer?" Ali asked, "Are you going to..."

"I really don't know. He wanted me to come early in the morning. I couldn't refuse, you know. He talked about how things are changing in Iraq, how his group was gaining control over bigger areas, and how other groups started recognizing them."

Mahmoud paused, made a half smile. "Then the Egyptian sheikh, the Ameer, told me that he wanted to reward my family, for being supportive for them and all... by marrying my daughter."

Ali was about to make a crack but thought better. There was an old saying that went, the worst crises is what makes you laugh. Ali thought about everything he went through today, Omar threatening him not to participate in the project, his brother-in-law being kicked out of his house, and what Mahmoud was going through. Wouldn't laughing be the normal reaction?

"What really repulses me," Mahmoud went on, "is not the fact that he is some twenty years older than my daughter and several hundred pounds more. The thing is, this man was the sheikh her fiancé brought to commence the engagement ceremonies."

"Oh my God," Zainab said, putting a hand over her mouth.

"He only saw my daughter at the engagement and I cannot stop thinking that he ... he... wanted her ever since."

"For Prophet Mohammed's sake, what sort of man is this sheikh?" Ali said, feeling something in the pit of his stomach.

"The kind of man who sends people to kick families out of their houses." Ayad sneered.

The four of them fell silent. Awkward as it was, but it gave Ali the feeling that they were all on one side. All facing the same problem. The anger in Zainab's eyes vanished. She too went into whatever world her brother and Mahmoud were in now. Desperation and acceptance.

A cell phone rang, breaking the silence, it was Zainab's.

She went to the other room to answer it. Two minutes later she came back, her eyes barely half opened, like when she got overwhelmed by something.

"I am sorry but I need to go to the hospital now." She gave her brother an apologetic look. "The police are there investigating the disappearance of two suspects I was treating yesterday."

Given all the craziness of this morning, this hardly made the news.

-29-
The Iraqi Perelman – The Green Zone
June 10th
10:20 AM

Luay sat back on one of the couches in the corner while Dafer finished his media interview with the Arabya.

He wasn't bored. Not when he spent the time watching the reporter. A busty woman wearing a white, almost see-through V-neck shirt and tight white pants. She was blond, although he doubted the hair color was natural. Anyhow, he didn't focus long on the hair part.

When the interview was over, the reporter turned around and looked at him. She smiled, he was still looking at her... um...not-the-hair-part. "Would you like a private interview?" he said, twisting his mustache. "To know what happens behind the scene."

She frowned, and spun around leaving the office with her camera man.

Luay walked back to his chair, the same chair she was sitting on.

"So," Dafer said, "let's go back to your plan."

"Yeah." Luay nodded, following the reporter as she walked out. The plan, today's operation, and Mujahid and the money Dafer promised him if he succeeded. Could he quit after that and have a normal life? How could he find the man Saud was looking for? And was the reporter wearing any underwear?

Dafer's cell beeped. Luay could see it was a message from Omar. Dafer took the phone and started reading the text message. His shoulder slumped.

"Omar was in the Green Zone," Dafer said, still looking at his cell phone, "the guy from the American company told him that we will not get the second phase of the project. Another loss."

Luay didn't know what to say, so he settled for the reliable, "Oh."

Dafer sighed. "Never mind, you were saying–"

"Yeah, I was working on another plan," Luay said then stopped, letting it sink in, enjoying the moment. Dafer leaned forward. Luay too, leaned forward, very conspiratorial... it felt silly. "The reason why those guys from Abu Ayob's group need the officer is to get the car through the security checkpoint of the target. Now if we have doubts that this officer will help us, then we need to find another way to pass through the security. Are you with me?"

Dafer nodded, Luay continued, "I am thinking that I can use a suicide bomber. Someone with an explosive vest to penetrate the security and then to get the car in."

"So you will bomb your way in!" Dafer said. "I like it. This plan shows... um... balls."

"Coming from you... it means the world to me."

"Shut up, Luay. So is that it? You're gonna use a suicide bomber then the car and the operation will be done?"

Luay made a yes-no gesture with his hand, leaning back in the chair. "Well, don't think it's that easy to get the suicide man in. There are still some details I need to work out."

Dafer did that left and right nod. Luay rubbed his neck, hoping whatever was wrong with Dafer's neck was not contagious.

"I see, it's a problem indeed," Dafer said, tapping on his chin. Very wise.

"I am working on it though." Luay couldn't hide the wide grin. He needed, from time to time, to show Dafer that his services, his expertise was crucial. Maybe part of it was that he also wanted to prove to himself that the years he spent acquiring his skills were not wasted.

He was smart, tall, strong, and fast. He wished he could add 'handsome' but that was a long shot. The point was, it wasn't his fault that he ended up being on the wrong side of the law and society. He had killed, he had tortured people but that was his job, his orders. It was the government's mistake, if there was a mistake at all, that he ended up this way.

"Have you forgotten that I was the sniper who made the Americans spin around like headless chickens for weeks in Amiriya district?"

Dafer squinted at him, his mouth wide open.

Luay waved him don't-worry-about-that then went on, "And my biggest challenge is the bombed car. Which is why I need Mujahid out. He is the only one–"

"Make another car man, we have TNT everywhere and I can give you any car you want."

Luay sighed, sometimes he just wished he could smash Dafer's head to the wall.

"Dafer, do you have any fucking idea on how long you need to prepare a fucking bomb car?"

Dafer mumbled something about not being rocket science.

"If we filled a car with TNT," Luay explained, the way he did to a child, "the only thing you would get is a strong bomb and expensive fireworks."

"So what do you put--"

"To make a good bombing car, one that really hurts, you need to take all the chairs and internal stuffing and fill them with nails, bullets, and sharp objects. Then you go to the car truck and you put some RBGs, mortars, and what have you. This will basically get you multiple explosions instead of one. You can put that in the car body as well but it might get spotted then."

Luay made a sketch on a newspaper on Dafer's desk. A rectangular box resembling the car. Okay, drawing was another thing he wasn't good at but hey, he was the muscles guy.

"There are some cases," Luay said, pointing at the middle of the rectangle, the car, "where we put gas cylinders, the same ones you use in the kitchen, cooking gas, this one is really funny, you can make a car jump while exploding. Imagine a jumping fireball... Pretty neat, yeah? Anyway, it depends on what you want to do and the target details."

Dafer made a tight-lipped smile that looked more like a frown. Then he nodded, tilting his head left and right. "Good, good." Mr. wise again. "Anyway, I will tell Saud to help us with Mujahid, but you need to help me with this Abdul Rahman guy. Oh by the way, this is his photo." Dafer gave him a passport-size photo.

Luay glanced at the photo and gasped. The same guy he saw today in the mosque. Of course, Abdul Rahman from Saudi, how many Jihadist could be in Iraq with this name from Saudi? Well, maybe a hundred. The name was common and Saudi Jihadists... Luay shook his head. Maybe Dafer was right, they better start worrying about the increasing number of the Jihadists.

"You know him?"

Luay nodded. "I can get him for you, but the thing is..." Luay paused, then, "Tell me again what Saud needs from him."

Dafer made something like a shrug. All Dafer's expressions were crooked somehow. Maybe he had serious joint issues.

"I don't care, I think this Abdul Rahman guy killed someone from Saud's family. And now he wants to get even with him."

"So he wants him dead?"

Another crooked shrug.

"Well, Dafer, if the idea was to get him whacked, I can think of really nasty ways to whack someone. The thing is, I can really use this Abdul Rahman in my team. And I will guarantee to Saud he will die in pain."

Dafer laughed. "Yeah, I know you can. But no, Saud stressed on getting him Abdul Rahman intact –cuffed and secure– but intact."

Luay sighed. "Okay, I will see what I can do. Tell him it's possible. Tell him I will have him today."

"I love you."

Luay made a face. "You sure we are not having a moment here?"

"Go to hell, Luay."

"Aren't we all in hell now?"

Dafer sighed, his shoulder slumped again.

"You know what, tell him to come to my place to pick him up," Luay said, considering an alternative plan.

Dafer mumbled something about the importance of Saud and he shouldn't wander around Baghdad.

It wasn't hard for Luay to convince him that Saud had to come to his place to get Abdul Rahman. Luay couldn't dismiss the possibility that when he would show Saud what he planned for Abdul Rahman he might change his mind and leave the young man with him.

Although being a savvy businessman-slash-politician, Dafer was very close to idiocy when it came to tactical planning. Some people were like this. Luay had seen it a lot. They were very smart and canny when given enough time to do long-term and strategic planning. But when they had to act spontaneously, or make a decision about small matters, they failed miserably. Maybe it was the other way around with him. With all the smart tactics he came up with, Luay failed big time to build himself a family. In his late thirties now, from the way things were going he would spend his forties and fifties in the same way. Alone. Then he remembered his sister, Enas, the only family he had been given, inherited really. And a warm feeling surged in momentarily. An anchor. The very same thing he avoided became the thing he craved most. An anchor.

Not a good sign. Maybe Dafer was right and he was really getting soft.

He shook his head. Focus, soldier.

Dafer mumbled about how important for his plans that he - through Luay– kept good relationships and open channels with all armed Islamic militia. Promoting himself as the political wing for those groups. The moderate. A figure that the American and the Iraqi government could negotiate with instead of the masked men. A peace messenger talking on behalf of the angry, uncontrolled, barbarian forces who answered to no one. And when the peace messenger's advice, read demands, were not taken seriously... Well, he could not be responsible for the increase in violence. He advised and they didn't listen. At the end of the day, the Iraqi government had to give him more power, which would make him even a better ally to the armed forces and the angry masses who became even more violent.

An endless ring. And Dafer was good at making the best of it. Luay didn't like it one bit. He preferred confrontation. Actions. And maybe that was what made them best allies. Yes, he worked for Dafer, he was on his payroll, but that didn't change the fact that they were allies, even partners.

"Anyhow," Dafer concluded in the same wise-man style, "our relationship with Saud is a strategic one. So it's important to keep him alive, those Saudis enjoy torturing the way we enjoy football."

Luay nodded. "No problem."

"By the way, I need your help in a similar matter, Luay."

"Torturing or football?"

Dafer pushed the newspaper on his desk. It was Al-Sabah, the most distributed in Iraq, funded and owned by the Iraqi Media Network, which had good support from the Americans.

The news headline on the first page was curious. The launch of a new water station at Al-Amel. A water station! Not politics, not bombings. Luay could understand why Dafer was upset, the article was a love letter to Al-Ghadeer Corporation and its outstanding performance. Right.

"This... This... Person, is bothering my son." Dafer pointed at a mug-shot photo in the article of a man in his fifties. "He is competing unfairly with him. Ali Al Kadumi. I need you to dispose of him."

"I will see what I can do."

"Great, now let's discuss today's target," Dafer said, making another left-right nod. The TV was showing a live feed from the Ministry of Planning, attendees from both private and government sectors were arriving.

"*Shinu?*" (What?)

"You heard me well, Luay, I want to change the target."

"I want some."

"Some of what?"

"Whatever you were smoking, or drinking, I want some."

"Shut up."

"We have been planning for days to attack this target. You can't... we can't just change it like this."

"Luay." Dafer's face reddened. Luay saw the Baath representative who ordered the execution of twenty prisoners in ten minutes. "There were some changes. Changes you and your *friends* cannot realize." Dafer spat the word friends. "We have to hit them where it hurts most."

"But we don't have time."

"You will have enough time. Besides, today is our only chance."

Luay sighed and listened to Dafer telling him about the new target.

-30-
The Green Zone
June 10th
10:30 AM

"You sure I can do that?" Enas asked her boss, Robert Taylor. "I mean I never did the preliminary comparison report for a tender. You sure I can handle something as big as the water project?"

Robert walked to the file closet on the wall, and started searching for something. "It shouldn't be hard," Robert said. "Only two companies are competing on the second phase of the water project."

"Two?"

"Yep, Alrasheed is out."

Alrasheed, that's Omar Al-Dayni's company. "But…"

"I just saw their representative and I told him they are out. I thought you were here when I met the guy."

She shook her head. Maybe that was during the time she went to the next-door financial department.

"Anyway," Robert said, flipping the pages in the file he picked. "Alrasheed company performance was way below the minimum acceptable, and that's only being polite. They sub sub-contracted their contracts to the level that nothing happened on the site. Giving them the job was a mistake."

"You are reading about Heavy Water," Enas said, pointing at the file Robert was reading. "The security contractor is giving us a hard time again?"

"More than you could imagine."

Robert picked up the phone and dialed a four-digit extension. The Cisco phone display showed the name Larry Gabriel, the head of the legal department.

"Hey Larry," Robert said, "listen, Heavy Water are putting us in a corner, I need to see you to discuss what we can do."

Robert listened, then said, "Great, see you in ten minutes."

"I met Richard Barn, from Heavy Water yesterday," Robert said putting the phone back into the cradle. "It was a blackmail, he wanted to treat all the buildings in one compound as separate locations, double the cost for us."

Enas wanted to say, so what? After all, security cost was charged back to the USAid funds. It would not be paid from G-plans.

"This money should be spent to help the Iraqis," Robert added. "Look at the schools and hospitals for God's sake, we still have lot to do here."

Enas nodded, feeling her cheeks flushed. Robert seemed to think about her country's interest more than... well, everyone else, including herself.

"He is doing that because the security situation is getting worse every day," Enas said. "And we don't have other options for protection."

Robert raised his index finger. "Well, he doesn't know about that."

"So?"

"I bluffed," Robert tried to chuckle, but the frown was still there. "I told him that we are going to use the US army to escort us if we want to go outside the Green Zone. I even told him that we scheduled a site visit to that water project of Al-Amel today and his company will not be involved."

Enas' jaw dropped. "Are you?"

Robert shrugged. "He bought it and that's what counts." He checked his watch. "Well, I am going to see our friend Gabriel to see what he can do about their contract. Richard told me they will stop any escort for now and I am sure Gabriel can sue their asses for this."

After he left, Enas decided that she needed something cold before starting on the assignment. Starbucks wasn't far. She zeroxed the price summary for each proposal, put it in a small file, and took it along with her bag. This way she could read it in the café.

Enas went down the stairs from the portacabin when she saw him. That emptiness in her chest, the accelerated heartbeat, the happiness. He was standing right outside their office.

Omar.

-31-
The Green Zone

June 10th
11:10 AM

Happiness was her first reaction.

But that soon faded to reluctance then confusion.

Enas didn't want Omar to see her in the Green Zone. He would figure out that she worked for the Americans. Which most probably meant blowing up her chance with him for good.

Omar fiddled with his cell phone. Probably texting. She peddled back. Too late. She toppled over the last step. Enas tried to grab something, but there was nothing to hold onto. She took the fall on her shoulder and elbow. It didn't hurt much. Not physically. But the embarrassment was overwhelming. Papers from her files were flying over her head. Muffled laughter came from the nearby employees who were smoking outside. Omar stood there looking at her, his blue eyes wide. One of those moments where she wished the earth would crack open and swallow her.

Several young men hurried toward her, handing her the papers she'd dropped.

"So, we meet again," Omar said with a half-smile she didn't understand, while giving her the last paper.

"Oh... Yeah... actually," she said, cleaning her shirt and pants. "I was just visiting a friend here."

She fought an urge to tell him the truth. Why lie? At least she was doing something good for her country. Not like his Alrasheed company. Taking payments for jobs that they never started. His company... could it be possible? Enas recalled what Robert had told her about someone from Alrasheed visiting him that morning. Could that be Omar? Did he see her? Why did she lie to him?

Omar might have nodded. But his face was locked in an annoying crooked smile. It reminded her of his old man, Dafer Al-Dayni. The know-it-all smirk, the I-am-untouchable arrogance. For Omar, it worked somehow. She liked people with self-confidence. The I-am-not-afraid-of-anything look. She had it, in the past. Now... well, she was living a lie.

In college, she studied that nations ruled by fear for a long time used to lie to survive. Lying became part of the way they thought and felt... natural. So natural that even the best lie detectors couldn't detect it.

That was very true for her.

Except today, her lie was awful.

"Anyway, I think she is very busy now," she added unable to stop. Why did she become so clumsy when he was around?

"Uh huh."

"I mean, can you imagine how consuming the work is here? Her friend came to see her for five minutes and she couldn't even come to say hello!"

She didn't feel convincing. To keep talking, babbling, in her case, was a sign of lying.

But who said he knew about that?

Enas credited her brother Luay, who was literally a walking lie detector, for her uncanny lying ability.

"And where is the company, I mean your company?" His tone was still flat. They were walking now toward Starbucks café across the street.

"It's in Karada."

They met there yesterday, near the Green Zone checkpoint in Karada, so it made sense to be working in Karada district.

Another non-committal nod. And what was with his look? If she was to speculate about it, it was pretty much that of repugnance. But why? Could it be possible that he saw her there? But she was sure he didn't. And even if, what was the big deal about it? There were hundreds of Iraqi women working in the Green Zone. She was not the first.

To hell with him. After all, he didn't mean anything to her. Except he was rich, handsome, and single and, again, rich. But it wasn't only about that. When she first saw him yesterday she had a strange, unfathomable feeling that it wasn't a coincidence. Something about destiny and things written in the stars and all of that. It wasn't love at the first sight. It was more of a hunch, an idea she couldn't stop thinking about, a daydream.

"Hey listen," he said, examining her as if examining a commodity. "How about an offer? Job offer, I mean."

Something in her chest bounced so hard it almost hurt. "Yeah...I mean, why not." The pounding sound of her heart was so deafening she feared he could hear it.

Keep it cool, girl, this is it.

"Very well, then." If not for her blinding happiness, she could swear that he was sad when she said yes. "Go to the Meridian Hotel tomorrow and ask for a man called Saud, he will conduct the interview with you."

"Saud?"

He looked at her with a flat eye.

"I mean… is he the guy who will interview me?"

Stupid. He just told you that.

Omar squinted at her, then just nodded.

Why this Saud guy and not him? But then she thought it might be his assistant or something. After all, he was the manager.

They were in front of the Starbucks now. The place was crowded with people, men and women, different nationalities, different colors, and different languages, listening to them felt like making a fast scan on the radio, picking a different station every time. She loved the smell of the coffee, the quality of the food. For a split second, Enas imagined her entire country being like this place. People who had time for late breakfast at a café, enjoying reading the newspaper rather than working under unbearable stress of explosions and power outages and traffic jams and cars with no cooling and dozens of other threats.

And for a split second, she thought she understood why some people, even educated people, decided to be suicide bombers. Or maybe that was just her being high because of what Omar told her.

Omar waved to someone wearing a white dishdash and a reddish shmag. Enas always associated these clothes with the desert. With people who raised camels, traveled on camels, ate, milked, and God-knew-what with camels.

Iraqi clothes were a tad different. Even when they wore dishdash for casual events, it had a different design and color. Enas didn't like either of them. She wasn't sure what she liked anymore.

"*Hala, Hala,* Omar," white-dishdash said. He was with another guy. Tall, reddish American who looked pretty much like an American version of her brother. Luay.

"Wait a second," Omar told her and sprinted toward Dishdash and the reddish hulk.

"Saud, how are you?" Omar said, his hands spread as if ready to hug.

They shook hands.

"*Hala,* Omar," Saud said, "I want you to meet Mr. Barn."

Omar Shook hands with the big guy. "He is the one who will solve all your dad's problems." Saud followed it with a loud chuckle.

The three men went inside the café. Enas wondered what the man called Saud meant by Omar's Dad's problems. What could it be? What she knew about Dafer Al-Dayni, his age, reputation, etc… well, it could be either this man was a hired gun, or a Viagra salesman.

She didn't like Omar's attitude; it reminded her of that follow-me-while-I-am-speaking stupid thing managers liked to do with their employees.

She wasn't yet working with him. She would have time to change that attitude. Enas smiled, her mind drifting to the house and the new car and the happily-ever-after.

Stupid girl, focus.

After two minutes, which felt like two eons, Omar joined her again. His face was resolute. "Can you go to the Meridian now… for the interview." It didn't sound like a question.

Enas hesitated. she didn't like his body language —nor any language he used today for that matter. But at the same time this was a once-in-a-lifetime chance.

A chance of what?

She couldn't answer the question.

Her lips moved. The words "I will try," came out almost a whisper.

"Good. Let me know how it goes once you are… done."

What made her body shiver was that he wasn't smiling.

A matter-of-fact tone.

She nodded, not sure what to say, and spun around.

Did she said goodbye? Enas turned, but Omar was gone. She tried to stop and think, to analyze, to figure out her next move. All that her brain could come up with was a mixture of images and sounds. Luay threatening to call the college, her dreams of a better life, her contempt for society, missing her father. Omar's face. His eyes, the way he talked, his self-confidence. Even arrogance.

Everything sounded like a cliché from a bad romance movie. But she wasn't happy. And she wasn't sure what to do. Forgo doing the right thing or not. And hell, if she knew why her heart was pounding like she was about to take a leap… a long leap into the unknown.

Enas was sure of one thing. She was heading to the Meridian hotel. And she had just tossed the report file in the closest bin.

-32-
Al Amel District
June 10th
11:15 AM

Luay examined the faces of the three young men gathered around him at the small house attached to Mahmoud's house.

He wasn't very optimistic about it, carrying out such an operation with inexperienced volunteers was pretty much like going to a formula-one car race with an old wagon.

He needed someone who had used a gun before, who fought in combat. Luay wished he could have one of those Mujahedeen whom he used to see gathering around Abu Ayob in better times. Somehow, when Mujahid was not around, Abu Ayob seemed to lose control of his group. But this was what he had and he should find a way to make it happen.

Why should he bother? He could drop the entire thing. But then the thought of what Dafer had promised him. There was a good deal of money if this explosion happened at the right time.

And he needed that money. Badly.

He examined his group again. The two guys who came through Abu Ayob, Amjad and Abdul Rahman, talked about something called human shields and if Islam allowed the use of civilians as human shields.

Amjad was very convinced –according to some Fatwa he heard from, ironically enough, a sheikh in Saudi– that Mujahedeen were allowed to use human shields in Iraq and Afghanistan to protect themselves. And at the same time, they were not obliged to respect the life of the shields if the enemy used them to hide.

Very convenient.

Just to complete the paradox, Abdul Rahman, the Saudi guy, wasn't sure about this.

"It doesn't sound, *Islamic*," Abdul Rahman said, scratching his ear.

Luay almost sneered at them. He had to admit, the way those guys understood Islam was very similar to the way Baath doctrines looked at human rights.

In short, they made the rules that fitted them best.

He didn't mind. Long since he had accepted that gray was the real color of life, that white and black, right and wrong, were just illusions people in power tried to impose on others.

Yousif, the son of the house owner, sat on another corner. He was busy cleaning some AK47s. Luay had known Yousif for some time now. The young man had nothing to do with Islam. He helped them for one reason, the best reason of them all– power.

Luay's gaze met Yousif's. Yousif pointed with his chin to Amjad and then smiled, sticking the tip of his tongue out. "Islamic nerds," He whispered.

Luay laughed silently. He liked Yousif. In a way, the young man reminded him of himself ten years ago. Different circumstances, different setup, different families but somehow they both made the same decisions.

"All right then," Luay said, rubbing his hands like a game-show host starting his show, "I want you all to gather around the table, I have something to tell you."

They did, vigorously, except Abdul Rahman. He was more anxious than the first time Luay saw him at the mosque. It could be normal, but then Luay remembered the discussion he had with Dafer an hour ago about the Saudi young man and wondered if it had anything to do with his anxiety.

"As you might know, we are about to have another battle with our enemy, the infidels and the Safavid." He tried to imitate the way Abu Ayob talked. Luay had sat a long time with the Egyptian sheikh, enough to pick up those Jihadi-jargon words.

The way they used the words reminded him of Al-Baath party jargon. Yet another similarity.

Every "operation" was an invasion. Suicide bombing should be called "martyrdom." The enemy should be referred to by long titles, hyphenated words would be even better. Abu Ayob liked to use the words Kafer, which meant infidel or unbeliever. And Mushrik, which meant polytheist or pagan. When the government or Shia were addressed, other words were better to be added such as Safavid and Parisians.

Learning the Mujahedeen jargon wasn't the hardest task in his mission as liaison between the old Baath organization and the Islamic militia –Islamic Jihadist, as per the jargon. His years in Sadam's secret services and elite forces, although they gave him an edge on everyone else, came with certain... habits. The sort of habits that didn't get along with the guys with the long beards.

The first problem was he used to curse when he got angry. It was very common where he used to work, to call the prophet names or even Allah. It wasn't personal, when you are angry you do things. What was the big deal? But his Salafism friends didn't appreciate his point of view.

Thank God he was good with martial arts.

The other thing that caused him problems was more surprising. Luay was trained to distinguish different Islamic groups in Iraq. The regime was more than sensitive when it came to… well, actually any other organization other than the Baath.

So when he first start working with Abu Ayob group, he had –he thought he had– a good idea on how the Jihadist spent his… spare time.

He was way wrong.

If the Baath got back to rule Iraq, and it would, eventually, Luay had to remember to speak with whomever was responsible for writing the manual about how to deal with Islamic groups.

Drinking, smoking Hasheesh, and practicing beheading were the easy things, which he didn't find problem accepting.

Another similarity –except for the Hasheesh– with Al-Baath.

And then there was the homosexual relationships issue. Something that wasn't very popular in Iraq.

Due to the fragility of the alliance between the Salafism and the Baath, Luay thought it better not to ponder the differences.

Mr. open-minded.

"Our target in this holy invasion will be a gathering for the Kafreen, the unbelievers who want to bring innovation to Muslims and spread ethical corruption. We have warned them many times but they are unwilling to obey the rule of Islam. It is inevitable for us to fight them."

He felt stupid.

No one said anything. Better.

"Because of the importance of the timing, we have to execute this afternoon."

Also no comments.

"The target will be very well protected by the Americans… I mean by the infidel Americans and the unfaithful Iraqi forces."

The now-familiar noise of a chopper cut him off, the sound grew uncomfortably louder. Surely nothing, but he stopped and looked out the window, trying to see if it was targeting them. He felt relief when the sound faded away. It was almost musical.

Another casual flight to enjoy the scenery.

Luay took out a paper from the file Dafer gave him about the target. He sketched something on it. He could feel all the gazes in room looking at his sketch. This wasn't helping.

He went on, pointing at the paper, "According to the information we received, there will be only one entrance protected by a temporary but strong fence, with only one checkpoint."

Everyone looked at the shapes on paper, which might be loosely referred to as drawings. A square in the middle was labeled: "The Target Building." Around the building/square were two thick lines, both totally surrounded the building except for small openings that were labeled "outside checkpoint" and "inside checkpoint."

"The first fence you see here." He pointed to the outside line.

"Ah, so that is a fence." Someone said.

"This fence is to prevent vehicles from driving into the target building." Luay went on. "So we would expect it would be a strong one. The outside checkpoint is there to allow only authorized vehicles to drive in. They will have the standard vehicle examination kit to make sure no bombed vehicles gets in."

Everyone nodded in unison.

"The second fence is to allow only individuals walking in; no cars allowed after the second fence. And as you might have guessed, the checkpoint here is to search people. This space here between the two fences will be used to park the cars that were allowed in. Mostly the VIP cars."

"So cars cannot get in to the building?" Amjad asked.

"With sharp observation like this," Luay said, "I am very happy we have you on our side."

Yousif let out a small laugh he immediately covered by a question, probably to avoid Amjad's glares. "So individuals will not be searched at the first checkpoints, is that right."

Good point. Luay had to think about it for a second before answering. "Not likely... No." He pointed at the inside checkpoint. "You see the one here, there is a small cabin that they prepared today, it's to search the women. And if you look at the outside checkpoint, you can see no cabin, so it means--"

"Since there is no way to search women, men will not be searched," Yousif added.

"Don't you love equality." Luay chuckled.

Now came the tricky part.

"By the will of God, we will be able to get a bombed car to explode in this space." He pointed at the space between the two fences. "And then… One of the holy martyrs will get inside, taking advantage of the chaos after the first explosion to detonate a bomb belt among the infidels who will be rushing outside through this direction to escape the place."

Luay paused, waiting for the plan to sink in. He was happy about his performance. He enjoyed planning the attacks as much as executing them. It was more than just his daily dose of adrenaline. It gave his life a purpose.

He took a look at the faces around him, at the small room they were in. Maybe it's not the best work ever, he admitted with a sigh. Trying not to let his mind wander to other possibilities. Possibilities such as sitting at one of those air-conditioned offices of the government and spending the day doing almost nothing; then he would get as much as he was getting now, without risking his life.

"Where is the target?" Abdul Rahman asked.

"It's in Baghdad."

Mr. Evasive.

They all stared at him.

"Not now," Luay said, holding up his hand as if stopping traffic. "When the time comes, I will tell you. We call it a need-to-know basis."

Abdul Rahman shrugged, he wouldn't know the location anyway. A big city like Baghdad would take a considerable amount of time to know well. And Luay doubted that Abdul Al-Rahman spent his time shopping in the city's main areas.

Amjad scratched his head. "You said the car will explode in the space here between the two fences, so that means it will pass the first checkpoint."

A real asset. Luay was about to make another sarcastic comment, but Amjad added, "So how will the bombed vehicle pass the first checkpoint?"

Luay make a slowdown motion with his hand. "You don't need to worry about it now."

As a matter of fact, he was worrying about this very thing. With what Dafer told him about Abdul Hasan, the officer in the commandos' forces, to predict how he was going to react was tricky.

A fair chance existed that the man would react the same way he reacted a decade ago when he refused going back to the army. Maybe he learned something from what happened to him? Who knew?

Fathers acted in a different way when the life of their own offspring were in danger.

He had seen —actually heard because everything was done on the phone— men negotiating the ransom amount as if discussing a business deal on a weekend afternoon. But when the father was on the phone, then the only thing he heard was pleadings and begging... no negotiations, no delays... just the please-don't-kill-my-son clichés.

"Who will carry the explosive belt? Is he going to be one of us?" Abdul Rahman asked.

Luay had seen such things before. People getting cold feet. And yet he sensed something else about Abdul Rahman. Maybe he wasn't here to fight after all.

"I don't think so," Luay replied, faking deep sorrow as if apologizing to them. "As you know, the honor of martyrdom, the right that will grant the heavens and all the blessings.... It is not easy for anyone to get it. You have to be chosen. It's a real honor."

Once again, he felt stupid trying to imitate Abu Ayob. Yousif gave him a get-real look. Amjad and Abdul Rahman both nodded in unison. Nice kids... really.

"What does that mean?" Amjad's question sounded like a protest.

He reminded Luay of a fat soldier he used to tease in the good-old days. An everyday prank was to take his bread while he was busy eating. The overweight man would stand in the middle of the soldiers' court and shout, "Who took my bread!" while his mouth was still full with food.

Luay managed not to smile, he faked a cough and carried on his role of delivering bad news. "As you know, there are lots of fighters... I mean brothers who want to get this honor and do the operation... the suicide... I mean the invasion." To hell with this jargon. "Anyhow, the rules we have here are that priority is given to those who joined us first."

"So we will not ... join ... this battle as martyrs?" Abdul Rahman asked.

Was that relief on his face?

"I don't think so, but again it's too early to know anything. There might be last-minute changes." He paused again, trying to put all his acting skills on the line.

Damn you, Abu Ayob, how could you do it?

"Then, my brothers. I might come here and tell you that Islam needs you. And the chance to be a martyr is within your grasp. And of course, I will leave the decision to you. No one would be forced to be a martyr."

Silence.

"*Wakt Al Salat*," (Prayers time) Amjad said, looking at his watch. He and Abdul Rahman excused themselves to go to pray at the nearby Tawheed mosque. He and Yousif stayed at the house.

Yousif held a device with an antenna and a coil with extra care. "What is this?"

"A detonator," Luay answered without looking at it. "It's an old-fashioned one. I am not sure how we got it. I think Abu Ayob or someone with him brought it."

Yousif nodded, now looking at the device as if he just discovered something grew unnaturally on his hand.

"The new ones we are using now are connected to a cell phone. You simply dial the number and boom. You can be anywhere, not like the one in your hand where you have to be close. We never used those."

Yousif threw the device away.

"Do you think I convinced them back there?" Luay asked.

Yousif was not much into religious campaigns so Luay decided to talk to him bluntly.

"No kidding, you are a master bullshitter. I was about to grow a long beard and start wearing those short dishdash of theirs."

They both laughed.

"Listen, Yousif, I want to tell you something?"

"You want to wear those short dishdash?"

Luay smiled. "No, I want to tell you about our target." He needed someone he could trust among the group in case the Salafism guys tried to play games.

Yousif dumped what he had in his hand and came toward Luay. His black eyes shone with interest, like a school kid invited by the teacher to take a look at the questions on the next exam.

Luay took the papers he was drawing on, then underneath the words "Target Building" wrote another three words and handed it over to Yousif.

Yousif stared at the paper for some time without saying a word. "So everything is decided?"

"Yes, pretty much."

"And the timing?"

Luay took the paper and start scribbling while talking. "The car should come from this road, enter through the checkpoint here." He drew a line, the only thing he could draw easily. "And explode at this time." He ended the line with a big X then wrote the time. "As for the suicide, he will come after ten minutes."

Yousif looked at the paper with something akin to awe. "So tell me, how can you get the car inside?"

Luay winced. "There was an arrangement, but I am not sure about it anymore."

Yousif just waited.

"I have a back-up plan."

Luay sat on a plastic chair facing the table. Yousif did likewise. Sunlight came through the window, reflected on the table, and lit the room. In the anti-terrorism campaign the national TV was conducting, terrorists were always shown to meet in dark and dingy places. Another cliché. Luay looked at the sunlight, the trees outside in the garden, the birds' call for mating, nope, it didn't fit in with the discussion. Maybe they would be better off in that dark place as the wise TV program had foreseen.

Luay took the drawings again, this time with no pen. "We can get the man with the explosive belt first. He can pass the first checkpoint easily. He will be in the yard between the two checkpoints."

Yousif said in a low voice, "Okay, but detonating himself there is not going to achieve anything."

"That's right," Luay nodded, "that's why I want to use this baby."

He reached to the couch nearby and grabbed a sniper rifle and held it in front of Yousif. "I have done wonders with this rifle," he said patting it gently. "I will have my eye on our suicidal, and when he approaches the second checkpoint, just before they start searching him, I will… take care of them." Luay made a motion with the rifle.

"What if there is another guard there?"

"I can take up to two guys in a very short time. This will create enough chaos for our man to rush inside and detonate himself."

Yousif looked at the paper again. He turned it in the other direction as if trying to figure out the perspective.

"This is the main street, right?" he asked, pointing at the line near the first checkpoint.

Luay nodded and then went on, "After our man bombs himself." He paused. How weird the words sounded. Then he shrugged and continued, "When he bombs himself, people will rush outside, there will be hundreds of them, even more, trying to get out of the place. Our bombed car will be ready to take them. Here in front of the entrance, we will kill many more than the first bombing."

Luay paused again, letting it settle.

"Too many people will die," Yousif said with something like a nod.

"Yes."

Yousif didn't say anything. Luay knew better than to rush him so he just waited.

"I mean, we don't know who will be there," Yousif said, "It could be anyone... not only government, not only Shia, even good guys will be there."

"Yousif!" Luay almost yelled. "This is a war, Yousif, I don't like it, you don't like it, but we didn't start it and none of us can stop it."

The young man swallowed, his Adam's apple bounced up and down, his gaze still on the paper.

"Look at it this way, those people are dead the moment they decided to go to this fucking place. It's not me and you who decided to kill them. We made it clear that any place attended by government or Americans is a target."

Yousif said slowly, "Like they are acting as human shields with their own will."

"Exactly, it's their own decision. They wanted to be on the side of the Americans and the government and the Iranians. This is their choice. We have a mission to carry out."

Yousif nodded. "You promised me that I will get paid once I start my first mission."

Yousif wasn't trained, albeit, but a young man like him could do lots of things.

"Is four hundred dollars a month okay for you," Luay said with a smile.

Yousif beamed.

Four hundred dollars was a good amount and could feed a small family for a month. Things were changing in Iraq fast; salaries were increasing to catch up with the new life. But for the next couple of months, this should make Yousif happy.

"There is one thing," Yousif said while packing all the paper in the file.

"Tell me."

Luay needed something to put the papers in. He searched the place. A blue paper bag lay on the floor. It was one of those transparent bags designed to carry papers. It looked perfect.

"Where do you want to position while using your sniper?"

Luay shrugged. "Anywhere with a good view of the checkpoint. Why, what's the problem?"

Yousif hesitated for a second. "You see, I don't know anything about using a sniper but I don't think you will have a good view at this checkpoint from anywhere. All the buildings around it would not be good."

Luay didn't like where this was going. He felt he didn't do his homework right. "What are you talking about?"

"What I am saying," Yousif said, "is that this building is in the middle of a residential area, all the houses in this area are too low for you to use them, the concrete wall is too high even if you got onto the roof of a house."

"Shit." Luay resisted an urge to throw the rifle at something. Or someone. "Shit... this idiot, I told him it's too late to change the target. Shit."

His face and head got hot, his blood boiled. He wanted so badly to get the job done and receive the money Dafer had promised him. Even Abu Ayob had promised him something. Both men needed to prove a point or deliver a certain message, or whatever sick reason they had. He didn't care. He felt tired. Exhausted. Nothing was going smoothly. He felt abused by the regime he served his entire life, and the lifestyle he had chosen or was chosen for him.

"We will work something out." He grunted. "And Yousif, I will give you the best advice that was given to me when I was your age."

Yousif looked at him.

"Don't think much about what we are doing. We are guns, weapons. Guns do not think, they just execute."

-33-
Al Karada District
June 10th
11:20 AM

Lieutenant Hussain sat in the big foyer of the waiting area of Al-Karada hospital. Hussain wasn't sure that his boss, Captain Abdul Hasan, was doing the right thing today. His son was kidnapped, true, and the man deserved all the sympathy in the world. But he shouldn't allow what happened to his son to cloud his judgment. After all, the lives of hundreds of people could be at stake and if the Captain was incapable of handling the situation, he should simply quit.

Quit! That was a bit harsh.

Abdul Hasan sent him to investigate a stupid escape of two suspects from a hospital instead of working on today's possible threat.

Despite his rank, Hussain, wasn't a real soldier. Far from it. His military training was a three-month crash-course in Jordan. This in no way qualified him to judge his Captain's decisions, with all the man's experience in real battles.

But what about Mujahid, the terrorist they arrested. There was no one interrogating him? How could this be justified?

Was his boss trying to keep him away from headquarters?

It didn't make any sense, and yet, it was the only explanation of his boss's behavior today. The way Abdul Hasan looked at him this morning when he arrived. It was as if he was an uninvited guest to a special party. And once this report about the escapees arrived, Abdul Hasan immediately assigned him to it.

Something was wrong.

Terribly wrong.

He shook his head, as if to cast away the suspicions. His job was to follow orders, not to question them.

Did he read that in the manual of the commandos force or see it in a movie?

Two male nurses entered the hallway carrying an unconscious fortyish man who wore a shirt that was soaked in blood. A black hole filled the man's waist.

Another shooting. He didn't have to be Sherlock Holmes to conclude that.

Hussain remembered a friend working in the city morgue who told him once that they used to receive more than forty bodies a day all killed by shooting. Bombing casualties and those who died due to natural causes were minor in comparison to assassinations. This was the real war, the hidden war.

It didn't matter if you were a Sunnie or a Shia, it would get to you. It didn't matter if you were a bad guy or a good guy, if you were a gangster or a law-enforcement officer or postman. It would get you. Or someone you cared about.

Iraqis had known wars. They had seen tragedies. But this one, this civil war, the mafia-style and yet almost-random killing, drove everyone crazy.

It didn't matter who started it, but it had to end. And Hussain had a strong feeling that it would get worse before it got better.

Before today, Hussain wouldn't worry about killing or anything else. He kept reminding himself of the old Iraqi saying –which everyone kept repeating lately as if people were reminding each other–

"The already-soaked doesn't fear the rain."

That was in the past, when he mentally accepted the fact that, statistically speaking, there was a ten percent chance of being killed.

Now... well, things were not the same anymore. He was going to enter another life. Marriage. Hussain wasn't sure if he felt happy or grateful or worried or scared. Maybe all.

It was very much like trying to forgo everything around you and hide inside this cozy, sweet and warm wrap with the love of your life.

Hussain's problem was, simply put, that everything around him, from his family to his neighborhood to his entire country, was living in continuous and apparently endless misery.

Hussain was unable to feel happy while he saw pain in the eyes of people he cared about.

He was no saint, but his religion told him that a true Muslim should wish for others what he wished for himself.

Right. And what have I done to help the others? Nothing.

He tried to help from his position. But it wasn't something to brag about. He'd arrested three terrorists so far. His squad had made an assault on a place suspected to be a hideout for one group. It turned out the terrorists had left it a week beforehand. Great intel.

In short, he had done almost nothing to make his city a better place.

It was difficult for anyone to do anything. Not alone. Iraq's problems required congregated efforts, something big, something equal to, say... save-the-whales efforts.

Recently, Hussain could afford buying a satellite receiver – somehow everyone in Iraq, even the poor, afforded satellite receivers and cable channels. He liked Animal Planet a lot. Especially the part of Animal Patrol where a group of soft-hearted, dedicated, and caring people would go in quest to help a limping dog, a sick giraffe, and the like.

Hussain looked at another group rushing through the hospital, this time carrying a young girl, five or six years old, blood splattered on her face and clothes. Hussain couldn't see any injury. The girl had a frozen, fixed, and freaking look on her face. One that you only see in a bad horror movie.

"What's wrong with her?" one of the young doctors asked, chewing gum, his hand in his blazer pockets.

"I don't know, we found her like that," a man said.

"I think she was with her father when he was shot," another man said. "This is his blood on her face. But we couldn't move his body… it was terrible, man… terrible."

The young doctor nodded.

Could Animal Planet send a patrol to Iraq one day? Maybe they could organize a save-the-children campaign.

"Lieutenant Hussain," a soft, feminine, yet resilient voice said. A woman in her forties stood at the hallway. She wore a white blazer, underneath it was a blue long dress. A white Islamic head scarf covered her head. There was nothing special about her clothes or even her face, but she was oozing with elegance and style. Or maybe he was just used to the sight of blood and dead bodies to the point that anything else looked as if from the Hollywood red carpet.

She must be Dr. Zainab. Hussain stood, deliberately making a move of checking his watch, then remembered he wasn't wearing one.

"I am so sorry, I know you were expecting me earlier but I had a family emergency."

Hussain cleared his throat, tried to say something wise about respecting the time but settled for a no-problem smile.

Why was he here? Oh yes, the big case of the two wounded men who escaped the hospital. Should he order the hospital surrounded by the police yellow tape until the situation was cleared? It was a good idea given the way his boss asked him to cover it.

But then, they didn't have yellow tape, they never used it actually. And with all the injuries from gunfire and other murder victims, this case hardly deserved a report.

Doctor Zainab led him to a room behind the reception area. The smell of the cleansing material sent immediate shock to his nose and brain. Compared with other hospitals, this one was in better condition. Bed sheets could use some washing but they were okay, the walls were pleading for a paint job but that was a luxury. Only one patient on the floor, everyone else on beds, two air coolers were at each end of the hallway, sending off cold, albeit wet, air. Lots of people, mostly in blazers, scurried around. Everyone shouted, instructing and complaining which seemed driven by the desire to feel important rather than any actual need.

They sat in a small room. He didn't like doctors' offices or clinics. Zainab sat at a desk with piles of books and papers on it. A plastic miniature for the upper half of a human body showed a colorful heart, lungs, stomach, and other organs. Why did doctors put things from six-grade biology on their desks? Was it some kind of trophy from elementary school? Or did they actually need a reminder of where the liver was? Just in case the doctor forgot or something.

Next to her, stood a nurse carrying some papers like those ancient Pharaoh servants who waved big sheets, acting as a human-air-conditioner.

The nurse was exceptionally beautiful, something that didn't fit with all the gloom and sadness engulfing the place.

Hussain gave her his best smile. She didn't fall to her knees and rather stared at him with a tight face. Hmmm, even she knew about his commitment to Sarah.

"We received a call from your hospital that two men who were brought by the local police escaped during the night."

Zainab nodded. She might have said something like that's right.

"I understand they were both suspected to be terrorists."

Another nod. She looked as if forced to have this discussion, pretty much like him.

"Would you please elaborate more?"

Zainab took the file from the nurse and started reading. Hussain was tempted to peek but thought it might be immature.

"Okay, in fact I was the one who worked on them," Zainab said. "The first one, who was wearing a mask, was shot—"

"A mask, as in those masks terrorists wear?"

Zainab sneered. "No, the Batman's mask."

Pharaoh-servant laughed.

Everyone was a wise-ass.

Zainab let out a breath and went on reading out loud from the file, obviously not appreciating the interruption.

Doctors! When would they learn that the real world was bigger than the hospital?

"He was shot in his waist, the shot came from the back. From a close distance. His injury was lethal but he survived. So did the other man whose injury was less serious. "

"Any idea how they got here?"

She shook her head. "No not really, the receptionist said the local police brought them, but you know how messy they are so I am not sure anyone knows for sure."

Hussain didn't ask who was messy, the local police or the hospital receptionist, probably both.

"But I doubted they were together."

"And why is that?" He managed not to smile. It always amused him when civilians tried to play detective. After all, not everyone took a three-month crash course like he did.

"Because they arrived with more than an hour time gap. If they were together, it would make sense for whoever found them to bring them at the same time."

Hussain pursed his lips. Okay, that wasn't bad.

A man entered the room. His ragged clothes and his wide smile told Hussain he wasn't a doctor. Doctors don't smile in front of the 'others,' they just nod. A nod full of wisdom, of course.

"I found it!" the man announced with the same pride George Bush displayed upon capturing Sadam.

Zainab's eyes lit up. "Aramis?"

"The original, everyone out there sells a cheap replica, this one is the original."

The man handed Doctor Zainab a small box wrapped in rosy gift paper.

"Oh, you wrapped it, thank you so much," Zainab said, putting the box in a drawer. Then answering her assistant's curious gaze, "Tomorrow is our twenty-second anniversary, and each year I buy Ali this cologne."

Hmmm, Ali must be her husband.

Hussain was born to be a detective.

After a couple sets of thank-you and you-are-welcome, the man left the room. Hussain was about to do the same when Doctor

Zainab stopped him. "There is something you might need to know, Lieutenant Hussain."

He sat back. She and the nurse exchanged glances, then she looked back at him. "The second man was a Saudi."

"How did you know that?"

"He talked… I talked to him."

Hussain motioned her to continue.

"He didn't say much, his name was Abdul Rahman, we figured out that he was Saudi from the accent."

"That's it."

Zainab nodded.

Hussain wasn't sure what he had hoped for, maybe a tip about where Bin Laden was hiding. That would be good.

"I gave him a strong shot of morphine, it should have kept him in bed till morning, but I guess the medicine was of a bad quality." She made an embarrassed smile. "Most of the new stuff we get is as good as sugar pills."

"What about the other guy? Did he say anything, did you manage to know anything about him?"

"Not really, it was just the face mask that made everyone here suspicious."

"I see."

"There was a long scar on his right cheek, the second guy I mean. He was your height, your weight, maybe, hard to tell."

"No personal belongings?"

She shook her head. "Anyway, this is the file, it's not much as you can see, just one paper for each of them. We don't keep records normally because of the amount of people we receive daily." She made another smile, this one too looked forced and weary. Dr. Zainab fumbled with one of her books. "It's just that the hospital management asked me to file one in case the police came to investigate."

The nurse added, "We asked for good computers to keep track of things and they give us nothing, when it comes to cover their backs they are the best to come up with solutions."

Yeah, yeah, everyone complained about everyone else. Hussain was in no mood to listen to this. Something caught his attention in the report. The bullet that was extracted from Abdul Rahman was caliber 5.5, the one used by an M16 normally. The bullet taken from the masked guy was caliber 6.

"That's weird," he murmured. "Are you sure about what is said about the bullets here?"

"I guess so, we have asked the hospital security to identify the bullets... another idea of our manager."

The nurse's phone started ringing. She excused herself.

"You must be very happy working with a creative person."

Zainab smiled. "Don't get me wrong, Lieutenant, the man is a great guy, very organized. We wouldn't get half of the beds and equipment here without him."

"Of course, I understand."

"But I didn't get what was wrong with the bullets."

"You see." He wouldn't lose anything if he explained. "M16 is used by the US army, we started using them as well, following our big brothers now. So that means the Saudi guy was probably shot by either us or the Americans. It makes sense."

Zainab nodded leaning forward, her elbows on the table.

"What doesn't make much sense is the other one. The American Army uses mostly Beretta, caliber 9, so does most of the Iraqi forces now. However, most guns you find in the street nowadays are caliber 6, which is what the militia use... and of course, half the population."

"So..." Dr. Zainab said, tapping her lower lip with her index finger. "Someone from another militia shot him."

Hussain shrugged. "There are other possibilities, as I said, this gun is very popular, it could be friendly fire, some people shot him defending themselves. But, yeah, I would bet my lunch money on what you said."

And the orange and the cookies my mother gave me.

"He was shot in the back. So it couldn't be self-defense," Dr. Zainab said.

"Yeah, sure, that's right." Hussain felt embarrassed.

Doctors, they wouldn't make it through medical college unless they had a big brain.

"Anyway, we don't have enough information to make a judgment but I still think there is something wrong."

"As with everything else in this country," Zainab said more to herself.

Hussain didn't pry, it looked as if the doctor had something on her mind.

"Yes, unfortunately," he said. "But as long as there are good and honest people we are still fine."

Zainab scoffed. "Yeah, right, that's only if they were not kicked out of their houses while you guys are just watching."

Hussain managed not to role his eyes. He took a deep breath. The truth was he –and everyone else in the force– was fed up with two kinds of people. Ones who thought the Iraqi army, especially the MICF, were too aggressive. And others like Dr. Zainab now, were just the opposite and kept asking for more severe actions.

"We are trying our best." His words, even in his own ears, lacked warmth.

The doctor nodded, not convinced at all. Her gaze moved around the room.

Hussain sensed she want to talk about something. "Is there anything I can help with?"

"In fact there is," she snapped. "I have a brother, living in the Amel district. He was threatened today to leave his house."

She told him what happened to her brother, including her nephew's difficult health situation.

"You have to do something about it. Not only my brother, but it doesn't make sense that people get kicked out of their houses and you are not doing anything."

Yet another case of forced displacement. The sad truth about it, Hussain had discovered, was that nothing could be done. Even if the bad guys were found and arrested, others would come in and terrorize the residents. It started with the western areas of Baghdad, because of people moving from Falouja to the west of Baghdad, the Salafism began with the Shia population and kicked them out. Then lately the Sader Army did the same to the Sunnies in the areas near Sader city in the east.

He gave Zainab his best sympathetic words. That and some promises he knew he wouldn't be able to keep. There was a time when his lack of ability to help caused him pain or even took sleep away. Not anymore.

Not a good sign. His boss, Abdul Hasan, told him on his first day in the force, "With our job, you either die saving people, or live enough to lose your sympathy to their sufferings."

Hmmm, not very encouraging but at least the health plan was good.

He gave his contact details to the doctor and left the hospital.

This small trip helped him to clear his mind. He made his decision. Whether Abdul Hasan was doing the right thing or not, Hussain had to do his duty. Not as a soldier but as a man.

He drove to the headquarters determined to do one thing.

The only right thing they should have done when Mujahid was first arrested.

-34-
Meridian Hotel – Near the Green Zone
June 10th
11:45 AM

Hotels, especially the four- and five-star ones, had that effect of bringing you to another dimension once you stepped inside. The cool and gentle air, the soft music, the plastered smiles, the shiny floors. Everything takes you to that dimension, where you are the honorable guest.

This wasn't what Enas felt when she entered the Meridian hotel in Baghdad.

The lobby was crammed with people of different nationalities, Arabs with Dishdash, Americans wearing sun glasses with tattoos on different parts of their body, Japanese with their sport back-packs and Nikon cameras, taking photos of everyone and everything around them. The lobby wasn't cold despite the two cabinet-sized air conditioners that guarded the entrance of the hotel like two mobster goons. Large and once-golden-colored letters carried the hotel name and logo fixed on the white marble wall. The 'M' was missing and was painted with a yellowish color on the wall that looked both tacky and idiotic.

The reception desk was packed, in front and behind it; most held cell phones, talking to each other and on the phone at the same time.

She didn't take long to get into the hotel, that was good. Her Green-Zone badge granted her fast access rather than the long queue others had to go through to enter the hotel. Security was as good as the White House due to continuous threats against the two hotels – the Meridian and the Sheraton– in the now-famous square where the first statue of Sadam was demolished by the Iraqis with the help of an American tank.

Enas remembered those days as if they were yesterday. How happy everyone was with the Americans coming. All the cheering, even songs were written about George Bush and Tony Blair. Ironically, she was very contemptuous at that time. Hating all Americans. Now, when the zeal had faded and Americans were not so popular anymore, she started seeing the other part of the picture. People like Robert. Honest, knowledgeable, and here to help. Even the soldiers were not that bad. They were more relaxed and cool and… civilized inside the Green Zone. Once out, starting from the checkpoint, they treated everyone as an enemy.

She smiled at one of the ladies at the reception desk. The lady nodded a hello, motioning for her to wait. She was on the phone talking to someone in a what sounded like English, reminding Enas of Abo from The Simpsons TV show.

Enas shrugged and waited. She felt cheerful again. She believed in signs, and all the signs she had encountered since yesterday told her that this was her opportunity. She wasn't sure how. Maybe working with Omar in his company would open some new venues for her. Maybe she would find that he was the right guy for her.

He is the right guy, you stupid. What else do you want?

But money was not everything; it wasn't the solution for all problems. Then she thought about her problems, her new depressing life, her brother and his gangster business… maybe money was the solution for ninety-nine percent only.

"Akder Asaedak?" (Can I help you) a groomed young man with oily hair styled back looking very much like a young Al Pacino in The Godfather approached her. His gaze was everywhere on her body except her eyes.

"I am looking for a man called Saud," she said with a conservative smile.

"Is he a resident here?"

"Not sure, I have a meeting with him here."

He stared at her a tad too; long she thought he was going to comment on her sense of fashion. She wore practical cloths. Okay, practical and fashionable were unlikely to be in one sentence, but this was the way she dressed for work. Today's choice was black jeans and a red shirt.

Al Pacino bent over the reception desk, examining a big record book. Then he said with the pride of someone who just solved world-hunger, "He is one of our guests, whom should I tell him?"

"Tell him Enas." She cleared her throat. "I am here after Omar Dafer Al-Dayni asked me to see him."

He dialed, spoke in almost a whisper, then hang up.

"He is in room 1607 waiting for you." He flashed another smile with a quick wink. "That's floor number sixteen."

A room? Well, many hotel rooms in the Meridian were turned into offices for different multinational companies.

She thanked him and headed to the big glass lifts, almost certain where his gaze was now. Men.

But didn't Omar tell her that his company was in Al-Mansur district?

Why then, was she meeting this Saud guy here, not in the company offices? Unless it was another branch.

The lift door opened. She hesitated then decided that she couldn't quit now. Her destiny, happiness, whatever it was, was very close. Steps away.

She entered the lift. Seconds later she was walking down the corridor of level 16. Most of the room doors where open. She heard people talking, discussing, laughing. Internet modems buzzed and beeped, photo copying machines hummed. Enas felt some relief, it was an office environment. What could go wrong?

The room 1607 door was closed. She knocked. A voice said, "Come in, it's open."

She stepped in. The room was tight and clean, as if the maid just finished. The curtains were closed, allowing only faint daylight in. The floor lamp and the two table lamps were turned on, giving an atmosphere that had nothing to do with work or any professional context.

The place was relatively big. A couch and two love-chairs fitted on one of the corners opposite the bed. Another corner had a big CRT TV –no plasma TV. A door to her left was the bathroom.

"Hala Hala," a man with a red Shmag on his head and white dishdash greeted her. He was the same one she saw Omar talking to in the Green Zone. "My name is Saud, you must be Enas, right?"

Enas nodded. "Hi," she managed to say.

He had that small beard covering only the chin. Saud was of average height and looked like he could lose a pound or two.

"*Hala Hala*, Enas." He flashed a full-wattage smile with all white teeth. Then he gestured for her to enter. She did, "Please have a seat, *Hala Hala*."

Word of the day, *Hala Hala*. Very welcoming.

Enas sat on the couch, putting her purse in her lap, holding it with both hands as if to look as small as possible, protecting herself from some unknown danger. Something didn't feel right.

"You are here for the job, am I correct?"

The job, working with Omar, a chance to have a new, better life.

"Naam" (Yes). Then she thought that she must speak more if she wanted the job. "Yes, Omar told me to meet you." Her stomach rolled. Probably the usual anxiety of the interview.

Saud sat on the chair next to her. Still grinning, his eyes, were X-ray scanning her.

She tucked a wisp of hair behind her ear. "I didn't have enough time to discuss the job details with Omar... so I was wondering--"

"You want to know more about the job, why not ... Sure," Saud said. He stood as if remembering something. "Oh, forgive my bad hospitality, would you care for a drink?"

He stuck his head in the mini-bar.

She told him that water would be fine. Saud raised both eyebrows as if to say are-you-sure. He came back with a small bottle of water with a glass.

"Tell me about yourself, how old are you?" Saud asked, handing her the water.

She answered him, avoiding looking directly in his eyes. Saud sat on the bed.

"And are you... married?"

She shook her head, forcing a smile.

Another question then another. All too personal. He asked if she was engaged, where she lived, her family. Whenever she was about to remind him that it was too personal he shifted to more professional questions.

It didn't last long. Actually, she was surprised when she checked her watch that less than five minutes had passed.

"Now you have asked me a question," he said, standing again and sitting in the chair next to her, repeating the *Hala-Hala* greeting, his eyes doing another full x-ray scan.

Enas suspected that *Hala Hala*, which basically meant hello, had some meaning in the Saudi culture, like a timer where you had to say it before it expired or something.

Either that or the man was sniffing gas.

"You want to know about our business, am I correct, Enas?"

Enas shifted to face him. She managed to say yes, tucking another wisp of hair. Her stomach rolled again.

"We are the biggest oil-export company in Iraq and the region. Our business is basically buying refined oil from Saudi Arabia and selling it to all countries in the region."

"Oil?" Hadn't Omar told her that he worked in construction?

"Yes, we have big contracts to export refined oil to countries like Iraq, Sudan, Syria, Afghanistan, and other countries."

"But all those countries do have oil. Why would they want to buy from others?"

Saud chuckled, he said stroking his small black beard as if a pet, "Enas, honey, those countries have oil, yes, but a pure oil, they just sell it and buy the refined oil from different places."

Enas nodded. She remembered the never-ending discussion about the gasoline crises in Iraq. The authorities were saying they were trying to buy more gas from Saudi.

And did Saud just call her 'honey?'

"So your company doesn't work in construction, because I am sure I heard Omar--"

"Come on, construction, oil, what's the difference, it's all money… right, good money."

Enas shrugged, trying a smiling. "Guess so."

Saud moved to the couch next to her. Enas recoiled to the corner while he kept talking.

"Enas, honey, this country is a gold mine. Anyway, the job is simple, I need you to organize my paperwork. I need someone here to arrange my bookings, and to manage the office here. And to help me with the personal things." His tone was slower now, his accent thicker. "You understand right, I can see you will do good."

A cold shiver crept up the back of her neck.

"And from what you told me, your experience is quite good."

"Yeah, I mean I have good experience with office management. But I am not sure I follow, you need a PA right?"

Saud frowned. "What is a PA?"

"Personal Assistant."

"Oh yeah, that, yes, this is what I need, a personal assistant. Your basic salary will be two thousand five hundred dollars."

"What!" She couldn't hold herself. Such a salary was too much, way too much. She was on eight hundred now, which was more than enough to support a medium family. And the salary was so high because of her work in the Green Zone and all the risk.

Saud raised his index finger, still grinning. "This is only the basic salary."

She tried not to salivate. He moved a tad closer.

"There will be bonuses, depends on your... Um... dedication and good work. You know what I mean, honey, don't you?"

What was with the honey thing? And she didn't like the way he was looking at her.

"So what do you say?"

She stared at the floor, covered with a bronzed-color carpet that was good only to hide stains. Enas didn't need to do complex math to know that with such salary, forgo the bonuses, she could buy a small house of her own after one year. Or probably buy a car, something she desperately needed to get rid of the inconvenience of the taxis or public transportation. Something with good air conditioning to save her on days like yesterday. Then she remembered Omar and yesterday's unplanned meeting. That brought her here. Enas knew she should feel grateful to him. But there was something more, maybe she didn't have the courage to admit it.

Saud chuckled, amused by her lack of words. "When do you want to start?"

Start... she tried picture herself working with Saud and then discovered that she still didn't know many details. Where was the company's location? Who else was working there? And most importantly, what did this have to do with Omar?

With a salary like this, why do you care about Omar, you foolish girl? But she couldn't just dismiss the question.

"I don't know," she answered, still looking at the floor. Then she turned to face him. "Am I accepted?" He was still examining her. She felt another shiver. Her gaze went immediately back to the floor.

"Of course you are, a gorgeous and lovely girl like you. How can I turn you down. And I am sure we will get along. And that you will take care of me and please me. What do you think?"

His words didn't sounded right. The strange tone, the hints.

His hand reached behind her head. It didn't touch her but it didn't make her comfortable either. He was too close.

"And what is Omar's role in the company?

"Omar?" He nearly scowled, then burst into a laugh like someone getting a joke. "No, no... Omar has nothing to do with this." He leaned closer to her. "It's gonna be me and you, darling, just me and you. And I will give you more money than you could imagine. And if you are really good, and take care of me, I will even take you with me in my travels. Have you seen Egypt, Morocco, Europe?"

She tried to shake her head, but her muscles were so stiff she couldn't. She could feel his breath now on her. She shivered again. Saud went on speaking about the travel and how nice it was and then he held her hand. His hand was warm, so warm and sweaty. She instinctively pulled her hand away.

And then Enas understood everything. Her heart sank. Omar didn't want her to work with him. Worse, he wasn't even looking at her the way she thought... or wished he was. Omar just gave her away to this man ... this salivating dog.

Saud's hands went to her hair now, gently touching. She stiffened. He was still chattering about how good it would be for her, money, travel. His voice sounded far away. The only thing she could hear was her heart beating. It might be anger. Fear. Or some other primitive instinct. Something that only kicked in when a woman was about to protect her... Honor? She looked at the room. The closed curtains, the faint lighting, the bed, the way he was sitting now, close, surrounding and touching her.

Shit.

Saud's hand touched her neck. He must have interpreted her silence as an acceptance. She moved her head away as rage consumed her.

"Oh, a tough girl." He chuckled. "Or is that because I was rushing things... do you want the first salary now, honey."

"Go away!" she screamed, standing up and facing him.

"Calm down, sweetie, calm down." He reached for her hand. "Although I must say your face is even prettier when you are mad."

"Don't touch me." Her voice was a grunt. "Do you understand?"

She had to leave. And fast. But she couldn't, she wanted to avenge her dignity, she wanted to show him, Omar, and whoever was in this plot against her that she wasn't for sale.

She was consumed with anger and disappointment. A painful mix. "You filthy scumbag, you think you can buy any woman with your money. Well, here is a newsflash for you, some are not for sale."

He stood up, eye bulging. The veins in his face and neck popped out. "Shut up, you whore!" His voice was louder than she expected.

"You think I don't know your little game, you come to my room, you sat here wiggling and giggling, showing me your goods."

"I ... I didn't ... you..." Words betrayed her, anger. Sometimes Enas wished she was a man. Punching Saud now would feel like taking a cold drink on a summer day.

"You don't think I know what you are trying to do here?" Saud scowled. "Trying to get more money out of my pocket." He grabbed her wrist. "I buy and sell a dozen like you in one day."

She slapped him.

He stepped back, letting go of her hand. He looked left and right, his hand on his reddened cheek. They were alone. "How dare you?" The angry animal surfaced again, angrier.

"Leave me alone!" Enas shouted, stepping back. She wanted to cry for help, but her dignity wouldn't let her. Who would hear her, anyway.

And before she knew it, she felt a slap, so strong that she found herself on the bed. It hurt. It wasn't an emotional thing, wasn't a pain in her dignity, just plain physical pain. Neither the surge of the adrenaline, nor her fear or anger helped ease the pain. She could still feel his fingers to her cheek. Enas put her hand where he hit her, holding back a tear. She called him names. Her voice trailing and choked with tears. She might have spat on him.

Saud circled around the bed, and whipped her with the thick black rope on top of his head cover, the eqal.

The first hit was on her thigh. Pain shot through her. Nausea. He whipped again. Enas rolled on the bed to avoid the slashes, but the second was on her shoulder. She saw stars. She kicked relentlessly. Her foot hit something solid, his leg. He cried, stumbling on top of her.

The good news was he couldn't beat her with his eqal anymore. But he was on top of her now. His hands everywhere on her. Nausea was back, worse than ever. She tried to do something, to push him away. He was too heavy.

"Let me go!" she screamed, but it came weak, muffled by his hands on her chest and mouth.

"You bitch."

His spitting, breath, and more were all on her.

Another hit, another slap, it didn't hurt anymore. Good. She hit him back, not sure where but he was screaming in pain.

It got him away, a tad. She kicked him with both her legs and rolled on the bed, trying to escape his grip. He caught her shirt. A tearing sound. Another back kick and she was completely free.

She sprinted out of the bed, but she was on the wrong side not facing the door. Saud stood on top of the bed, or maybe he was on his knees, hard to tell with the dishdash. He spread his hands like a goalkeeper preparing for a penalty.

He wouldn't let her out, she could see it in his eyes. The mad look, something had snapped inside his head.

In her peripheral vision she saw something on the bedside table. She snapped it and threw it at Saud. The bedphone hit him on the chest. Saud covered his face with the hands, which made him lose balance and crumble on the bed.

Enas sprinted to the door. Saud cursed and yelled behind her.

Enas ran through the corridors, room doors were still open. She could still hear the laughing, discussion and the internet modems buzzing. She reached the lift area. Her shaking hand pressed the down arrow repeatedly. She turned toward the corridor. Her heavy breathing made everything look as if jumping up and down. Her eyes were wet and teary. But no one followed her.

Had she killed him? No way, she didn't hit him hard enough to cause any serious damage.

The elevator dinged. The doors opened. It was empty. She rushed in, pressing fast on the close button. The doors started closing. She watched them with her heart thudding like a drum. In the movies, the bad guys always managed to catch the heroin at this moment. She could see the bloody hand reaching to stop the doors from closing at the final second.

But nothing happened. The doors closed. The lift started moving, the small yellow light danced from one number to another.

The lift stopped abruptly at the sixth floor. Enas' heart leapt, fear anew. Two Americans, holding cameras with lenses the size of small canons stepped in. The doors closed again. One of the Americans said something like hello. Enas just stared at him, eyes wide, still unable to control her breath or shaking hands.

The two men glanced at each other and then at her, stepping away as if she had a contagious disease. The glass lift had no mirrors, but she caught a reflection of herself on the glass. She covered her mouth with her hand so that she didn't cry. Unable to recognize herself. Her shirt was torn, reveling her left shoulder and part of her body. Her hair was like those cartoons when an explosion blasts someone. But the worst part was her face, pink bruises were all over it. She looked like hell.

Once the elevator door opened, she hurried up to the exit doors. Even in the street she kept looking back, waiting for someone to follow her, someone to stop her, for Saud to appear. Nothing. And she wasn't sure if that was good or bad. She looked for a taxi and spotted one. There was only one thing in her mind.

Home.

The only place where she could feel safe again.

-35-
Tawheed Mosque – Al Amel District
June 10th
12:05 PM

Abdul Rahman stood in the line ready for prayers.

It was the Duhur prayers, they were doing it in Jamaa, which meant praying in group after the Emam, a person leading the group.

Something didn't feel right. Abdul Rahman always found a solitude in the prayers. In those five or six minutes he would forget about everything in the world expect for God. For five minutes he had a chance to remember what he was doing in life.

Praying was the reason.

Mankind was created to worship God. Allah. Through this prayer and other duties. Until man could reach, through his worship, the status of mind and body that God created him for.

To cleanse his thoughts from evil.

His heart from hatred.

And to free himself from worshiping others.

Worshiping the evil inside him, greed, money.

And to help his brothers to reach the perfect society where no one suffered. Where everyone loved everyone else.

This was what brought Abdul Rahman to Islam. He was a Muslim by birth, but his parents didn't raise him to pray or to follow any of Islam's teachings. They just left him alone. And he spent a good part of his young life like any other adolescent in the world.

A slave to his desires.

Until he started listening to the lectures about Islam. He liked it. It gave his life meaning. And it was all about helping others. Working with other brothers and sisters to ease the pain of people around the world. So what happened to him? For the caring young man to turn into this life-taking mercenary. He used to feel God watching him. Not only in prayers but all the time.

The caring and merciful God. Protecting him, guiding him.

And now?

He wasn't sure. Things changed. He wanted to move from the ordinary Muslim who tried to ease the pain, to the one who fought the evil that caused the pain.

Two years ago his friends in college recommended special classes for him. Nothing to worry about, taking more classes about Islam in the college, from a professor with recommendations and certifications that filled his wall. What possibly could go wrong? The lectures were a tad harsher than his normal taste. But he got used to it. He got used to the fact that he should do more. The fact that fighting evil was more important than helping the good. That who didn't agree with them was a misguided person who needed to be brought back to the guided-way.

Then he joined another group at another mosque. And with each group the tune was harsher. Not much, it didn't repulse him, but he started wondering if he was doing the right thing. They told him that skeptical thoughts are of the devil. And he needed to fight them.

He was told that God would grant heaven and afterlife happiness for those who obeyed what the sheikhs said. After all, all their teachings were from the grand books of Islam and the Quran. They were trying to make his life closer to that of the prophets.

So he should be on the right path.

Still something was amiss.

His heart was supposed to be full of love and yet all he knew, all he felt was hatred. Everyone was the enemy. But this was understandable. They kept telling him that. He had done a lot of bad deeds in his old days. Even now.

Redemption was what he needed. Redemption of giving one's life for the higher cause. For Jihad.

Was this the answer to his hesitation?

To kill the enemies and die in the process.

They kept telling him to look into his heart and he would find God. But all that he could find were doubts, suspicions, and darkness.

The prayer was over. Another tasteless prayer. Another day of disappointment. A day when the prayers were no longer his connection to God. A day when it was dark even in mid-day, when he felt alone even when surrounded by people, when he looked at the faces around him and saw no kind smiles or a caring looks.

Abdul Rahman glanced at Amjad. "Do you think we will have a chance to be martyrs today?" He tried to make the question casual, but even his ears could hear the trepidation in his voice.

"I don't know." Then after a beat. "I just can't wait to get even with those tomb worshipers."

Abdul Rahman nodded. "But what if some Muslims die or get seriously hurt in the process?"

"I told you before," Amjad nearly scowled, "this is allowed in Iraq war, many sheikhs had given their judgment in the matter and they said if a good person died as a casualty in Jihad, he will go to heaven. Bad people will go to hell. Simple, no brainer." Amjad knocked on his head.

No-brainer, like many other things.

Abdul Rahman always liked the fact that the Muslim had to follow the teaching of the clergy and whatever went wrong was not his fault. Not all Islam schools agreed with this. Some gave the individual a crucial role in selecting whom to follow and what order to follow, to question and to debate.

Those were the ones misguided by Satan.

Two young men in the row in front of him were laughing. They were younger than him, probably sixteen or seventeen. One was showing his friend a music clip on his cellphone. Abdul Rahman could hear the noise they called music. He sighed. No one around him believed in Islam's real teachings anymore. Did they believe in life after death? If so, why waste their time? Why not utilize every single moment to be a better person. Like he was doing. He looked at the two guys again. One nudged his friend's shoulder, the other did likewise. More laughing. Abdul Rahman couldn't remember the last time he felt happy and relaxed.

"So why don't you ask Luay to give you the explosive belt?" he asked Amjad.

Amjad tilted his head, rubbing the back of it. "Yeah, maybe... good idea... Inshalla... everything is by God's will."

Sheikh Abu Ayob approached with a wide grin. He was the one who led the Jamaa prayer. People started leaving the mosque and he had time for them now.

"How are my two heroes?"

"Um..." He tried to think of something to say. He didn't want to say "fine" because he wasn't. He needed to talk to the Sheikh, to ask him his advice.

"Good, good I can see that you are both doing well."

Amjad said something like Alhamdulilah (thanks to God).

Abu Ayob grin widened. "Well, I have something for you, both of you."

The Sheikh looked left and right. No one was in the mosque except for two men with long beards. The same guys he saw this morning. Part of the group, he guessed.

Abu Ayob got something out of his pocket. No way. It couldn't be. They shouldn't be doing this. Especially not in a mosque.

The small plastic bag held a white powder.

"What is this?" Amjad asked.

"Don't ask, my brother," Abu Ayob said with the disappointment of a teacher hearing his best student make a mistake in the multiplication table. He shook his head, looking Amjad in the eye. "Put your trust in God." Then he took Amjad's hands and put a sprinkle of the white powder on his wrist. "I am giving this to you because I know you will need it," Abu Ayob said in ceremonial way. "Sniff this now."

Amjad shrugged and sniffed.

Abdul Rahman watched while his new brother was getting high in the mosque, the Sheikh watching him.

He would be next.

-36-
MICF Headquarters –Karada District
June 10th
12:25 PM

"I need your help," he told Shaker.

He never thought he would need his help, but if Abdul Hasan learned anything from his five decades, it was that life would keep finding ways to surprise you, and teach you.

They were sitting in his office on the second floor. Alone. Ironic enough, from all the five officers working for him, he could only trust Shaker for this matter. Shaker, the most reckless officer in his team, wasn't a bad man. Abdul Hasan could tell that. But Shaker too had problems with authority, among other things.

Abdul Hasan watched the young lieutenant long enough he could almost touch that aura of violence and anger surrounding him, despite Shaker's attempts to hide it behind his sarcasm and careless behavior.

"Me?" Shaker tilted his head like a dog that couldn't understand what his master was asking. "Sure thing, Sir. I would be glad to help, Sir."

He didn't need a mirror to know how he looked. His unshaven beard, red eyes, untidy cloths from yesterday, and God-knew-what other zombie features on his face.

But appearances were the last thing to occupy Abdul Hasan's mind. He'd spent the last three hours sitting here, in his office, holding his mobile, urging it to ring. Well, that and he wanted to make sure the damn device had coverage. He didn't know how to start; hell, he didn't even know what to do yet.

"I need you to do one thing for me."

It wasn't an order.

The Captain still remembered his decision more than ten years ago. When he refused to join the army again as a desperate attempt to save his brother. Abdul Hasan had seen a lot in the eight years of the Iraq war against Iran. More than a human could tolerate. He had seen young men die; read, he ordered young men to die. He buried Iranian soldiers alive after one battle following his general's orders.

He followed orders that brought nothing but destruction to other human beings. Iraqis and Iranians. The keyword here is followed, but what difference would that make? So going back to another war was something he couldn't do. He couldn't live with the ramifications of another order that could take the lives of more soldiers. Isn't that what his brother did after all? He couldn't relay the orders to execute a bunch of Kuwaitis. Iraqis, Kuwaitis, or Iranians, the tragedy was the same.

Going back to war would be much more horrible than leaving his brother to his fate. Or so he thought.

Another thing that he learned from life.

That he was wrong.

"The kidnappers called me half an hour ago."

Shaker said something. Abdul Hasan didn't pay much attention to him, already lost in his thoughts.

"It was another one, not the same guy who called me this morning."

Shaker raised both eyebrows. "This morning?"

Abdul Hasan filled him in about the first call.

"So why do you think this one was another man?"

"The first one had an Egyptian accent. The second one was Iraqi."

Shaker nodded with a thoughtful "hmmm."

In other parts of the world, where real police were equipped with real police gismos like voice identifications and super computers with enormous database of every single scumbag on the planet, in those places kidnappers used voice changers and untraceable cell phones. In Iraq, there was nothing like that. Abdul Hasan had even added the number of the kidnapper (yes they were using the same cell phone) to his phone contact list. Maybe after all this finished he could text them some seasonal greetings from time to time.

"He told me to go to Mansur district, The Rowad intersection." He could still hear the sound in his ears, something like an endless, painful echo. "I asked him to prove that my son was alive... they hung up."

"Do you think the... um... car will be there?"

The car.

Even Shaker was thinking the same now, he could hear it in his voice, it had to be a bombed car. They were not asking him to drive some kids to school or to bring their clothes from the laundry.

Abdul Hasan was about to shrug but he couldn't pull it off. "I don't know. But what I need you to do is to take the man you have arrested, Mujahid or whatever his name, with you and help me get my son back."

Shaker shifted back in his chair. "Mujahid?"

"Yes, I will give you a place where my son might be held, they will try to make an exchange, my son for … you know…" Saying it was harder than he thought. "Driving their car to the specified destination."

"I am not sure I follow, sir." Shaker frowned, he rubbed his face with his enormous hands. "What makes you think they will give you the place where your son is… I mean they could just…"

Their gazes locked for a second. He could see the question in Shaker's eyes: Are you going to do it?

After the execution of his brother and then sending him to Abu Gurayb prison, everyone looked at him as a hero. Or a mad man. Abdul Hasan saw the awe in the faces of the inmates, even the guards which didn't change the way they treated him, no double standards or special treatment in Abu Gurayb, everyone had to suffer– even when he told them why he was sent to prison after years of serving in the army as a high-ranking officer. But the truth was slightly different. He did believe that he made the right decision, at least in the beginning. But there was no way in hell he could anticipate all the pain that would follow. The slim chance to help his brother wouldn't be worth risking going back to the army and being responsible for another mass-murder.

But Abdul Hasan didn't, couldn't anticipate other things.

Things like how he was going to answer his mother's continuous pleading to save her younger son. Or how to answer his brother's little children when they asked him why their father didn't come back from his travels. How to look those angels in the eyes and lie at them.

But that wasn't all.

The worst was yet to come.

When Dafer Al-Dayni, the Baath inspector at that time, advised him to enlist in the army again and that might help his brother's case, Abdul Hasan didn't think for once that not doing that would initiate another series of actions. Someone had communicated this to Sadam –or one of the blood-thirsty royal-family members– and soon after his brother's execution, Abdul Hasan was sent to jail with charges of… well, there were no charges really, not official ones, but who needed them in the great Iraq of Sadam?

The risk of going to jail wasn't going to change his mind, but again Abdul Hasan couldn't see it coming. In every corner of the endless sea of gray concrete, in every minute of his long nights in the cell… his brother was there.

He knew he was dead. He knew that his little brother with his loud laugh and kind spirit was rotting in some pit in the secret-service buildings. He knew it was all hallucinations of his tormented soul. He couldn't shun him away. Maybe he didn't want to. He could see him standing in front of him. He wasn't talking, he wasn't even reproaching him. He was actually smiling at him. That knowing, and understanding smile.

They were raised the same way. Both to be soldiers. Like their father. And the way Sadam and his Baath gang mutilated the Iraqi army from the best army in the region to a collection of miserable mercenary groups changed nothing of the way they looked to the army.

Abdul Hasan knew in his heart that his brother would understand his decision. That he wasn't thwarted by what he'd done. He actually even suspected that his brother was there just to lessen his pain.

It somehow made it even worse.

He kept asking himself, was there anything he could have done to help his brother? Crazy scenarios popped into his mind every night. Each with different possibilities and sometimes Mission-Impossible-like complications. At the end of the day, he wasn't able to convince himself that he could have done nothing.

He couldn't help his brother and nothing in the world would make him feel better, not what his wife was telling him, not what the inmates were telling him, and not even what his brother's smile and kind eyes were saying.

Whatever the case, the ghosts from the past were haunting him again.

For what he was about to do today.

He thought about driving this car again. Would he really do it? To be responsible for killing sixty, seventy, maybe even eighty innocents? To help the terrorists in their plans? And betray everything he believed in and was trusted for? But then did he have the courage to send his own son to death?

If he survived the guilt of his brother's death, he wouldn't, couldn't do it with his son. When it came to protecting your off-spring, you don't think. You simply act. Instinctively. You don't think about whether to jump in front of a speeding truck to protect your child and whether your sacrifice would be meaningful or not. You just do it. As if humans were hardwired this way to save them from the painful thinking process of weighing the different options, while the result couldn't be anything different.

You had to protect your children even if that meant you lost your own life, check that, even if you knew that you couldn't do anything really.

Abdul Hasan could understand that now.

He was about to drive this car, to whatever point they wanted, even for exchange of the slightest hope that this could help his son.

He just wished, hoped, prayed that he wouldn't live to regret his decision.

"I am still working on a plan," he said in his low and calm voice. "What I need from you is to help me by getting ready with some force."

"And Mujahid?"

"Keep him with you. He knows a lot about all their places, and their methods, try to use him to your advantage."

He stopped, listening to what he just said. Why didn't he push more on the suspect to get some useful information from him that might save some lives?

But the answer was in front of him.

Just a chance to save his son.

"Do you think he will cooperate?" Shaker did the head tilt again.

"He will if you make him believe that his life is on the line. Let him see that you are really about to kill him if he doesn't help you and he will do what you want."

Shaker nodded, a slight smile parted his thick lips. "Okay, in that case," Shaker stood, "let me go back to him to prepare him for some cooperation."

Abdul Hasan didn't want to pry into Shaker's meaning. Let him do what he could. Abdul Hasan had other things to worry about.

He needed to go to the Rowad intersection to get the car. The caller told him to be there as soon as possible.

He had to leave now.

What a considerate gesture from the kidnappers, to allow for some delays for traffic so they didn't give him a time, just, "Be there as soon as possible." Another reason for him to send them seasonal greetings later on.

If he were to survive the day. Odds were good that the next few hours would be his last on this planet.

He shivered.

His office was piled with papers of different cases he was working on.

It would be someone else's problem.

He would not come here again.

His wife, his friends, his other kids.

He thought about calling his wife to say goodbye.

But the idea looked very TV-like. The last thing he wanted now was more melodrama.

The only thing he wanted to do was to jump in front of the speeding truck to save his son's life.

Abdul Hasan closed the door to his office. Shouting came from downstairs.

"What's going on?" he asked one of the soldiers who was hurrying toward him.

The man took several seconds to catch up, eyes wide, hand pointing at the general direction of the main entrance. "Sir... they ... the Americans... they are here... they want ... the terrorist we captured... yesterday..."

Another primitive instinct kicked over. Anger, fear, maybe both. He sprinted toward the shouting.

They were at the area where the terrorist was detained. To one side stood Shaker with other soldiers and officers surrounding the suspect who was still cuffed.

On the other side stood a hulking ruddy man with five other soldiers. All tall, all armed from top to toe. The two groups facing each other, the tension in the air, hands on the guns' holsters ready to fire at the slightest move.

Very intense and very western-movie style.

"What's going on!" Abdul Hasan shouted in the best English he could muster under the circumstances.

The ruddy man turned toward him glaring, then grinned, recognizing his rank. "Captain, this man is coming with us." The ruddy man pointed to the suspect with his chin. "He is accused of attacking an American convoy and thus we have the right to investigate him first."

The same old story. According to the protocol between the coalition and Iraqi forces, if a suspect was detained in an Iraqi facility and was suspected of assaulting coalition forces, they could interrogate him first.

Somehow, almost none of the terrorists returned back to the Iraqi forces.

The problem was so common that even some real terrorists started playing this game. Admitting attacking American forces and when interrogated, the Americans found him clear (as far as they were concerned), and there was a good chance that he got released, playing the police-brutality card.

"You sure he wasn't the one who killed JF Kennedy," Abdul Hasan scoffed.

"Good one." The ruddy man chuckled. "But we are still taking him."

"You do not represent the coalition forces, you are merely a hired gun," Abdul Hasan fired back. Closer to the man now, he could read his badge. Richard Barn. The black symbol on his right arm indicated that he was working for Heavy Waters, the biggest security contractor in Baghdad.

"So?" Richard said. Their eyes met. Richard beamed, confident he could take the prisoner. They both knew it. All he needed was to talk to someone who would talk to Abdul Hasan's boss, or his boss's boss and force them to release the terrorist.

But Abdul Hasan wasn't about to give up easily on this one. There was a lot at stake.

Shaker snapped his gun and pointed it at Richard's forehead.

Richard looked at Abdul Hasan, raising his red eyebrows as if saying "Are you really up to it?" Then he grabbed Shaker's gun hand and twisted it upward in a way his wrist never meant to move. Richard spun away from the line of fire. Shaker was on his knees, his face red from either pain or embarrassment. Richard was on top of him, putting his own gun to Shaker's forehead.

"I am not here to play, kid," Richard said too loudly for just Shaker. "But if you want to play I'm game."

Their eyes met again.

This time Abdul Hasan didn't hold the look.

"Stop it!" No point endangering other lives. "Take your man and leave now."

Shaker grimaced, looking at Abdul Hasan. He was trying to help, it just backfired.

Two Heavy Water personnel stepped forward and took the terrorist, who grinned, extending his arms toward Abdul Hasan.

"Un-cuff him," he ordered. He didn't need to look at their faces to see how low their morale was.

For the first time, he saw Shaker shrinking. He thought about saying something but then it wasn't the time or place so he just looked away.

Another Heavy Water soldier cuffed the terrorist again. He was only one foot from him. They both exchanged looks. The terrorist smiled, he wasn't glaring at Abdul Hasan, not threatening, it was more of curiosity, as if looking at a painting he couldn't understand.

The terrorist had refused to give them his name, only insisting that he wasn't Mujahid. It didn't matter now. As a matter of fact, Abdul Hasan wished he wouldn't come to know that the man they'd been detaining for over eighteen hours was Mujahid and they hadn't managed to get any useful information from him. He didn't worry about the implications of such failure on his career, it's just he couldn't be responsible for any more killings. The words of the Syrian young terrorist echoed in Abdul Hasan mind. Mujahid was a psychopath who enjoyed knowing his victims before killing them.

He looked at the terrorist again, his eyes, the curiosity, even a regret, as if sorry he didn't stay long enough to know Abdul Hasan better.

"Mujahid," Abdul Hasan whispered.

The terrorist arched an eyebrow, his smile widened. Then despite the two men grabbing him he leaned forward, close enough to whisper to Abdul Hasan, "Do what you have been told, or I swear to God you will wish the reaper got to your son before I get to him."

-37-
MICF Headquarters –Karada District
June 10th
12:40 PM

"What's going on?" Hussain asked, unable not to notice the gloom on everyone's face. No one gave him an answer, just an angry murmuring, head shaking, or a collection of invented Iraqi swear words.

From the bits and pieces he heard, something bad had happened. It didn't take him long to put it all together.

They'd lost the terrorist.

This, and the entire Iraqi forces got another slap of reality today, reminding them that they were still not the ones who called the shots in their own country.

What disturbed him was another thought. That his captain might be involved in releasing the terrorist somehow. After all, nothing he did made a lot of sense.

Then he saw Abdul Hasan in the small parking lot in front of the headquarters.

The unruffled and calm man, the man who just seeing him walking was enough to give confidence that the Iraqi Army still had pride, still had what it took to take control, this man was walking with his head lowered. His back bent, like a boxer who just lost ten rounds in his lifetime match.

"Sir!" Hussain cried.

Abduul Hasan turned, a tad too slow to be interested in anything.

Hussain scurried to reach the Captain. "Is there any news about your son?"

How broken the man was.

Abdul Hasan sighed and shook his head. He then opened his white Camry door and was about to step in before he turned toward Hussain as if remembering something. "Hussain, I have noticed something odd today," he said, as if reciting a dream; not much like Abdul Hasan. "Yesterday a man called Ayad Al Mousawi came here to report a terrorist gang in his neighborhood. It wasn't much, pretty much like dozens of other reports we have nowadays about Al-Qaeda gangs threatening Christians and Shia, and we are struggling to do anything about it. Anyway," Abdul Hasan made a dismissal motion in his hand, "what I remember well, which was the odd thing, is that Ayad told me that one of the gangsters had threatened the owner of the house."

Abdul Hasan paused, rubbing his unshaven beard, frowning, as if embarrassed how long it grew. "What he told him, and these were the exact words: If you talk about that again you will pray to God that the reaper gets to your family before I do."

"Looked to me like another gory psychopath." Why was this important?

Abdul Hasan nodded.

Two ambulances passed them in the street. The ominous sound of the sirens rose up, forcing both of them to hold for a moment.

Before the two sirens faded away, repeated gunfire sounded from the distance.

Just a normal day in the new Baghdad.

"I beg your pardon, sir, but what has this to do with–"

"They are the same words he used," Abdul Hasan said in his calm voice, watching the two ambulances drive away. "He just told me something similar."

Mujahid.

But why was Mujahid threatening Abdul Hasan, unless...

"He told me he was going to kill my son, but he used the same words. You understand what this means, don't you?"

Hussain did. Part of their training was about forensic evidence. He still remembered the part about linguistic forensics. Recent studies suggested that people tended to use the same words or phrases in their oral or written communications. Whether in a love letter or office memo, similar words and writing structure reflect the person's way of thinking, culture, personal taste, which collectively form some kind of unique style that can almost be a match to a particular person or at least a very small group of people.

The American instructor -or was he British? Hussain couldn't be sure. For him, all white and blonds are Americans– told them about cases when the police in the United States managed to arrest a kidnapper by matching the linguistic style in the ransom note with that in a post card he previously wrote to the same family as a friend.

"But I don't understand what Mujahid has to do with your son's kidnapping?"

"Maybe nothing," Abdul Hasan admitted, sitting in his car and lowering the side window to talk. "But this is the only clue I have left, Hussain."

The Captain was always a father figure for everyone who worked for him. It wasn't only his kindness, the man also managed to surround himself with an aura of respect and awe. He was the most senior officer and perhaps the only one who had seen a real war; everything in the man spoke of generations of military training. He was the kind of man, the kind of commander, to whom soldiers would look during battle and follow his orders no matter what.

But now, Hussain could only see the friend, the father, not the commander asking for help.

He might be wrong. Perhaps he just wanted to think this way to prepare himself for the next mission. Helping the man, not the officer.

"I need you to go alone, Hussain, undercover if you can, find me this Ayad. I have a hunch that the terrorist group he was talking about yesterday had something to do with my son."

Abdul Hasan looked at his watch then back at him. "I know I sound crazy but really this is the only thread I have."

Hussain wanted to say something like "Yes Sir," or even more intimate like "I will search for your son like he was my own son," but it all sounded very cliché or very ass-kissing.

The Captain drove away. Hussain didn't even ask him where he was going. He wasn't sure he wanted to know. He didn't ask him what really happened with Mujahid and why he didn't let them interrogate him.

Was his boss... what was the phrase? Emotionally compromised? Hussain didn't really know what it meant exactly. One of the terms those wise-ass instructors kept repeating. How could a soldier, no, an officer, be emotionally compromised. A man who dealt with life-and-death decisions all the time could not be compromised, not emotionally anyway. This work teaches you to compartmentalize, to live a different personality, one that could look at children's burned bodies after a bombing near to their school and the only thing you worry about is how to secure the location and move the wounded to hospital. You think with your mind and teach your heart to cave. You leave the human at home, and at work, you put on the mask, the other person, the machine. Because it's the only way you could look at a six-year-old child crying in pain and you don't go and set fire in the nearby Salfism mosque where the terrorists responsible for the bomb were hiding. The only way you could ever put human rights and interrogating a terrorist in one sentence.

This work had taught Hussain how to live with those two personalities. But seeing his Captain today, well, Hussain saw how a soldier could be emotionally compromised. He saw what would happen if that thin compartment fell apart. When the human cannot hide behind the facade of the machine.

He wanted to help Abdul Hasan. But he didn't have the courage. Today among all days, he never wanted a work day to be shorter, safer, so that he could go home to the biggest step of his life.

He also had this worrying feeling, something that those wise-ass instructors might describe as happiness anxiety. When you are so happy and everything is good around you, too good. Something doesn't sound or look like your normal miserable luck. So you keep walking on your toes, unable to hop or dance happily because something keeps whispering that you are walking on thin ice, that it will soon shatter to reveal the same old shit again.

Hussain wasn't the most optimistic man in the world.

Despite all of his feelings, his suspicions, and even his fears, he couldn't turn his back on his Captain.

Love to others what you love for yourself.

Maybe, or maybe he just couldn't get the image of the now-broken man from his head.

He looked at the digital clock in his cell phone. Not yet one in the afternoon. So he still had time to help his Captain and go back home to go to Sarah's house with his mother.

But first he had a couple of things to do. So he headed back to the office with some sort of plan materializing in his head.

Minutes later, a civilian sedan car carrying Hussain in civilian clothes headed towards the address mentioned in the report filed by Ayad yesterday.

-38-
Al Amel District
June 10th
12:55 PM

Six Machine guns.
Four hand grenades.
An explosive belt with cell phone detonator.
Two, just to be on the safe side.
One RPG launcher.
And ammo, lots of ammo.

That was Luay's grocery list. Everything had gone well so far. He had to pay more than he had budgeted. The dealer told him that prices had increased because of the demand. He didn't have time to negotiate or argue. Maybe he should have. Those arms dealers are the worst type of parasites ever. Buying the old army's stolen weapons at half the real price and selling them at double the price.

A rip off.

They should be put in jail for this. Yeah, right.

Anyway, what mattered was that he finished his shopping, loaded the car with the weapons, and was heading to the safe house now. Everything was ready from his side. He just needed Mujahid released to get the bombed car.

As if on cue, his cell phone rang. It was Dafer.

"Luay, I have very good news for you."

"I could use some good news now," Luay said, the traffic was slower than usual in Al-Amel main street.

"I met Saud," Dafer said, as if this alone was an achievement. "And you know what he told me?"

Luay wasn't in the mood now to play a guessing game. "Mujahid is out."

"Yeah, how did you know?"

Luay shook his head. "Dafer, unless Sharon Stone joined your party, I cannot imagine what other good news you could bring me."

"Oh, shut up. What's it with you and Sharon Stone anyway?"

"Have you seen her last movie?"

"Huh?" Dafer said. "No, I am not sure. Did you?"

"Well, not really, but I have seen the movie trailer. She is hot. I am telling you, Dafer, she is so fucking hot she could trigger a bombed car if she just walked by it."

"I don't know. I thought she was getting old."

Luay held the cellphone in front of him, glaring at it. Old, he said. He wished he could throw the cellphone and Dafer from the window now.

The traffic was crawling like a wounded soldier. This wasn't good.

"What do you want, Dafer?"

"Mujahid is released, you are right but this is not the only good news I have for you."

Fucking old, he said. He was about to tell Dafer to put on his telescope-like magnifying glasses next time he watched TV, but now wasn't the time.

"What else?"

"Saud told me that he met a guy called Richard Barn from this mercenary company—"

"Heavy Waters."

"Yeah, those, anyway, the man and Saud go long back when Saud was working as… you know… in Afghanistan, anyway, I think we can make use of the man."

Luay switched the cell phone from one ear to the other. The traffic still not moving. "*Kayf?*" (How.)

"You see, I was telling Saud that finding this Abdul Rahman for him was a very hard job. It was like finding a needle in a farm."

"Haystack you mean."

"Yeah, right, finding a haystack in a farm, so he should give us something more than just Mujahid."

Sharon Stone?

"So you know what Saud told me?" Dafer added, so excited Luay feared that the man was going to wet himself. "Richard Barn was having a problem with G-Plans, you know G-Plans, don't you?"

"Sure." He never heard the name. The car in front of him moved a few steps, then the red brake light lit again. Luay moved his car quickly not to leave a space between the two and tempt someone to change lanes.

"Those idiots in G-Plans believed that they could do things alone without their security contractor." Dafer chuckled.

The cars moved again. Now Luay could see it. A checkpoint. Oh shit.

Only three cars between him and the checkpoint.

The weapons in the back trunk. How could he be so careless?

"Luay, You still there?"

"Yeah, yeah, so what does this have to do with us?"

Two cars now.

"Saud said that this Barn guy is eager to do anything to cause some disturbance."

"Oh, really?"

One car now. At least four soldiers manned the checkpoint. One of them behind a heavy machine gun fixed on top of a police car. They'd put up road blocks as well so that cars had to slow down, turn left and right before getting out of the checkpoint.

Damn.

"And this man had some good connections. Saud said that it was Richard who got Mujahid out. Is he really out by the way?"

"Who?" Luay had to put the cell phone on the passenger seat and use the speaker phone. Talking on a cell phone was not allowed in the checkpoints.

"Mujahid. Is he out?" Dafer's raspy voice came like static on the line.

He was in the checkpoint now. If they checked his back trunk he was doomed. If they checked his stolen car registration he would be doomed.

The soldier motioned for him to roll down the window. He did.

Their eyes met.

All the sound was muted, the traffic noise, Dafer's shouting on the cell. Just his heartbeat.

What a shitty job he had chosen.

"Salam Alycum, officer, how are you?" Luay said, putting on the best friendly smile he could master.

The officer, he was really just a soldier, nodded. Looking at the soldier on the other side.

This is it.

He would tell his colleague to check the car.

But the man just motioned for him to move on.

Luay waved a thank-you. "Hot day, yeah?"

Mr. Social.

"Move on." The soldier yawned.

Fine, he would not invite them to his next barbecue.

Luay pressed on the peddle, the car roared. Dafer was still yelling and bitching on the phone.

"Sorry boss, I was in a checkpoint," he said, reaching the phone that somehow got under the passenger seat. "You were saying?"

"Man, you could at least say something. I don't like yelling on the phone like this. Where was I? Yes, I was telling you that this help from Richard Barn could solve a lot of challenges for us."

Luay tried to remember what Dafer was talking about. Something about Heavy Water and creating some disturbance.

He almost missed his exit. Luay veered to the right. A police car came out of the same ally he was going in. He pressed on the brake. The tires squealed. He turned left. So did the driver in the other car.

Too late.

The car jolted, almost throwing him through the windshield.

Shit. That's why they were yelling about using seat belts.

Both cars stopped now. He managed to kick open the door and get outside.

"Are you okay?" one of the soldiers, with a big nose the size of a hand grenade, asked him.

Luay turned back, thank God the checkpoint was not in their line of sight. "Yeah, I am fine."

"Open your fucking eyes next time, will you?" another soldier, fat with white skin that looked like something from a doughnut commercial said.

Luay winced. "I will, officer."

He checked his car bumpers and front lights. This Korean shit didn't stand a chance against the cops' Ford truck.

Ah, American cars.

In his peripheral vision, he saw the third soldier, a short man with black skin moving behind his car.

Uh oh.

"We have to issue a ticket for you." Big-nose said.

Luay nodded. Then he smiled to the soldier, two smiles in one day, what a torture. "Can we settle this here?" He took out his wallet a tad too slow. His looked to Shorty in the back, who was close to the car truck.

"Well," Big-nose rubbed his chin, "we are all in a hurry, so we might just take the fine now."

A civilian car passed next to them, the driver slowed down, looked, and drove away.

Luay took out some cash and handed it to the officer.

"Oh, shit!" Shorty yelled, his hand moving to his gun.

Doughnut-commercial reached to his gun as well. Luay grappled big-nose's hand, pulling him as a cover. He snapped the soldier's gun and fired at Shorty. Shorty fired at the same time. His bullet hit Big-nose's chest. Luay threw Big-nose body at Doughnut-commercial, who fired twice. Luay shot back, hitting Doughnut in the head. He fired another at Shorty who was on his knees from the first shot. Headshot.

Luay walked back to his car. Good thing it was still running. He pulled away from the police Ford and drove off.

Dafer's static-like yelling made it easy to find the phone, again.

"Yes, Dafer," he said, ignoring the cursing and shouting. "This Richard Barn could open a whole new world of possibilities for us."

-39-
Al Amel District
June 10th
1:00 PM

Luay and Mujahid stood in the small house attached to Mahmoud's. Although a crucial member of the group, Luay was never comfortable working with Mujahid.

Arrogant psychopath.

Mujahid was talking to Abu Ayob on his cell.

"So, where is the car then?" Luay asked him after he finished his call, using the coldest tone he could master.

Mujahid shrugged. He examined the dual magazine attached to an AK47 machine gun. "Do I look like a car dealer to you?"

"Fuck you, Mujahid, you know what car I am talking about."

Shit. He wouldn't let Mujahid get on his nerves.

"My my, someone is nervous," Mujahid said with his crooked smile. The bruises on his face made it even sicker. "Calm down, Luay, the brothers will bring it soon."

The brothers. This was what Mujahid called his group. Luay couldn't help but notice the nice coincidence of how all the brothers were back in the group once Mujahid was back. More proof that Mujahid was the real leader. The Egyptian sheikh was just a front, a religious figure to the junior members.

"You have to excuse me now. There is a mission we have to do for Sheikh Abu Ayob," Mujahid said, putting a handgun in the back of his pants. "Be a sweetheart and take Yousif and the two new brothers and go back to your house."

"Perfect," Luay scoffed. "I woke up this morning asking God to give me the honor of helping Mujahid. Anything else I can do for you? Maybe rub your shoulders?"

Mujahid reached to his right shoulder. "You know, it's not a bad idea, yesterday in the cell they didn't give me the extra pillow I asked for."

"Fuck you."

Mujahid smiled again. Damn him and his stupid, psychopath grin.

Luay took two steps toward Mujahid. He wasn't very good at keeping his temper in check. He didn't care much either.

"Give me one reason not to take this machine gun and stuff it up your ass?"

"Because you'd like to rub my shoulders?"

He poked him in the chest. "You think you are fucking funny?"

"What about the dozen brothers in this house and the Mosque?" Mujahid's crooked smile became part of the background now.

"Do you really think that those brothers scare me?" Luay spat.

"Oh, stupid me, for a moment I forgot you were a super agent. What about if you screw with me your operation will fail." The smile was still on his lips but his eyes were serious, empty, as if made of glass. "Come on, Luay, you think I don't know how desperate you are to get this job done."

Luay stepped back, biting on his lower lip. Mujahid was right.

"Abu Ayob wants to marry Mahmoud's daughter," Mujahid said in his flat tone. "He told me to bring her to him now. It will be messy, I believe, so it's better to take the new guys with you, especially her brother Yousif."

"He is fucking what?" Luay scowled. "Those people are our allies, for crying out loud, they helped you countless times, they gave us shelter, their son is working with us." He couldn't take more of Abu Ayob and his perverted desires.

Mujahid put his hand on his chest. "Please remind me to feel bad about it."

"Fuck you. You idiot, you are going to risk everything for that walking-hormone."

Mujahid chuckled, but there was no humor in it. "This walking-hormone is the only point of contact with the big guys in the organization."

This was something new. Luay couldn't hide his bewilderment.

Mujahid went on, same smile but Luay could feel something there now. Anger maybe. "I don't know why? Maybe some big master there likes his fat ass. Maybe his wife sleeps with a big shot. I don't know and I don't really care. What you need to do is to make him happy. Rub his shoulders maybe." Mujahid snickered. "Or suck his balls. Do what you can to make him happy because you know well that without the organization, you can go nowhere."

"You know what," Luay said, "when I first saw this Abu Ayob, I expected a man who only worries about his stomach. Kind of the way to the man's heart is through his stomach... Now I know I should have lowered my expectations several inches."

They both chuckled. Then Luay added, "Mujahid, listen, I have killed people, raped female prisoners, I have done things that even you would think was extreme. Shit, we were trained to eat a man alive. But there are things that are wrong even for a man like me. Those are our allies. You do not fuck your ally. Why do you risk them for this idiot?"

Mujahid just shrugged. "Who said it's not the right thing to do?"

Luay wanted to say something but couldn't find the words.

"You need to look at things objectively, Luay."

"Objectively?"

"Indeed, the instructions we have are to establish the Islamic state in this region, so we need an Ameer. And Abu Ayob is the only candidate. But as you might have noticed, our friend is not the most charismatic leader in the world. So what he needs to do is the old Qaeda trick."

"Let me guess. Make him lose some weight?"

"To use the stick, not the carrot," Mujahid said. "Iraqis care about honor and all the protect-the-women thing. So when the Sheikh takes one of their girls and bangs her, people will feel humiliation more than they can tolerate and what will happen is the same thing that happened everywhere with Qaeda."

"Shall I win something if I finally guess the right answer?"

"People will start justifying it, they will say it's marriage, and it's good to have the Ameer as their in-law. Those things happen as a defense mechanism when people face something they can neither accept nor avert."

Luay tried to make a sarcastic comment but once again words betrayed him.

"We want to break them to the point that they will start loving us because this is the only way they can keep living." Mujahid's smile came back. If there was one thing more intimidating than serious Mujahid, it was happy Mujahid. "I have seen people running after the bone we gave them not because they wanted it, but because they wanted to please us."

An image flashed into Luay's mind of when his team was assigned to accompany Saddam on his public visits to schools or factories. The crowds were hopping around him, clapping and cheering. Luay and other agents had to hit them hard, sometimes even semi-lethal hits to get them away. He always wondered why those people –most of them hated Saddam and rebelled against him– were doing this. Hypocrisy, fear, greed –sometimes Saddam was throwing money– it didn't really fit. Luay could see a different angle now through what Mujahid was saying.

Maybe... He shrugged. Sometimes it's better not to stop and think. You have to keep going. The moment you stop, your demons will find you.

"Yousif, Abdul Rahman, Amjad!" Luay yelled in a military voice. "Come with me, we are going to my place." He was about to say move your asses fast, but the gloomy look on the men with long beards —Mujahid's brothers for sure— caused him to refrain. It was hard to know with Salafism which words they liked and which ones they wanted to chop your head off for.

"I will call you once the car is ready," Mujahid called after him.

....

Luay gave his house keys to Yousif and asked him to take Abdul Rahman and Amjad and wait for him there. Enas wouldn't be home for hours.

Odd to suddenly miss the family bonds. After his mother passed away ten years ago, his father abandoned his responsibilities toward him and his sister. He wasn't much of father anyway. With all his authority in the Baath party, his father provided him with nothing but that job in the private security force. His mistresses got more money out of the old man in one day, or night for that matter, than he and his sister got in a month.

Luay stood in the street, watching Mahmoud's house. He wasn't sure why, but he couldn't just go. He wanted, needed to see what would happen.

Mujahid and three more dishdash came out of the small house carrying machine guns and heading to Mahmoud's. Something about the sight of a man with a dishdash above his ankle and a long black beard carrying a machine gun was unsettling. It was as if the two shouldn't be together. Like a child carrying a gun. The sight of weapons was fairly scary, but having them in the hands of someone with whom you couldn't reason, someone who understood nothing but blood... well, it looked like something of a bad joke.

The four men didn't wait for someone to open the door. Mujahid just kicked it open and they rushed inside. Seconds later, desperate crying came from the women. Then two dishdash came out dragging a woman. A yellow sheet over her head made it impossible to tell her age.

Luay had no idea why the sheet was yellow and why they covered her this way. But everything looked like something out of a low-budget war movie. The woman stumbled while being dragged by the neck by one of the dishdash.

Behind her, an elderly woman rushed out, crying for help and striking her head and face with both her hands. The third dishdash pushed her back home.

Neighbors peeked out, too afraid to come out. The two men didn't rush inside the attached house, just the opposite. They slowed, making sure everyone saw them.

Mujahid and the third dishdash walked behind, firing some rounds up in the sky. The shy heads behind the neighbors' doors hid as bullets echoed in the street.

The woman in the sheet tripped and fell to the ground. The two dishdashs didn't help her out. They stood watching and waiting for her to stand up. She was stalling and they knew it. The woman stood up and sprinted, trying to escape. It wasn't easy with her head covered with the sheet. She toppled and fell again, this time it looked serious. She cried, calling for her mother. The mother answered with more cries, still hitting her face with her hand.

Mujahid signaled to the men. From where he was standing, Luay wasn't sure if one of them had kicked her but her body suddenly jerked forward. The two dishdashs lifted her from the ground.

The scene was provocative. Even to a man like Luay.

Luay thought about Mujahid's words. And looked back at the faces of the people in the neighborhood. Men, women, kids of different ages, different shapes but one look.

They were all terrorized. You could almost see the question in their eyes watching their neighbor being dragged like an animal: will my daughter be next?

Luay didn't like what he was seeing.

He wasn't big on righteousness and wickedness. or good and evil but could still see something wrong. Something utterly cowardly.

Luay's memory threw out images from times he couldn't remember anymore. Images of people with exactly the same look. Different scenes, different cities, the only common thing was himself. He was there right where Mujahid was now. He was taking people, men and women, from their homes. Most of them never saw the light again.

Suddenly all the justifications seemed ridiculous.

Flashes of the faces he killed, tortured, raped came to him. Was he like what Mujahid was now? A coward, intimidating helpless people?

The crazy train of memory didn't stop. It took him in tunnels. Searching for one memory of himself he could be proud of. Darkness.

Then it finally stopped at one single memory. Twelve-year-old Luay helping his baby sister after a tough day at kindergarten. Carrying her all the way back home.

He could remember how other children and people on the road looked at him with admiration. Not fear.

Like a hero. Not the Baath dog.

The lady, no doubt she was Yousif's sister, the young man he liked not only because he reminded him of himself but because he was the only one in the herd of Abu Ayob with whom he could share a laugh or a dirty joke. He watched her now as she took another poke in her back by the tip of the machine gun.

For a second he considered helping her. Yousif was like an assistant to him, right? But he couldn't allow himself to get emotional now.

They got the girl into a parked car. The two dishdashs got into the car, Mujahid stayed with the other man.

He had a lot to win out of this operation. He couldn't risk everything now. And for what? He didn't know what he wanted anymore.

It is my last operation, he told himself, going back to his house. After that he would take his money and open a small grocery shop. Maybe even get married. As for Yousif's sister... well, another daemon to haunt him.

-40-
Al-Amil District
June 10th
1:30 PM

If you were lucky, and your path crossed no army convoys or road blocks, it was pretty easy to move around Baghdad. The problem most of the Baghdadis faced, however, was that they were not lucky.

Just like everything else with him today, Hussain's luck with the roads was perfect. It only took him several minutes to reach Al-Amil District.

He looked at the car clock, impressed. So this was how life could be when luck smiled on you.

While searching for the house, Hussain couldn't help but notice how the area looked... different. Baghdad wasn't in its best shape anyway. The temporary arrangement for the basic services of water and electricity made every street in Baghdad look like one of those modern-art drawings, where you couldn't tell whether it was a flower, a house, or the milky way. One street was completely blocked by the electrical generator someone had brought and left in the middle of the street next to what was left of a car chassis. In the main street, shops in different states of abundance had those big billboards on top of them. Black paint had covered most of the Pepsi sign. Another billboard featured the guy from the Lord-Of-The-Rings movie smoking a cigarette as if sucking on a life-support tube. This one was partially covered with a white sheet with a big "Death to invaders" scribbled in red. Citrus and olive trees stood along the street, dried, bent in an awkward way, as if grieving what once was a decent neighborhood.

The deeper he drove into the district, the more it looked like a scene from a western movie where the hero arrived to an abandoned town. Lifeless streets, open doors, shadows behind the windows. And those creepy white banners.

The banners were everywhere, on the house doors, fences, trees, and every post available. The red writing carried slogans about killing infidels and Americans, some threatened Iranians and Safavids. The houses looked deserted, gardens were yellow instead of green. He drove past a soccer field, one that, a lifetime ago, used to be the biggest in this part of Baghdad. Burned tires were left in the middle of the field. The two goals were covered with the white sheets, perhaps threatening the infidels that they would lose the next football match.

After another ten minutes, he managed to find Ayad's house. Nothing special, a traditional house with a six-foot brick fence. And a big yellow main door. Tree branches peered over the fence, at least those were still green. Second-level windows were visible from the street, nothing unusual except for the open main door.

Not a good sign.

He parked the car in front of the house, knocked hard enough for the people inside, if any, to hear it.

Nothing.

Trying the doorbell would look so naive and... preppy. No one used them anymore. Probably no electricity anyway.

He knocked again, this time using the car key.

Ayad didn't provide his phone number in the police report. Maybe the officer who took the notes forgot to ask him for it. Bottom line, he had no way to contact Ayad now but this house address.

Hussain wasn't sure about his boss's theory —that Mujahid was connected to the gang that kidnapped his son and somehow also connected to the gang that Ayad talked about. Just because he used the same words. Seemed a long shot at best.

Desperate measures. Hussain tried to imagine how life would look if his son was kidnapped. He didn't have a son, but he pictured one of his nephews getting kidnapped.

A shiver, of anger or fear or some sick mix of the both, spread all over his body.

Okay, point taken. It's ugly. But how could he help?

Two men were working on a red Corolla parked at the house next door. Both stared a bit too long now. He wasn't wearing the police uniform so maybe they stared because he was knocking on their neighbor's door. Iraqi were very curious about their neighbors. Very might not be the right word. Extremely, tremendously, were still tad short.

Hussain thought about asking them about Ayad. He was already walking toward them when a tingling feeling crept onto the back of his neck. He stopped. Someone was watching him. He turned but saw no one. Was it just his spider-sense? After all, if Ayad were right, there was a terrorist group hiding —or living or working, depending on how secure they felt— in one of those houses.

He continued toward the two men. Both were bending over the open-hood car engine. Only the lower part of their backs was visible. Another typical Iraqi scene, a mixture of passion for car mechanics and old-car problems.

His spider-senses tingled again. Not sure what to do, he bent down, pretending to tie his shoe lace.

Great. He forgot to replace his military boots when he changed his clothes. Then, it didn't really matter, Iraqis were not slaves for fashion. He looked back again. Nothing in the street. Just one small grocery shop two blocks away. One of those now-common shops that were part of the houses.

During the last six years, the economy slowed so people were opening shops from a partition of their houses. They were so common, especially in the poor neighborhoods, that one shop could only serve five houses to the left and right before another house-shop came in.

Damn you, Saddam.

He found it much safer to check out the store owner first. If neighbors were curious, then the local shop owners were the official holders of the gossip hub for all the neighborhood. Besides, if he were to exclude anyone from being a terrorist, it would be the shop owner. Hard to imagine a short dishdash Wahabbi working in a place where the stuff, according to Salafism beliefs, were all innovations that had to be thrown away.

Plan A, try to open a discussion. He approached the small shop now. Plan B, coming soon.

"*Salam Alyckum*," he greeted the shop owner. Another man sat with him. Both were the same age, the wrong side of forty. The owner sat behind a table filled with pre-paid cell phone cards and lolipops. Both men had the Homer-Simpson-five-o'clock shadow.

The man mumbled something. Both his and his friend's faces were gloomy. Iraqi shop owners were not the funniest people in the world –it was hard to expect a man broken to the point that he opened a shop out of his house to smile. But Hussain had the feeling that there was something more to it. They had that look. The look he had become familiar with now. The look he saw hours ago on the face of the little girl. Of someone who had seen a tragedy. Of someone shocked.

Plan A, failed.

Where was plan B? Nothing came.

"Err… Do you have… cigarettes?" Hussain asked, putting on the most charming smile. If those men were women he would get the cigarettes for free.

"A cigarette?" The man's eyebrows furrowed, he made a gesture to a shelf behind him. The shelf was empty though. "What kind of cigarettes?"

Hussain fought the urge to slap his forehead, you don't ask for cigarettes, no one does. You ask for your brand. The problem was, he wasn't a smoker. The only reason he asked for a smoke is because he figured it was the best way to open a chat. And no, this wasn't his three-month-training. Sometimes he liked to improvise.

He remembered a billboard he saw today, of the guy from the Lord Of The Rings movie. What was the ad for?

"Marlboro," he said with a triumphant sound as if he just answered the million-dollar question.

"How many?" The man reached out to a drawer below his table.

"Just one."

Cigarettes used to be on the nearest shelf, now they were hidden below. Another sign of the Al-Qaeda-was-here: everyone was afraid of everything.

He heard a heavy breathing sound to his right. A man sat on a small crate next to the chilled cupboard, holding a Pepsi Cola can. Hussain didn't notice him when he entered because of the big refrigerator. The man was in his early thirties or late twenties. His face twitched with something Hussain couldn't really comprehend. The veins on his jaw were popping in and out as if about to explode.

The shop owner handed him his one cigarette. He thanked him, not sure if he should put it in his mouth before lighting it or light it first.

They put it in their mouth first and then they light it, you idiot.

But he wasn't about to start smoking now.

Hussain tried to engage in social conversation; he never had a problem doing that before. Not with his charming looks and easy-going personality. This time, the air looked so intense, so... electrified.

So he tried one of Iraqis all-occasions and always-successful ice-breaking phrases:

"Shku Maku", literally, it meant "What's there and what's not there," but basically it was the Iraqi version of what's-up.

The shop owner frowned, then he just said, "Quarter. For the cigarette."

"Oh, sure," Hussain said, smiling while paying the amount, "I came here to say hello to a family friend who lives here."

Silence.

"His name is Ayad."

Still silence. The shop owner glanced at his friend. The other slightly shook his head. The move was fast and subtle but Hussein caught it, fear. They said you can see fear on someone's face, probably in some situations, but most of the time you just feel it, smell it maybe. Trained or not, you feel fear in the other person even if his face and eyes betrayed nothing.

Hussain could smell their fear; he felt it in the pit of his stomach like a heavy brick of cement.

The shop owner swallowed. "They left."

"Traveled," the friend added.

Traveled? But he was just yesterday filing a report at headquarters.

Silence again.

There wasn't even the mind-your-own-business usual response. Nothing.

He looked to his left again to the man sitting on the crate. Their eyes met. Hussain didn't know what to make of him, was he angry? In pain? Sad? But there was one thing was sure, those eyes were what triggered his spider-sense.

Hussain took his unlit cigarette and left the store. His three-month-training didn't teach him how to handle such a situation, nor did the movies he watched.

Hmmm, what would Arnold Schwarzenegger do in a situation like that? Hussain debated using the 'I'll-be-back' line, nah, he didn't have the black sunglasses.

"Excuse me."

He spun around, even before that he knew who was calling him. The man with cola can.

"Do you have a lighter?" the man said, waving his right hand with a cigarette in it.

"No, not really."

The man took out one from his trousers' pocket, and extend it to him.

"I don't feel like smoking today."

Right, he bought the cigarette just for fun.

The man smiled knowingly then made a suit-yourself shrug.

"You were asking about Ayad?"

Hussain was taken aback. "Yes." What else to say? "He was my brother's friend." Stick with the lie.

Another knowing smile. Another shrug. This time looking at his army boots.

"You are in the army." He pointed with his chin to the boot. It wasn't a question.

"Would that make any difference?" Hussain resisted an urge to check the gun he hid in his back.

The man didn't look intimidating. He was pale, barely standing, and kept glancing at the direction of Ayad's house.

"Let's talk there." He pointed to a big olive tree outside the house-slash-shop. "It's safer."

The man walked, Hussain followed. He could now see a long scar on the man's right cheek. He also had difficulty walking. His steps were too elaborate, his hand on his side. Wounded. Hussain could almost see the bandages under the white shirt.

Scar-face looked left and right. They were under the olive tree now. Another tree to their right blocked them. The place was a perfect observation post. No one could spot whoever watched from here.

"I need your help," the man said finally, but with the difficulty of a hard confession. "And in exchange I can give you a lot of information about this area."

"What help?"

"There is a terrorist group in this area, their hideout is in the Tawhid mosque," the man said in a low whisper, gaze fixed on something across the street where the two guys and the red Corolla were.

"So?"

"I need your help to assault the mosque."

"Just that? You sure you don't want to assault the White House as well?"

Scar-face stared at him, not slightly amused.

"I am sorry." Hussain held up an apologetic hand. "But we can't just assault a mosque."

"Whom do you work for?" Scar-face asked.

"It's not about whom I work for," Hussain tried to explain. "Assaulting a mosque will cause problems, a lot of them."

Scar-face grimaced and put his hand on his side again.

His discussion with Dr. Zainab! The two wounded men who escaped from the hospital. He remembered her words: "A long scar on his right cheek." If this was a coincidence then it was a hell of one.

"Listen to me," Scar-face pleaded, still trying to keep his voice low. "They are kidnapping people, they have just kidnapped–".

The world kidnapped got Hussain's attention. After all, this was his mission, to find a lead, any possible lead on a terrorist group who kidnapped Abdul Hasan's son.

On the other hand, mosques were sacred places in Islam. Assaulting one without proper approval which went all the way into the administration of coalition forces, especially in the case where a Shia-controlled force such as the MICF, attacked a Sunnie mosque in a Sunnie-controlled area. Jurisdiction was only a small part of the problem. Realized by the terrorists, mosques were more and more turning into a safe haven for them. Still, attacking a mosque was a rejected idea by both Shia and Sunnie.

"Look, pal. It's just so complicated," Hussain tried to explain.

Scar-face held up his hand as if stopping traffic. He let out an impatient puff. "First, don't call me pal. My name is Malik." His swollen face reddened. "Second, it's serious. Those men kidnapped a woman now, and I swear they have more than one hostage inside."

There are moments where you know someone is saying the truth. The pain in his eyes, the tune that speaks of the complicated feelings trying not to say something but doing just that. The sign of saying the truth. Or a good actor.

But this wasn't why Hussain decided to help.

Maybe it was the image that kept flashing in his mind, of the broken Abdul Hasan.

Or he trusted his new luck, and could share it with others.

Stop with the whys, there was no time.

"I will do what I can, Malik, okay. I need you to tell me about Ayad."

"I met him once, when I was in visiting his neighbor... wait a minute– I thought you were asking about Ayad because of his neighbor and the people living in his house."

"I am very interested in finding a twelve-year-old boy, and I thought Ayad, or his neighbors, knew one of the kidnappers."

Malik rubbed the back of his head, maybe he was thinking of guarantees of some sort.

"Okay," he finally said, sitting on a small concrete brick, clutching his side again. "I will tell you everything I know about the group who lives next to Ayad's house, but you have to promise me that you will help the woman they kidnapped from Mahmoud's house."

"Fair enough, but who is Mahmoud?"

Malik looked at him as if he told him the earth is flat. "The neighbor."

"Oh, yes, him." Hussain never heard the name.

"He is a decent man, honest, and his family is respected by everyone in the neighborhood. Everyone likes them. He has a son and a daughter."

"The daughter was the woman who got kidnapped?"

Malik nodded. "Mahmoud had hosted some people from the resistance in his house."

"You mean terrorists."

"Whatever, Mujahedeen, terrorists, resistance. The point is, Mahmoud was trying to help them so he gave them the house attached to his. Then they got so powerful now they kidnapped his daughter."

"For a ransom?" Hussain asked, still thinking about the connection between this and Abdul Hasan's son.

"No." Malik shook his head, looking down. If he was acting, then it was a hell of an acting job. His face twitched as if some invisible force was torturing him mercilessly. "The sheikh at the mosque wants to marry her."

Hussain wasn't sure he heard it right. "So why kidnap her if he wants to marry her?"

But the answer came even before Malik said it. A forced marriage. But how come this man knew so much about it?

Malik looked up, his scar was more prominent, his eyes moist. "Of course he had to force her because she is already engaged."

The words made Hussain shiver.

"I am her fiancé, and that coward hypocrite wanted to kill me to have her for himself."

-41-
14th of Ramadan Street - Baghdad
June 10th
1:40 PM

A lifetime ago, Abdul Hasan used to enjoy going to Mansor district. All Iraqi families did.

And they still did.

Not him, not now. He was late and the traffic wasn't helping.

Ahead was an American convoy. He knew the drill, a distance of 500 feet had to be maintained between the last vehicle in the convoy and other cars. That wasn't the problem, it was the twenty mile-per-hour speed of the tanks.

The convoy stopped. Right after the intersection he should take to go to Mansor. He estimated the distance between the tank and the intersection to be less than 200 yards. Maybe they would let him drive to the exit. He was already late and he didn't want to risk it. He drove slowly, making sure the right signal light was on. Hopefully the soldier on top of the tank would see the signal and allow him to take the exit.

Nope. The American pointed his machine gun at him. Okay, got the message. He stopped and waited.

Abdul Hasan felt alone. Vulnerable. No troops, no guards. Somehow reminding him of his days in jail. A man in the car behind him kept honking for him to move ahead.

Some people wanted to try for themselves. Abdul Hasan veered the car to the right, allowing the new hero to pass him and try his luck. This time the American fired some rounds in the air. Who could blame him? Now everyone just sat in their cars and waited, no honking. Good, sit there and enjoy the lovely Baghdad streets.

He was close to Mansur district. Asiacell, another cellular network provider, had a big billboard announcing their new family package. One that would allow calling three other lines for less than half the price. The billboard showed a family of a young couple and a child. All with shiny smiles, all healthy, all beautiful. Never be away from your family, the board said.

Another billboard, smaller though, showed Showtime's (the cable channel) next movie. One with a man with metal claws on his hand

and a funny hair cut that looked like something from the '70s. His son would love this one. In a nearby large electronic store, an LG sign told him that life was good. Right.

A young couple sat in a car next to him. College students probably. He glanced at them. The temporary traffic stop didn't seem to bother the young couple. They both sat on their heels, facing each other. Both in the same way, chins rested on hands, their arms wrapped around the seats. The man was saying something, the young lady laughed. Her head tilted back when she did. She had shoulder-length black hair. Now, it was her turn to talk, the man listened, no interruption. When she finished they both laughed. Abdul Hasan could hear the giggles, that worry-free laugh. The one only youth could do. Full of confidence, of trust in life.

The traffic still didn't move. People started honking again, some yelled. More laughter from the couple, hearing it almost hurt. There was a time, too far away as if in another life, when he and his wife used to laugh this way. That was before the jail, before the execution, before the war with Iran. Before life showed him its true nature, its real face.

There was a time when he used to laugh this way. When he used to believe the LG slogan that life is good, that all difficulties and pain were just temporary, and eventually everything would be just fine.

Now he knew better. Yes, sadness and happiness took turns in life. But with a twist, misery and despair were the reality, the actual fabric of life, pleasure was just a mask.

A mask that Abdul Hasan once knew. Once he saw the ugly face underneath, he never trusted life again.

Some might think that his gloomy outlook was because of the war and death he saw. They would be mistaken. It just opened his eyes to see the truth. The reality behind every happiness was the ugly sadness.

Happiness was temporary, surrounded by misery, by despair that waited around every corner.

The couple in the car next to him was an obvious example. They were laughing, holding each other's hands. But would their happiness last? Could it last? The answer was so simple, he wondered how others couldn't see it.

A stray bullet from the convoy ahead, an explosion in the road, a heart attack, an accident, cheating, even a simple lie, it only took one small thing to go wrong for their laughs to change forever.

The truth was that all happiness was surrounded by misery and sadness. We just chose to ignore it. The awful truth is once the unpleasantness occurred, the thin ice is shattered forever. You celebrate your birthday, but your health is in continuous decay. You look at your child's smile and it makes your day, but deep inside, you know that this moment is over, there might be others, even better, but they won't last either. And soon, the next day or next year, something bad will happen, maybe your child will grow up and leave, maybe they will get sick or even kidnapped, something will happen and you will not be able to enjoy this smile again.

And when life shows you its true ugly nature, no mask, no make-up can hide it anymore. Enjoying life would be living a big lie, in a dream you know would end. They tell you to live in the moment, to enjoy life as long as you can. You might do that, you might try, but that nagging feeling won't let you. It will keep reminding you that you are living in a dream, that the ugly reality will soon find a way to turn all happiness into misery. The once-happy memories will haunt you as your worst nightmares. Your kidnapped child's smile will be your worst and cruelest tormentor.

The traffic finally moved. Abdul Hasan hit the gas pedal, trying to make up for the time lost. He almost hit another car and drove on the wrong side in a small street to make a short cut.

He thought of an excuse if the traffic police stopped him.

"Sorry, officer, I have a bombed car to drive."

That wouldn't help him much.

Abdul Hasan thought about the bombing attacks carried out by the Salafism gangs in Iraq... were all the suicidal bombers under threat as he was now?

He had seen video where the bombers, the terrorists, talked about why they wanted to do this.

Maybe they were forced to do that as well.

No, that was a long stretch. Those people came from different places to Iraq. No one forced them to come here. They came here to be martyrs. Or at least to participate in the war.

Jihad. He sneered.

When he was a kid, this very word meant a lot to him. Jihad meant a holy fight. He remembered the story he once read about how Mohammed the prophet and a few of his true companions had fought the Arab unbelievers, defending their city. How when they came back, victorious, Mohammed told his followers that this was the small Jihad, and the big Jihad was yet to come. The fight against the evil inside them. Fight to be better persons. Fight against lying and cheating, injustice and lust. The fight with one's desires so that one doesn't hurt others, and wish for others what he wished for himself.

That was a long time ago. Before the United States started supporting the Afghani warriors in their Jihad against the Soviet Union. Before the Islamic groups in Egypt started killing tourists and before the three thousands innocents in New York died just because Bin Laden wanted to prove a point.

Perhaps it was another side of life's ugly truth? That even things he used to believe, words that used to represent good, could turn into evil.

Take the word Islam for example. The image he had in his mind was of Emam Hussain, the prophet's grandson, instructing his companions not to harm even the animals and plants. And when Emam Hussain was surrounded by the army that came to kill him and what was left of the prophet's family, the great hero was all tears, sorry for those who tried to kill him. That was the Islam Abdul Hasan knew.

Not anymore.

This image was taken away, replaced by something nightmarish.

Islam became the cloak under which innocent people could be killed by the thousands. It became another tool for politicians to get more power. A reason why the incompetent could get a better position in the government than the competent.

He tried to draw a line between the Islam he knew and this Islam.

He used to say the Qaeda-Islam and this was fine for a while. Until the contamination was passed to ... well, almost everyone else. The Sader Army, the Shia and Sunnie parties, the government, even the people he knew.

Everyone was using Islam as a cover. As a justification. Abdul Hasan thanked God that he had known the religion decades before all of this happened. He knew it when it was a felony. When Sadam was sending people to prison when caught praying. Back then people were trying to hide their religion. Not to use it in their election campaigns.

And God, he missed those days.

His cell phone rang. He didn't have to look at the number to know.

"Yes." Good he didn't have to say, "Yes, Sir."

"Are you there yet?" A new gruff voice.

Maybe they had something like a terrorist's call center and every time a different customer-service agent answered or made the call.

"I am in the Rowad intersection. What do you want me to do?"

"Get out of your car and walk toward the old central market." Silence. Still Abdul Hasan could hear some muffled sounds then the voice was back again. "We are watching you and if we see any of your men, we will disappear and your son will be sent to you–"

"I got it… I am alone." He managed not to sound angry. What lack of creativity. Phrases such as "send him in pieces to you," or, "kill him slowly," were worn out, yet he still trembled. Maybe he still could feel something, numbness hadn't taken over, something inside him was still... human?

"Good."

The call ended.

Abdul Hasan examined the street. There was no way he could find a parking place. The right lane was already filled with parked cars, which left only two more lanes in the street.

Why should he care anymore? A parking ticket would not look good on his resume, yes. Anyway his resume would have more serious charges today.

He parked in the middle lane and stepped out of the car. Angry honking and yelling came behind him.

Abdul Hasan walked in the street. The Rowad intersection was one of the most famous spots in the Mansour district. A luxury neighborhood. The name, Al-Rowad, was after the ice-cream shop on the corner of the biggest block. In the old days, this street was one of the most visited shopping places in Baghdad.

Maybe that was still the case nowadays.

The street started from the old and large central market building, built in the late '70s. The early forms of shopping malls. Quite the awe at that time. Closed for the last fifteen years.

Shoppers used to park in the lot of the Magic Lamp children's cinema. Kids were left either watching a movie or in the cinema playground. The cinema was changed to a warehouse, two rusted slides were what was left of the big playground. Gone were the big swings and the colorful merry-go-round.

Then the street extended to a Lebanese fast-food restaurant –at least it was Lebanese in its hey day– after that the fashion and gold stores. They took four big blocks before ending with the Rowad ice-cream shop where shoppers entertained themselves with one of Baghdad's best pistachio and vanilla ice creams.

The shopping trip normally ended back at the Lebanese restaurant near the parking lot where shoppers bought take-out dinner and headed back home.

The street was also famous because of the failed assassination attempt of Oday. Saddam's elder son. Oday was known for his night adventures. Chasing women; kidnapping and raping them was his hobby. Twenty ladies were found in a basement beneath the Iraqi Olympic Community building, all belonging to Oday. But his real hobby was discovered later. After the regime fell, people found tapes recorded by Saddam's son showing him...um... making love, with married women in front of their husbands. The women were all crying, but it wasn't rape. No... not even a slight struggle.

Abdul Hasan was now right next to the spot where Oday's car was assaulted by some mysterious attacker who emptied a full magazine into his body while Oday was sitting in his car watching women shopping and most probably wondering which one he would take home tonight.

The son of a bitch didn't die. Just crippled.

A voice brought him back to the real world. Someone was calling his name. A black car stopped in the middle lane of the street. They must have gotten the parking tip from him. Three men stepped out, all carrying machine guns. All of them with long beards. All dressed alike. One of them was tall, another was fat, and the third was relatively short. Some nightmarish version of the three bears, which...what, made him Goldilocks?

Drivers in the other cars didn't honk nor yell at the three bears for blocking the street.

Double standards.

Daddy bear beckoned to him. Abdul Hasan walked toward them. Mummy bear gripped him by the collar. Baby bear punched him in the kidney. Abdul Hasan tasted the blood in his mouth. Another punch at the back of his head. Nausea, but he was lucky it ended soon. The last hit pushed him inside the car.

The door slammed and the car darted at full speed.

-42-
Al-Amel District - Baghdad
June 10th
1:50 PM

Enas couldn't understand. Why, of all places, she ran home. The very place she wanted to escape now looked like a safe haven, where she knew what she was and what she wanted.

She threw herself on the couch in the living room. Her tears had long since dried. She could cry no more. What was the point anyway.

Then she remembered his hands on her body. His breath on her face. She shivered. Her entire body shook. Tears ran again.

She hated herself. Hated every single minute she spent thinking about Omar. How could she be so stupid? How could she let him use her like a prostitute? Sending her to his friend.

Her blood boiled. She wanted to hurt someone... herself, Omar, Saud, anyone.

You wanted to work with him, you stupid.

Footsteps thudded in the front yard. Luay? The kitchen door squeaked. Her pulse accelerated. Her brother couldn't see her like this. She sprinted to her room upstairs, changing her cloths. Maybe for the first time in her life, she missed her elder brother. She changed her shirt, looked in the mirror to make sure everything else was okay. She still look like hell with her reddened eyes and nose. He would probably think it was her dust allergy. She went back downstairs.

"Luay, is that you?"

More footsteps, now inside the house. What was going on?

She reached the small guest room where the sounds were coming from. No, she wasn't afraid, she probably should be, but somehow what happened in the hotel brought to the surface a part of herself she always fought to keep buried. But she needed it now, the primitive her.

Her hands tightened into fists ready to launch at whomever might be there if it wasn't her brother. She yanked the door open. And almost gasped. Three men, young men actually, sat in the guest room. They jumped when she entered.

"Who are you?" she cried out.

The young men looked at each other rather than at her.

"We... we.. I .. just..." a skinny guy tried to explain. He looked at the others as if asking for them to help.

"We are waiting for Luay," another young man said. Enas recognized him from the neighborhood. "He gave us the keys and he is coming right behind us."

"Okay." She nodded slowly, not knowing what else to say.

Enas then closed the guest room door and went back to the living room.

What should she do now? Sitting there in the house alone with three other men wasn't really something the friendly Iraqi society would cherish.

Screw them.

And yet, this wasn't like Luay. He never gave the house keys to anyone. What was going on? Was he in danger? Enas didn't know what her elder brother did for work. He paid the rent. He gave her pocket money and put food on the table.

Enas was making good money but, unless she had a death wish, she couldn't share this information with him.

Despite all the rough and violent life he lived, and all the things he did –which she could only imagine– deep inside he was a good man. Well, maybe very, very deep, but there was something there.

Something, maybe the elder-brother figure, maybe the man who protected his family, or maybe just her desperate imagination that kept seeking shelter. But she could only think of her brother now. She wanted to tell him what happened to her. She wanted his help. Like she used to do when she was in first grade and other children picked on her. He beat the hell out of them and their elder brothers if they had any.

She imagined telling him about Omar. What that bastard did to her. She imagined Luay bringing Omar, here in front of her, and beating him for what he did.

Strange how all the feelings could turn into hatred so fast. What she had in her heart about Omar was love. Stupid and unjustifiable, but love. Why did she still feel pain, and all this vengeance if he was just an opportunity? Iraqi girls were the fastest to fall in love. She read that somewhere.

Love or no love, she didn't care. All she cared about now was to get even with Omar. To see him humiliated. To see him in pain.

But how?

Her imagination took her to places. Dark ones. From one idea to another. The thing about dark thoughts was you could not control them. You didn't know where they would take you. She could see her life now, her past, present, and future. It was as if flipping the pages in a sad story.

"What are you doing here?"

She jumped from the couch. It was Luay.

"I… I am not okay." She couldn't look him in the eyes. Even her voice sounded different. Exhausted.

"What's wrong? Are you sick?"

The thing about Luay was that she couldn't tell whether he was worrying because he cared or because he was suspicious.

Maybe this was his way of being a brother.

"I don't know." She choked. Tears stung her eyes. She wished she could hug him right now, cry on his shoulder. Tell him what happened to her.

He was her family.

He tilted his head. "Are you going to throw up? If you are, better go to the bathroom," He smiled. That was Luay. "Enas?"

"I am not okay, okay." She wiped something from her eye with the back of her hand. She wished he could read her thoughts. Even if that meant he would beat her up. God, she needed someone to care about her. Even if that care was only expressed by beating.

Luay stood there, his head cocked, his hand rubbing the back of his neck. He never liked to show sympathy. Something he learned from their father. But she could feel his puzzlement, the way his tight grip squashed the blue paper bag he carried.

A knock came on the outside door. Then a honking sound.

Luay peeked from the window. "Shit." He sighed, then looked at the files in his hand, another honking, he hesitated then left the bag on the table and hurried out.

More honking and knocking on the door.

What the hell was Luay doing with files?

She reached for the first one with her finger, slightly pulling it outside the bag and started reading.

Enas held her breath. A sketch of what she assumed was a building surrounded by security checkpoints. Her heart sank as she read the captions on the arrows. Two arrows, one with the caption, "explosive belt," and on the other one, "bombed car," and below at the bottom of the page, three words. Three little words of where the bombing would happen.

He should have written 'Big Clue' on that file.

Luay's heavy footsteps came. She wasn't sure why, but she hid the papers behind her back.

"Enas, go up to your room." The same old commanding tone. Hitler was back, or in this case, Saddam was back. But then he added with a gentler, more human voice, "I have a guest... I don't want to put him with the men in the other room. It's ...er... complicated."

Luay was giving her an explanation. Oh, God. Next, they might go shopping together.

She nodded and stood up, still holding the papers behind her back. He was too busy to notice.

Enas went upstairs, still listening to Luay. Once he went out to bring in his mysterious guest, she hurried back to the living room on tiptoes. She had to put the papers back.

Enas put the file back on the table. Her heart pounded so loud that she didn't hear the footsteps. She headed back to the door, still off balance because of what she just read.

He stood at the door of the living room.

Wearing his white dishdash and his red shmag.

On his face a purple bruise.

She gasped. Unable to believe her own eyes.

Saud.

-43-
Al-Mansur District - Baghdad
June 10th
1:55 PM

"Is he awake?"

"No."

"Wake him up. Come on, we don't have the entire day."

His senses started coming back. The pain. His kidney was on fire; his head still hurt from the blow.

Someone slapped his face.

He was in a car. He could feel the movement.

Abdul Hasan opened his eyes. He was sitting in the back seat, between two men. In the front sat the driver and the third guy of the three bears.

"Wake up."

Another slap.

How romantic.

"I am awake, stop it."

Mommy Bear, the chubby guy, was sweating as if in a sauna. His hairy chest smelled of old socks on a hot day. He had a six-inch-long beard, his arm surrounded Abdul Hasan, putting a knife next to his face.

Abdul Hasan's face was an inch from the man's sweaty chest and beard. Nausea.

Baby bear, held a gun pointing it to Abdul Hasan. He was about to slap him again when the tall guy, Daddy bear, ordered him to stop.

"Where is my son?"

No answer.

He repeated the question. Sweaty Mommy Bear to the left gave him another blow to the kidney.

Pain almost blinded him.

"*Ya Kafer,*" (You infidel) Daddy bear spat. "We know nothing about your son, we are just following orders, okay. And our orders are to drive you to some place and give you a car. That's it. So don't keep asking questions."

"Yeah, stop asking," Mommy bear added.

A different group. Abdul Hasan thought about asking for their phone number to add it to his contact list. But three bears would understand if he didn't send them seasonal greetings.

"Where should I take the car?"

"Stupid infidel. Are you listening to what I'm saying?" Daddy bear rubbed his face in frustration. "We don't know nothing."

Abdul Hasan nodded, trying not to think of the obvious. Were those the same guys who kidnapped his son? Did they beat him as well? How?

And the most important question: was his son still alive?

Abdul Hasan looked out the car window; they were still in Mansur, the luxurious and big houses stretched all the way, with three or four cars parked in front on the clean streets.

They were driving in the alleys now. It made sense that the car, the one he had to drive, was in Mansur district. Otherwise they had to drive the main roads, which meant passing security checkpoints. Even though a trivial inspection, it was still inspection and five men in a car —not to mention the weapons and the long beards— was always suspicious.

And he was right. The car took a turn into a smaller alley to park in front of a wide unoccupied piece of land between two houses. There was no fence. Sand and left over construction material filled the area, two stray dogs coiled in a corner. A four-wheel-drive police car parked a few feet away.

"Get out!" Daddy bear yelled.

Abdul Hasan did. Hairy-chested Mommy bear stepped out the car with him. "Take this key. You will find a cell phone inside the car." He extended his hand with the key.

Abdul Hasan looked at the man's hand. Too big. Too beefy. He imagined him beating his son with it. Something boiled inside his chest.

He saw himself grabbing the man's hand, twisting it, and kicking his kneecap. Then standing behind the fallen man with the knife to his throat, threatening to kill him if he didn't give him some information about his son. He might kill him anyhow after that. One terrorist less.

"Man, what's wrong with you. Take the key."

It was all in his head. He was too old for all of this action. And they had his son, holding Abdul Hasan's balls.

He took the key. The four men immediately drove away.

No goodbyes. No kisses.

Even Salafisms were too practical nowadays.

The neighborhood was so quiet it was almost dead. All Baghdad luxury areas were like that. You could be jumped and assaulted and no one would even notice or hear your screams.

Except that those areas used to be the safest places in Baghdad.

The car had all the signs and colors of a real Ministry of Interior car. Nothing special about it. He didn't know what to expect.

Maybe a big bumper sign with big letters saying, "Bombed Car."

Yeah, that would be nice. Even with that sign the checkpoints might not notice it. He should have expected to find a police car. If he was to drive it to a high-security area, then it should look like an authentic MICF car.

Abdul Hasan got in. Even from the inside it looked normal. Then he started noticing things. Like the wires behind the steering wheel that went all over the car. And the strange car interior. Seat covers were all taped with a gray duct tape. They looked jagged and uneven, as if all the internal stuffing was taken out and replaced by something else, then covered by the duct tape. He sniffed the air, half expecting to catch a whiff of gunpowder, but his nostrils were still aching from the unpleasant smell of hairy-chest in the car.

Some things just stuck in your senses' memory.

Anyhow, he wouldn't live long enough to complain about this.

People didn't realize how important their lives were until near the end. The last few hours became the most precious ones. They looked for things to take with them or to leave behind –depending on their beliefs. As if all your life would be paraphrased with what you did in your last minutes on earth.

Abdul Hasan thought about that, then he looked at the wiring in the car.

His last deed. His last action on earth.

After a life full of battles. After giving up so much for his principles. He was to drive this bombed car. And this wasn't what troubled him. The hardest part to accept was that he was going to sacrifice everything and yet he wouldn't see his son again.

Another thing about last minutes in life. They always came with regret. Regret about doing things and not doing others. Especially when those things were right in front of you all the time.

He regretted not hugging his son yesterday. Not wishing him a happy birthday a little early. He missed his boy's scent, he missed his playful smile, he missed his son's repeated question about when he would buy him the new PlayStation. The simple things, the things he took for granted, those that became part of everyday life, were the hardest to leave behind.

Maybe he was just getting emotional because of all the circumstances. He spent his entire life as a soldier. And now in his last hours, it was okay to get soft.

He didn't have to wait long. After a few minutes, a cell phone rang. It sat on the passenger seat. He picked it up.

"Drive the car to Saydaia district," a voice commanded him. Then "Be careful–"

"No," Abdul Hasan said resolutely

"What… what do you mean?"

"I will not do anything. Unless I talk to my son."

"Then… then we will send him to you in pieces."

"FedEx."

"What? What are you talking about?"

"Use FedEx, they are faster."

"Are you crazy, I am going…"

"You know what, you are not going to do anything. You can't even come up with new threats."

"Do you want me to tell you that I am going to kill him now? Is that what you want, you ass-wipe? Because I can shoot him right now!"

"No you will not, you know why? Because I have your car now and I will not go anywhere until I make sure he is all right."

Silence.

"Your son is all right."

"And I have to take your word for it?"

"Yes, he is fine."

Abdul Hasan laughed, really laughed. "And you swear on that?"

"Yes."

"You swear by the scout's honor?"

Angry cursing came from the other side. Abdul Hasan smiled. Something had surely snapped inside his own head.

"Let me talk to your boss," he finally said.

The call was ended.

Abdul Hasan drove. Not going anywhere in particular, he just wanted to be away in case they sent the three bears after him.

He kept looking in the rear-view mirror to make sure that no one was following him.

Anxiety crept in. What had he done? What if they really killed his son now? Or beat him? The man on the phone sounded really angry. What? He expected that low-life-terrorist wouldn't avenge himself by beating a helpless boy.

Oh my God.

He imagined someone like fat Mommy Bear beating his son. Punching his kidney, as he did with him.

Finally the phone rang again. The same voice grunted. "Your last chance."

"And yours," Abdul Hasan said, realizing that he was biting his lower lip. "Now, do you want me to take the car and disappear and leave you to explain it to your boss or let me talk to him."

Silence again. The call ended.

Abdul Hasan had no other options. They had the detonator connected to a cell phone, most probably. This was their style. If he drove to the place they wanted, it would be suicide. No, a meaningless suicide. He wouldn't have any leverage.

At least now he had a bargaining chip. Their bombed car.

He also had another thing now. They wanted him to drive the car to Saydia area. It could be the final target, possible, but most likely just a way-point so they could watch him and make sure he was not replacing the car or taking any backup force with him.

He continued his aimless driving, passing an elementary school. Boys played football in the empty school yard. He could hear the cheering, the shouting, the cursing. A kid missed a chance to score. His teammates where all over him, all angry and red-faced and shouting. Would the target be one with children? Would he have to look into their innocent faces before the car blew up?

After a long ten minutes, the phone rang again.

He picked up the phone and casually said, "So, are you the boss."

But the sound he heard made him press on the break so hard he almost hit the glass.

"Dad!" He was crying.

"Mohammed."

"They are beating me."

"I will get you out. Be strong, I will get you out."

But his son was gone. Then he heard the Egyptian guy from early this morning. "Now listen to me or I will let you listen to your son while we are chopping his fingers."

Hearing his son's voice was so painful it pushed him off balance. So he just listened to the man giving him the instructions of going to Saydia and the old don't-bring-anyone-with-you threats.

When the man finished, Abdul Hasan demanded, "I need some guarantees that he will be alive."

"Put it this way, you infidel. You can either drive the car to the destination we will tell you about and take my word for bringing him back to you. Or you can listen to him right here, right now while the brothers here skin him alive. And I swear to God I will do it and I don't care about this car you have."

In the background his son cried for help, begging them not to hurt him.

Abdul Hasan's heart sank. Fear, rage and worry consumed him. He opened his mouth to speak. Nothing came up. His eyes were moist with tears and pain, a pain he never experienced before, not even in Saddam's prisons.

He wanted to threaten the man, to scare him, to tell him something like the heroes in the movies did, something like, "I will find you and kill you."

It didn't come out. A pleading "please," was the only sound he could make.

Then he started sobbing.

-44-
Al-Amel District - Baghdad
June 10th
1:55 PM

"This is the place where they took her," Malik said in a low voice, pointing at the high-fenced mosque at the end of the street.

Hussain nodded. "You sure she's here?"

"Of course I am sure. This coward mole never comes out from his pit."

It wouldn't be easy. Even if they somehow got the green light to search the mosque, the terrorists wouldn't be sitting there drinking tea. There would be resistance.

"Lieutenant Hussain, you have to help me, help my fiancé. Please, time is running out."

Hussain let out sigh. "Do you know how many terrorists there are?"

Malik looked at the mosque then at him. "Not sure, I know that there is a room in the small house attached to the mosque. This room is used by the Ameer, I mean the Sheikh, to execute the Shareea."

"Decapitation?"

Malik closed his eyes and nodded.

"You been involved in this shit?" Hussain couldn't hide the disgust he suddenly felt.

"Lieutenant," Malik said, his hand on his side, holding the wound, I will tell you everything you want. I will turn myself in if that is what you want, but please you have to—"

"Malik I understand your—""

"You understand nothing!" Malik shouted, his face red. Hussain instinctively took a step back. "I watched the only woman I care about in the world being dragged by that monster. I have seen what he does with prisoners and it's beyond sick. Look at what he had done to me." Malik pointed at the wound on his side. "How do you expect me to stand here and talk while my fiancé is with Abu Ayob alone."

Hussain felt as if he were hit on the head. "You said Abu Ayob, the Ameer from the Islamic States of Iraq."

"Yes, he sent his right hand, a man called Mujahid to…"

Mujahid!

This time he felt it on his chest.

Hussain reached to his cellphone and dialed. Shaker picked it up from the first ring.

"Shaker, Mujahid is free and I know where he is." Then, remembering what Abdul Hasan told him about how Mujahid threatened him, "He might be connected to the Captain's son's kidnapping."

"Hussain, what are you talking about? Where are you?"

"No time for explanation, just come with some men to Al-Amel district, I will call the Captain to get us a warrant."

He gave him the address.

"Ten minutes," Shaker said then hung up.

Malik scrutinized Hussain's face. He opened his mouth. Hussain held up his hand. He need to make one more phone call. Abdul Hasan.

But the Captain's cell phone was out of coverage. He tried once more, no use.

"You said there is a kidnapped child?" Malik asked him.

"Yes, a twelve-year-old boy, do you know anything about it."

"They don't kidnap kids, as a matter of fact, they only kidnap men to behead them."

"You said that this Abu Ayob wanted your fiancé…" Hussain wasn't sure how to put the question.

"It's all my fault." Malik winced. "I am the one who brought him to Mahmoud's house to do the engagement party, you know, bringing a sheikh to conduct the ceremonies for—"

"The blessing." Hussain sneered.

Malik leaned against the nearby fence and closed his eyes, his hand still on the wound. "She told me, my fiancé, she told me that

Abu Ayob's looks gave her the creeps. But I told her that she was just nervous, that the man couldn't do this. Not to me, forget about his religious status. I mean how could you not trust your sheikh?"

A car passed. A man in the front seat stared at them a tad too long. Not uncommon when two strangers show up in a neighborhood, but given the circumstances, better to be careful.

"Let's walk to the shade," Hussain said, heading to a nearby large berry tree and sitting on a small brick that was left there. Cigarette butts, lots of them, were scattered on the ground along with cans of Pepsi and Seven Up. Malik sat on another brick next to him. They could barely see Mahmoud's house from here.

"So Mujahid shot you so that Abu Ayob could marry your fiancé? Why didn't you warn them when you get out of the hospital?"

Malik let out a long exhale. "I thought Mujahid shot me because I wanted to leave the group."

"Ah, so you wanted to leave the group. I see." Somehow, all the terrorists they caught were just about to leave their groups.

"I promised Esraa, that's my fiancé, that I would quit working with the group." Malik shook his head and scoffed. "The truth is I was a fucking coward, I just couldn't do it."

"Do what? The killing you mean?"

"*La Lais Al-Katel*" (no not the killing) Malik said, closing his eyes. "The decapitation."

They both fell silent. Hussain continuously checked the street and the mosque. Nothing abnormal, a woman walked to her neighbor's carrying a basket of dates. Three boys played football in the middle of the street. The neighborhood was too quiet, which, given the hundred plus Fahrenheit, was expected.

"In the beginning, they gave me chickens to practice the slaughtering," Malik said, his gaze fixed on the ground. "Two days later me and Mujahid went to a place outside Baghdad. There was a guy selling sheep, you know, one of those people you see on the road with a lamb or two to sell. Mujahid put a gun to his head and told me to slay the animal."

Malik's voice trailed off, he rubbed his face, "For a week after that, I became vegetarian. I know it will sound odd that a man working with the resistance cannot stand the sight of blood, but it wasn't about that. Slaying is a different ball game, you look in the eye of the animal, you have to hold it tight not to move, you feel the warmness of life in his veins, you watch the blood splattered and listen to the poor animal making that noise... fuck."

Malik spat on the ground. "They made me do this again and again until the day came when Mujahid came to me and told me that I would participate in the decapitation of the Australian business man."

His stomach rolled. He had watched the video, the execution was best described as a disaster.

Malik closed his eyes. "We were in a room attached to the mosque, where the killing normally happened. I didn't know the man, they kept telling me that he deserved killing because he was Christian. I told them that the Prophet Mohammed use to trade with Jewish and Christians, and ruled a city with a twenty-percent Jewish population. They just laughed at me and asked if I want to be the new Ameer. Mujahid told me that I would be surprised how easy it is to kill a Kafer. Mujahid had spent the week before talking to the Australian guy. I don't know, he gets off on that stuff."

Hussain nodded, the same thing the Syrian terrorist told them about Mujahid.

"We were all covering our faces, you know, because of the filming. As soon as I got near the man, I lost all my courage. My feet started trembling. I asked them to stop and spare the poor guy. At first he was sitting there on his knees, closing his eyes and waiting for the thing to happen. Once he heard me saying that everything changed. As if he was holding his tears. He broke down. The guy behind the camera started yelling at me because what I said wasn't part of the script. Anyhow, the poor bastard saw a window of hope, he start screaming, and begging. It was something I will not forget, his red face with the veins popping out about to explode, his reddened eyes. And his voice... God... all that gurgling and struggling. He begged me to kill him with my gun. I tried to tell him I couldn't do anything to him... no use... he wasn't listening... he was on the floor kissing my foot."

"Oh my God."

"One of the brothers came and spat on the Australian guy. The others did the same. The man didn't wipe it away, he pleaded them. Mujahid showed him the knife and told him how he would feel it. He asked him if he would prefer to cut his neck from the back or from the throat. The knife was not sharp and this was what made all the mess later. This lasted for ten minutes. Finally, on a signal from Abu Ayob, two men grabbed the Australian by his hands. A third guy sat on his legs, pinning him down to the ground on his back. His last words was to me, "Shoot me," he cried. I told you before how hard was it to slay an animal. Looking into its eyes... the thing is, every creature fears death. And this fear, this realization of death changes them. This man... I don't know..."

Malik shook his head. "Anyway, I assume you guys have to watch the videos for executions."

Hussain nodded.

"So you will understand when I tell you that once this was over I told Mujahid I could no longer work for them."

Hussain nodded again, trying to cast away the images from that video.

-45-
Al-Amel District - Baghdad
June 10th
2:00 PM

"What are you doing here?" Saud's scowl brought his eyebrows together. His hand reached to his eqal. "How much do they pay you here? You whore."

She scrutinized the man's face, the purple bruises, the red face, the shaking hands, his heavy breath. He was real. But she wasn't afraid. Not here, not in her own house. Not with her brother a few steps away.

Saud stepped toward her, the eqal now in his hand. His red shmag fell down on his shoulders.

She stood. Looking at him in the eye. Her thigh and shoulder still ached from the last time he whipped her with this eqal.

Whipped her.

As if an animal. A slave.

And why? Because she didn't allow him to touch her. But what really got on her nerves wasn't the pain, or the humiliation, it was that rage in his eyes. The rage of someone denied what belonged to him. He truly believed that he had the right to do what he did.

"What are you doing here?" she grunted, tightening her fist and ready to launch at him.

Saud stopped, squinting at her, as if trying to understand her attitude. He still had his eqal, his face was still blood-red, but she could sense the hesitation now.

"You bastard!" she shouted.

He stepped back, his lips parted into something like a smile. "How... you..." He shook his head, as if amused by her boldness.

Behind him, like a giant shadow, Luay stepped in. Her brother looked at Saud. His eyebrows rose up in a half moon.

Saud said in a commanding tone, "Luay, take this bitch away from here." He pointed at her. "I came here for business, not to be entertained." Despite Saud's attempt to sound confident, his voice trembled.

Luay's jaw dropped. He glared at Saud as if trying to make sure he was for real. "What?"

Saud forced a nervous chuckle, still talking to Luay without looking at him. "This whore is not my type anyway."

"How dare you." Enas grunted, her hands reaching out at Saud, fingernails pointed like daggers.

Saud rose up, ready to fight back. Luay's hand moved like a predator's claw and grabbed Saud's dishdash. He pulled him back spinning him around.

"What the hell... What—" Saud cried.

"What did you just say to my sister, you pig?" Luay lifted Saud with both hands from his collar. His dishdash made a tearing sound.

"Your sis—"

Luay pinned him to the wall. The veins on his forehead popped out, turning his red face into something barely human.

"Get your hands off!" Saud protested, then, trying to force a smile. "I think there was a misunderstanding here... I will not tell Dafer about it and if she wants some money, I can give it to her."

Luay's eyes popped. Saud flew over the table and landed with a thud on the floor.

"You son of a bitch!" Luay cried, kicking Saud's coiled body.

Saud shouted, "I am sorry!" His words were mixed with cries of pain and interrupted by the heavy blows to his gut.

The man sobbed on the floor. Blood splattered from his mouth. His hands moved relentlessly from his belly to his face in a desperate attempt to predict where the next blow would land.

Men like Saud, men who sat in bullet-proof cars watching the world from the shaded glass, had seen a lot of violence. They were not new to human cruelty, they watched people get beaten on their orders. The keyword was watched. They never experienced the feeling. Never been on the other side of the glass. On the receiving end of the beating and pain.

Now, Saud's protective glass had shattered.

"Give me the black bag." Luay pointed at his sport bag in the corner.

Enas did.

He emptied the contents on the floor, took duct tape and held Saud's hands firmly. Within a few seconds, Saud was tied and gagged.

"Come with me, you scumbag, let's see if Abdul Rahman knows you."

Saud's eyes widened in terror. His legs resisted, trying to stand while Luay dragged him to the other room.

Enas followed.

"Do you know this piece of shit?" Luay cried to Abdul Rahman, grabbing Saud from the hair to keep his head up.

"What in God's name..." Abdul Rahman rubbed his eyes and looked again. "He... he is my elder brother."

-46-
Al-Amel District - Baghdad
June 10th
2:05 PM

"What are we waiting for now?" Malik said. "You have to break in the mosque before the Aser prayers starts and people arrive."

He was right. If they were to break into this mosque, now was the best time. Still they could not do military operations in this part of the city without the proper approval. The last time Hussain tried to get the approval, it took two weeks, during which the terrorist group they were after changed locations maybe twice.

"Only if I can get Captain Abdul Hasan," Hussain said in a low voice, almost to himself. He and Shaker both tried countless times to call Abdul Hasan but his cell phone was switched off.

Finally Hussain's cell rang. He didn't recognize the number, yet he answered, hoping it was the Captain calling from another line.

"Lieutenant Hussain," a female voice, definitely not someone who could help him with the warrant he needed.

"Speaking."

"I am Doctor Zainab from the Karada hospital. I have been trying to reach you for the past half an hour."

She was the one who treated the two men. He looked at Malik again. He remembered what Zainab told him about the bullet found in Malik. His guess was right after all, Malik wasn't shot by the American or Iraqi forces.

But what difference did that make? Not much. It just gave him peace of mind to eliminate the possibility of Malik setting them up.

"Yes, hello, Doctor... have you remembered anything about the subject we discussed today?"

"What subject?" Zainab asked. Then she said, "Oh, you mean my brother Ayad and the threat. No, he and his family are going to stay at our house until he finds another place."

An image flashed in his mind, a realization. But it didn't last. A car headed right in their direction.

"Actually," Zainab continued, "I wanted to tell you about something else... something you might be able to help with."

Now that the car was closer, he could recognize the MICF colors and signs on it.

"Umm... I really." What the hell was an MCIF car doing here? "I am sorry, Doctor, I am in the middle of something... I will call you back soon."

The car parked, four men were inside.

"Okay, thanks, anyway." She hung up.

Hussain reached for his gun. He held his breath, watching four men stepping out of the car.

Then he saw Shaker.

"Finally." He exhaled. "How did you get the warrant?"

"We didn't." Shaker chuckled, looking at the other guys. "But we were feeling bored and thought, yeah, why not shoot some Sunnie bastards."

Hussain gave him a disapproving look.

"Just kidding, man." Shaker laughed. "I wish you could see your face."

The other three laughed with Shaker. It was difficult for anyone to stare into Shaker's eyes and keep frowning.

Despite his size, Shaker had an innocent face that could fit a six-year-old boy. He had that let's-kick-life's-ass smile, a reckless and idiotic and boyish look that made it hard to be angry at him.

"Anyway, I announced at the headquarters that I was going to help you and I needed volunteers and I got the guys here." Shaker gestured to the three men who came with him.

Hussain knew two of them, they were brothers, Mohammed-Ali and Mohammed-Jawad. Two-word names were common in many Muslim countries. Most likely to have Mohammed as the first and then another name. In Iraq, Shia used these names a lot.

The third soldier was a new recruit. Hussain couldn't remember his name. Something like Khalil.

"So?" Hussain asked. "Are we going to search the mosque with no warrant, no approval?"

Shaker rubbed his chin. "Let me think about it, I have a chance to kick some terrorists' butts for free and maybe as a bonus we can save the Captain's son. On the other hand," he pointed at Hussain, "you want me to wait for some lazy-ass politician to give us the warrant because otherwise I might be fired?"

"It's about following the rules. Maybe the Captain will get our messages and be able to get us the warrant in time."

Shaker made a face. Then he looked at Malik. "Please tell me you are not a reporter."

Malik shook his head. "No, actually I –"

"Hey, your face looks yellow," Shaker said. "I hope you didn't get your lunch from the Falafil shop at the corner, it's horrible."

"Please." Malik pleaded looking at Hussain. "She is alone with him now. You have to do something."

"Who is alone with who?" Shaker asked. "Are we talking about the Falafil?"

"His fiancé," Hussain snapped. "Shaker, it's serious."

"Your fiancé is in the mosque?" Shaker's eyes bulged.

"Yes! They kidnapped her, for God sake."

Shaker shook his head, turned back to Hussain. "Damn it... man, I can't believe it. You are here waiting for a warrant when there is a woman in danger in that place?"

Hussain tried to say something, but Shaker was already running toward the mosque, pulling off the safety from his machine gun.

"Come on, guys, I am going alone if I have to!" Shaker shouted without turning back.

Malik ran.

"Shaker!" Hussain called after him but Shaker was already half-way through.

"Okay, Mohammed and Mohammed, you two go with Shaker and support him. You," he addressed the third guy, "come with me. Let's try to find a back door to surround them."

The Mohammed brothers made what-the-heck shrugs and hurried after Shaker.

Hussain and Khalil ran toward a small alley that went behind the mosque. At the end of the road, Hussain saw a small yellow door at the corner of the mosque's high fence. The door was close to the small house attached to the mosque. It must be meant to serve the small house so that the Sheikh and his family could come in and out without using the main door.

"There, to the door." He pointed to Khalil, who ducked in and ran toward it.

On the other end of the street, a group of boys was playing football, arranging bricks to mark the goal. Once they saw the guns, they signaled each other and disappeared.

Better.

"It's locked!" Khalil, called out.

Before Hussain could answer, gun shots rang out from the other side of the mosque.

Shaker and his team already engaged.

"Khalil, do you have any explosives?"

Khalil nodded quickly and took out a small rectangular box, the size of a cigarette pack from his front pocket. He fixed it on the yellow door near the lock.

"Hurry up!"

More shooting came.

"Clear out!" Khalil shouted,

They stood away from the door, their backs stuck to the fence.

The small charge exploded, throwing dust and small particles from the wall in all directions. Except for the metal clanking of the door, the bomb didn't make much noise.

Khalil sprinted into the mosque's back yard. Hussain wanted to follow.

He couldn't. His legs trembled.

He suffocated. Something pressed on his chest.

They were outnumbered. Not even well equipped.

Did Malik tell the truth?

Who knew?

His knees buckled, the suffocating feeling got worse. Cold sweat ran on his forehead.

Breathe.

Like in a dream, anxiety paralyzed him. His mother... his engagement... his youth. He managed to move one leg. In slow motion like walking in water.

He needed to breathe.

God damn it! People inside were about to die.

His friends!

Hussain took a long breath. Then another. Good. His heart still pounded. His legs still trembled. But at least that suffocating feeling stopped. He peaked through the opened door to the yard. Khalil now stood at the door of the small house. Trying to pry the door open. To the right stood the main door of the mosque, where Shaker's team must have entered. Khalil got the door open. He fired randomly. But before he could get inside, a stream of bullets came toward him. He ducked. The bullets came from the mosque's main door. Two armed men, both wearing dishdashs, ran toward Khalil, shooting at him.

Hussain hid back behind the fence. He checked his gun. Loaded.

Footsteps clattered, they passed him.

Another deep breath.

Now or never.

Hussain dashed right into the yard. The two armed men in front of him aimed at Khalil. Hussain trained the gun at them. One spun around. Hussain fired five rounds.

The two dishdash lay on the ground. Both dead.

"Are you okay, Khalil?"

"Yes." Khalil stood, checking himself. "And please stop calling me Khalil, my name is Kais."

More shooting came from the mosque.

"Kais, let's break into the house."

This way, Shaker could make it through the mosque.

Two more armed men entered the mosque through the main gate.

Shaker and his team would be trapped.

"Hurry, let's get in."

Kais kicked open the door. They got in. Hussain found himself in a big empty room. Nothing there except one rag on the floor and some white banners on the wall with slogans about killing the infidels, the Christians, the Shia, and the Americans.

Thank you so much.

In the middle of the room, a man lay motionless on his back. His eyes opened. Blood formed a small pool beneath him. Shot by Kais' bullets when he first broke through the door.

The room had one more door. Hussain opened it carefully. A dark corridor had rooms to the left. At the end stood three armed men behind a metal door. The men blindly shot through small holes in the door.

"They broke through the house!" one of the men spotted Hussain and shouted.

The others spun around.

Hussain fired. He ducked behind the wall. Kais kicked the door closed. Shots hit the wooden door, making holes in it.

"I think you hit one of them, Lieutenant," Kais said, out of breath.

"Do you have grenades?" Hussain shouted above the shooting.

"Only one smoke grenade."

"Use it!"

Kais opened the door slightly. Hussain fired some shots to distract them. Kais threw the grenade.

A muffled explosion followed by a hissing sound.

The smoke grenade worked perfectly. Coughing came from the corridor along with cursing. Shooting still came from the mosque. Shaker's team must be fighting with whoever came in the front door.

"Now, on my count," Hussain whispered to Kais who nodded. He counted, one... two ... three... They peeked from the door and shot into the shadows.

Two shadows fell. The third vanished into one of the rooms.

The metal door exploded. The blast knocked Hussain to the floor. Shaker and the Mohammed brothers ran into the corridor, weapons ready and aimed at them.

"Stop!" Shaker commanded. "He is Hussain." Shaker looked at the two dead terrorists on the floor and whistled. "Nice job, bro."

The soldiers cheered. Mohammed-Ali and Mohammed Jawad hi-fived each other. Hussain smiled, trying to hide his embarrassment.

No! The third man was in the room.

"Careful, someone is hiding in the room!" Hussain shouted, but his voice got lost in a new stream of fire coming from the mosque.

"Take cover!" Shaker shouted. "They have reinforcements."

"This way!" Kais ran to the big empty room. The others followed.

A cry of pain erupted. Then a low voice. "I'm hit."

Mohammad Jawad lay on the ground. At the end of the corridor near the metal door, a group of armed men took positions.

"Cover me," Shaker said, throwing his machine gun. "I will go and bring him here."

"No!" Hussain called after him.

Shaker had already sprinted toward the wounded soldier.

"He is still in the room!" Hussain shouted.

Kais and the other Mohammed didn't have a clear shot without risking hitting Shaker.

Shaker made it to the end of the corridor and carried Mohamad Jawad. No one shot from either side.

Why weren't the armed men in the mosque shooting?

Unless...

A fat man with a long black beard sprinted out from the room to the left, shooting in all directions, heading to the end of the corridor toward the mosque.

Shaker pushed Mohammed to the wall, shielding him from bullets. His face twitched in agony.

"This is the Ameer! Don't let him escape," Malik shouted.

"Don't shoot!" Hussain held up his hand. "You might hit Shaker and Mohammed."

No one fired, the corridor was too narrow to shoot without risking hitting their colleagues. Once the fat man reached the corridor, the armed men started firing again. They had waited for him to come out. It didn't last. It was just a cover fire.

Shaker, still on the floor, did not move. A bad sign.

"Shaker!" Hussain ran to him. He carried his big friend in his arms. Shaker opened his mouth. There was no blood from his mouth, no talking in a low whisper. But Shaker's face was pale, his whole body shaking. The crooked smile, the playful boyish look wasn't there anymore. A peaceful look, one you see on the face of a sleeping child, was all Hussain could see.

"Shall we chase them?" Kais asked.

Mohammed Ali went to check on his brother. He was shot twice in the leg.

"No, leave them, just check out the rooms."

But Malik was already there. They could hear his cries from the room the armed man came from. Kais hurried inside.

Shaker looked Hussain in the eye. One corner of his mouth curved up. "I do not regret anything," he said, his black eyebrows brought together in a grimace.

"Someone call the ambulance!" Hussain shouted. Life was slipping from his friend's big body.

Malik and Kais came in, each holding someone else. Malik held a young women in her twenties. She was crying. Her eyes shut, her hand clenched onto Malik's shirt as if afraid he might run away.

Kais held a boy. The boy looked so scared he kept his hands up as if expecting someone to hit him. His face was filled with bruises, blue ones, yellow ones, and purple. The boy was crying too. Begging them to leave him.

"This boy says he is the Captain's son," Kais said.

"Do you see what I mean?" Shaker said, his voice now sluggish and whispery. "We saved two families, kicked some terrorists' butts... think about it... okay... a man like me, I would never dream of doing all of this in a life time. Could an English teacher do that?"

"Not even the best in the world." Hussain shook his head, tears slipped down his cheeks.

"It's gonna be okay, bro." Shaker smiled. A thin, crimson-red line of blood ran from his nose. "No one will mourn me, no children, no family.... you... you better find a wife...okay."

"Shaker, hold on, the medic's on their way." Then he turned to the soldiers near him. "Someone calls the goddamn ambulance, for God's sake."

"Tell the mother-fucker terrorists that..."" Shaker laughed, amused by what he was going to say. It turn into coughing. "No point of suicide anymore... I... I am gonna take all the virgins in heaven..."

Hussain laughed. His tears dripped on Shaker's blood-covered neck. "Save one for me, bro."

Shaker held Hussain's hand, his hand was cold and weak. "Just for you, bro."

He smiled, that peaceful smile, his eyes open, his hand still holding Hussain's.

"Lieutenant... you have to see this," Kais said, this time from another room.

Hussain put Shaker down on the floor very carefully as if he were asleep and he didn't want to wake him up. He didn't even dare to close his eyes.

"What?"

Kais stood in the middle of the room. The air was so intense Hussain almost gasped. The smell of decay made it even harder to breath. The small room was painted in dark yellow. A chair and one big closet positioned next to the wall. A thick velvet curtain divided the room into two halves.

"Look at this." Kais pointed to a bed inside the room, pushing away the curtain. Chained by her wrist to the bed was another young woman, same age. Blood covered all her body. Her eyes were wide open with that hollow and glassy look of death, her lips were parted, her teeth tightly closed as if biting on something. Her face screamed of pain... lots of pain.

"I think she was beaten to death with this belt." Kais pointed with his chin to a thick belt on the floor. It too was covered with blood. "A bad way to die."

Hussain's cell rang, another unrecognized number. He hesitated but picked up.

"Hussain, it's Abdul Hasan. Please tell me, have you found Ayad."

Ayad! Yes, that was it. He figured out what Doctor Zainab had mentioned to him and why he thought he heard something interesting.

Ayad was her brother's name, her brother who was threatened into leaving his house in Al Amel district. Ayad wasn't a very common name. Same man.

"Hussain, can you hear me? Did Ayad tell you anything about Mujahid?"

Hussain smiled with bitterness remembering Shaker's words: "I have saved two families."

"I couldn't find Ayad... but I found your son, Captain."

-47-
Al-Amel District
June 10th
2:15 PM

Abdul Rahman was sober now. He had inhaled very little of the powder Abu Ayob had given them, just enough to please the Sheikh. Drugs were forbidden by Islam. But since the Sheikh himself gave it to him, he couldn't say no. He didn't want to cause any problems. And to be fair, it helped in overcoming his anxiety.

For the past hour, Abdul Rahman enjoyed this relaxation and peace of mind. He could hear people talking around him, but everything looked strangely fine and non-threatening. He understood why people described taking drugs as being high. He was really floating, high in a vanilla sky.

Not anymore. He was back to the ground. And most likely he had completely lost his head.

Where did his brother come from?

Abdul Rahman looked again to the man on the floor near his feet. The sense of distance was back and things started to look... real. Good. But what was Saud doing here?

Maybe he was still high?

He looked at the man Luay had just thrown on the floor. Yep, Saud, no question about it. But he'd never seen him like this before, no head cover, his white dishdash torn in two places revealing his hairy shoulder and chest. And his face, my God, full of bruises of all colors. But the worst of all, the way he looked now, not only gagged and bound, so humiliated as if someone had just wiped the floor with him, literally.

Luay asked him something. Abdul Rahman answered. He wasn't sure what he had said. Something about Saud.

But Saud was in Saudi Arabia. What could bring him here? To this hell where there was nothing but death.

When was the last time he saw his brother?

Three or four months ago. Man, it felt like three years now. He came home at night after Eshaa prayers. Still living with his sick mother in the big villa in Riyadh. He remembered his bewilderment when he saw the fancy SLK Merc Saud drove parked in front of their house. Saud never visited them for the last two... maybe three years. He was just too busy.

His first guess was that his brother wanted to see their mother before she died. Doctors gave her a year at best. But when he saw his brother sitting next to his mother's bed, when he saw the looks on their faces, he finally understood.

Saud wasn't here to see his dying mother. He was here because she called him. Her last resort to hold him back from joining the Salafism group at the mosque.

"Abdul Rahman, there is something I need to talk to you about."

269

He didn't need to listen to what Saud wanted to say. He already knew. The way Saud and his mother exchanged looks, the way he sat next to her bed.

Abdul Rahman sat without saying a word. They warned him that his family would try to hold him back. They all did at one stage or another.

Saud started talking about Jihad and the Islamic organizations. The same old lies people just repeated nowadays. That Jihad was just a way some Arab governments used in order to get rid of internal issues, by channeling the anger building up inside the youth to other countries. But it backfired on them big time. That most of the people who were calling for Jihad, especially the sheikhs and other member of the clerks, were doing that because they were paid to do it.

Same old lies.

That the war and the fighting, all the slogans about getting the Americans out of the Islamic countries, was really serving the interest of the big corporations in the region.

Abdul Rahman had already heard those false accusations.

Except that Saud was backing up his accusations with numbers, names, and details. Saud said he was revealing such confidential information just so he could see the truth.

A desperate attempt.

He couldn't believe him. Saud told him that he himself was part of a big network to create, support and control war in different parts of the region. That he worked with corporations like Heavy Water to smuggle weapons to Afghani Talaban, the very same militia Heavy Waters fought and Saud was *officially* there to encourage the peace talks.

Abdul Rahman's relationship with his brother wasn't so strong. In the last three years, they had spoken only three or four times tops. Saud traveled a lot. But this… hearing his brother saying all those lies about the people who were giving their lives for the cause. It was just too low and too mean.

"Have you ever asked yourself why the Qaeda is not attacking Israel?" Saud challenged him. "Don't they keep saying that fighting, no not just fighting but exterminating, Israel and the Jews is their goal, how come then there was no attack, never against any Jews by Al-Qaeda?"

"Okay, let me guess." Abdul Rahman didn't try to hide his sarcasm. "Maybe because Bin Laden and the grand rabbi were best buddies in high-school or something?"

"Shut up and be serious, will you!"

"What do you want me to say? They are fighting the Israeli interests all over the world, not directly but they are doing what they can. And then there is the support Al-Qaeda is providing to Hamas in Palestine."

"You thick head! Hamas is not supported by Al-Qaeda, they are supported by Iran. Everyone knows that. Your Mujahedeen had never committed any attack against Israel, not only Israel but also some other countries and corporations in the region. You know why? Because that was one of the red-lines they were told not to cross."

"Nonsense!" Abdul Rahman fired back. "We... I mean the Mujahedeen have no red or green lines. All the infidels are targeted."

"Right." Saud scoffed. "And what do you call the thousands of Brits and Americans living here in the gulf? Cheap labor? Hell, they are living like kings here with privileges me and you don't have. Can you tell me why not one of your friends ever targeted them?"

"They have been attacked in Khubar."

"A rogue group that was exterminated and they kicked our asses because of it. My point is simple, Jihad and fighting is only directed at certain locations where it can best serve our interests and our allies' interests. You find Jihad in Afghanistan and Iraq because there are Americans, fine, but why is no one calling for Jihad against the biggest American base in the region? And please tell me you know it's in Qatar."

"Special interests? In Iraq?" Abdul Rahman frowned.

"Right, and this interest only came after the war. You remember how all the clergy here declared Sadam as Kafer. Yet no Jihad was called to Iraq, and in one night after the regime fell everyone was calling for Jihad in Iraq to fight the Americans who were coming from Qatar, Saudi and Kuwait. Don't you find this at least ironic?"

"Sadam was strong, that's why no one dared to call Jihad in Iraq. Now it's easier to establish an Islamic state."

"Bullshit." Saud sneered. "Do you think anyone really cares about establishing this Islamic state of yours? Yes, we do support the armed groups, all of them because they are serving our interests. And for Iraq, it's very simple, we don't want America to build a democratic country. We don't want the Shia to rule there. You can see everyone now is asking why we don't have elections here in Saudi. The same discussions are taking place in Egypt, Tunisia, Kuwait, everywhere. They are asking this with all the problems in Iraq. Now, imagine if Iraq was truly prosperous. People would rebel against their rulers. It's better to keep Iraq as a fighting ground for different militias, giving them some space for expressing their anger, failing the American project in Iraq. And who knows? Maybe those idiots of yours could really rule the country and then we demand some rights for oil extraction."

Saud stopped. He gave an apologizing look to their mother. As if to say sorry to bother you with all of this. She nodded for him to go on.

"In short, my young brother, don't be carried away by the slogans and the shiny banners. Your Jihad is just a tool for our politics."

"Jihad is not a tool. Religious leaders do not take orders from anyone."

"Have you ever wondered who gives you the money, all the money you are spending everywhere?"

"Charity, donations," but before he could finish he imagined what Saud would say.

"My dear brother, those charities and donations are all owned by different governments in the Middle East. Even your dear sheikhs are on our payroll."

"Yet, they are only making the orders for what's best for the religion."

Saud just laughed. Then he started mocking him, giving him other detailed examples about known names and known events.

Saud was like this. Always arrogant, always full of himself. He had no respect for anyone. Abdul Rahman always resented this about him.

Yet, seeing him like this, on the floor... broken, touched Abdul Rahman deeply. He always thought that his brother needed someone to humiliate him, to break him. Maybe he would stop talking to people in his haughty way.

But now, seeing him this way, Abul Rahman felt something for his brother he didn't think was there before. Compassion. He was his brother after all. Despite all his arrogance, all the coldness in their relationship, he was his brother. And his only brother for that matter.

"Your brother!" Luay exclaimed, turning from him to Saud as if trying to find some resemblance. "But... but this man was looking for you, saying that he wanted to kill you because–" Luay fell silent, looking now to Saud who was still on the floor. His nose dripped blood on the duct tape.

Abdul Rahman shook his head. Everything got hazy again. "Kill me? No ... no way, he came here to take me back to Riyadh." His head was about to explode. Was this a hangover of the drugs? Or all the mess he found himself in?

Luay made something like a smile, no... more of a wide grin, revealing a set of white teeth. The most frightening grin he had ever seen. It could be just the drugs hallucination. For all he knew, Luay might be wearing Honolulu dancing clothes now and doing a belly dance.

Abdul Rahman rubbed his eyes. Nope, it looked pretty much real.

"So," Luay said to Saud, punching his left hand with his right, "all of this was a play to get to your brother. But I don't get it, Dafer would help you anyway. Why did you have to lie?"

Saud made some undecipherable noise through his gag.

"I don't think so," Abdul Rahman found himself answering. "He couldn't... he would lose his reputation and maybe even his job if his superiors found out that he came to Iraq to... to talk one of the Mujahideen off the Jihad."

Abdul Rahman's eyes met with his brother's. For the first time, he saw something there that was not arrogance. Apology, regret, something like that. Was he trying to tell him something? Abdul Rahman closed his eyes, wishing he could clear out his thought.

Damn that drug.

"Whatever," Luay waved him off, "I don't care about any of this." Then he kicked Saud hard in his back. "This bastard insulted me and my family and I am going to–"

Abdul Rahman charged at Luay. Luay didn't move. He just poked him with his middle finger in the center of his chest, below the rib cage. The pain was excruciating, pushing him several feet back.

Luay snickered. "Yes... where was I? Oh yes, this son of a bitch insulted me and as you religious fellow says, an 'eye for an eye' right? So I am going to pay him back."

Abdul Rahman tried to breathe, he couldn't. Tears stung his eyes. The pain in his chest was unbelievable.

Luay sat at the couch. His gaze swept through the room, as if checking on all of them. Yousif was still sitting in his place. So was

Amjad, who took a larger dose of the powder and kept staring at them with a stupid smile.

Abdul Rahman exchanged looks with Amjad. I need your help. He tried to tell him through his eyes. Some Mujahedeen brain-wave communication kind of thing.

Amjad smiled and gave him a thumbs up.

So much for brain-wave communications.

"Abdul Rahman," Luay addressed him. "It looks like the honor of carrying the explosion belt will be yours."

A sudden drum beat in his ears. Loud, so loud as if his ears were about to explode.

It was his heart.

"Not this one, please... I am not ready," he managed to say despite the fogginess in his thoughts.

"What do you mean not this one!" Luay yelled. "Do you think we are in a fucking soccer club here so you participate in the match you like? You are going to do what I am telling you to do."

A knock came on the door. Loud and urgent. Luay stood up, looking out the window. The smug smile was replaced by a frown. Abdul Rahman tried to look as well but couldn't see anything.

Luay went to check but not before he gave Yousif a gun and gestured for him to watch Saud. Once Luay was gone, Abdul Rahman ran to his brother, trying to take the gag out of his mouth.

Yousif yelled and trained the gun directly toward him. "Step back."

Luay came back with the man called Mujahid, and another masked man. Mujahid's breathing was too fast, panting while talking. "They took over the mosque, those sons of the devil." Mujahid said, gulping for air. "We barely saved the Ameer Abu Ayob... Someone betrayed us."

Mujahid, glanced at Yousif.

"Where is he now?" Luay asked, with the concern of someone asking about the stock market in Japan.

"We have moved him to a safe house."

"Good, so we have to carry on our mission and fast. I am going to call the officer and tell him where to take the bombed car. I think this is our best shot. As for the explosion with the belt..." Luay turned toward Abdul Rahman. "I think the best one to carry it is Abdul Rahman."

"But I need some rest... you see... my body didn't recover yet from the accident."

Mujahid, Luay, and the masked man all laughed. Then Mujahid pointed at Saud, who was still on the ground and asked, "Who is that?"

"His brother," Luay answered. "I think he came here to talk him off the Jihad and ask him to go back to Saudi."

Mujahid made a tsk-tsk sound. This time Abdul Rahman could swear he could read Mujahid's mind. And once Mujahid spoke, Abdul Rahman knew he was right.

"Why then don't you use the brother to carry the belt."

Saud made that grunting noise again, his eyes bulging with fear.

"Leave him alone!" Abdul Rahman shouted, staying where he was.

Nevertheless, Luay grabbed his collar and whispered, "Listen, boy, your brother will not live to see the sun tomorrow. He insulted my sister and I don't care if he is Sadam himself. So I am going to be merciful and let him die like a martyr."

Bullshit. Abdul Rahman sneered. Luay threw him back on the couch. "You son of a bitch, you don't believe what I am saying. I will show you. Have you ever heard of the Baath torch? No? I don't think so. I will show you."

"I...I..." He didn't know what to say.

"Yousif!"" Luay shouted, "Go and bring me that gasoline pack from the front yard."

Yousif hurried out then came back after a minute carrying a small plastic container and handed it to Luay. Luay opened the cover and pushed it next to Abudl Rahman's nose.

"In the good old days, the days of Saddam, we used to soak the traitors with gas and flame then watch them running while on fire. The Baath torch, we used to call it. I wonder how long a man like your brother will take to burn all his fat."

Mujahid and the other masked man chuckled. Abdul Rahman couldn't say a word. He tried to plead, to remind them of Islam ethics. He couldn't. He just stood there watching Luay pouring the gas on top of his brother.

Saud started to scream in a heart-shredding voice despite the gag on his mouth.

"Please, leave him… help!" Abdul Rahman cried. The overwhelming smell of the gas was making him sober and dizzier at the same time. If such thing was possible.

"What happened to you, brother?" Mujahid whispered in his ear. "You have a chance to get to heaven, to revenge all the enemies of Allah, and also to spare your brother. Why don't you take the belt yourself."

Abdul Rahman wanted to cry, to protest, or even to fight. Saud, soaked with gas, wiggled like a dying fish while Luay grabbed him hard by the hair. He never stopped making this noise through the mouth gag.

This wasn't the memory he wanted to keep of his elder brother… especially not the last one.

Maybe it was the drug, or the entire bizarre situation or maybe both. Images of himself and his brother flashed in his mind. A long time ago, when he was a kid trying to learn how to ride a bicycle, feeling frustrated at how many times he fell down. How Saud helped him. Running beside him, holding the bicycle. Damn it, why did the good memories come at the most inappropriate times, why didn't you remember bad things about people when you wanted to hate them, to turn away, to leave them to their destiny.

Or maybe there was a reason for that. Something to remind him that this man on the floor was his brother, like it or not. No matter what happened later between them.

"Luay," Abdul Rahman found himself saying the words as if on auto pilot, "you don't have to give Saud the explosion belt. I will wear it."

Luay let go of Saud's hair letting him fall on the floor again.

For the first time since he came to Iraq, Abdul Rahman felt good about something he did.

There was something in Islam about family connections and blood relationship. And how important it is to honor them.

Whatever.

He knew now it was his destiny since the day he decided to come to Iraq. Maybe even before that.

"Why should I forgive him?" Luay said, "I want to see him suffer."

"Because you know that I will be better than him. You can force him to wear the belt, true, but he might go and ask for help or I don't know what. I will carry out the plan to the end for the exchange of his life."

It was one of those moments of sudden clarity. You know what you want, you know how to say it, and you know you will get it.

Luay pushed his lower lip forward.

"It's my destiny to be a martyr, and I can do it."

And before he took back his word, before fear got him, before doubts about heaven and hell crept back to his mind, Abdul Rahman looked again at his brother. Saud looked back, eyes red because of the gas and the beating. Apologizing. Definitely not the result Saud wanted from his trip. Abdul Rahman gave him his best comforting smile, tears in his eyes.

No need to worry, brother.

Well, there might be such a thing as brain waves after all.

No point in fighting his destiny. His brother had risked his life to save him. True. But that wasn't the reason he was doing it. Abdul Rahman could see more and more clearly now, as if looking at a prophecy coming true. The moment he stepped into Iraq. The moment he traveled to Syria and joined the Jihad recruiting agency, or even before that, when he first joined the Salafism group in Saudi... he could feel it back then, that his life was going down a road with less and less options. Drifting on a river with an accelerating current, why fight? It was easier for everyone if he just gave up.

Luay and Mujahid both nodded, both smiling in satisfaction.

A cell phone rang. Every one turned to Yousif's phone. The young man walked to the end of the room then answered. Mujahid signaled to Luay, who just nodded an okay.

"Yes, I was in a bad coverage area," Yousif said. "What? No way? He is here next to me, how is that?"

Yousif hung up and strode to Mujahid, eyes filled with rage.

"What have you done to my sister, you mother-fucker?" he cried, putting the gun Luay had just given him to Mujahid's forehead.

The two men stood like this. No one moved.

Mujahid, his expressions still calm, finally said, "Yousif, put your gun down."

Luay said something similar.

Yousif's entire body was shaking, anger... fear. "This mother fucker kidnapped my sister!" His gaze was everywhere, making sure no one was going to surprise him.

Saud moved, probably because of all the gas he was soaked with, trying to breathe clean air. Or maybe he wanted to escape, to free himself of his ties. Abdul Rahman inched toward his brother, taking advantage of the fact that all the eyes were on Yousif. He bent toward his brother.

If he could just untie him.

"Hey, stop it!" Luay shouted. Stupid idea. Desperate. Luay grabbed Abdul Rahman's neck. His iron-like fingers sunk deep in a spot between his neck and shoulder. The pain was paralyzing.

Yousif momentarily spun in the direction of the quarrel.

The last thing Abdul Rahman saw before everything turned to darkness was Yousif aiming the gun at them and pulling the trigger.

-48-
Somewhere in Baghdad
June 10th
2:30 PM

Abdul Hasan sat in the fake police car. Praising and thanking God for saving his son, and his own life. He couldn't imagine this could happen. He kept praying to God to interfere somehow, to help at least ease the pain of what he was about to do... but this...

"*Alhamdu Lilah*" (Thank God), he said again.

The cell phone the terrorists gave him was a pre-paid one. They deliberately left it with no credit so he wouldn't be able to make any phone calls, just to receive. Without his wallet and money, it wasn't easy to put money in to make a call.

When he finally made it and called Hussain, he just hoped that he could get him any useful information about Mujahid, but this... everything had changed now.

Abdul Hasan took a deep breath. Air smelled different, fresh, reminding him of the life he was just given back. He thought about someone to thank. He didn't have to think long. Hussain and his team. This young officer was up to what Abdul Hasan saw in him.

Since the day he met him for the interview, when Hussain was enlisting in the new MICF, he saw honesty, a sharp mind, and commitment. A typical example of Iraqi young men.

Not because of his nationality, or because of the extreme happiness he felt now, but Abdul Hasan always believed that Iraqi young men were the best people out there.

Well, maybe that was a bit of an exaggeration, especially with his not-very-broad experience with other people from other nationalities.

Still, with Iraqi youth he saw hope, to the point of madness where everything around them was consumed in flames.

He saw that unique altruism; giving when one didn't have anything to give. Being generous when everything you had in life was your own life.

They had seen nothing of life. Chased by Saddam and his gang to either enlist in Baath or in the army and war —mostly both— no freedom, poverty, and threatened to be sent to trial and immediate execution if they did as much as fart.

Hussain passed the crash course with an excellent score. He didn't have military training before. Yet, he knew Hussain would do good. Iraqis were all good once they put their minds into something. Once they were loyal to something.

Gee, he was really emotional today.

And Shaker. Hussain told him he was killed while saving another colleague.

There were a lot of people, young men especially, like Shaker. The first impression they gave was that they were the black sheep, but once put into a real-life test, once you dug into their real metal, you would find pure gold.

Abdul Hasan's years in the army showed him a lot of those.

But now wasn't the time to moan or write poetry about Iraqis. Rude as it sounded, Shaker was the eleventh soldier he'd lost during the last two months.

Abdul Hasan was sad and sorry, but at the end of the day, even death and the loss of a fine young man lost its edge.

He needed to focus now, this car was mostly connected to a cell phone detonator. Terrorists could blow it at any time.

Problem one.

Problem two was less urgent, but he still wanted to know about this group and what their real plan was. Terrorists didn't give up easily. Yet, he had two advantages now; they might assume that he didn't know his son was found. Possible… especially considering the fact that they hadn't bombed this car yet, they still hoped he didn't know.

Encouraging. The second advantage was even more encouraging. He had their bombed car now. And the last time he checked, car agencies didn't sell bombed cars. Not yet.

So what was his first step? No need to think. Secure this car. He couldn't leave it here, it might hurt pedestrians. So he had to drive it to any empty or deserted location and dump it there until the bomb squad arrived.

Then he could look for those bastards who were behind this.

Abdul Hasan pushed on the accelerator and then veered onto a side road and into a small alley, looking for any suitable place where he could leave the car.

Five minutes later, he spotted a fairly empty area, an old and deserted car park. His cell rang. The caller ID showed Kidnapper2. Whoever was calling was using the second number.

Abdul Hasan didn't have time to compare this with what he used to see on TV. The kidnapper called and a dozen FBI agents listened to the call and looked at some monitors with the map, and then the usual keep-him-talking-as-long-as-you-can line and they tracked the location.

Man, that would be handy.

They tried doing that once, during their first kidnapping case. The cellular network provider wasn't very keen on helping them. They gave all the excuses not to. Then after several escalations and mediation efforts, it turned out that the company didn't want to piss off the terrorists who had apparently threatened the management that any cooperation with the Iraqi local government would mean a war on all the transmitters and towers of the company.

There was no way to verify that, but it was a dead end. Some people in the Ministry of Interior believed that there was more going on in the background between the provider and the terrorists.

Conspiracy theory.

Why not think of something simple, like a business-discount package for all terrorists. Or free threatening text-messages.

"I need to talk to my son," Abdul Hasan said once he hit the receive button, making his voice as nervous as possible.

"If you do not reach the Saidyah district within five minutes, I will cut off his hands."

You should cut one after five minutes and the other after the next five minutes. Not both of them together. But he didn't say that. Funny how he could make fun of those threats now.

"Damn it. How can I know my son is still alive?" he demanded, his tone so emotional that he scared himself for a while.

"You have four minutes and forty seconds left. Do you want me to start cutting some fingers first, you son of a bitch. Move now and when you are there, I will bring your son somewhere you can see him alive."

The call ended.

Abdul Hasan's heart still pounded. Maybe it wasn't very funny even when your son was safe.

Saidyah was an area in the middle of the road between several other areas. You could go to Al-Karada if you took the Saidyah bridge, to Al-Adel district in western Baghdad, and also to Al-Amel district.

So maybe they were asking him to go there as a way-point and once there, they would instruct him as to the final location. Maybe they would have someone there to report his location.

In this case he needed to go there and let them spot him and reveal the real destination.

The other possibility was Saydiah was either the target or the target was on his way there. In that case, they would trigger the bomb at any time.

So what was the best course of action?

Well, despite the fact that he was ready to drive a bombed car half an hour ago, he wasn't so crazy about having himself killed. Things would be safer for him and everyone if he just parked here and let the bomb squad take it. .

And so he did.

After calling them, he stood in the area, keeping a safe distance from the car in case the terrorists tried to detonate it.

He called Hussain to check on his son.

"I will send him to your home, Sir," Hussain said, "then I need to contact the doctor from Al-Karada hospital."

Abdul Hasan felt sudden embarrassment. He had sent Hussain there earlier this morning to keep him away from Mujahid.

"But you already interviewed her, didn't you?"

"I did, but then she told me about her brother who was forced to leave his home by terrorists and I think he is the same Ayad who you met yesterday." Silence filled the line for some time. Then, "I am not sure, I don't think we will need Ayad, especially since I have found another man working with the terrorists and he knows a lot about them. It's just—"

"Hussain, if you think there is something down that avenue then you have to chase it and see."

"Exactly, we ignored Ayad and his sister twice and both times it turned out that they had useful info. So I just want to check with her. She called asking for some help."

"I understand." He didn't, but thought after what Hussain did today it wouldn't hurt if he did things his way, for one day. "Do what you think you should do."

They hung up. Abdul Hasan stood there in the street, waiting either for the bomb squad to come or for the fireworks party to begin.

-49-
Somewhere in Baghdad
June 10th
2:35 PM

The four-car convoy of Dafer Al-Dayni started from the Green Zone heading to his home at Al-Adel district. Dafer sat in his bullet-proof car, listening to his assistant summarizing today's session.

Dafer wasn't very interested in wasting his time yelling at other counselors in the Parliament.

"Some parliament members discussed a legislation proposal that will guarantee to all members in the council a life-time full salary, even if he wasn't elected in the next election."

The thirty-year-old assistant, Atheer, read from his small journal. He reminded Dafer of a Boy Scout, too well groomed and too smartly dressed. A shiny gray suit, with razor-sharp creases. Red tie and a white shirt. Wire-thin glasses and buzz-cut hair. Even his facial features were all sharp and pointy. Today he looked more a like robot than a Boy Scout. One of those human-like cyborgs.

Dafer nodded. He'd heard this proposal before and was interested to hear more about it.

"Any sign of accord yet?"

Atheer adjusted his glasses, moved to the other page of his journal, and started reading the names of all members strongly supporting the legislation. More than fifty names of individuals and groups were listed in the paper.

Really a robot.

"You are talking about three hundred grand a year for life," Dafer said. "Even my grandmother will rise from her tomb and support this legislation. Tell me about those who oppose it."

Atheer flipped through more pages then moved backward, looking for something. "Well…" Atheer closed his eyes, biting on his lower lip, "there was some shy opposition from a few Shia members. I am sorry sir. I didn't take their names."

Dafer suspected that Mr. Cyborg would initiate some self-destruct sequence.

"You know why those members are showing this hesitation?"

Atheer shrugged.

"It's because of the Shia higher clerk. He is opposing the legislation, saying that it is overloading the state budget. So our friends in the Parliament cannot disagree with the big guy and that's why they are taking this position. Wait for the real voting and you will see that everyone is going to vote for the legislation with no exception… Hell it's a salary for life. If I'd known about that, I would have put Omar with me in the party."

"Omar was under thirty-five during the previous election, so you couldn't do that anyway. But he will be thirty-five right before the next elections."

Mr. Facebook.

Dafer watched through the tinted glass as one of his bodyguards shot a warning bullet for other cars to stay away from the convoy.

"So we will not insist on passing this legislation?" Atheer asked.

"Never…let it take the normal route. See, from my first day in the Parliament, I have found out that money is the only common language all the members understand. So why bother using our influence to pass something everyone wants? As a matter of fact, I think our official stand should be completely neutral for this proposal."

Cyborg tilted his head in puzzlement. Dafer could hear: does-not-compute, does-not-compute.

"All the Shia members got to the parliament because of the support from the grand Ayatollah. But at the end of the day, they will vote for the legislation. At the same time, I don't want them to defend themselves by saying that we have pushed them to that legislation and that for-the-sake-of-Iraq-unity crap. I want everyone to know that it was their decision and they have chosen not to listen to the big guy in Najaf."

Atheer smiled. "You want them to disobey the Ayatollah so that he pulls out his support."

"We won't be that lucky, the guys in Najaf do not rush into publicizing differences. Unfortunate for us but we have to live with it. Anyway, by the time we reach the next election, I think many deviations will surface between Shia clergy in Najaf and the politicians here. Maybe one day we will have a fair competition with them without the support they have."

It wasn't as easy as he made it sound. His party didn't win enough seats to give him the same influence as the Kurdish or Shia parties. Still, he hoped this could be rectified by the right coalition.

The other thing that paid well was the alliance between him and the armed resistance. It gave him not only some credibility among the voters by attacking the Americans, but also valuable leverage when he negotiated with the government. Today he was about to explore another avenue of such an alliance. He had thought long about it, and given all the circumstances today, decided it was worth a shot.

"Listen, I want you to contact this person and arrange a meeting with him as soon as possible."

"Okay." Atheer blinked, waiting for instructions.

Dafer gave him a piece of paper.

Atheer examined it as if it were a communiqué delivered by pigeons. "Richard Barn? Who is that?" he asked with a frown.

"Let's say a potential ally," he said, remembering what Saud told him about Richard and the situation of Heavy Waters with G-Plans. "I want you to sit with him and see how we can help each other. You know everything about my business, and I think this man needs us more than we need him."

"Is it about today's operation?"

Many people believe that talking about terrorist attacks takes place in secure rooms, ones that have been swept for listening devices around the clock. And even then, the involved... conspirators, talk only in metaphor, looking left and right while whispering to each other.

Silly. Dafer hardly fought the temptation to brag about the last operation he arranged when he was on a live TV interview.

After all, it's an armed resistance; the people's right to fight for their freedom… and a couple other shiny slogans.

Anyhow, Dafer trusted his assistant for most of his business so he briefed him about his discussion with Saud and the challenges they were facing in executing today's operation, including the last update from Luay that Abdul Hasan didn't show up in Saydiah, which most likely meant he got his son back and they lost the biggest part of the plan.

No explosive belt could match a bombed car. Not only the size and severity of the explosion but the ramifications of getting a bombed car inside a protected area, the size of the infiltration, the amount of resources required to equip the car and deliver it.

The message would be totally different. There would be no impression, no wow.

And he wanted the wow effect.

Atheer didn't comment for a minute, computing, Dafer thought. Then he finally said, "I will do my best, but I think it's better to meet him now."

"You are right, call on the radio and take one car and go back to the Green Zone," Dafer said, looking through the window. A butcher shop recently opened next to the big Hawajis supermarket, what was left of it anyway. A decade ago, the three-story building had everything a family might need. Today, broken windows and peeled-off paint was all that was left of the supermarket.

Maybe it was a good idea to put some banners with his party slogans on the supermarket building.

Nah, this place was so miserable he couldn't use it even as a free advertisement space.

They were almost in Al-Adel district now. "Call Richard to arrange for the meeting while you are on the way."

Atheer opened the radio transmitter that made a cracking sound. He asked all the drivers to stop immediately.

Their car slowed abruptly. Tires screeched on the other cars. Then honking came from other vehicles. No one appreciated five cars immediately stopping in the middle of the road.

It was all normal except for the crashing sound that came from the last vehicle in the line, followed by shooting.

"What is it now?" Atheer shouted getting out of the car, Dafer watched through the bullet-proof glass.

A small gray sedan had bumper-hit the last car. The crash wasn't hard enough to damage any of the vehicles. But still there was a big noise and people gathered around the two cars.

Atheer came back and Dafer lowered the window glass. "Nothing to worry about."

"So why the shooting and all the people gathered?"

But the answer came from an old woman who rushed toward Dafer's car. She wore one of those black dresses that covered her entire body, revealing only her wrinkled face. Her eyes and mouth were wide opened, her face red. She had that crazy look of someone who wanted to hurt, to kill.

"Dafer, you bastard!" the woman cried in a piercing sound. "You pig, what did my son do to kill him... you criminals... you will bear his blood!"

Oh shit, not again. He had to talk with his bodyguards about shooting civilians.

"Go away, it was your son's fault." His assistant shoved her away.

She made another piercing cry and tried to launch at Atheer. Other bodyguards helped him to push her away. She was still crying and cursing, fighting the two goons who pulled her. Her muffled voice reached Dafer. "God damn you... Let God avenge my son... God..."

A cold shiver went up his spine. It lasted only a second, what could a woman like her do to him? Nothing.

Unjustifiable fears, unreasonable fears, feelings when you look at them that were totally ridiculous. Maybe the look on a madman's face or a curse by a gypsy or a weak woman praying to God to hurt you.

Nonsense, yet it somehow got to you.

All the bodyguards in the world could not protect you or ease the gnawing fear deep in your soul.

Everything was going okay for him today, coincidences were all on his side.

He reached to the front seat and gave orders to the man sitting next to the driver. "Call the house and have them put extra security measures... now."

He sat back. The cars started moving again. Guards communicated through the radio about tightening the already tightened security.

Yet, that didn't ease his fears.

-50-
Al-Amel district
June 10th
2:40 PM

In her room, Enas expected Luay to come any minute. He didn't show up. Hard to believe that he just took her side without even a question.

Luay was always very sensitive about foreigners in Iraq, especially when it came to the way they treated Iraqi women. Saudis in particular had a very bad reputation for looking at all women as inferiors. Luay once told her that he saw a Saudi in Jordan offering money to a lady walking in the street to come with him to his hotel. She was walking with her husband and pushing a baby stroller!

Not surprising at all, given the way Saudi treated their own women. Enas received an email once, one of those forwarded emails, about stores in Saudi Arabia. Photos showed one big door for men, and another smaller, always to the far side of the store, everything about it screamed "service entrance" for women.

Her brother wasn't a prince himself, especially when it came to treating women. But it was something similar to dating the girl-next-door, okay for the local boys but not for a stranger.

Iraqis and their rules.

So maybe Luay didn't suspect any relationship between her and Saud. And given the way he tied him and took him to the other room, Luay wouldn't let him speak to explain what happened between them.

Luay.

Enas couldn't deny the thrill she felt when Luay was beating the hell out of Saud. Anti-feminist as it might sound, it was nice to have a brother like him.

Full of surprises. She thought about the paper she snapped from the bag Luay brought with him today.

She didn't have to be Miss Marple to know that this was a plan for a bomb attack. The drawings showed the plan. And the writing described the detail of the explosion.

It was a shock.

She had suspected Luay was working with the resistance a long time ago. He kept defending all the killings and all the attacks. He wasn't the type to brag about his work. He also wasn't the type who liked to chit chat with his little sister.

But planning for a suicide bombing?

Somehow it sounded a tad too evil even for a man like Luay.

For Enas, a fine line existed between resistance and terrorism. A line most of her people started forgetting. Shia, for example, were calling any armed action against everyone –including the Americans– terrorism.

Somehow they forgot all about the Al-Sader army. She snickered.

Sunnie, on the other hand, were calling everything resistance. Even when they assassinated businessmen or sent suicide bombers to high-density Shia areas like Sader city and Karada. Even when other Sunnies died, it was Jihad and resistance.

Collateral damage had a very broad definition with those guys.

Another snicker. You can have a lot of snickers when you live in Iraq. If you manage to keep your head.

She always thought about starting a blog. Blogging had just become popular and internet access was available at her work. She wanted to write about love and life, and the love of life in her country, not the terrorists, militia and Jihad.

For Enas, the fine line between terrorism and resistance was if the act was against American troops or the government troops. Americans came here to conquer the country and it was only fair to fight them back.

That was her point of view before working with Americans. When she dealt with them, when she found how sincere and professional most of them were, it was hard to maintain the same mindset anymore.

She refrained from going to the extreme and saying that having the Americans, at least American companies, was the best thing that happened to Iraq. Because this wasn't the truth. There were still many pros and many cons.

All in all, justifying any armed action against anyone was very difficult for her now. It was easy to make generalizations about people and prejudgments. But once you knew the individuals, once you touched bases with them, you could not be so agnostic anymore.

Unless there was something to fuel this hatred.

Something like what happened to her family.

Or something like the bruises on her hands.

People like Omar were enjoying the new situation in Iraq, doubling and tripling their money. While people like her family had lost everything.

It wasn't fair at all.

The worst part was when the rich guys started treating the less fortunate as commodities. She stood looking in the mirror. She was lucky Luay didn't see the purple marks on her shoulders or left cheek where this Saud bastard had slapped her. That son of a bitch.

Despite all that she witnessed of Saud's ass being kicked, Enas still craved more. Revenge. She needed to take revenge on Omar.

Ashamed to admit it, but seeing him suffer was the only thing that would comfort her.

At this very moment, destiny, her destiny with Omar had once more spoken. This time as her cell phone rang.

It was him.

She picked up the phone, looking at the cheap mirror on her wall. Her reflection was smiling a crooked smile, mostly because of the dents in the mirror.

"*Hala Hala*," she said, maybe Saud's greetings were contagious. Her voice was soft and welcoming. Enas was surprised to hear it.

"Enas… how are you? It's me, Omar Al-Dayni." Omar's voice was weary if not anxious.

"How could I mistake your voice." Her tone was even lower and softer. She sat on the stool in front of the mirror still looking at the paper that contained the attack plan.

"Listen, Enas, I was trying to reach Saud with no use… er… I was wondering if you know where he is?" He paused, as if trying to put it in a polite way. "I know he was supposed to meet you today at noon but I don't really know what happened afterward."

"Is that so?" She stabbed the paper with a pencil… God, she wanted to stab him in the heart.

"I need him urgently, so please if you know where he is I would really appreciate that. By the way how was your… meeting?"

The way he said it sounded like how was your date.

"Great…and memorable." She looked at the bruises in the mirror.

Omar was silent for a minute. She could sense the surprise in his…silence, or breathing or whatever supernatural waves the cell phone could carry.

"I am so relieved and glad that everything went fine," Omar finally said with a chuckle. "I mean, Saud sometimes acts funny with ladies... even primitive," he said the last words with a laugh.

"Oh, don't worry about that." She turned toward her room door where Saud's cries for help reached her again. Then she added in her most seductive tone, "He is tamed now...I am sure you will like it."

"Wow...I didn't know you were that expert." Omar chuckled but she could sense the lust in his tone. "But you didn't tell me where he is."

"I have a better idea. Why don't you meet me and Saud in an hour. Let's say... at four or before that." Then she added, speaking the words slowly, "I have a surprise for you, something to make you happy. Saud has something for you too."

This time his silence was all desire and excitement. "But can I speak with him now?"

"Don't rush, honey, just come and you will be...rewarded."

She gave him the details of the location at which she and Saud would supposedly meet him. She ended the call with more spicy words just to make sure he wouldn't be late.

When she finished, she took another look at the mirror, she couldn't recognize the girl in the reflection.

And it wasn't because of the dents.

She could see something she'd tried to keep locked for years inside herself. Deep inside. A monster. But that monster was what she needed now; what the weak Enas needed to avenge herself. She tried to think of the innocent people, of all the moral reasons, she couldn't. The monster, the dark passenger who took the wheel now, wouldn't let her.

She sat on her bed crying, the same bed she slept on yesterday dreaming about Omar.

The paper was still in her hand, full of stabs, but most of the penciled little holes were around one line. One line that had those six words:

"Time of first explosion: 4:00 PM."

-51-
Al-Amel district
June 10th
2:45 PM

"My my…" Mujahid said, looking at Yousif who was now on the ground, unconscious. "Empty gun, I'm impressed."

Luay examined Yousif's head. When Yousif turned toward Abdul Rahman, Mujahid immediately hit him on the head, sending him unconscious to the ground. Luay wouldn't need to kill him.

"I had no choice," Luay said, "after what you did to his sister, I knew it was a matter of time before he turned against us."

"Indeed," Mujahid said. "So, are you sure our friend Captain Abdul Hasan will not cooperate?"

Luay sat back on the couch, watching Abdul Rahman pulling himself together.

"Yes, the man watching the intersection in Saydiah told me that the car didn't come yet." Then he added, "Anyway, I wasn't counting much on your plan about Abdul Hasan. I was working on a backup plan."

Mujahid smiled. Luay felt the hair on the back of his neck standing. He was trained to kill a wolf with his bare hands and eat it alive, but somehow this off-centric smile of this skinny son-of-a-bitch gave him the creeps.

Luay knew that Mujahid looked at him as his future enemy. The future when the armed groups and the Salafism militia won the battle against the Americans and the Iraqi government.

The future when today's allies started fighting with each other for power.

No one ever mentioned that possibility, well… except for Dafer, but everything was possible with Dafer, the man suspected his own shadow for that matter. As for everyone else from the old Baath, they were always referring to the Mujahedeen from Qaeda as allies, even brothers in arms. But Luay started seeing Dafer's point. A war between different Salafism groups and Baath forces financed by different neighboring countries was on the horizon.

That would be interesting.

"Glad to know you were spending your time planning while I was in prison."

Luay made a yes-no gesture with his hand. "You can say I was spending my time fixing your plans and getting your ass out of prison."

"Touché, now I feel guilty I didn't send you postcards from there."

"Oh, don't worry." Luay waved him off chuckling. "Your sister was taking good care of me."

Mujahid didn't smile. "My sister died ten years ago in Gaza."

Luay shrugged. "Don't worry, I am sure your mother was… er… busy enough giving you a dozen brothers and sisters you don't know about."

Amjad laughed, he was getting sober. "Good one."

Mujahid glared at him.

Amjad turned away.

"Shall I get the privilege of hearing your fantastic alternative plan?"

"It's not finished yet, we are still facing some difficulties getting the car through the first checkpoint but I am waiting for Dafer to help us out," Luay glanced at Saud. "Once the car passes the first checkpoint and explodes, we can send the explosive belt to detonate him outside while the people rush in his direction," Luay pointed with his chin to Abdul Rahman who was next to his brother.

"Would it be possible that mighty God has finally answered my prayers and this big-mouth Dafer could actually help?"

"See Mujahid, I have known Dafer for some years now. And I have seen people lose their lives because they underestimated him. So my advice is…"

"Let me guess, would that be: Not to underestimate him?"

"Wow, Mujahid, you are not as dumb as you look. Yeah, don't underestimate the man. You know what, it's better to leave the planning for this operation to us."

"If I only had my notebook." Mujahid shook his head again, faking a sigh. "Too much wisdom from Luay and I don't want to lose it."

"Okay," Luay shrugged, "if you don't like me giving advice, we can talk about your mother instead."

Amjad laughed but he put his hand on his mouth immediately.

Mujahid glared at Luay, then shook his head. Maybe a sick bastard but he knew better than to engage in a fight with him. Mujahid then turned to the masked man who came with him. "Brother," Mujahid addressed the mask man. "Bring the explosive belt and teach brother Abdul Rahman how to use it."

"Mujahid, we forgot about one last problem," Luay said, remembering something. "What about the car itself? I mean we lost the bombed car."

"Oh, I wouldn't bet on that." Mujahid smiled.

Luay felt the shiver again.

-52-
Al-Amel District
June 10th
2:55 PM

Hussain looked with more than a mild curiosity at the way Malik helped his fiancé get into the car. Esraa, that was her name, kept holding Malik's hand even when in the car. Mostly it was because of what she just went through, but there was something in the way they looked at each other, the way their moves synchronized, the way they talked to each other, as if they had rehearsed everything over and over until it became so smooth and so tuned.

Hussain scoffed at terms like "meant for each other" and "soul mates," but when he came across a couple like Malik and Esraa, he couldn't help but wonder if he and Sarah would have such a relationship, such harmony. It used to be a hypothetical question, now, well... things might get really interesting. Life suddenly had a totally different meaning when one was in love.

"We need to hurry," Hussain said, looking left and right. "Terrorists might come any minute."

Malik glanced a look at Esraa. She nodded.

"Let's go, Lieutenant, anywhere but not in this area," Malik said.

Hussain started the car and drove, heading out of Amel district to the main highway leading to Saydiyah bridge. He had parked the car in the shade, yet, it was so hot it felt like sitting in an oven.

"Where are we going?" Malik inquired, looking through the window at the blue river of Tigris.

""First I want to make sure your fiancé is safe. So maybe the best place would be the MICF headquarters, then," Hussain pointed with his chin to Malik's waist which was soaked with blood, "I will get you back to the hospital, your wound is bleeding."

"I will stay with Malik," Esraa said from the back seat, her voice trembled as if the mere idea of leaving Malik was terrifying.

Malik turned and extended his hand to hold hers.

"In that case, we can go to Yarmok hospital. It's only ten minutes away," Hussain said, taking the U-turn after the bridge and heading back in the direction of Mansur district. "But I need your help as you promised me, Malik."

"And I am at my word."

"What help?" Esraa asked, leaning forward to put a hand on Malik's shoulder. "What are you going to do, Malik?"

"Nothing dangerous, sweetheart," Malik said, patting her hand. "I will give the Lieutenant information about the... the people I used to work with."

Hussain suddenly felt lonely.

"What do you want to know?" Malik asked.

Hussain remembered his discussion with the Captain about the plan to bomb a car. "Tell me more about the group."

Malik hesitated, probably because of his fiancé. "The Ameer is an Egyptian guy called Abu Ayob. He was the one who shot Lieutenant Shaker."

Shaker.

Hussain felt a steel hook reaching into his chest. He pretended to look in the rear mirror as if to make sure no one was following them.

How could a man so young, so vibrant, so ... alive, be taken by death?

"Abu Ayob was assigned by the leaders of the Islamic State of Iraq. Yet, he is not the mastermind of the operations in Baghdad."

"Mujahid is the mastermind."

"Bingo. He is always the one who contacted other people and makes plans. I am not sure where is he from. He speaks pure Iraqi tongue. But I remember him once telling me that his mother was Jordanian and he came to Iraq when he was a little boy. You know, one of those Hayfa-street guys."

Hayfa street. The resistance-slash-terrorist stronghold in Baghdad. Hussain nodded. Hayfa district had the most modern vertical residential buildings in all of Baghdad. Built in the '80s by the best European companies to be home for university professors. Instead,

Saddam gave most of them to the fellow brothers and sisters from Syria's Baath party.

Refugees from Al-Assad regime.

They were immediately hired by Saddam's intelligence agencies and secret service. Loyal to Saddam, he used them ferociously against Iraqis when needed.

After the war and the fall of the regime, many Iraqis insisted that all Arabs livings in Hayfa district should leave Iraq. Everyone knew what they had done and keeping them was keeping a time bomb, not to mention the old wounds.

Despite the fact that many were evacuated abroad, back to Syria or Jordan, a large proportion managed to stay, as they had been given Iraqi passports by Saddam.

Not unexpectedly, they formed one of the most brutal armed resistance that killed both Iraqis and Americans on Hayfa street. The buildings were the perfect cover for the snipers. And the "common interest" made their groups impenetrable.

"There is another important man in the group. His name is Luay," Malik said, pressing on his wound. "Technically, Luay is not with the group, he is a sort of liaison between the Islamic militia and the old Baath and secret service agencies. The man is really dangerous – lethal."

"The elite forces."

"I think so, yes…I saw him killing a man with bare hands. It was…horrible." Malik closed his eyes, shook his head, and took a deep breath.

Hussain didn't want to ask if the poor victim was a fellow law-enforcement personnel or a civilian. What difference would that make anyway? Had Malik himself killed Iraqi soldiers? What about American soldiers? He hated to admit it, but fighting side by side with American troops against other Iraqis still felt... weird. Not wrong, just weird. Hussain had seen the burned bodies of pilgrims killed by terrorists, the so-called Iraqi brothers. He couldn't allow this to happen again. And whoever fought with him to stop this madness was more than just a friend.

Still, it felt weird.

"Anyway," Malik went on, "he is very valuable to Abuy Ayob as he used to give us intel and even men when we needed, experts, men like him."

Hussain reached a dead end. It looked as though it was recently blocked by concrete blocks. Other cars started reversing back to the main street. So did he. Nice to have flexible traffic rules.

"I joined them because I hated what the Americans did in Abu Guraib. I mean, I saw the photos on the Internet. It wasn't fair. Someone had to stop this. Our government is no good. But I don't hate Shia or anything like that. I have a sister married to a Shia man. We are all brothers."

Hussain nodded. Malik went on. There was no point of arguing. Maybe he needed to talk about it. People who were involved in violence needed to talk. To justify themselves.

"Then it was too late. It was too late from the first day I joined them. They killed people for almost no reason. They were all hypocrites. They talk and talk about Islam and they treat blood as they do water. No respect for people's lives."

He turned to face his fiancé again. Maybe he was talking to her more than to Hussain. "But after we got engaged, I made a promise that I would not get involved in killing any Iraqi anymore." He scoffed. "Never thought they would reward me like this, shooting me and kidnapping the woman I love."

"Never mind," Hussain said. "Do you know what target they were after?"

Malik shook his head slowly. "Not really, no."

"But there is an operation today, right?"

"Yeah, I guess. Abu Ayob, Mujahid and Luay talked about something painful to the government, something that would kill many people. But they never shared the location with the rest of us. They don't trust everyone with everything, you know."

"But it's today, right?"

"I guess, yes." Malik lacked the certainty Hussain wanted to hear.

His cell phone rang. Hussain looked at the caller ID. Dr. Zainab. He didn't want to ignore her anymore. She might really have something.

"Hello, Doctor."

"I am really sorry for bothering you, Lieutenant," Zainab said. "But it's an important matter and I don't know whom to speak with."

There was a code of Iraqi law-enforcement agencies, something like, "To serve and protect." Hussain wanted to tell Zainab that. But it sounded stupid.

"Tell me, Doctor," Hussain said.

"Actually, it's about my husband, he is the chairman and the owner of the Ghadeer company. A big contracting company. And they are doing lot of projects with the Americans."

"Uh huh."

"He was threatened," she said.

Hussain sighed. Threatening, blackmailing, kidnapping and even killing businessmen or anyone working for Americans was very common now. If you had a lot of money, they'd threaten you to give them money for your safety. Refuse and you were either kidnapped or killed. If you didn't have money, then they killed you to prove the point that everyone's life was in danger.

"Well, I am sorry, Doctor, but there is little we can do in these cases."

So much for 'serve and protect.'

"What case?" she asked.

"I mean, most threats are done by gangs specialized in kidnapping and threatening. They know what our resources are and it's not difficult for them to evade us and we cannot track them."

The problem was people watched a lot of TV.

"But my husband was threatened by a person face to face!"

"Even in this case, we don't have a database for known criminals—photos or anything like that—so that he can take a look and identify who threatened him. We are working on that but–"

"Lieutenant, how about letting me finish?"

Doctors! They always like to do all the talking. "You are right. I am sorry."

"My husband was threatened by a person he knew. The son of Dafer Al-Dayni. He is a competitor and…"

"Then let him submit an official statement and we will bring Omar in to question him." Oops. "Sorry, Doctor go on please."

"The problem is, I don't think we have time for this. Omar had threatened my husband to back off from some project. And today my husband will meet the manager from the American company to discuss the new project during the launch of the first one. So as you can see, if the threat is serious..."

"They will hit him before he meets the American guy."

"Yes, I am afraid so..."

"Well, if that man was serious… you said he is Dafer's son, right?"

"Yes, Omar."

"Shoot... They are serious people," Hussain said. Gone were the days were Iraqi were afraid of the government. He hoped it was a good thing. "Doctor Zainab, the best thing for your husband is to stay low for couple of days. Even if he wants to meet the American, let him do it in hush-hush way."

Zainab sighed heavily. "He insists on going today to the meeting, and the worst part is it will be during a big ceremony. A public one."

"Public?...As in anyone can come in?" He sounded asinine but he couldn't picture anything for the public in the Green Zone. Malik almost laughed despite the pain.

"Yes, it's in the Amel district water station," she explained. "My husband will meet the manager from G-Plan, the American company, there. Lieutenant, I'd really appreciate if you can put some protection on my husband or watch Dafer and his son... I don't know, put some bug on his phone or monitor their calls. Something like that."

Again, the TV... Hussain now understood why Saddam didn't allow satellite dishes.

"Don't worry, ma'am. If an American company sent a manager, then it pretty much means all the US army will be there. Those people don't take risks. I don't think they can get to him while he is there."

"I am not sure..."

The old white building of the medical school attached to the hospital was visible now.

"But my husband's partner talked to the American guy and it looks like they have problems with their own security company."

"Problems?"

"I didn't understand exactly, I told Ehab, that's my husband's associate, to persuade him not to go and he told me that the American guy just called him telling him about how he was risking to come because their security company, Heavy Water or something, has a dispute with them of some kind."

"Don't believe that, Doctor," he said with a laugh, trying to sound assuring. "American companies do not let their employees go into the Red Zone without proper protection. They value the lives of their people."

"Maybe," she said. "But I would really be grateful, Lieutenant, if you could put Dafer under surveillance or something. You know how dirty they are, the whole Adel district was shut down because of them."

"Okay, Doctor. I will do my best."

Malik gave him a we-don't-have-time-for-this look. He might be right. "I need to go, Doctor. I am sorry."

She thanked him and hung up.

Hussain smiled at Malik with a what-can-you-do shrug. Malik winked to his fiancée. "Some women, you cannot make the call short with them."

They reached Yarmok intersection, cars lined up bumper-to-bumper. Everyone was honking, yelling, and shouting. A young girl carrying cigarette packs came next to the car window. "*Afya Eshtri Fadshi*" (Please buy something) the girl said.

"What do you have?" Hussain asked, keeping an eye on the road ahead in case the traffic suddenly moved.

The girl's gaze slid to the back seat where Esraa was. She moved to her window. "Please, Madam, I am starving."

Esraa, made a move of reaching to her handbag. She didn't have it.

"Come here, I will buy from you," Hussain called after the little girl. She was seven, maybe eight years tops. Her face, and it wasn't an angel-like face, begged for washing. Her big eyes were filled with rheum from what could be days or even weeks. She wore a rosy dress and had her hair tied in one long brown lock. The lack of personal hygiene made her look older than she was.

She was back at Hussain's window. "Please, I am starving."

"And I want to buy whatever you have, just tell me."

She gave him a bored look. "Cigarettes, bubble gum and mint gum."

He didn't like any of these, but the idea was just to buy something. "Okay, I will take bubble gum… no… wait, mint, mint is better."

Another bored look, maybe she even sighed. Innocence was long gone from this little girl. It didn't matter if she were eight or seven or even six years old, streets had a way of changing grown-ups. What chance did a little girl have? No education, no medical care, and the only parental control was someone at the shithole they lived in taking whatever money they got after working in this heat.

"One thousand dinar," she said in a very practical tone. Then she added, pleading, "Please... I am so hungry and I have to feed my little brother—""

"Okay, okay," He gave her a bill of ten thousand Iraqi dinar, which was around ten dollars.

She flashed a smile, "Thank you, thank you... may God bless you." She took the money and put it in a small pocket in her waist, Hussain didn't have the courage to ask for the change.

Some people got out of their cars and started helping the volunteers in the street to direct the traffic.

The girl handed him a greenish gum pack that looked more of radioactive waste than anything else. Before he could say anything she scurried to another car.

Talk about customer satisfaction.

The traffic was finally moving. When he reached the intersection, the volunteer acting as a human traffic signal signaled Hussain to stop. He ignored him and crossed the street. He couldn't lose more time. The man shouted at him.

Sorry, pal.

He felt bad. Assaulting a mosque then disregarding those volunteers, he might as well have shot some children on the way.

The hospital parking was full as usual but he managed to park.

"Oh, shit." Malik winced. The wound, blood was all over his shirt now.

"Don't worry, Malik, I will arrange a doctor fast. Anyway, we have a lot of time now."

Malik gave him a skeptical look. "I thought you were worried about the next operation of the group?"

"Well, I am, but I also know that they are crippled now."

Maybe he shouldn't tell Malik about it. Trusting an ex-terrorist was more than naïve.

"You caught Mujahid?" Malik's eyes widened with joy.

We caught him and he was released. "No, not really, but we got their bombed car. So they won't be able to do any serious damage, at least until they get another one."

Malik's face became blank. His eyeballs dilated as if he just remembered he left the gas on at his place.

Hussain didn't like it when people did that. "What?"

"I hate to bring the bad news to you, Hussain, but the only thing I am sure of is that Mujahid was asking another group for a second bombed car for this particular operation."

-53-
Al-Amel Water Station
June 10th
3:00 PM

Ali Al-Kadumi arrived at the water station, shocked by how Al-Amel district had changed, less people in the streets, less open shops, and more white banners.

"This is nothing, we are still on the main road," the company driver told him when he asked him about the area. "If you went down in the middle of the houses, you would see the real disaster."

"This way," someone called. It was Ehab. "You have to leave the car here and we will walk."

The driver dropped him and went back. The moment he stepped out a gust of hot air greeted him, as if someone had turned on a giant hair dryer.

"Glad you could make it," Ehab said, showing him the way to the checkpoint. Another maze of concrete walls in the new Iraq.

"Are you kidding, half of the staff is here doing some work and the other half asked for permission to come here to visit the first half."

Ehab laughed. "Maybe you should have told them you would be here and see how many would still want to come."

"Are you saying that my charming character is not appreciated by our employees?"

Ehab looked at him from top to toe, then shook his curly head. "No...I think you need to add more colors to your clothes and maybe some make-up to have a wider smile."

Once they passed the checkpoint, the two large water silos greeted them like two giants guarding a mythical castle. Ali remembered how this place was eight months ago before their company took over the project. The single-story building was severely damaged by the war, the eastern part was wrecked after being hit by a missile. The western part was burned by the Baath forces after the war, like many other buildings in Iraq. No one really knew why they did it.

There were theories, rumors, and speculation; Iraqis were never short of any of these.

Now, the old building was completely removed, replaced by a new two-story one. The two water silos were repainted. A big fence surrounded the venue except for one opening for access, with a security checkpoint with a small but air-conditioned cabin for security personnel.

There was a lot of unused space between the building and the silos and the inner fence, so they decided to fill it with grass. Today a big tent was pitched on the grass where the celebration was planned. A dozen water coolers were installed in different locations of the big tent to provide air circulation.

They approached the checkpoint where two Iraqi soldiers hand-searched them before they entered the main space.

"Have you noticed something odd today?" Ehab asked. "I mean back there at the security checkpoint."

Ali tapped on his nose with his index finger, nothing was special except, "I still have my cell phone!"

For some highly classified reason, no one in the world seemed to understand why cell phone devices were strictly prohibited inside state government offices for visitors. Whenever Ali tried to ask why only the employees there got to keep their cells, he was risking being at the receiving end of the dagger-like glares of state employees. The universe was full of secrets, maybe this was just one of them.

Ehab smiled. "I have talked to the operations manager from the Ministry of Water Resource and asked him to allow people coming to the celebration today to keep their cell phones."

"And he agreed just like that?"

Ehab lit a cigarette, took a puff, and then looked at him with a wider smile. "No, but then I reminded him that the building is not officially yet under their control so that even his employees and himself should check in their cell phones." Ehab laughed. "Then somehow he was more relaxed about people carrying their cell phones."

"Next, you should work on solving North Korea's threats."

The enormous white tent could fit around five hundred people. A big stand with four big sound amplifiers and speakers was stationed to the front.

"How do you find the preparations, sir?" a tall and wiry young man who worked in the logistic team of his company asked.

"Wonderful," Ali replied. It was indeed wonderful, Ali watched three other employees fixing eight big signs that showed eight photos each of a different month during the eight-month project.

The password: eight.

"Finally the man we all hear about, Mr. Ali Al-Kadumi."

Ali turn to see a big man with a large stomach, nine-months-pregnant big. He wasn't fat, except in the belly and face, typical government-employee symptoms. The man was in his fifties, nearly bald (another symptom), and had a Saddami-style mustache. What was left of his hair and his mustache were dyed dark black, the kind of black you can only get from a shoe-shine.

Ali shook hands with the man, whom Ehab introduced as the operations manager for the water station appointed by the Ministry of Water Resources.

"How are the preparations?" Ehab asked the man after the pleasantries.

"Oh, great, still ongoing to the last minute," the man, Ali forgot what his name was, said, tapping on his big belly. Very proud of it. "Of course, all the credit goes to your people, Ehab. I never saw a staff so motivated as yours. Ah.. by the way, some media reporters are here. I am not sure how they knew about it."

Ehab and Ali exchanged smiles. Ali knew about Ehab's behind-the-scenes efforts to get the media.

"I heard many people talking about the minister of the Water Resources attending the opening," the man added, waving hellos to some reporters, "but I really doubted it as all the ministers will attend the big conference in the Ministry of Planning today. I have one of my colleagues there who just called me saying that it looks like a parliament there, people from all over Iraq attending the conference."

"What is that?" Ali pointed to a long table where small statues and other miniatures were displayed.

"Oh, this is one of our surprises for today!" Ehab said with an ear-to-ear smile. "Can you guess what those statues are?"

The operations manager frowned, tapping now with both hands on his belly. Clearly not an art fan. But to be fair with the man, Ali didn't blame him. For the last three decades the only art permitted was that glorifying the bloody Baath and Saddam. A regime that killed four million Iraqis coupled with art… They just did not go together. The other reason was that the economic situation and wars made arts a luxury very few could afford.

"It's abstract art," Ali said, examining the statues closely. "But what I don't get is the material used. It's not brass or tin.. It looks like… ""

"If it was rocks then I would have said it's Madonna of the Rocks," the operations manager said, still frowning.

Ali blinked. "Um… Madonna of The Rocks is a painting."

"Well… clearly this thing is not the Mona Lisa."

Thank God, the reporters were not here yet.

Ehab gestured to a young lady in her early twenties, most of her golden hair was covered by a thin scarf. She was petite and walked with grace. She was fixing description cards next to the statues.

"May I introduce Miss Sundus from the Academy of Arts," Ehab said in a game-show-host tone. "Miss Sundus, would you please tell the gentlemen here what those statues are."

"With pleasure!" She almost jumped in excitement. "We are a group of students of the Academy of Arts. We volunteered to work in an NGO, a non-government organization, which has the main mission of safely disposing of all guns and bombs Iraqi forces confiscated from the terrorists."

Ali couldn't help but smile. Sundus was moving a lot and standing on her tiptoes while speaking. Other students, boys and girls, her colleagues, gathered around them.

"What we did," Sundus said, "is that we took those materials, the bullets, bombs shells, and what have you, and turned them into artwork."

"But who wants to see a statue made of shells from a bomb that killed or was intended to kill hundreds of people?" the operations manager said. "My young lady, we want to forget about violence and destruction, not to celebrate it."

Sundus smiled, a charming smile of child-like innocence. She must have answered this question a zillion times before. "We also don't love guns and weapons. We hate destruction like any other Iraqi. But this is our way to say to the world that we Iraqis can make creativity out of our tragedy, life and beauty out of death and destruction. This is our way to say we will not bend to terrorism, but at the same time, we will not fight it with violence, we will fight it with life, with art, with creativity and culture… we will not be dragged to their level."

Cheering came from the people gathered.

She blushed, then stepped back, allowing one of her male colleagues to take the lead. The young man had long black hair and wore chains around his neck. even his clothes screamed "I am an artist!"

"Look at this statue, for example," the young man said. "It's a miniature of the famous Assyrian winged bull, made of two RPG shells, hand grenades, and an explosive charge, all confiscated from a terrorist hideout in Yousifya. Those weapons were meant to kill people, to inflict death and pain. Someone financed those weapons, and we all know who. We want to say to them, and to everyone, that those tools, those resources could be, should have been, used for good and culture instead of death."

Another young lady added, addressing one of the reporters, "We want to say that terrorists and Salafism groups' dark and sick view of life will not prevent us from living and creating despite everything."

Impressive. The looks on their faces, the hope, the challenge, the spirit, things that he always admired. "That was really interesting," he told Ehab while walking toward the stand where another group gathered.

"There is more."

Ehab pointed to a group of children wearing some strange attire, all too shiny, lots of colors, lots of symbols. Some wore hats, cylinder and cone-shaped ones, some carried swords, others carried long ornate canes.

"This activity was prepared by another local NGO, which prepared those children to present a short play about Iraq history."

Ali got it now, the clothes represented different eras of Iraq history. Four or five wore very bizarre clothes; it must be the Babylonian, Sumerian, Acadian, and Assyrian, unable to tell who's what. Ali was a bit young to remember what the Sumerians used to wear.

And there was the pre-Islamic state of Manathera. He knew that because the child had a tag on his costume. Another for the early Islamic state in Kufa ruled by Imam Ali, and another for the Abbasi Islamic empire.

The children all stood in a row. Two women were helping the kids rehearse their roles.

"It looks like they ran out of costumes here." Ali pointed at the last two children who were wearing modern clothes and standing at the end of the queue.

"Maybe." Ehab called for one of the teachers and gestured what-is-this, pointing at the two children at the back. One of the two children, a chubby child with a big white circular face and sun-burned red spots on both his cheeks caught Ehab's gesture and hurried to the front, probably thinking it was his cue.

Before the teacher could say anything, the child shouted his part, both his eyes closed, "My name is Ahmed and I lived in the Republic of Iraq in the year 2005. By the will of our men and women, our country will be back again to its proper place in the world."

People applauded. Some cheered, some just laughed. Little Ahmed went back to the end of the row.

"There will be a band that will play the national anthem and some songs. We will serve cold refreshments as well." Ehab pointed to another long table where people gathered around, "Although by the time the ceremony starts, I doubt anything will be left."

"It's hot." Ali shrugged.

"No, it's free food and drinks, that's the problem." Then as if he remembered something, Ehab put his hand on Ali's shoulder, "But the most important thing is your role."

"You know I don't tap dance anymore." Ali grinned.

Ehab made a face. "It's easier than that."

"Samba?"

"Tell you what, Ali, I will leave it up to you. I thought it would be good if you could come and say a few words, you know, kind of a PR thing. But if you feel like dancing, I am sure you would entertain us better."

"I didn't bring my flute." He sighed. "I don't want to do it, Ehab, I don't feel like talking to people."

"Come on, Ali, I promise I won't laugh, and I won't do any funny faces. I will do nothing, absolutely nothing."

Ali stared at him.

"Okay, maybe I will only pick my nose."

"Ehab, it will be just so boring especially with this weather."

"Okay." Ehab stuck out his lower lip, "I will ask mister shoe shine here to entertain us with half an hour of his wisdom, I am sure he has a lot to share."

Ali gave up. "You win, how much time do I have to prepare something?"

Ehab grinned, "It's 3:10 now. Your welcoming keynote is scheduled at 4."

-54-
MICF Head Quarter – Karada
June 10th
3:15 PM

Abdul Hasan listened to Hussain on the phone briefing him on the latest update.

Bad news.

For the last hour, he was under the impression that everything was settled and the day was saved. Now he had to live the horror again. The horror that it was Mujahid from day one and he was the one who postponed the interrogation in order to save his son.

All their suspicions about Mujahid were true.

"Are you sure about that?" he asked again, maybe for the third time.

"Yes," Hussain said over the phone. "The young man whose fiancée we saved, Malik, assured me that Mujahid was preparing two cars. It's just that Malik didn't know what was the target and execution time."

Mujahid. He tried not to think of the name. Still, the word hammered into his brain, bouncing inside his skull.

"But it's today."

"Yes, Sir"

How trivial. Of course it was today. The car he was given to drive was to be detonated very soon.

What if the explosion happened in a market place where one of his sisters, his wife, his friends, used to shop? What about other innocents? Was he that selfish to care only about people he knew?

When a grieved woman prayed to Allah asking to avenge her son or husband, to punish those responsible of the explosion, would he be one of them?

His mind was not clear, this entire thing about Mujahid gnawed deep inside him.

"Okay, let's see, what are the possible targets?" Abdul Hasan said. "I can only think of the convention at the Ministry of Planning, which will last till 4."

"Well, maybe then they want to do it when the people are dismissed, you know, to kill as many people as they can."

"Possible," Abdul Hasan said, not really convinced. Killing people after the conference would not have the same political impact.

Abdul Hasan could hear the background noise of the street, Hussain must be still in the Amel district.

"I know it sounds racist," Hussain said. "But maybe they are targeting a highly populated Shia area or some other target of religious nature. I mean, Salafism groups normally attacks places where the Shia are concentrated like Sader city, AL-Shaab, Karada."

"Hussain, they wouldn't need me to drive the car if they wanted to go to Sader city, would they?" It had to be some high-security place, and that was why they chose a police car with him to drive it.

"Okay, let's try from the beginning," Hussain said. "We know that Mujahid is the mastermind of the attack now, and we also know that Heavy Waters got him out, which cannot be a coincidence, right? There has to be some reason why they wanted him out."

"Go on."

"Let's assume that Heavy Waters had motive to get Mujahid out, and maybe this motive has to do with this operation today. Like they wanted the operation to be carried out or something like that."

Abdul Hasan took a long breath, sighed, and then said, "It's a long reach, but let's go with this assumption for now. I still cannot see where it can lead us."

"Do we know anything about Heavy Waters' movements outside the Green Zone during the last twenty-four hours?"

Abdul Hasan looked at the map on the wall. No creepy sounds in his office today. After what he did, no self-respecting creature would ever visit him. Even ghosts had standards.

"Captain, you still there?"

"Yah, sorry..." What was Hussain asking about? Heavy Waters movement. "No, nothing significant, you know how they refuse to coordinate their operations with us, saying that our lines were infiltrated by Baathist and terrorists and unfortunately this is true."

"You said, 'nothing significant'?"

Abdul Hasan inhaled, shuffling the papers on his desk. Shouldn't he feel happy going back to his work? "I just got a report about

American vehicles crashing two civilian cars in Karada. The driver sent us the plate numbers and the number is not a US Army number, it belongs to Heavy Waters."

The Ministry of Planning was so close to Karada district. Just one street away.

"That's near the ministry," Hussain said.

"Listen to this." Abdul Hasan was reading from the paper on his desk now. "The report says that the armored vehicles drove over two cars and crashed a small stand for magazines and cigarettes before entering Street 44."

Abdul Hasan stood up, looking at the big map on the wall. He followed a thin brown line of Karada's main street, where the two cars were run over then searched for the 44 Street where the magazine stand was crashed. "Oh my God!"

"Their path leads directly to the ministry, right?"

"Let me call the forces responsible to protect the ministry, I have to check what Heavy Waters did there."

"I think it won't be a bad idea to send some forces to enhance the security. What do you think, sir?"

"Good idea. Heavy Waters might have some interest in helping the terrorists carry out their plans against the Ministry of Planning. Who knows? Maybe a dispute against one of the companies participating in the conference and they thought that an explosion might solve the problem. Damn it, I don't know… there is something here, I can feel it…"

He looked at the small glass door in the wooden cupboard. Nothing reflected in the glass. If it did, Abdul Hasan was afraid he would see a monster. A hideous beast that scared even the spirits haunting this place.

What had he done?

Nothing happened yet. And if they could be at the ministry in time, nothing would happen.

But Mujahid's words and the look in his eyes kept haunting him.

"Sir, do we have a list of the locations and companies under Heavy Waters' protection?" Hussain asked just before Abdul Hasan hung up.

"Yeah, not an updated list but it should do. We have it as part of the security coordination between us, the US Army and the private contractors… But why do you need it?"

"I am not sure," Hussain said, "but maybe we could conclude something if we compare the locations and clients they are protecting. Maybe something will come up."

Abdul Hasan thought about it, then, "I will ask someone to look into that. In the meantime, I will try to find out what those mercenaries were doing in the ministry." He paused. "As for you, Hussain, you did a great job. I just want you to be on standby for the next hour. Maybe something will come up."

After a hesitation, Hussain said, "I will be here, sir."

-55-
Water Station – Al-Amel District
June 10th
3:20 PM

Bored, not any boredom but the kind that made reading the phone book very exciting.

Ali kept listening to the Water Station's operations manager talking to Ehab about how they used to run things in Sadam's days. Very inspiring experience... it was, if you were looking for one hundred way not to make things work.

But that all changed when Ehab stood up and nudged him in the shoulder. "He is here."

Ali turned to the direction where Ehab was looking and saw a man dressed in a Lacoste light blue shirt, similar to what he was wearing himself, and khaki pants. His face sun-reddened, his gaze searched the yard until it settled on Ehab, then on him. The corners of his mouth turned up in a smile.

A young American soldier accompanied Robert. He was tall, six-two probably, his off-white helmet, boots, and vest made him look more like a part of the building than anything else.

"How was the trip from the Green Zone?" Ali asked him after they were done with the introductions.

"It was okay." Robert flashed a set of white teeth. "But I have to admit that I expected to see the city in a better situation. At least better than the last time, six months ago."

"Yeah, I think you are right," Ali agreed. "Every day passes with a worse security situation and worse services."

They walked toward the big tent. More people were inside now, people of different ages, their clothes indicating different professions. A woman pulling a baby stroller asked them if the band coming would do the national anthem only or there would be a DJ as well. Ehab told her that there might be a DJ if time allowed.

"What caught my attention," Robert said, looking at two kids playing with a tennis ball. Where did they come from? "Is that the preparations people take to avoid security threats are close to nothing."

Ehab nodded. Shoe-shine said in a gruff voice, "If you are soaked you won't fear the rain, Mr. Taylor."

Robert chuckled. "You know, I wish I had a dime for every time an Iraqi told me that. Whenever I ask people why are you not afraid of the bombings and killings, they tell me this thing about soaked and the rain."

Everyone laughed. Inside the tent, the air was colder thanks to the air coolers distributed around the place. It was also considerably more humid, again thanks to the water coolers. Schoolboys and girls in uniforms carried leaflets about the project and distributed them to the visitors. Ali gave Ehab a skeptical look.

Ehab shrugged. "They are volunteers from a nearby school."

"You are brave people," Robert said, addressing no one in particular.

"I think we were left with no choice," Ali said. "Throughout the past three decades, Iraq moved from one war to another. People adapted, had to adapt to this situation."

"They accepted the life threat?" Robert arched an eyebrow.

"In a way...yes," Ali said, showing Robert his designated seat in the front row. "Don't forget, the other choice would mean that we gave our country to the Baath gangs and Al-Qaeda militia," Ali added, taking a seat next to Robert.

Ehab and Shoe-shine sat on the other side. The American soldier just stood with his hand resting on the machine gun. Robert beckoned for the young man to take a seat.

Ehab moved to the next seat to make a space. "It's a long speech, my friend. Trust me, you cannot spend the day standing," Ehab told him.

"His name is Ben," Robert said to Ali, pointing with his chin to the young soldier. "He should be back home now, in the States I mean, but his flight got delayed and he insisted on joining me today. Especially after what our security contractor did."

"I heard about the difficulties you are going through because of them."

"It might be my personal mistake," Robert said, holding up his hand. "But they made it sound like blackmail. I bluffed about us having an agreement with the US army to protect us, Ben was there by chance, so he backed me up on the bluff."

Ali nodded. "Costs of security are making everything ridiculously expensive. But you still need to work out something with your contractor. You cannot go around anywhere without them."

"Tell me about it," Robert said. "Everyone in my company, including my personal assistant, thinks I have taken sick leave for the rest of the day. No one will approve me coming here without Heavy Waters' escort."

A ten-year-old schoolgirl came to offer them cold drinks. He took water. Robert asked if they had Red Bull. The others settled for Pepsi. A minute later, the girl came back with a cold can of Red Bull.

Everywhere you go, same drinks and same food.

The World Trade Organization should be proud.

"You know, Ali, can I call you Ali by the way?"

Ali chuckled. "We Iraqis use only first names."

"Yeah, I noticed. What I wanted to say is that it's sad how things ended up here, with all the violence and the so-called resistance. I am not saying the United States government didn't have its shares of mistakes, but still—"

"Slow down, man," a man sitting behind them wearing a white flannel shirt and jeans, interrupted.

Another thing about Iraqis, they loved to participate in any discussion, or more often, *hijack* any discussion.

"You are criticizing the only friend Iraqis had since fucking thirty-five years."

Robert turned around to face the man. "I...um..."

"And who might that be?" The operation manager demanded, his hand on his hip.

"*Ayatollah Sayed Ali Sistani,*" an old man said. He wore thick glasses that could be as well mistaken for a telescope. "Without this man, we would have a civil war no doubt."

Lots of people murmured in approval.

"This is not what I meant," white-flannel waved him off, "I meant the friend who, alone, stood on our side when everyone else in the world just stood and watched."

Robert whispered to Ali with a playful grin, "Please tell me it's not Superman."

"George Bush!" a young man with sunglasses shouted from the back seats as if it was a competition.

"Hell no," the operation manager said.

"I salute you, my friend." White-flannel raised his hand and waved for the young man with the sunglasses. "He is the only one who cared about us."

"He is just after our oil."

"As if everyone else were after your mother. Everyone is after oil, man, at least this man actually did something," white-flannel answered the operations manager.

The argument continued, Ali and Robert sat and listened. More people participated in the discussion.

"What can you do," Ali smiled to Robert, "the US election was only six months ago. People are still in the debate mode."

"I prayed to Allah that Mr. Bush wins," a lady wearing a white Islamic headscarf sitting two seats next to Ali said, flashing a smile. "People think I am naïve but, they just cannot see what the alternative would be."

"And you can?" Robert asked. If he aimed for sarcastic, he managed to hide it well.

"He might have a slight cowboy style, but he is a believer." She flashed another charming smile, all white teeth.

"In what?" Robert asked. Behind them, the discussion went on, the operation manager was shouting now, accusing someone that he was anti-Muslim.

"In his war against terror," she said. "He is the kind of man who will not back down and leave us in the middle of the road like his father did after the war against Kuwait."

"Or like this John Kerry guy would have done if he won the election," white-flannel said, joining their discussion again. "Man, wait until some democratic wimp gets to the office and he doesn't have the balls even to fly here."

"But—" Robert shook his head. He opened his mouth to talk, George-Bush-autobiographer held up his hand, as if disappointed that an American was arguing against Iraqis' best friend.

"Okay now, enough with politics," Ehab said with a perfect salesman laugh. "Let me take all of you on a tour inside the station. It's time to brag about what we have done on this project." He turned to Ali and said teasingly, "And if Mr. Tyler enjoyed all the political mumbo-jumbo, then I am sure Ali will put some in his keynote."

He winked. Ali chuckled waving him off.

In a few minutes they were all following Ehab and the water station's manager for a tour inside the water station.

-56-
Al-Yarmook Hospital – near Al-Amel District
June 10th
3:30 PM

Lieutenant Hussain watched the young resident doctor re-suturing Malik's wound.

They were lucky they managed to find an empty bed in the over-packed hospital, filled with people with different levels of injuries. The hot weather and the fuming odors of blood and God-knew-what nauseated Hussain.

Malik's fiancée, he forgot her name, watched Malik with a frozen stare, like someone in another world. Hussain thought about her, about what she went through today. He wasn't sure what Abu Ayob did to her, did he touched her? Did he hit her? Would she be able to forget this one day?

Malik was staring at the ceiling, he too looked distant. Would he remember Abu Ayob and his group every time he looked at his fiancée?

A lady in a nearby bed cried in pain, she had burn marks on her arms and forehead. The man next to her, probably the husband, shouted at the nurses. They shouted back.

Two hospital visits in one day… that was too much for him.

"Is it always full like this?" he asked the young doctor. Why were all doctors in the emergency rooms young?

"Worse."

"I can't imagine how on earth this could be worse. I mean, we barely found an empty bed and as far as I can see, all people here are injured not sick."

"Explosions," the doctor said, signing a paper a young nurse had brought.

Hussain noticed the way the nurse looked at the young doctor. He had no idea why nurses always had that thing for doctors and if that was only in Iraq. But at times like this he yearned to be a doctor.

"But no explosion happened today or yesterday." Hussain tried to remember. "Or even day before yesterday."

"Last week," the doctor murmured, opened the wound and started cleaning it again. Some white liquid oozed out of wound.

Okay, maybe he would re-consider being a doctor for now.

"Man, if this was the situation a week after the explosion, I can't imagine what the hospital looked like the day of the explosion."

But he already knew the answer.

"Worse."

"Do you always answers all question with one word, Doctor?"

The young practitioner looked up, his mouth's corners curved up in what might be considered as a smile. "No."

Even Malik couldn't help but laugh. His laugh immediately turned into "ouch" as the doctor started suturing.

"Our biggest problem is the morgue," the young practitioner elaborated. "They are unable to cope with the body count. You see, in the Karkh side of Baghdad, the morgue can only fit four hundred bodies. And as you might know, Lieutenant, we get this number of bodies in one week."

"So the morgue has to dispose.. I mean bury, four hundred bodies a week."

"And you didn't even need a calculator," the doctor said with a mocking smile.

Why were all doctors in the emergency rooms young and wise-ass?

"We couldn't bury them," the doctor said, almost done with the wound. "Then people volunteered to take the bodies and bury them in Najaf city, at their own expense, and of course, at their own risk."

Risk... going to Najaf wasn't safe these days because of the Salafism groups blocking the roads and killing anyone going to the holy shrines in Najaf and Kerbela.

"Why Najaf, why not bury them in Baghdad?" Malik asked.

The doctor stared at Malik as if he was asking why one plus one equals two.

Hussain explained, "Because it's close to Imam Ali's holy shrine, Shia believe that burying in Najaf cemetery has a special spiritual benefit, especially for the deceased. People used it since the first days of the Islamic empire."

"Actually, the history of Najaf cemetery goes way before the Islamic state," the doctor added. "Archeologists had some evidence that Adam and Noah and several other prophets were buried on that very spot. That's why it is called Wadi Al-Salam."

"The valley of peace. I've heard about it… but…" Malik wasn't buying it. "I mean, come on, how could one cemetery fit for all the Shia, or according to you, doctor, for all those people since God-knows-when? It's millions of tombs we are talking about."

"Well, first of all, it's by far the world's largest cemetery, even bigger than Baghdad city itself," the doctor replied, walking to the bed where the woman with burned hands lay. The husband was still shouting at the nurses. He immediately went silent, giving the doctor a polite smile. "And it's a known fact that after ages of wars and different weather conditions, many parts of the cemetery were re-used to bury new people after the old tombs were obscured due to different reasons. It's a multi-layer cemetery, if you like."

What do you know? Doctor-one-word turned out to be a scholar.

"We buried my three brothers there," Hussain said. After years of being afraid to talk about the subject, one of the new era's benefits for Hussain —and thousands of people like him— was that they could not only talk about their lost family members but could also get people's sympathy because of it.

And yes. He craved for that sympathy… not sure why though.

A stunning young woman wearing a white blazer came and whispered something to the doctor. She had coal black hair and white, porcelain-like, delicate features. The doctor nodded, then she padded away.

Okay, I want to be a doctor, Hussain thought with a sigh.

Then he remembered, he was so taken by all the excitement and completely forgot about his mother and the engagement. He checked his watch. It was 3:30. Maybe he still had some time, not much but still some.

He went outside and dialed his mother's number from his speed dial.

"Son, you okay?"

With all the killing and death he saw today, hearing the voice of the only person in the world who cared about him, really cared… to the point of panic, was something beyond comforting. It gave him the feeling of safety. The feeling of everything-is-going-to-be-all-right. Although weak and old, she always had that strength saved for him. He never asked her for help. Of course, he was a big boy now, a man who took care of himself and the entire family. Nevertheless, it was good to hear her voice. The tone of the mother ready to do anything to protect her child. The tone that made every word sound like "I am here for you."

Okay, that was a tad too soft for a commando officer. But for someone who just saw his friend shot dead, Hussain believed he was doing well.

"Everything is fine, Mom." Yeah, right…"Some boring job." He forced a chuckle that sounded like someone was about to burst into tears.

"What time are you coming then? Don't forget the appointment, son, the people are expecting us at five today."

There was no such thing as mother knows everything, or mother's intuition. Hussain had thought about it a lot, she couldn't even sense the trembling in his voice.

"I will try."

"Try? Hussain, don't try, you have to be here, son, it will look bad if we don't show up. And don't forget you have to take a shower and dress up."

Take a shower and dress up. Suit and tie. Perfume. It sounded bizarre and nice and so unreal.

"Okay, Mom, I will be there… *Inshalla*."

"*Inshalla*," she said with the happiness of a child who was promised a trip to Disneyland.

"Lieutenant, would you please do us a last favor?" Esraa asked.

"Sure."

"I called my mother. She is staying at my uncle's, two blocks away from our house…"

He had spent a lot of time with Malik and his fiancée, and needed some time to concentrate on the mission in hand.

"I will drive you there," Hussain said with a smile. Hard to say no to a lady.

On the other hand, there was nothing he could do for the case they were working on. The Captain was going to send reinforcements to the Ministry of Planning and it should be fine.

Even if the terrorists really had another bombed car, the forces in the area would be highly alerted.

The only thing that he could think of now was to break into the terrorist's house next to Mahmoud's. It might help either arresting some terrorists –if anyone was dumb enough to stay there after what happened in the mosque– or at least it might help him find some clues left by the group.

Hussain felt sorry for the people in that area. Mahmoud and his family, Ayad who had to leave his home, and God knew who else had to suffer because of them. They were like cancer, once it started it was so difficult to stop it… Multiply… that's what it did.

Salafism, Wahabisim, Qaeda and a dozen other blood-thirsty ideologies, that 'invaded' Iraq in the last decade brought only death, pain, blood and poverty. There was no prosperity there. One look at the fifty beds filled with people suffering, because of this cancer-like ideology of Qaeda, was enough to prove the point. No, it couldn't be religion that caused all this pain and misery. It couldn't be anything related to God. And whatever it was, Hussain wanted so desperately to end it, to fight it. But most importantly, and this was something he didn't really pay much attention to before, he wanted to stop this disease from using the name of his religion to kill innocents.

A man cried in agony, a child wept. Hussain felt the blood rising into his head. Rage. He couldn't really explain what it was. After all, it was hard to keep emotions checked while looking at people who lost hands and legs, the agony on their faces, the pain on the faces of their families, he could almost see the ordeal of their future life. How a poor family would manage with the only supporter now handicapped? Or dead?

And it was hard to keep thinking logically when your friends' blood was still wet. All you could do to ease the pain was to look for something to do. A way for revenge, justice, whatever it was.

He had promised Dr. Zainab that he would check into the threat her husband got from Al-Dayni. Maybe it wasn't a very urgent thing. But what if this G-Plan company couldn't provide real protection to the area? What if Al-Dayni sent someone to kill the doctor's husband?

He was ashamed of thinking this way, but when he compared the life of one man to the life of possibly hundreds of victims… well, it all came to numbers at the end of the day, didn't it?

They checked out of the hospital, not that they did any paperwork of any kind. Hussain just helped Malik to stand and he said goodbye to the hospital staff.

Mahmoud's house was maybe ten minutes away. While he drove, his cell phone rang. It was the Captain's landline.

"Hussain, I have two things for you." The Captain's voice was weary. "I am not sure how it will help but anyway… first, Heavy Waters company is not protecting any company we know about that is participating in the conference of the Ministry of Planning."

"Sir, do we know if Heavy Waters has a contract with the American company G-Plans?"

Through the phone came the shoveling of papers. Hussain wasn't very comfortable asking his boss to look for something for him, even though Abdul Hasan was always very practical and down-to-the-earth. It just didn't feel right.

"They are their biggest client," Abdul Hasan said. "It says here that they are protecting more than… let me see… more than twenty projects for this G-Plans."

Hussain's brain was thinking in two directions now: Mujahid and his group and what target they possibly had. And on the other side, Heavy Waters and how they fitted into that.

They were involved somehow. They sprung Mujahid, didn't they? And placing them near the Ministry of Planning on a day like this when they had no assignment was suspicious.

"Hussain, just to bring you up to speed," the Captain said, "I have spoken with the man in charge of protecting the Ministry of Planning, an American officer, a fine man and I trust him for that matter. He said that Richard Barn, the same guy who took Mujahid from our headquarters, came to the location and took an Iraqi soldier from the front lines because he was involved in a very urgent investigation. The officer said that the soldier was immediately replaced by another and everything is normal as far as he could tell."

"You said took him?" Hmmm. "Is it possible he was trying to undermine the security there?"

It made even less sense to his own ears. The soldier was replaced by another anyway.

"Actually, it might be the other way around."

"What do you mean, sir?"

"Do you remember the case with that officer from the Iraqi Army who was accused of receiving paychecks from unknown sources."

Of course he remembered him, the bald officer who caused a lot of problems for everyone. The memory also brought back another painful one. Shaker had once engaged in a fight with that man, accusing him of taking bribes to pass information to the militia... Shaker always wanted to take the law into his own hands. It was just hard to accept that he was dead. Such a man, so strong, so vigorous.

"Yes sir, I remember the man."

"Well, he is the one Richard took with him. I wouldn't say that taking such a man would undermine any security. If anything, it would make it better."

"Not if he put him somewhere else?" Something crossed Hussain's mind for a brief second and vanished. A glimpse of an idea. It disappeared now but he knew it would come again.

"What do you mean?"

"I am not sure, sir, not yet anyhow. I need to think about it... just give me couple of minutes and I will call you back."

"Hussain."

"Yes, sir."

"You have done great today. Me and my family are alive because of what you have done."

"Sir, it's my..." Hussain tried to say something, but it sounded like a worn-out cliché.

"My point is," Abdul Hasan said, "you have done well and I am sure whatever those bastards are about, we can stop them. I have sent everyone to protect the ministry."

He thanked him and ended the call, not sure of what else to say. They had reached the uncle's house. Everything was quiet. Probably the terrorists had left the area.

"I want to help you, Hussain," Malik told him, his face still yellow and drawn.

"You rest," Hussain told him and stepped out of the car to help him get out. "I am not sure there is anything we can do right now."

He helped Malik out of the car. His fiancé thanked him. He said it was nothing.

Music came from somewhere behind the houses.

"What is that?"

"I think it's some celebration about some water project," Esraa replied. "Everyone in the neighborhood is there now. My father was supposed to go but I guess because of what happened to me..."

It hit him...He understood everything...All the different threads...the bits and pieces...everything was connected...the problem between G-Plans and Heavy Waters...releasing Mujahid... taking the bad officer to put him in another location...the celebration of opening the water project of Al-Ghadeer company...Al-Dayni's threat to Al-Ghadeer...the competition between the two men and the rumors of Dafer Al-Dayni's connections to the terrorists.

"Oh my God... How can I get there?" he cried.

Malik and Esraa jumped.

She pointed at a turn to the right. "Take that turn and keep moving forward, it's so close.. you can't miss it, just look at the water silos."

Hussain thanked them and hopped into the car, pressing the gas pedal. He dialed the office and asked for Abdul Hasan. When he finally got on the line Hussain, could see the water silos of the new station.

"Sir...I think I know where the terrorists will hit today," he said trying to control his fast breathing.

His entire body was shivering.

"And sir, I think we were wrong."

-57-
Al-Adel district
June 10th
3:40 PM

"That's great, call Luay and relay these details to him so he can prepare himself." Dafer hung up on his assistant. The results were better than he anticipated. He would be able to hit his opponents in the government with a blow that they wouldn't forget for weeks. Not only that but he would get rid of that Al-Kadumi, who cost them a lot of money.

Nothing better than hitting two birds with one stone.

In the beginning, their plan was to target the convention at the Ministry of Planning. But then some of his allies told him that they wanted to participate in the conference.

"If we don't secure a quick win out of that conference we'll make sure it fails," one of the leaders of a big group told him early that morning.

Then Dafer thought about it. With all the bureaucracies and the conflicts of interest, he was pretty sure that this conference would not have a snowball in hell's chance of success. It would be a circus, just like the Parliament.

He didn't need a bomb to fail this conference. He just had to let them fail.

On the other hand, he read the newspapers this morning. The opening ceremony looked to be a big event. Which made it a perfect target, from many perspectives.

The celebration would be held in a poor area, which meant a lot of people would come. A lot of people would be killed. And more contempt against the government.

The project would also be a blow to the American companies. And most importantly, it would get him a better position among the Salafism groups for the amount of the Shia that would be killed. Al-Amel district was, after all, full of Shia. It was full of Sunnie as well and the amount of Sunnie people who would die would be as high as the Shia, but who was counting. The word would go to the armed groups that Shia were killed and they would buy it.

As if they cared.

It was also the best way to get rid of Al-Kadumi. Each businessman now had a small army of bodyguards, and this Al-Kadumi guy must be the same, which would only make killing him more difficult.

"Mr. Dafer." One of his bodyguards approached him. "Your son Omar called and he wanted—"

Dafer waved him off, he was about to call Omar anyway to tell him he had fulfilled his promise and he didn't have to worry about Ali anymore. He wanted to tell him that he was planning for this a long time ago and he always cared about him. That what happened in Dubai, Dafer's marriage to another woman was nothing that could affect their relationship as a father and son. Dafer's pulse raced. He could stand in front of two hundred members in the Parliament and lie without skipping a heartbeat, but when it came to telling his son the truth about how much he truly cared... it was silly.

"Why is his cell turned off!" Dafer yelled at the people around him after the second call attempt failed.

He felt the unease again, the cold shiver.

"I tried to tell you, sir. He ask me to deliver a message for you."

"A message? And what are you waiting for? The postman? Tell me what did he want?"

The bodyguard cleared throat. "He said he is at the Al-Amel water station and that the...um... bug still bothers him. I think he meant Al-Kadumy guy, sir."

The air was sucked out of his lungs, he couldn't breathe. His eyes bulged. He tried to speak, tried to swallow. Nothing worked. No, he must have heard wrong. His hands trembled while he dialed his son's number again.

"I think his cell ran out of battery," the guard said.

"Sir, are you okay? Your face is pale," another guard said.

Voices echoed in the distance. As if they were in another room now. He was still trying to call Omar... no success.

Several guards were around him, talking to him, talking to each other, some of them where laughing.

"My son... you mother fucker, my son!" he finally shouted. He managed to breathe.

They just stared at him.

"Take me to Al-Amel district right away... now... call Luay ... tell him to abort the mission."

Blood wanted to burst out of his head and ears. They were just staring at him in bewilderment.

There was no point in talking to them. He ran to the car.

It was only then when they started moving, trying to stop him... the idiots...

-58-
Al-Amel district
June 10th
3:50 PM

Christmas came in June.

Luay had received all the details. Odd how Dafer was useful for the first time in the execution.

Luay used to deal with Dafer as a nagging client, asking for results and not even caring about the details. Today for the first time he was helping them in the execution. Not only the part when he managed to get Mujahid out, but also when he gave them the solution to penetrate the security and get the suicide man inside.

"You will get in from the line where a tall bald man stands. They say that you cannot miss him and he will not wear his helmet so that you can recognize him," Luay told Abdul Rahman, who nodded in surrender, kissing his brother on the forehead and putting on the explosive belt.

Luay looked with resentment to the still-bound-and-gagged Saudi. Saud tried to say something. Probably the standard pleading. Or it could be the also-standard threats, depended on which level of breakdown the man was in.

Never mind.

Dafer would not be particularly happy about what happened to Saud if he knew about it... if anyone ever knew about it.

"Amjad, are you ready?" Luay called. Amjad was sober now. "The car you will drive is parked outside."

"I will have the chance to kill them, of course I am ready, I am going to Allah... to heaven."

Whatever.

"Those hypocrites, those tombs-worshipers ruined every good thing in my life. I have to kill them."

"Yeah, sure... keep up the good spirit but let's save it for the filming, okay."

Luay ushered them to an empty corner in his house where Mujahid fixed a small digital camera on a stand. He always wanted to keep the formalities, every operation had to be filmed and sent to the big rug-heads in some underground shithole hideout or cave in some forgotten mountain.

"I will start now," Mujahid said, "turn off your cell phones, I don't want to redo it all over again because of a cell phone ringing. We have limited time."

Okay, Spielberg. Luay turned off the cell phone.

Mujahid, who was standing behind the camera, blathered something about Jihad and resistance. Luay kept yawning. Then he gestured for Abdul Rahman to step in. Abdul Rahman did and started reading from a paper Mujahid gave him.

When Abdul Rahman finished his weather-forecast presentation, which was all predictions and promises of death and bombs, Luay checked out the belt again, making sure it was well hidden under the clothes, and finally added one small thing to the belt.

"What is that?" Abdul Rahman asked.

Luay pulled a wire from the belt and show it to Abdul Rahman. "Look at this wire carefully, this is the detonator. When you reach the designated place, you have to pull it and the belt will... well, you know."

Abdul Rahman nodded. He might have swallowed as well.

From the diaries of the abandoned city.

Strange are those feelings that react within humans. Trepidation... fear... panic... anxiety. They can be paralyzing, preventing them from living a normal life. Force them to hide, waiting for the storm to pass, to bend in front of evil... to lie low to the ground. But those feelings can also push them to seek a way out, to fight to save someone they care about, to stand out in front of danger to protect those they love most.

A reminder that they are still human... weak... incapable of facing the growing evil around them and always in a need of God's merciful care, the care they only see when despair prevails, when the painful mix of hope and fear leaves nothing in the soul. It is in their weakest moments, when all the illusions are gone, that they can see a higher and merciful power.

Zainab tried to talk to Ayad, Hussain and Ehab, none of the people around her could understand her irrational worry about her beloved husband.

It was fear that made her push her brother to take her in his car to Al-Amel water station where Ali was.

It was also fear that made Abdul Hasan leave everything and rush to Al-Amel district with whatever was left of his resources... he feared for the lives of hundreds. But he feared most his remorse.

Fear for his son's life made Dafer run like a madman, followed by his bodyguards heading to Al-Amel district... to the place where he condemned innocent people to die just to find out that the cruel sense of humor of God's justice decided to give him a taste of his own medicine.

And it was the fear for the lives of those innocent people that made Lieutenant Hussain speed up to the belly of the beast, ignoring his nagging feeling that he had run out of luck today.

And Abdul Rahman's fear for his brother was what prevented him from running away and saving his own life. His fear that those criminals would catch him eventually and torture him and his brother to death, made him go on toward his end.

Humans might not understand their fear, they might ignore it, deny it... and they can find all the reasons to convince themselves that it's irrational. But at the end it will prevail and make them take action. Fear is, after all, the greatest motivator.

Enas kept convincing herself that she didn't care about Omar, despite that she was running toward the water station, consumed by her fear of the repercussions.

Malik couldn't fathom why he had that nagging feeling whenever he thought about Hussain. The man who saved his fiancé. The man who was his enemy a few days ago. Fear had paralyzed Malik, he couldn't think of anything, couldn't speak, and didn't know what to do.

It was then when his fiancée looked at him, and as if she could see the pain, the fear of the unknown, twitching in his head, she motioned to him. And the next thing he was running with her toward the station.

Fear doesn't come alone. It always has another companion. Another feeling.

Hope...

Faith...

Man's trust in a higher power, a power he can only see with the eyes of his heart when the darkness of fear consumes the heart... when despair paralyzes the brain.

It is then when a glimpse of hope touches the heart, strings of faith extended from heaven for their beliefs to stand out, stronger than ever... and clearer than they ever were.

They knew that the disaster would happen... there was no way around it.

But their faith was driving them.

Pushing them not to surrender.

-59-
The Water Station - Al-Amel district
June 10th
4:00 PM

Abdul Rahman carefully approached the checkpoint, unable to refrain from patting his waist to conceal the explosion belt.

On his way there, he didn't give up trying to remind himself what the scholars, and teachers and lecturers and sheikhs keep telling him about Jihad and heaven and the virgins waiting for him.

He couldn't remember anything. It was strange, because he could remember the words, one by one, but somehow something was amiss. Oh yes, the part that made all of this interesting, that made it real. Everything sounded just like a politician's promises now. Eternal life, big palaces, forever happiness, they could say whatever they wanted… but he couldn't see it, couldn't feel it as he used to. Like he was feeling death now.

But he didn't stop walking.

His fear inspired by Luay's menacing words forced him to go on. At least he would die fast, not tortured. Alone… saving his brother from that Baath torch.

He had safely passed the first checkpoint. No one even noticed him, only cars were being inspected. He was now inside the concrete walls. A voice came to him; someone talking on a loudspeaker. The opening ceremony must have started.

"We've been through crises no other country has seen. Our people suffered thirty-five years of a barbarian dictatorship… The dreams were confiscated, the sons were sent to pointless wars, the land was sold, the honor was violated. We stood watching, filled with fear, all people around us, all countries helping the dictator against us." The disembodied voice continued…

"Torturing Iraqis was a competition for companies to make better instruments and world organizations to issue more suitable covers. Everyone looked proudly at the increasing hills of mass graves in the north and south."

Abdul Rahman reached the manual-inspection queues. He spotted the tall bald officer Luay told him about. The bald guy was in the middle row, so he took that one. Twenty other people were in front of him. Mostly children.

327

Casualties of war.

The sound still came from the loudspeaker.

"But history has to move on, and as it usually does, it left Saddam and his gang in the trash and granted us freedom again. The freedom our seniors almost forgot, and our juniors never knew. So we started again, building our land, claiming back our dreams, trying to put behind us all the madness and to mend the old wounds."

Abdul Rahman reached the bald officer. His heart pounded so hard he feared people around him could hear it.

What if he wasn't the guy?

The officer passed his hands under Abdul Rahman's arms, down to the waist. His heart was going to explode now, he could feel dizziness, drums in his ears.

The officer's hand stopped on his waist for a fraction of a second. Their eyes met. Abdul Rahman opened his mouth. Nothing came out, it felt dry as hell.

The bald guy winked at him, beckoning for the next guy to come in. He almost tripped and fell. He gained balance again. Abdul Rahman looked left and right. No one even cared about him. But that annoying voice, the man was still speaking, it was louder now.

"But yesterday's executioners came back to us. Never full of our blood. Annoyed by our happiness, aggravated by a smile on the widows' faces. Provoked by a dream of an orphan child to have a home that wars would not burn again. They came back again. In a different cover, preaching death and bombing. Preaching killing and slaughtering… what a preacher."

Shut up. Please for God's sake, shut the hell up.

Abdul Rahman could see where the voice was coming from. A man in his fifties stood on the big white stand. Behind him were a dozen children in strange costumes, ready for their cue. Abdul Rahman walked toward the stand.

Closer now. The man kept talking. Abdul Rahman had to push his way through the crowd in front of the stand. People were on chairs and couches under the tent. And more were around the stand.

Why did people want to gather around the stand? But it was the best place for him to go. Even though people started looking at him suspiciously.

He headed there, to the center of the crowd. The man sounded more agitated now. His face wasn't red or angry, maybe the opposite.

Sad and concerned. He truly believed in the bullshit he was saying. All the same.

"Haven't they read our history? A nation that refuses to fade away in the darkness of the terrorists' night. We are the Iraqis, we are the Sumerians, we are the Babylonians, we are the Assyrians, we are the Acadians, we are the early Muslims and for the glory of our ancestors we'll not let a bunch of ignorance lead us. We will live life. And if our destiny is to die, let all the terrorists know that we are not afraid of death.

"We will choose life, we will choose to write yet another page of history. The history that longs for our glory as we yearn to its everlasting fame. From this place, my brothers, we tell terrorists that we will not die even if they kill us.

We will live even if they bomb us.

We tell them that your days of terrors are over and there is no place for you here.

Because this is Iraq, our Iraq."

Storms of cheering and applauding came from everywhere.

Teenagers made strange sounds, supposedly encouraging.

It was now or never. He took out the wire from behind his belt. People noticed it. They ran away from him. Others ran toward him, preparing to jump him.

Noise, sea-shell noise in his ears, mixed only with his heartbeats and muffled voices of the people nearby.

Now...

But he didn't have the courage. He just couldn't do it. He let the wire go and closed his ears. He wanted to block the voices.

Two men jumped him, they all fell to the ground.

"Secure his hands!" someone shouted. More came in, pinning his hands and legs to the ground. No way he could do anything.

Relieved, there was nothing he could do now... he was saved.

Amid all the noise, he felt a vibration, a cell phone ringing. The men holding him noticed it as well...

"Under his shirt!"

He could see it now, the white screen. A cell phone under his shirt. Attached to the belt.

It wasn't his... he didn't have one.

Then he knew it was the end.

-60-
Near The Water Station
June 10th
4:05 PM

Hussain pressed on the gas pedal as if it personally offended him.
He heard the blast coming from the direction of the water station.

So he was right. Not that it gave any comfort.

A cold shiver went down his body.

Black smoke started ascending into the sky.

His eyes filled with tears. He wanted to cry... he was late.

God knew how many lives were lost now, how many dreams torn
apart.

Just because they couldn't stop the bad guys.

He didn't know what he was doing.

The blast wasn't strong. It couldn't be a bombed car. Like many
Iraqis, he'd had the privilege of hearing a bomb car explode. His ears
stopped functioning for days after.

People, lots of them, ran out of the concrete walls, out of the
water station to the parking area.

The smoke came from inside the station. No car could go inside.

A small charge?

More people poured out, waves of people, men and women and
children. Some of them covered with dust, stumbling over each
other.

Why did he still have that feeling?

That pain in his chest. The feeling prior to a blow to the stomach.
When your body tried to brace for the pain to come.

He sped toward the entrance of the street that led to the station.
People ran out of the checkpoint.

His phone rang for the third time now. It was his mother. He
recognized the ringtone. The national Anthem, "*Moutiny*" (My
country).

He couldn't answer, what would he tell her? He could not lie
now.

The cell phone kept ringing. The lyrics sounded sadder than ever.
My home... My country...
Glory and magnificence,
Beauty and brilliance...

330

I found in your lands…
In your grounds…

He pushed harder on the gas. Less than a hundred yards to turn left, where the unpaved street would lead to the station entrance. From there, it was another three hundred yards to get into the checkpoint. Three hundred yards full of panicked people running toward the main street where he was.

Some made it to the main street. Others stopped, feeling somehow safer, turning to look at the station and asking what happened.

A few took photos on their cell-phone cameras.

Police forces tried to shove people into the empty land that separated the station from the main street.

On the other side of the street, in front of him, a red car slowed to take the turn into the unpaved road.

Why would someone want to get into the station now?

There was something about that car, something familiar. People waved to him to go back, it wasn't safe. Hussain ignored them and continued. Then he noticed the make of the car. A Corolla. The same red Corolla he saw in front of Mahmoud's house, the car the two men were working on. He remembered what Malik said about the group having two cars. It was there all the time, in front of him, being prepared for its lethal mission.

His cell rang. The anthem again.

Shall I see you?
Safe and triumphant and dignified.
Shall I see you, where you belong.
High up in the sky.
My home… My country.

"I am sorry, Mom," he whispered, looking at the phone. "I have a more important appointment."

He couldn't let the red Corolla take the turn.

He couldn't let him reach the wave of people coming from the station. More than a hundred now.

"*Ya Allah!*" he cried out, pressing on the gas, veering his car to cut across the road to the red Corolla.

They crashed. Hussain jolted in his seat. The steering wheel smashed against his chest.

He saw the flames, or he imagined that. He might also have imagined hearing the banging sound of the explosion.

What he was sure of, was that his body was shredded into pieces, flying in the air.

He felt no pain, nothing. The only thing he felt was joy, overwhelming joy.

It might also have been his imagination that he saw hundreds of people running away from the car explosion, safe and sound.

Never mind...

He had found peace.

....

A few miles away, in the nearby Bayaa district, the thunderous sound of the explosion shook the glass of a small house. The children who were playing with a blue balloon looked up toward their grandmother, seeking her usual don't-be-afraid confirmation. Except, this time their grandmother put her hand on her chest, her mouth opened, her eyes about to burst into tears.

"Oh God... not Hussain," she called, tears filling her eyes.

She stood up. Her gaze swept the room as if following something.

Her lips quivered in a smile that was soon turned into a grimace of pain. She dropped the cell phone from her hand. "Why?" she called out, and started sobbing.

Everyone in the house gathered around her.

She examined their faces, one after another moving relentlessly to settle finally on it.

The blue balloon Hussain blew up this morning.

She grabbed it from the children... hugging it close to her heart.

"Keep away from it!" she cried out, shoving them away, still sobbing. "My son's breaths are still in it... Hussain."

-61-
Somewhere not on this planet
June 10th
4:20 PM

Abdul Hasan was the first to arrive. He ran toward the crash site. Although burned and turned into a skeleton of black metal, he could still recognize the car. The rear registration plate was intact.

Abdul Hasan tried to get closer. The firemen pushed him away. Flames rose from the car, gnawing at what was left of a burned body. Of a young man who saved his life today.

Of course, the pile of coal in the car that resembled what was left of Hussain's body could be anyone's body. Nothing to identify him. Gone were the handsome features, the delicate nose, the wavy hair, and certainly this horror-movie-like scene of a burned-out skull staring at him from the shattered car window had nothing to do with Hussain's smile.

Abdul Hasan wished he could do what people on TV did, they fell to the ground, on their knees. They said words of wisdom or regret, or even something with a deep and obscure meaning like, "It's not over."

But he did none of that. He looked around. Some people were hurt by the second explosion, not too many, the number would be terrifyingly more if the bombed car managed to get in. He counted ten bodies. Others might survive, but given their injuries, he wasn't sure it was good news for them.

A fireman came in with a big hose. He yelled at someone and a strong beam of water came out of the hose at the burning car, Hussain's car. Abdul Hasan looked away so that he didn't see the body pushed by the water beam.

Another fireman with another water hose was washing the ground. Blood, pieces of flesh with blood, clothes soaked with blood and some other substance with blood mixed together with the dirt from the unpaved ground.

Abdul Hasan wanted to stop the fireman, to tell him that his work might remove important evidence, but he could hear the man's answer, "What evidence?"

In a few seconds he was shouting orders to his soldiers to evacuate civilians, clear the way, secure the area, and be alert for any further attacks.

Abdul Hasan didn't leave the area where Hussain was. Couldn't. From time to time he glanced back at the charred remains of his young lieutenant and among all the feelings of sadness, guilt, sorrow, regret, anger, and many others he couldn't name, one idea couldn't leave his mind...

That if not for Hussain, he, and hundreds of other innocents, would look like this.

. . . .

Two Iraqi men carried a blond American man in his forties. They moved him away from the stand where the explosion took place. One of them kept asking, "Anta Zain?" Finally, the second man realized that the American couldn't understand what they were saying so he asked him with a thick accent, "You are okay? Help?"

"I think so," The American replied.

They nodded and left to attend other people.

In his peripheral vision, Abdul Hasan could see a man on his right, his hand covered his face, his shoulders heaved while sobbing.

Before Abdul Hasan could offer help, the man turned toward him. He gestured in front of him at dozens of children wearing what looked like colored costumes, now covered with blood and ashes.

They were all dead.

At least this was what he wished, for their own sake.

"I am their schoolteacher," the man sniffled, looking at Abdul Hasan as if he had a magic wand. Then he showed him two cell phones in his hand. Both were ringing continuously.

Nineteen missed calls. One of the screens showed.

"Their parents are calling to check on them." He pointed at the pile of blood and flesh, "What could I tell them? What could I say?"

The blond American ran to a spot not far away from them. An American soldier lay motionless on the ground.

"Ben. Oh God, no!" The American wailed.

Three men carrying a wounded child bumped into Abdul Hasan. He moved away, his gaze fixed on the American holding the body of the young soldier, shaking him, as if that would bring him to life. Ten minutes later, a squad of armed men, security contractors led by Richard Barn, came and picked up the American, taking him back to the Green Zone.

. . . .

Enas looked left and right. People screamed and cried in agony around her. Everywhere.

She saw a group of men. Some wore uniforms, some didn't. They were gathered around bodies on the ground... mostly remains. Holding out heads, body parts, burnt arms and legs. Trying to match this hand to that body. All were puzzled, all were shocked... in the sadistic, most grotesque version of mix-and-match she would ever see.

Then she saw him, shouting and cursing frantically. But his cries were lost with all the noise around him. His face had multiple scratches, some of them dripping blood.

It was Dafer Al-Dayni, and in his arms was the upper half of a young man's body, covered with blood. From his neck dangled a golden necklace in the shape of the map of Iraq.

No lower part to the body.

…………

Doctor Zainab ran to the stand, what was left of it. Ayad followed her. Her cell phone was set on auto-redial, so it kept calling back.

Her husband wasn't answering.

Where are you, Ali?

She didn't want to think of the possibilities. There was still hope she could find him… alive, injured maybe but please, God, alive.

She bumped into a woman carrying a little child. The child's left hand was cut and most of the left side of his body was burned. The child was crying and the woman just didn't know what to do. Zainab looked at the woman, the doctor inside her wanted to help. She was about to suggest something when she heard Ali's mobile ringtone. She hurried to the sound. "He is here, nearby!" she called to Ayad.

Ayad didn't answer. He stood on the other side of the stand, staring at the ground.

"Ayad…"

His gaze remained on the ground. Not a good sign. She flew toward him.

Ayad stood looking at a body on the ground…she stepped closer…it wasn't necessary…she already knew.

Zainab sat next to him…on the ground. Cradling his head in her lap. She wanted to cry, to scream, to call his name for the last time, her mouth was open, her face contorted but there was no sound.

There was one big wound in his neck. Probably what killed him. She put her palm gently on his cheek, as she used to do when he was sleeping.

His cell was still ringing, somehow it was louder than any other sound. Everything else faded into the background except for the words that kept repeating and repeating.

My home… My country…
Glory and magnificence, beauty and brilliance…
I found in your lands… in your grounds..
Shall I see you?

335

As I want to see you?
Safe and triumphant and dignified.
Shall I see you, where you belong?
High up in the sky.
My home... My country.

-62-
Headlines from Iraqi newspapers
During June 2005
-Slightly Modified, very slightly... really-

-A senior member of the Iraqi Parliament mediates the efforts to free a Saudi Business man. He also commented that keeping communication lines open with armed groups paid off in releasing the kidnapped hostage.

-Two terrorist attacks in Al-Amel district.
The Islamic State In Iraq announced their responsibility for the two explosions at Al-Amel district that targeted the opening ceremony of Al-Amel water station project. According to official sources, more than forty people were killed, most of them children. Casualties exceeded one hundred.

- Parliament member hides a bombed car.
The Commandos forces of the Ministry of Interior caught a bombed car that was traced to the parliament member (...) the head of the (...) alliance. After inspecting the politician's own residence in Adel district, another bombed car was found in his garage.

-Iraqi citizen buries bodies in Najaf city at his own expense. He volunteered to receive forty bodies each week from Baghdad morgue to bury them in the cemetery of Najaf.

-Fine Arts challenges terrorism:
Our Reporter (...) met a group of students from the College of Fine Arts, who collaborated with one of the civil society institutions to hold an art exhibition. The exhibition demonstrated some art work by using the remnants of the improvised explosives and weapons seized from terrorists groups.

- A true martyr hero (…)

Baghdad municipality with cooperation from the Ministry of Interior named an elementary school in Baghdad after the heroic lieutenant (…) who saved hundreds of citizens by sacrificing himself to stop a terrorist from detonating a car bomb. Our newspaper found out that the hero martyr was the only provider for a family of seven, including three children and his elderly mother.

-Finding hostages in a mosque.

The Commandos Forces of the Ministry of Interior found several hostages abducted by the armed groups connected to Al-Qaeda. There were several women among the abductees with signs of torture on their bodies. A hideout for machine guns and explosives was found inside the mosque.

-American private security firm suspected in the emancipation of terrorist suspects.

A high-ranking officer in the Ministry of Interior (…) accused the private American security contractor (…) of conspiring in the emancipation of several suspects arrested by the ministry forces during the last months.

-Failure to issue a new investment law cripples the attempts to rebuild Iraq.

Although two years passed since the regime fall, the new Iraqi government is still unable to make a new investment law more attractive to foreign investors.

An official in the Ministry of Planning (…) expressed deep disappointment of the bureaucracy enmeshed in all parts of the government, which contribute, along with the new sectarian quota system enforced by the American ambassador, to bringing incompetent staff to critical government positions.

-The remains of thirteen members of an Iraqi tae-kwon-do team kidnapped last year have been found in western Iraq.

The team was traveling to a training camp in neighboring Jordan, when their convoy was stopped and all fifteen athletes abducted along a road between the cities of Fallujah and Ramadi, in Anbar province. Two of the athletes remained unaccounted for.

....

Abdul Hasan folded the paper and put it aside on his desk. A knock came on the open door of his office in the MICF headquarters.

Ayad stood on the step. Abdul Hasan welcomed him, shaking hands, and gesturing him to take a seat.

A stream of memories flooded in.

"So, you went back to your house?" Abdul Hasan asked.

"Actually no... I couldn't." Ayad shook his head looking everywhere but at him. "The situation is still bad, other groups replaced the old one and..." his voice trailed off, leaving the obvious.

"You will go back... I am sure of it. There is a proposal for a wide-ranging operation to clean all west and south Baghdad areas. Once we are done with that, it will be much safer for everyone."

Ayad nodded with a sad smile. Abdul Hasan wished he could share with Ayad all the details about the plan, which would include tremendous support from the US Army. They merely awaited the approval from the American congress to send re-enforcement forces.

"How can I help you?" the inevitable question.

"Actually my sister, Doctor Zainab, left Iraq after her husband's death in the bombing. And she has decided to join the UN refugee program so she was asking for some official papers proving what happened to her ... her husband, I mean." Ayad's fingers tapped on the desk a tad too fast.

"Sure, I can help with that." Relief. Finally he could help this family. "But may I ask something, if you don't mind.. I know it's personal but.."

"Why refugee?"

Abdul Hasan raised his open palms. "I am not making any judgments here. It's just I am a bit curious, as my understanding is your sister has no worry for money."

"She is a wealthy woman, very wealthy as a matter of fact." Ayad nodded. "But it's not about money. You see.. the problem is that she doesn't want to live in any of the Arab countries. She believes that those countries are making use of Iraqis' difficult situation and not giving any rights, not even basic ones to Iraqi expatriates. On the other hand, European countries respect everyone no matter what his background. They are just more..."

"Human," Abdul Hasan finished with a sad smile.

"Well, I was about to say civilized, but I guess they are the same, kind of."

He didn't comment on that. There was no need to share his views of living as refugees. But then in one way or another, even people living inside Iraq were refugees.

Abdul Hasan took a piece of paper from his drawer, one with the logo and signs of the Ministry of Interior, and wrote. When finished, he called out for one of his assistants and asked him to print it and bring it back to him to stamp it.

"By the way," Abdul Hasan said, "what happened to your neighbor...what was his name?"

"Oh, you mean Mahmoud?" Ayad smiled. "Well, he still lives there. The man calls me weekly as he is taking care of my abandoned house so that terrorists don't take it. His daughter got married and his son..." Ayad paused for a moment. "Well, he is fine, but I bet he learned a good lesson from that day."

"And are you planning to leave Iraq as well?" Now that he said it, the question didn't sound as casual and friendly as he intended.

"Migration is not for me." Ayad's brow furrowed. "Despite what happened to me, I want to stay here and see those bastards kicked out of Iraq once and for all. And maybe I will live long enough to see this country get back to us for the first time."

His office assistant came in with the paper. Abdul Hasan stamped it and handed it to Ayad.

"Here you go." They shook hands. Abdul Hasan wanted to say that he was sorry for not taking Ayad's statement seriously that day. It didn't matter now.

Ayad left and his secretary came in.

"Sir, Dafer Al-Dayni is asking to see you," the young sergeant said.

Dafer. Abdul Hasan had no doubts now that Dafer was involved in the bombing attack. Because of him, Hussain and Shaker died. "Let him go to hell, if he wants to see me let him come here."

"Um... actually, sir, he is—"

A man wearing a hideous triangular hat and a brown jacket rushed into the room. "Abdul Hasan, please..."

"What the hell are you doing here?"

Dafer said, "I need your help Abdul Hasan—"

Hussain, Shaker, his son who almost got killed because of this slackened-faced old man.

"Get out of my office. Now!"

"I want to cut a deal," Dafer said, with a toothless smile. The bastard looked as if he aged twenty years. "We both want the same thing."

"Was it you?"

Dafer shook his head. "Abdul Hasan, I am not following…"

"Was…it…you?" Abdul Hasan grunted.

Something in Dafer's face gave away. "Ah… you mean the thing with your son."

"Yes, the thing with my son. And the operation in Al-Amel district."

"I swear by God–" Dafer held up his palm ready to swear.

Rage, he could hear nothing but his heart, Abdul Hasan saw his hands gripping Dafer by his jacket.

"This is the deal I am offering," Dafer cried, his eyes pleading. "I will give you the terrorists behind everything."

Abdul Hasan let go of Dafer. "In exchange for what?"

"Immunity, you drop all the charges against me."

"Why don't you ask for an airplane and five million dollars as well?"

"Think about it, Abdul Hasan."

Abdul Hasan looked at his desk. Hussain's cap lay there. Hussain had changed his clothes that day. Not sure why, Abdul Hasan kept the young man's military hat in front of him.

"Get the hell out of here."

"You will save innocent people from their next attacks."

"We will do that by hanging you to dry in public. After your diplomatic immunity is suspended, nothing will stand between you and jail. No deal can save you."

"I lost my son because of them, Captain, don't you understand? I fucking lost my son." Dafer's shoulders heaved, his eyes closed into thin slits, but no tears. "Do you have any idea what it means for someone my age to lose his only son?"

As a matter of fact, he did.

"Give me names, locations, phone numbers, everything."

"I don't know much about the Salafism, but there was a man from my team, the man who planned the whole thing. His name is Luay, he is hiding in Dyala city, I will give you the exact location."

Dafer took out a piece of paper from his jacket and handed it to Abdul Hasan.

"He knows everything," Dafer said. "Now I have fulfilled my part, it's up to you if you want to keep your part of the deal." Dafer turned and started walking to the door.

If he didn't know Dafer, if he didn't serve with the Baath gladiator for one year during the war with Iran, he would have bought it. But he knew Dafer, knew him so well that he called out for him before he reached the door. "You are unable to catch him, aren't you?"

Dafer stopped. He sneered without turning. "The son-of-a-bitch killed the second group I sent after him. Nine men this time, can you fucking believe it?"

"So you thought... what? We might be able to do it."

"Eventually." Dafer sneered again shaking his head. "After he kills a squad or two, maybe you will be smart enough and send the entire force after him. And maybe then I will have my closure."

All that to avenge his son? Abdul Hasan could understand that, but something didn't add up.

Dafer left the office and was on the stairs now.

"So it was just an act?" Abdul Hasan called after him, "Coming here and asking for immunity, and for the charges to be dropped, you just wanted to give me Luay, to make us hunt him, kill him for you?"

Dafer's sunken eyes were bloodshot. "Leave it there, Hasan," Dafer said and continued his way downstairs.

Why wasn't Dafer concerned about all the evidence against him? All the charges? Did he accepted his destiny? Had his son's death given him some kind of death wish?

No, he knew Dafer better.

Dafer's words echoed in his ears: "Leave it there, Hasan."

Shit.

He jumped the steps, two at a time. "Don't let him leave!" he cried out to the soldiers gathered in the ground floor. "Stop him!"

They did.

Abdul Hasan reached to him. Two soldiers stood between Dafer and the exit.

"You haven't told me everything?" Abdul Hasan said, panting.

"I told you to leave it." Dafer gave him half a smile, his eyes almost closed.

"How did the terrorists know that I am authorized to get a car without inspection into the area?" Abdul Hasan asked.

Dafer tried to push the two soldiers away. They held their ground. He turned back to Abdul Hasan. "You cannot arrest me."

"Why not? Your diplomatic immunity is suspended. We didn't do it before because we were not allowed to come to your area. Now you are here..." Abdul Hasan pointed at Dafer. "Arrest this man."

Three men approached Dafer, all eager to execute the order.

"How did they know where I lived? How did they identify my kid? His play time?"

The room was spinning. He lived the nightmare again.

"I gave them this information," Dafer said, raising both eyebrows. "Happy now, Hasan?"

But how could Dafer know all of this about him? There was no way even for a parliament member to gain access to this personal information. No way, unless...

The room kept spinning. He had to lean against the wall. "Dafer, what did you just call me?"

Dafer gave him another one of his half smiles. No one called him Hasan, except for...

Abdul Hasan shook his head.

No way.

"I am leaving now," Dafer said.

"Arrest this son of a bitch!" Abdul Hasan shouted at the men.

Dafer shrugged. He walked. The soldiers grabbed him. Dafer reached for his cell and quickly dialed a number. They knocked the phone from his hands and cuffed him.

On the floor, the cell was still calling. The screen changed, showing that the call was connected.

"Take this call...Captain." Dafer laughed. It was loud and joyful.

Abdul Hasan took the phone with the tips of his fingers, keeping it a safe distance from his ear. "Hello?"

But he knew who was on the line.

"Hasan?" the voice said, surprised. A brief silence, then a sigh. "Let Dafer walk away, Hasan,"

Abdul Hasan dropped the phone to the ground. He could imagine the empty justifications, the pathetic excuses, it wouldn't change anything, Abdul Hasan finally understood everything.

The voice on the other line, the man Dafer called, was General Kenani.

Epilogue
Place: Al-Najaf Cemetery
A year after the bombing

She stood in front of the four graves, putting one rose on each tomb. Her gaze moved from one stone to another. Memories flooded in a maddening rhythm. Uncontrollably.

One wound after another, none of them healed yet.

They said that troubles, pain, make you stronger if they don't break you.

It wasn't true... each loss was harder. Made her weaker. She swore she could still feel the pain of the loss of the first son. Losing the second son, then the third just added another section to the poem.

But Hussain was different. Losing him... it wasn't painful... in the beginning yes, but then there was something else.

She was past grief, she couldn't feel it anymore.

The only thing she could feel was the emptiness, the dark pit in her heart that turned into a black hole sucking everything else into it.

They were in a better place. Heaven, or whatever it was, didn't matter to her. Wherever they were it was a better place.

And she prayed to God to take her to them. She had more offspring beneath the ground than above. So why should she care about life?

Nothing could make her feel sadder than continuing to live.

In a way, she was stronger now.

A tear escaped her eye; she tried to explain to people that she wasn't sad. Or sadness wasn't what worried her.

She worried about how long she had to live and who else she would lose.

"Put your trust in God, they are in heaven," Malik's wife, Esraa, told her compassionately, putting her palm on her shoulder.

Why were those words always empty? Why did they only make the condemned feel lonelier? No one understood his pain.

She nodded. What else was there to say.

To her right was a man with an Iraqi Police uniform, sitting on a stone block reading Quran. Glancing at Hussain's grave every now and then. He stopped reading. Looking at her with a smile.

"I saw him yesterday in a dream," Malik said. He always called her to tell her he saw Hussain in his dreams. "He told me he longs for hearing Quran."

Another tear escaped. "He always liked it when someone read Quran to him," she said. "When I was pregnant, I used to read lot of Quran. They say it's a blessing for the baby."

"He was a good man, ma'am."

A baby cried. Esraa cuddled him in her arms, smiling at him. "Little Hussain woke up."

The baby cried louder, demanding. Something about infants she always admired. They have their way to get everyone's attention. They didn't care about how tired people were around them, how sad, how miserable, as if they understood that life had to go on. It could not stop. And somehow you would find a space in your heart for them, the patience to take care of them.

The baby's cries blended strangely with the scene... the endless sea of tombs, the hills and the valleys, covered with that carpet of gray stones.

"I think it's better to go now," Malik said, closing the Quran and standing. He stretched. "We have one hour to visit Imam Ali's shrine and go back to Baghdad before the curfew."

She whispered goodbye to her sons.

Nodding in respect for the silent sea of tombs.

It wouldn't be long before she joined them.

And maybe then, she would have peace.

The End.

ABOUT THE AUTHOR

I.M.Hussaini is an Iraqi novelist and human rights activist. He worked as a reporter in Iraq and the Middle East during the war that ended Sadam's regime by the US-led collation. I.M. Hussaini is the author of the controversial series of Edward Fleming that attempts to bring to light the stories behind the scene of the new Arab revolt and discuss tabooed details from the Islamic history of the region. The author's decision to write in English came after his most famous book *The Detour* was banned in many Arab countries. For more details about the author and his work you can visit his website at www.imhussaini.com